A VINEYARD SEASON

JEAN STONE

KENSINGTON
PUBLISHING CORP.

www.kensingtonbooks.com

To the countless islanders who continue to teach me about this magical place called Martha's Vineyard and who help me get the details straight.

I will forever be grateful to you for making this series come alive.

Prologue

To everything there is a season—
On Martha's Vineyard, there is a high season,
an autumn season,
an off-season.

And there is spring. That glorious time when
tulips burst forth in Cannonball Park in Edgartown, and the *On Time* ferry is spruced up in
the harbor;

When throughout the village, scents of new
paint and freshly cleaned windows mingle with
soft chirps of robins and warm yellow sunlight;

When neighbors greet neighbors in sidewalk
conversation, and the island is reborn, and all
things are possible.

At least, that's how it's supposed to be.

Chapter 1

Home. At last.

As the big ferry rounded the jetty and headed into Vineyard Haven Harbor, Annie closed her eyes and waited patiently to feel the subtle bump against the pier. She smiled. She'd been gone all winter, working with screenwriters and producers in the exciting, energetic, exhausting realm of Hollywood, transforming her best-selling mystery novels into scripts for a dream-come-true TV network series.

But Southern California wasn't Martha's Vineyard.

Oh, sure, Annie thought, both places have lovely beaches. And, yes, unlike the Vineyard, SoCal has sunny skies and hardly any humidity. And palm trees and flowers blooming in February. And convertibles with their canvas tops down. And movie stars all over the place (which islanders could boast having in summer, if any of them cared about that sort of thing). In truth, Annie had fantasized about permanently living in L.A. About reinventing her entire career into writing for film, about brainstorming with others instead of sitting at her keyboard plink-plinking in solitude, about having a year-round tan, a preposterous notion for a woman her age, but there it was.

Greg Williams hadn't helped. An illustrious wizard of Hollywood, head of a multi-Oscar- and Emmy-winning production company, he was always on the lookout for seasoned writers to lure into his stable, using flattery as his bait especially when they seemed vulnerable, unsure of themselves. The way Annie had been when she'd arrived. After all, though she'd penned numerous novels, film scripts had eluded her. Until she was caught in Greg Williams's web.

"Your ideas are brilliant."

"Your scriptwriting instincts are outstanding."

"You could have a real future here."

Annie supposed his lines were well practiced and polished, like those used in any bar, in any town, anywhere, though he wanted talent and not sex.

It had been tempting. But Annie knew she belonged on the Vineyard. On the opposite coast. Which was why she'd spent Thursday night into Friday flying toward the sunrise, then boarding the early Peter Pan bus from Boston south to Woods Hole to catch the boat. It had been a long journey, and she'd been gone too long. But John would be waiting on the dock, his arms outstretched, eager to embrace her. And on April 23—only three weeks away—they'd be facing one another, holding hands. And Annie Sutton and John Lyons finally would be married.

That, too, had been a long journey.

"Hey, Annie!"

The voice jolted her. It took a second for her to recognize the woman standing in the aisle: She worked at both the post office in Edgartown and the thrift shop. But Annie couldn't recall her name. Betsy, maybe? Bonnie? Her bottle-blond hair was in a ponytail and she looked to be in her early forties, younger than Annie by a decade or so.

"Haven't seen you for a while," the woman said.

Apparently the island grapevine hadn't notified the residents of Annie's whereabouts. Thank goodness. "I've been away," she replied, "on business."

With a flick of her ponytail, the woman sat on the armrest of the seat opposite Annie's. "That's right. You were in . . . California?"

So the grapevine remained well oiled, after all. "I was." She seemed like a nice woman, but Annie had wanted these last moments alone to help her make a smooth mental transition from the palm trees to the pinkletinks—the latter being tiny peeping frogs that alerted the Vineyard as soon as spring arrived. She'd also wanted to freshen up before seeing John. As his bride-to-be, who'd been on the lam for three whole months, she did not want to resemble a ragtag, jetlagged traveler who'd left LAX more than twelve hours ago, counting the plane, the bus, the boat. And the waiting in between.

"It wasn't a bad winter here," the woman went on. "Not much snow. A little ice. And the infernal wind. Otherwise, it was kind of boring. So I took a third job as an assistant admin at the Boys and Girls Club. Speaking of which, John's girl, Lucy, was a big help after school in the arts and crafts room."

Annie smiled. "I know. She told me it's a lot of fun." Annie had made it a point to frequently contact John and his family, even Abigail. And, of course, all her friends who formed the rest of her "island family." Staying in touch had helped her keep her priorities in balance, a yoga exercise for her mind.

"Lucy's a good kid," the woman continued. "Smart, too. Too bad she can't keep coming. What with everything going on."

Annie didn't know that Lucy had stopped going to the club. But between maintaining straight A's in school, having a boyfriend, and lending a frequent hand to her grandparents (though they maintained they did not need help), it wasn't surprising. "Lucy's sixteen now," Annie replied. "And I swear her life is busier than mine."

The engines slowed to a low growl. Annie slid forward on the seat and glanced out the window, its glass hazy with salt spray from the perpetual trips between Cape Cod and the island. Back and forth. Seven days a week. Year-round. And now the houses that graced the hill above the shoreline grew larger as the *Island Home* drew nearer into port.

Annie hoisted her purse. "If you'll excuse me," she said with a smile, "I need to duck into the ladies' room and comb my hair. And try to look civilized."

Stepping aside so Annie could navigate around her, the woman asked, "Is John picking you up?"

It seemed like an odd question. "He is."

The woman looked over Annie's shoulder and out the cloudy window. Then she nodded slowly. "It's good that you've come home," she said.

Before Annie could ask what she had meant, a voice blared from the loudspeaker, notifying drivers to return to their vehicles, and for walk-off passengers to exit on the starboard side of level one.

"Gotta go!" The woman gave Annie a quick wave and darted toward the iron staircase leading down to the freight deck.

For a moment, Annie was befuddled. Why was it good that she'd come home? And yet, as she grabbed her carry-on and headed to the restroom, she reasoned that Betsy/Bonnie was only being friendly, a common trait among true Vine-yarders.

Yes, Annie thought. *That must be it.* Surely there was no need for butterflies to start flapping their wings in her stomach.

★ ★ ★

John's arms weren't exactly outstretched, but his pearl-gray eyes locked straight on Annie, and that was good enough. They skipped the "hi" and "how was the trip?" and hugged only a little longer than if Annie had been shopping on the Cape for a few hours. His daughters often accused him of not doing public displays of affection.

"So," he said, with a half-cocked smile once they'd collected her suitcases from the luggage cart and were buckled into his SUV, "you're back."

"So it seems."

He reached over and tucked a lock of her hair behind her ear. "I'm glad."

He didn't mention that the silver strands Annie had left with had disappeared, or that her hair's dark brownish-black "natural" state had been revived. Some things he didn't seem to notice, including that she was a little slimmer, thanks to snacking on fresh oranges instead of Lucy's fabulous cookies. Then again, she knew that looks were of little importance to him. He no doubt didn't even realize that he was tall and handsome, and a heartthrob to many, especially when he was in uniform as a detective sergeant of the Edgartown Police Department.

She leaned over, straining her seat belt, and kissed him. "I'm glad I'm back, too." Through the nylon of his jacket, his shoulder felt less muscular, as if he'd lost weight, too. Perhaps he'd stopped feeding on pizza and had finally learned to cook. Or, more likely, one of his daughters had.

He pulled away, halfcocked a smile again—his face looked thinner, too—started the engine, and became occupied with the rear camera and the mirrors as he backed out of the space.

"Mom and Dad want to throw you a welcome-home dinner tonight," he said, maneuvering onto Water Street and driving toward the five corners. "I said tomorrow would be better, that you'd probably be tired today."

It was only ten thirty in the morning, and Anne was eager to see John's parents, Earl and Claire, who had been like family to her since she'd moved to the Vineyard. "I can do tonight," she said. "As soon as we get to Chappy, I can sleep for a few hours. And I'd love to see everyone."

He nodded but said, "And everyone wants to see you. Including Lucy, who has the science fair today. I think it goes until seven or eight, so she'll be getting home too late to join us. And you know she'd hate that."

Putting her hand on his, she said, "Okay, then let's do tomorrow. There's no rush. I'm not planning to go anywhere for a long time." She said that not only to tell John but also to reinforce the fact that any California daydreams she may have had were just that.

He lifted his arm and rested it on her shoulder, while keeping his eyes fixed on the road. "I've missed you, you know."

Annie moved a little closer; his hand felt warm against her cheek. Then she drifted into a half-sleep, where she remained all the way across the channel from Edgartown to Chappaquiddick—the quiet, smaller island that was called Chappy by many, and "home" by only about two hundred residents. Including Annie.

"Did you tell her?" Earl's voice whispered.

Annie stirred and opened her eyes. They were parked in the small clamshell lot at the Vineyard Inn—the wonderful place that she owned along with Earl and her brother, Kevin. John's window was down and Earl was crouched, squinting beneath his spikey white brows as he peered inside.

"Told me what?" she asked, sitting straight up, her thoughts blurred like the glass of the window on the boat. She realized she'd slept all the way from the boat and had missed crossing the channel on the *On Time*, the tiny, open-air, raft-like ferry that held only three vehicles, two, if they were big.

John cleared his throat. "Dad's asking about dinner." He turned back to Earl. "We need to come tomorrow instead of tonight. Annie's tired. And Lucy has the science fair."

Earl scratched his chin and slipped his hands into the pockets of his L.L. Bean wool jacket. Just because it was April didn't mean it was time to put away cold-weather clothes on Martha's Vineyard, where that infernal wind, as Betsy/Bonnie called it, sometimes made spring feel like January.

Shaking off the remnants of her catnap, Annie lifted her carry-on, which she'd parked at her feet, and got out.

"I really am tired," she said, circling to Earl and giving him a hug. "But it's great to see you. So, yes, let's plan on tomorrow, if that works for Claire."

Earl raised his fingers to the horizontal lines that skated across his forehead and saluted. "Count on it. She's dying to hear about your adventures with those movie folks."

Annie laughed. "My adventures mostly dealt with work. Not very exciting, I'm afraid." She was determined to downplay what she'd been doing; she didn't want anyone to think she preferred California to the island or that she thought the people she'd met there were more interesting—"cooler," Lucy might have said—than anyone back home. She did not want people to think that, because it wasn't true. Well, it almost wasn't true.

"In the meantime," Earl added, "your mother-in-law-to-be stocked up your kitchen. She'll get you to eat one way or another."

"I'm glad. Because as well as being tired, I'm hungry." She wasn't hungry at all, but neither Earl nor Claire needed to know that.

He grinned. "You also might like to know I gassed up the Jeep for you, had her oil changed, had her checked out, so she's good to go. I even put fresh water in your water bottle on the console and replaced your hand sanitizer."

"Thanks, Earl. You think of everything." She took his hand and squeezed it.

"You won't get to see Francine and Jonas and Bella until later; they're at a gallery on the Cape. The place is going to show some of his paintings. That boy's doing real well." He said it with a note of pride, as if Jonas were one of theirs, because he—and Francine and, of course, little Bella—couldn't be closer to their hearts if they were blood relations. They'd had prime slots on the list of essential people with whom Annie had stayed in touch.

"That's wonderful," she said. "I'll watch for them to come home. If I'm awake, that is." Jonas and Francine now lived on the property of the Inn. Just before Annie had left, Kevin started converting the old workshop into a home for them. She'd been looking forward to seeing the finished product.

"Are you coming in?" she asked John, who was still gripping the steering wheel.

"Sorry. I can't. I've got to get back to the station. Besides, you need to sleep. We'll talk later."

"I'll get your bags," Earl said as he lumbered to the back, lifted the tailgate, and said loudly enough for Annie to hear, "Looks like there's more here than you left with."

That was true. She'd found so many cute things to buy: clothes for Lucy and Abigail, lovely scarves from the Huntington Botanical Gardens for Claire and Taylor, a baseball cap from NASA's Jet Propulsion Lab in Pasadena for Kevin, and an Edward Gorey jigsaw puzzle for Earl, because during one of their phone calls, Claire had mentioned that his winter project involved developing an addiction to puzzles. "Like he's an old fuddy-duddy," she'd said. Annie had also picked up gifts for others, including Francine's baby, who was due to arrive in a few weeks. John had been the most difficult, because he was not a souvenir kind of guy; he certainly wouldn't wear a T-shirt with HOLLYWOOD silk screened on the front, or would want a refrigerator magnet of the big sign up in the hills. She'd been thrilled to find a very nice vegan leather wallet, though she skipped having his initials tooled into the front.

"I'll help you, Dad," John was saying as he finally got out.

He lifted two of the suitcases and let Earl take the lighter one. Together, they ambled down the slope to Annie's cottage and brought the bags inside.

"Get some rest before you unpack," John said. He gave her another hug, kissed her forehead, then left with his dad.

Annie stripped out of her travel clothes and took a quick shower. The water was blissfully hot, no doubt thanks to Earl, who must have seen to that as well. She pulled on a warm nightie, slid under the comfy covers of her much-missed bed, and tried not to feel disappointed. Between the woman on the boat and John and Earl, Annie sensed that something was different, that something had changed. Or maybe she simply needed time to recalibrate to the rhythm of the island and the people that she loved.

Then again, because she'd been up all night, maybe she wasn't thinking clearly yet.

Yes, she decided, that was all it was. Things would seem perfectly normal after she slept.

If Murphy, her long-deceased friend and self-appointed guardian angel, cared to offer advice (as she often did from her place in the heavenly clouds), then Annie fell asleep before she heard it.

Chapter 2

It was after three o'clock when Annie awoke, no longer tired but by then very hungry. After quickly dressing in jeans and a long-sleeved sweater that had hung untouched in the closet since early January, she started to prowl through her beloved tiny kitchen with its natural stone counters and wide-plank floors—a far cry from the white-walled, white-marbled, wide-windowed space of the sunshine-drenched bungalow (complete with French doors that led out to the pool deck)—where she'd spent the winter. Blinking back that lovely image, she found some bread and a container of what appeared to be fresh chicken salad that Claire must have made; it emitted an aroma of dill, Claire's favorite herb.

Annie made half a sandwich, set it on a plate, then noticed a large cookie tin on the counter. A Post-it note was stuck to the top: the only message was a smiling emoji hand-drawn in a thick marker. Prying off the lid, Annie was greeted by a generous stack of jumbo-sized chocolate-chip cookies, the ones Lucy had become famous on Chappy for baking and, fat and calories aside, tasted better than a Clementine plucked right off a tree.

Lucy, she thought, her heart warming a little. She wondered how the teenager was making out at the science fair; she'd told Annie that her entry examined the long-term effects of beach erosion and the keys to preserving the habitats of Sengekontacket Pond, the Barrier Beach, and Trapp's Pond. It seemed like a big undertaking for someone her age, but Annie had no doubt that the teenager was up to the task.

John had said the fair went until seven or eight; Annie decided it would be fun to see Lucy's entry and the others. Being in a room filled with energetic, Vineyard high schoolers might help Annie reacclimate. So she wrapped her half sandwich and two cookies—one for her, one for Lucy—grabbed her keys and her purse and headed out the door.

She had barely stepped onto the porch, however, when she remembered she needed a coat—something she'd rarely thought about in sunny California.

Nothing's perfect, Murphy commiserated. *And no place is, either. Except, of course, where I am. But you can't come here yet. You still have work to do.*

Annie growled with exasperation. She went back inside and found a jacket that she likewise hadn't worn since January. "By the way," she addressed her old friend, while zipping up, "where have you been? I haven't heard from you in three months." She'd missed having the spirit of her sidekick nearby.

You had your work to do; I had mine. I kept an eye on things here for you.

"Good things?"

Murphy paused, a habit of hers that Annie found annoying because she couldn't tell if Murphy was still there or had whirled back up to heaven.

Let's just say "things," came the reply.

"Murphy . . . ," Annie began, but the air in the cottage suddenly went still, a signal that her old friend had vacated the premises. Annie growled again and went out the door.

But on the short drive to the Chappy ferry (aka the *On
Time*), Annie realized she was smiling. She nibbled on her
sandwich as she thought about Murphy, her bright, red-haired,
life-of-the-party friend since college, whom she dearly missed,
though she was grateful for her occasional ethereal presence.
After graduating, Murphy had become a well-respected behavioral therapist, then the wife of a prominent Boston surgeon and the mother of twin boys who, like their mother,
were rambunctious. Annie and Murphy's final fabulous ad-
venture had been the weekend that they'd come to the island
to celebrate their fiftieth birthdays. Annie still couldn't pass
the Charlotte Inn in the heart of historic Edgartown without
remembering when they had whiled away an afternoon on
the patio, sitting in wrought-iron chairs under shady blue um-
brellas, sipping cosmos instead of plain Chardonnay because
Murphy claimed that vodka dressed up with Chambord and
orange liqueur showed more enthusiasm than plain old wine.
They wore floral sundresses and open-toed sandals that
showed off their fresh pedicures; as usual, they shared lively
conversation about some things that mattered and more that
didn't. That was the day Murphy suggested it was time for
them to make bucket lists.

"What would you want to do if you weren't such an infernally sober stick-in-the-mud?" Murphy asked between sips.

Annie had a good laugh at that. "Okay," she said after taking a few moments to think. "The first thing I'd do would be
to move here. To the Vineyard. At least for a while."

"Do it," Murphy said in an uncommonly serious voice.
"Make the move. It's time to reinvent your life." Annie knew
it was Murphy's way of telling her to stop wallowing in the
past, to shed the baggage of too many losses and disappointments that she'd amassed from living in the city all her life.

In hindsight, Annie wondered if her friend had had a premonition, because a month later, Murphy had been diagnosed

with a rare, swift-moving cancer. And yet it didn't stop her: between her family, work, and chemo treatments, Murphy managed to carve out a day or two here and there for Annie. Together they found a cottage on Chappy that was perfect for Annie, then, with her bald head cocooned in a gaily striped turban, Murphy accompanied her on moving day. She said she needed to see her best friend settled and to know that she was safe. That had been on Labor Day. Four weeks later, Murphy was dead. And Annie's heart felt irrevocably broken.

Thanks to her friend's prodding, however, Annie stayed true to her dream. And she was still there, surrounded by unending beauty and the peaceful rhythm of the place she now called home. Besides, she suspected that if she dared to leave, Murphy would come back to haunt her in a rap-on-the-knuckles kind of way. Even worse, she might take her Irish stew of witticisms, serious talk, and often snarky humor elsewhere. Of course, Annie still wasn't sure if Murphy was a real ghost or a figment of her overactive writer's imagination. Over time, however, she'd decided it didn't matter; she liked to think that Murphy was still with her.

But now, as Annie drove into the lot at the high school in Oak Bluffs, she wondered if her old friend had nudged her to remember that afternoon at the Charlotte Inn for a reason.

Finishing her sandwich, Annie gathered her things and decided that if Murphy had been hinting at something in particular, it must not be terribly worrisome, or she would have explained.

Wouldn't she?

The Science and Engineering Fair was held in the high school cafeteria. More than two dozen foldout poster boards sat atop six-foot lunchroom tables scattered around the expansive space; some featured drawings and hand-lettered descriptions of numerous topics, from sea glass to ancient tribal relics unearthed up-island at Aquinnah; other entries spanned topics such as marine life and wind farms and had in-depth Power-Point presentations accompanied by informational handouts. Exhibitors were stationed at their booths, greeting a hearty throng of meandering people, which included teachers, other students, and visiting parents, as well as neighbors and supportive islanders.

Annie walked around, keeping an eye out for Lucy. Soon she spotted a large poster with a bold headline that read: SENGEKONTACKET, BARRIER BEACH, TRAPP'S POND: WILL THEY BE HERE TOMORROW?

Annie went toward the booth, but Lucy wasn't there; instead, a young man stood next to the table, his back to Annie. He was tall with slim shoulders; his light brown hair crept over his collar. He turned as Annie got closer; that's when she realized it was Kyle, Lucy's boyfriend, who had shot up in height while Annie was away.

"Kyle!" Annie said, trying to hide her surprise at his growth spurt. "It's so nice to see you."

"Hi, Annie," he replied shyly, because that was Kyle. "You're back."

She nodded. "At last. Is this Lucy's project?"

"Yeah. Pretty cool, huh? She did the posters and a Power-Point. Too bad she wasn't here for the judging. She won first place in the Investigative category. Look." He held up the large wood-and-brass trophy on the table in front of him. When he smiled, his adorable dimples in both cheeks smiled, too. "I was going to text her about it, but I figured I'd wait till she got back. Let her see for herself, you know?"

"Wow," Annie said. "This is wonderful. I'm sure it's well deserved."

"Yeah," he replied. "She's so crazy-smart. But I thought she'd be back by now."

Annie looked around. "Where'd she go?"

"To check on Abigail."

A what-on-earth-had-Abigail-done-now feeling swept over Annie, despite the fact that before Annie had left, the eighteen-year-old had cleaned up her act, finally pointing her life in a positive direction. But as badly as Annie wanted to grill Kyle as to why Abigail needed checking up on, she quashed her runaway thoughts.

"Is Lucy at the house?" Annie simply asked. The "house" was John's town house in Edgartown, the lovely two-bed, two-bath place he'd won in the affordable-housing lottery long before Annie had met him. Even though he was a hard-working, well-respected police detective, John would have been hard-pressed to come up with the kind of deposit that new homes on the island now commanded.

"I guess. You wanna text her?"

Pretending to be interested in the posters that framed Lucy's exhibit, Annie tried not to show concern.

"Thanks, but I'd rather surprise her. And I'll have a chance to check in with Abigail, too."

"Don't tell Lucy she won first place, okay?" He swept his hair off his brow, unveiling his bright blue eyes.

Annie held up three fingers. "Scout's honor. I'll save that for you."

He grinned, picked up a handout of Lucy's project, and said, "Here. You can tell her you read this. She'd like that." Kyle was a sensitive, well-mannered boy, which partly explained why both John and Earl had approved of him as Lucy's choice for a first boyfriend.

"Great idea. I'll tell her to let you know when she'll be back, okay?"

"Yeah, thanks."

Yes, Annie thought as, printout in hand, she headed from the fair, Lucy had found a really sweet boy. Unlike some that Abigail had been entwined with.

But those days were over; Abigail was on a good path now. And Annie had no reason to believe otherwise.

"Knock, knock," Annie called as she opened the front door. She was still uncomfortable barging into John's town house; she still wouldn't retrieve the key from under the planter on the right side of the porch if the door was locked, even though in three weeks she'd be officially entitled to do those things, once she was John Lyons's wife. She wasn't going to take his last name as hers. He'd seemed disappointed when she'd first told him, but later he agreed that they were old enough to forgo that tradition. Besides, Annie had a writing career built on her name. And Sutton was the surname she'd been born with; it wasn't as if it had belonged to one of her two previous husbands. Of course, John would never guess that the real reason she didn't want to change her name was that she didn't want to have to change it back if things didn't work out. Twice bitten, third time shy.

Restless, the part-Bernese mountain dog, part something unknown, bounded down the stairs that led up to the bedrooms, whimpering with excitement, just as Lucy appeared in the doorway that led from the living room to the kitchen.

"Sssh," Lucy cautioned him.

The dog shushed but continued to wriggle from one end to the other. Annie bent down and gave him a big hug, then stood and gave Lucy one, too. Like Kyle, Lucy seemed taller, more mature, than when Annie had last seen her. How did such things happen so fast?

"Abigail's asleep," Lucy said, her voice still a whisper. "But welcome home!"

Restless rolled onto his back, as if begging for a tummy rub. Annie obliged, while saying, "Thanks. It's great to be here. What's wrong with your sister?"

Rolling her pearl-gray eyes that were identical to John's

and to John's mother, Claire, Lucy replied, "Good question. She keeps saying she's tired. And that she feels 'off-balance,' whatever that means. Dad says she's probably bored with her classes and doesn't want to admit it 'cuz of all the money he spent between buying her the car and paying rent on the garage apartment on the Cape so she wouldn't have to commute. I figure he thinks she's drinking . . . or worse."

The presumption was reflective of the old Abigail, the party girl with an attitude, so the possibility wasn't without merit. But by the end of last year, she'd become responsible, sensible, and nice to be around. She seemed to love the community college and was looking forward to transferring in the fall to the Rhode Island School of Design, where she planned to focus on fashion design.

Studying Lucy's face now, Annie tried to read her thoughts about what really was going on. But the changes in the younger girl's appearance were distracting: her caramel-colored, trademark long braid was gone; her hair was neatly clipped just below her ears, as Annie's was; she wore eyeliner and mascara. In short, Lucy looked grown up. If Annie told her that, however, Lucy most likely would roll her eyes again.

"How long has she been . . . tired?" Annie stood up again, a crick in her hip, no doubt from having been squished for too long on the plane, the bus, the boat.

"A while."

A while? Why hadn't John mentioned it?

Because unless it's about cop stuff, he's a crappy communicator, Murphy, or perhaps Annie's inner voice, acknowledged.

Shifting on one foot, she asked, "What about today? How long has she been asleep?"

"I don't know. At least since I came home like an hour and a half ago. I don't think she's eaten today, so I'm heating up tomato soup and making a grilled-cheese sandwich. They're her favorites."

Pampering her sister indicated that Lucy was worried. The two girls were very different; they had not been close. Unless that, too, had changed over the past months.

"I'll tell you what," Annie said. "How about if you keep cooking, and I'll go upstairs and try to rouse her. And, speaking of favorites. . . ." She dug into her purse and pulled out the baggie of chocolate-chip cookies. "Have one of these. I believe they're the best on the island."

Lucy laughed. It was a small, quiet laugh but a laugh, nonetheless.

Annie hugged her again, then Restless led the way upstairs. She hoped she might be able to tell if Abigail needed medical attention. Over the years, Annie had been around sick people—her parents, Murphy, and Donna, her birth mother. And yet, when she reached the landing and went down the hall to the girls' bedroom, Annie was not prepared for what she saw.

Chapter 3

Though the sun was out and the temperature had climbed above sixty degrees—a perfect combination for early April—the bedroom that the girls shared was dark. Gloomy. And silent, except for the soft, steady breaths coming from Abigail's side of the room.

Annie went to the pair of tall windows and slowly opened the drapes to let in some light. She was greeted by more changes—this time, the room's décor. It was a large space, able to nicely accommodate twin beds with matching bureaus, two desks with chairs, and two sizable, freestanding wardrobes that, in addition to the generous closet, provided storage. Annie knew that for high school and college-age girls, storage was a must-have.

Because there wasn't a bathroom off the bedroom, John had relinquished the one in the upstairs hallway to his daughters; though the main bedroom also was upstairs, he used the other bath on the first floor. It was something Annie intended to tweak once they were married and she moved in.

She went to Lucy's desk and sat in the adult-sized, office-type chair with lumbar support, armrests, and wheels. It was no longer the small, wooden chair that Annie remembered had been painted pink, with the name LUCY spelled in glittery crystals across the back. In fact, the entire room was no longer pink but soft ivory. The wall on Lucy's side was covered with posters of salt ponds and marshes, oysters, and quahogs. The opposite side—Abigail's side—featured a variety of fabric samples, which Annie suspected Abigail had painted by hand. The samples were surrounded by large sheets of paper filled with fashion illustrations, mostly of skirts that were long, short, and in-between. The colors were vibrant and happy, unlike the pale complexion of the girl who was breathing softly, her once-shining blond hair, now stringy and in need of a wash, splayed on the pillow in assorted directions.

After ten or fifteen minutes, the warmth from outdoors seeped into the room and seemed to stir Abigail.

"Good morning," Annie whispered.

The girl in the bed lifted her head, rubbed her eyes. "What time is it?" Then she looked at Annie. "Annie? Is that you?"

"Yes. I'm home. And it's almost four in the afternoon."

Abigail's head dropped back to the pillow. Her eyes were the color of warm brown cedar, like the trees that grew in abundance on the Vineyard. They stayed open, looking at nothing.

"Lucy says you're not feeling well. Do you want to talk about it?"

"Not really."

Annie understood the hesitation. Like Abigail, she never liked people hovering over her, especially when she felt lousy, physically or emotionally. She drew the chair closer to the bed.

"What's different?" she asked. "When I left for California, you sure seemed healthy."

Beneath the comforter, Abigail muttered, "I'm just tired." Which was evident from her weak voice.

"Have you seen the doctor?"

"Yeah. I had blood tests." She turned onto her side, her back to Annie now, as if speaking had worn her out. Perhaps she wanted Annie to leave.

Then Lucy appeared, bearing a food tray complete with a small vase in which she'd stuck a plastic blue hydrangea blossom.

"Lunch!" Lucy declared. "Tomato basil soup and grilled cheese. With applesauce for dessert because you love it, even though I think it's gross."

After a moment's hesitation, Abigail slowly rolled back and faced them. That time, she wore a limp smile. "Awesome. I might even be hungry."

"You won't be as tired if you eat," Lucy said. "Even bears come out of hibernation to pig out in the spring. Of course, there haven't been any bears on the island for decades, unless you count the Polar Bears at Inkwell."

Annie laughed; Abigail offered a small smile. Inkwell Beach was in Oak Bluffs, a neighboring town, where a community group, open to all, had been convening every day between Memorial Day and Labor Day since the 1940s. It had become an island tradition that was started by a few African American women who'd dubbed themselves the Polar Bears. The group now boasted a couple of hundred "regulars" of all ages, genders, ethnicities, and so on, for swimming, talking, and/or walking the beach at seven thirty in the morning. Annie knew that Lucy liked to ride her bike there and join them whenever possible.

Pulling herself up, Abigail pushed her hair away from her face and picked up the sandwich.

Annie waited until she'd taken a few bites before asking, "Did you get the blood test results yet?"

"She has to go to Boston," Lucy said.

Though Annie loved Lucy, she found it mildly irritating that sometimes the girl could try to run things when she should not. Perhaps this time, it was because she was scared that her sister was really ill.

Abigail lifted a spoonful of soup. "They want me to see a specialist. A neurologist. My dad has the details." It was impossible to know if she didn't know or if she did not want to talk about it.

"That's great," Annie said, searching for positive words. "Specialists can get to the bottom of things. When are you going?"

"Tuesday," Lucy answered for her sister again.

After a second, Annie said something generic that she hoped would be reassuring but was probably a cliché: "I'm sure everything will be fine"; "the hospital up there has wonderful doctors"; something like that. Then she excused herself, saying she needed to get home and unpack, and telling Abigail she hoped she'd feel better. Restless accompanied Annie downstairs to the front door. Then she left John's girls and his dog and his house and made her way back to Chappy, annoyed that he hadn't told her about any of this and feeling left out of the family before she was legally in it.

Once home, Annie texted John and asked if he could pick up a pizza and have dinner with her. She didn't want to have the conversation on the phone about what was going on with his older daughter. Nor did she feel like plowing through the rest of Claire's food containers.

He quickly responded: 7:00?

She agreed. Then, before being tempted to wallow in self-pity, she texted her brother: **Hey. I'm home. If you're around.**

Kevin didn't respond right away, which she also tried not to take personally. But within minutes, two knocks came on her cottage door. She opened it; her brother was standing there. He was holding a fat bouquet of daffodils.

"I missed you a bunch," he said, holding out the flowers.

It was ridiculous, but tears welled in her eyes. Kevin, her brother, had brought her daffodils; John, her fiancé, had not. In fact, John had barely kissed her. She now knew that he must be distraught, worried about Abigail, but wasn't he glad Annie was home? Didn't he think she could offer a calming presence that might help quiet his fears?

Kevin set the flowers on the counter and gave her a hug. "Don't cry. I'm not that funny."

Which, of course, made Annie laugh and wipe her tears. "You're an idiot," she said, giving him a shoulder bump. "But thanks for the flowers."

"They were free. I picked them in our meadow."

He had no way of knowing that made the situation worse, that he'd been thoughtful enough to take the time to pick the perfect daffodils when John hadn't even bothered to grab a ready-made pot from the sidewalk rack at Stop and Shop.

She sighed and chalked up her sensitivity to too many hours spent traveling.

Backing up a step, she took Kevin's hands in hers, scanned his round, happy cheeks, and looked into his hazel eyes, which were clones of hers, clones of their mother's. His hair was still a shade lighter than hers; he was still only slightly taller than she was. And though he'd built up a solid set of biceps from a career in construction, unlike his older sister, his middle was a little round, a little soft. All in all, Annie was grateful that he pretty much looked exactly as he had when she left in January. Maybe it meant that not everything and everyone in her world had changed.

"I've missed you, too," she said with a grin. "How about a cup of tea and one of Lucy's cookies? Then you can tell me what's been going on that you didn't tell me about when we talked because you did not want to worry me."

He plunked down in a chair at the small kitchen table.

"Deal. But there's not much to say. There haven't been any disasters since you left. Hmm," he added, folding his hands and pressing his chin into his palms, "Do you suppose that's a sign? That you're the troublemaker in the group?"

"Very funny." She put the daffodils in one of Claire's glass canning jars, which doubled as a perfect-sized vase. Then she put the stainless-steel kettle on the stove, dropped two Earl Grey tea bags into mugs, and handed him a cookie on a napkin.

"I suppose there is one thing," he said with a mischievous smile. "I'm still waiting for final approval from Boston, but there's a pretty good chance I'm going to be a captain of the *On Time* ferry."

To say she was startled was an understatement. She grabbed the cookie she'd just given him and took a big bite. "You're kidding." She brushed a crumb from her shirt.

"Nope. You might recall that since I've been here, I filled in as a deckhand every summer?"

"Well, yes. But I thought you were just helping out because you can't sit still."

"That's how it started. But I really liked it. While you were gone I took the training course for the Coast Guard requirements. I passed the physical, and now there's a good chance that I aced the exam; I'm just waiting for the final word."

"You're serious! I didn't even know you liked boats that well. Or simply being on the water. Do you even fish?"

He laughed. "Not since I've been here. But, yes, I like boats. I owned a couple in my previous life—I mostly took my clients out and cruised around the harbor. We came down to the Cape a few times, and over to the Vineyard once or twice. Anyway, all those hours I spent navigating on the water counted toward the experience I needed to take the Coast Guard course. Who knew that would happen, huh?"

"And you found time to do that in addition to finishing

the house for Francine and Jonas." She took another bite before handing back the cookie.

He shrugged. "I had lots of time to study. Not much else is going on in winter. But you already know that."

Apparently not everyone enjoyed the peace of the winter as much as Annie did. She laughed again. Having her brother around was the best panacea for her worries. "Like I said, you can't sit still. But congratulations. I believe that having a captain of a ferry is a first for our family."

He sank his teeth into the cookie. "It's the *On Time*, Annie. Hardly the *Island Home*. But I was amazed at how much I had to learn about the channel and the currents and what to do when the wind picks up and how to navigate around the boats moored in the harbor in season . . . and you're not listening, are you?"

She hadn't realized he could tell that her thoughts had drifted. "I was," she replied. "I'm excited for you, Kev. I think it's amazing. And I'm sorry, but I'm a little preoccupied. Have you heard anything about Abigail?"

"John's daughter?"

She set the vase on the table and responded to the kettle that had begun to whistle. "Uh-huh."

"What about her? Like, if she's done something wrong?"

Pouring the water into the mugs, Annie tried to act nonchalant. "More like if something's wrong with her. If she's sick. And if so, how long it's been going on."

The small frown line between his eyebrows deepened. "I haven't heard anything. You want me to ask my wife?"

Kevin's wife, Taylor Winsted, and Annie had finally become friends of a sort, meaning that Annie had become accustomed to the woman's often irascible personality and had learned that Taylor had her reasons. And her good side, too. But Annie didn't want to bring her sister-in-law into it unless John asked her to. If he ever decided to talk to Annie about it.

"Thanks, but I think the fewer people involved, the better. Besides, I'm probably overreacting. It's just that John hasn't told me what's going on yet, and I think Lucy's concerned."

"Maybe Lucy's the one who's overreacting."

"Maybe. But I saw Abigail. And, honestly, she doesn't look well."

He frowned again. "Should I ask Earl?"

She shook her head. "No. If they don't know, it will only upset them."

"Then unless you hear otherwise, I'd chalk it up to Abigail being . . . what is she now? Eighteen?"

Annie nodded and he chomped on the cookie again.

She decided not to belabor the topic. After all, she hadn't seen her brother in three months, and she really wanted an update about his life and the Inn and the rest, including how Francine and Jonas were settling into their new house. So she carried the tea to the table and sat across from him, and they had a long talk about this and that, and he gave her tons more details about what it took to be a captain of the *On Time*, and somehow she felt a lot better.

John was late and the pizza was cold, for which he apologized. He said he'd been delayed by an issue at the station. He did not elaborate. Annie turned the oven to a low temperature and slid the pizza in, remembering that Claire once told her that "police business" was something Annie had better get used to if she was going to marry John. Over time, Annie had figured out that on the job, his communication skills were well honed; off the job, he was like many other men who needed to have their emotions pried out of them.

"So," she said while setting the table, hoping if she stayed in motion, she'd be able to hide her frustration, "Abigail's not feeling well?" She set a plate, silverware, and a napkin in front of him while his brain cells presumably scrambled for an answer.

He cleared his throat. She knew it was his way of stalling while he conjured up a reply. "That's what she says," he said. "At first I thought she'd been partying—hitting the booze maybe or doing stupid drugs. I know she really likes college and her grades are good, but . . . ."

"But your assumptions are based on . . . ?" She supposed she should give him a chance to tell her in his own words but she wasn't in the mood to be patient.

Then the wide, strong shoulders that Annie loved resting against—especially in tough times, as if she could absorb his strength—slumped. Yes, she thought, he had lost weight.

She waited a moment, hoping to come up with the right words. "Do you have any evidence that she's been . . . acting up?" *Evidence* was a word he'd be able to relate to, because he was a real detective, not an amateur like Annie was when she dabbled with mysteries, mostly murders, in her books.

He didn't clear his throat that time. He merely looked at her, his alluring eyes now dull and sad. "No," he said. "Besides, if she was drinking or drugging, it would be easier for me to spot." He sighed and lowered his eyes. "The blood tests ruled out a bunch of things like lupus, Lyme disease, a handful of infections, and other stuff."

Waiting for a heartbeat or two, Annie then said, "Okay. That's good." She had no idea whether or not it was. "So, you're taking her to Boston?"

"Right. An MRI, a spinal tap, more blood work. First we'll see a neurologist. But you know what it's like today—sometimes it feels like the medical people do too much poking around." He paused. "Or at least that's what I've been trying to tell myself."

Annie's instincts told her he was trying to avoid getting

too apprehensive. Her gut also warned her that Abigail might have something serious. Suddenly, Annie regretted having felt bruised that John hadn't given her—and her homecoming—more attention. When had she become so self-centered? Had it grown out of having been heralded so much, too much, in Los Angeles?

She fussed with silverware and napkins, plopped the salad fixings into a bowl, added dressing, and tossed. She turned her thoughts back to John, where they belonged. "Is she scared? Has she had an MRI before?"

He laughed. "She fell on the playground when she was six and needed three stitches in her arm. I think that's the only time she's been in a hospital. Except in the wing where the doctors' offices are. And only for regular stuff—vaccines, school physicals, a bad cold one year. Both the girls have always been healthy."

She poured a glass of wine for herself and got a beer for John. But as she set them on the table, she had a sudden thought that he might be in denial. The first time that had happened to Annie was when her first husband, Brian, was killed in a car accident. It had taken months of therapy for her to be able to face what happened—after all, Annie Sutton was a stalwart third-grade teacher who carried on, no matter what, because everyone had problems, didn't they? Even then, she knew it was a very long time before she recovered. "Denial is the shock absorber of the soul," her therapist told her. Annie at once thought that that should be carved on her tombstone.

But now she had an idea.

"Maybe they'll let you bring Abigail to the hospital here first so she can at least see the MRI machine. I'm sure one of the technicians would be happy to explain how it works, so she'll know what to expect."

"She'll be fine, Annie. She's not a kid."

We all become kids again when we're scared, Murphy whispered in her ear.

Annie hesitated half a heartbeat. "We all become kids again when we're scared," she said, echoing her wise friend.

Toying with the beer bottle, John said, "Maybe. But neither of my girls are crybabies."

In that moment, Annie decided it was time to take the pizza out of the oven, whether it was hot or not. She knew that John was a great dad, knew that he loved his girls and would do anything for them. She also knew he was a smart man. Even though sometimes . . .

"And I'm not saying anything to my parents right now," he continued. "I want to wait until there's something definite to tell them. No sense worrying them for no reason."

Yes, John was smart. Most of the time.

The pizza wasn't hot, but warm enough.

Grabbing a spatula, she carried the box to the table and slid two slices onto John's plate and one onto hers. She brought the box to the counter, then returned to the table, trying to gauge how to express her feelings in a way that might help without pissing him off.

"When are you going to Boston?" was all she came up with, though Lucy had already told her.

"Tuesday. We're on the six o'clock boat. She's not happy about having to get up so early."

Annie sipped her wine. "I'll be glad to go with you. If you want." If Lucy was the one who was sick, Annie wouldn't feel a need to ask. With Abigail, however, sometimes she still felt like an interloper.

John bit into his pizza, chewed, and swallowed, another tactic Annie recognized as a diversion. Finally, he blurted out, "Thanks, but there's no need."

"It could be a long day, John. Maybe Abigail would like

some extra support. And maybe you could use the company. . . ."

He took another slug of beer. "Well, it's true she would. And it's true I would. But it's also true we've got that covered." He cleared his throat again, that time, more slowly. "The fact is, Jenn's going with us. She said she should be there. As Abigail's mother."

Annie blinked. Jenn was the ex-wife who lived in Plymouth—a forty-five-minute drive from the ferry terminal in Woods Hole—where the Pilgrims had supposedly landed and where Jenn had been born and apparently raised. Even before the divorce, she'd returned to her hometown on the mainland, close enough to stay mildly engaged with Lucy, far enough that Annie often conveniently forgot that the woman existed. Until last year, Abigail had lived with her mother.

Nodding now, Annie did not know what to say; it wasn't as if she could refute John's comment about Jenn being Abigail's mother. But along with a small bite of pizza, an unexpected lump landed in Annie's stomach.

Chapter 4

Ever since he'd been a kid, John tried to do everything right. Sometimes, it didn't work.

He'd been wrong when he was eight and kicked Davey Blodget in the shins because Davey was ranking on Tracey Morley, who at the time was the prettiest girl in Edgartown Elementary School, even though she wore braces, which Davey had pointed out, loudly, laughingly, made her look like she had teeth made out of tin.

John also had been wrong when he went to college and majored in pre-law because he thought he'd make a better attorney than a cop.

And he'd been wrong when he married Jenn, though he'd been right when he thought he'd love being a dad.

He'd also been wrong these past couple of months for not telling Annie that Abigail was sick, or that Jenn had come to the island a bunch of times. And that she'd stayed at the town house that wasn't hers but his. That would soon be Annie's, too.

There were probably other times when John had been wrong, but those were the worst ones, the ones that stuck in his mind, mostly because each time he screwed up, his dad vocalized that he was "disappointed" in him: disappointed because Davey Blodget was a kid who was small for his age, a lot smaller than John, and that Earl hadn't raised John to be a bully; disappointed because, though John was smart enough to get into law school, Earl thought his son knew he was cut out to keep people safe on the Vineyard, not to convict people who might be innocent or to defend criminals because that's what lawyers did. Mostly, Earl had been disappointed when John married Jenn, though that time, he didn't say a word. Still, John had known his dad all his life, and deep down, he, too, had known that Jenn wasn't right for the island, or rather that the island wasn't right for her, that she'd never be happy there, that she'd wind up being miserable and that she'd make John's life miserable, and Earl's and Claire's lives, too.

Earl also had asked if Abigail was sick—which he'd deduced without John having told him, because Earl was good at sensing problems within his family. John didn't deny it but said she probably had mononucleosis. And when Earl asked if he'd told Annie, and John said he'd wait until she was home, because what could she do about it out there in L.A, Earl shook his head, got into his pickup, and drove off. Worst of all, he didn't mention it to John again.

For a guy who always tried to do the right thing, Detective Sergeant John Lyons had a way of screwing things up.

And now, when what he really wanted and needed was to spend the night with Annie, so that she could let him hold her close, let him tell her how scared he was and to cry if he could, well, the look on her face when he told her Jenn was going to Boston with them—a look not of anger or bitterness but one of disappointment that, thanks to his dad, John knew well—was why he finished his pizza and said he didn't want to leave Abigail for the whole night. Which was when he left Annie's cottage and took the On Time back to Edgartown.

He sat on the long sofa in his living room now, the TV on, the sound muted, while he mindlessly scratched Restless behind the ears and wondered what the hell was wrong with Abigail, and if, somehow, he was going to mess up everyone's lives because he didn't know what the hell to do.

Chapter 5

On Saturday morning, Annie walked up to the Inn. Before going inside, she took a moment to look around, to remember how lucky she'd become. Only a few years earlier, she'd come close to not having a home of any kind; she'd been without a family of any sort; she'd been completely alone. And then the world had opened up and enveloped her: suddenly she had a mother and a brother and a passel of new friends. And now there was an Inn—the commodious, picture-perfect waterfront place that blended subtle luxuries with the rustic charm of Martha's Vineyard and stunning views of Edgartown Harbor and the lighthouse. Best of all, within its lush, first-class décor, it also was homey and welcoming, from the grand, two-story great room, the custom-designed chef's kitchen, the library, the media room, and the laundry room on the first floor to the seven rooms with private baths upstairs. They called it the Vineyard Inn—a memorable name for a place where they hoped visitors and year-round islanders would feel at home. On Memorial Day weekend, they would open their doors for another season. Things had been going well.

She crossed the stone patio, which, come summer, would again abound with planters of colorful, local flowers and boast comfy chairs and a fire pit to encourage outdoor evening conversations among guests and the staff. Upstairs, three rooms were reserved for year-round islanders and three for visitors in season; the visitors' rooms were then leased to islanders from October through May for what were called winter rentals. The seventh room had once belonged to Francine and Bella; now they kept it available for emergency situations, when someone had nowhere else to stay. So far, it had been used often.

With her long legs striding up the back steps, Annie opened the door and went into the mudroom, which, despite its name, was spotlessly maintained by their dependable cleaners. She knew that Francine (who'd taken on the management duties while Annie was in California) would make sure the Inn was kept pristine.

Reaching the door into the kitchen, Annie took a deep breath. She expected—hoped—to see either Francine or Claire, busily making breakfast. But when she went in, there was only Rex Winsted—Taylor's brother, Kevin's brother-in-law. A former multi-Michelin-starred chef, he was taking a muffin tin out of the oven, humming a cheerful song. An aromatic blend of rosemary and sage filled the room.

"Hey!" he said, lifting his gaze from the muffin tin. "Welcome home!" He grinned a big grin that matched the bigness of the rest of him.

Annie moved inside as the bald-headed lumberjack of a human being set what looked like herbed egg-and-cheese quiches on the marble-topped island. Having known Rex only since Thanksgiving, Annie was still amazed that the large man was so skilled at crafting such delicate, delicious dishes.

"Thanks, it's great to be here." She looked around the gourmet kitchen. "I didn't think I'd see you here this morning."

He shrugged. "Doing my civic duty. Otherwise known as helping out when help is needed."

She decided to wait to ask where the others were. Maybe Claire was busy preparing for her dinner guests; maybe Francine was with her. So Annie matched Rex's grin so she wouldn't look disappointed.

"How are you?" she asked. "Have you found a place for your restaurant yet?" Rex had owned an upscale restaurant in Boston before the Covid pandemic put him out of business. Though his skills had once been sought after, he'd once said that plenty of good chefs were still out of work in the city. So Rex had come back to the island where he'd grown up and was trying to jump-start his life by opening a restaurant in Chilmark or Aquinnah.

He gave her a nonchalant shrug. "It's hard to find a spot up-island where a restaurant can survive year-round. Maybe that's why there haven't been many." He'd traded the family home on Chappy with Taylor for the plot of land in Aquinnah that their late father had won in the fishing derby decades earlier; Rex had been living there, in the small but pleasant cabin that the elder Winsted built. "I'm not discouraged, though. I keep telling myself when the time and place are right, I'll be ready."

At least he had a good attitude.

"Absolutely," Annie said, then couldn't hold back any longer. "In the meantime, while I certainly don't disapprove of your being in this kitchen, would you mind telling me why you're here, and not Francine? Or Claire?"

Usually, Francine was the breakfast chef, except during the previous off-seasons, when she was at college in Minneapolis, majoring in hospitality and tourism management. When Francine was away, Annie had taken care of breakfasts: She'd provided their year-round tenants and three winter renters with a simple fare of yogurt and cereal on weekdays, scrambled eggs and toast on weekends. But with Annie being gone and the baby due in May, Francine and Jonas had decided to stay on the island all year; the school agreed to let her finish her degree remotely. And she no doubt had been spoiling everyone with dishes like the savory quiches that now tempted Annie.

"Claire said she was busy," Rex said. "Whenever she says that, I don't ask what she's doing." He snickered. "I'm still not sure she's happy to have me around. Anyway, Francine asked if I'd come in today and do breakfast for the renters and make something special for you and her. I expect she also wanted to sleep in. Her back's been aching a little. As I'm sure you know, the baby's due soon."

So Rex had melded into the island family—at least that was one nice change while she'd been away. But no matter what Rex thought Claire thought about him, Annie knew she'd slowly begun to trust that he wasn't the same rabble-rousing, unlikable boy as when he'd been growing up. As for Francine, at least she had a happy reason to ache a little. Annie smiled at the thought of a tiny baby joining the troops, as Kevin had dubbed the group. A baby was far more pleasant to think about than whatever was going on with Abigail. Or John. Or his ex-wife.

Then Annie realized it was nice of Rex to come all the way from Aquinnah for this special chore.

"Thanks for doing this. And, by the way, it smells delicious."

"You should have been here the other night when I made Wasabi crab cakes and tarragon crab and avocado. I vowed to spend the winter making sure I don't get rusty." Taking a small copper fry pan from the overhead rack, he laid a few strips of bacon in the pan, then removed a colander from the sink and transferred freshly rinsed greens into a bowl. He picked up what looked like a small leather briefcase, set it on the counter, and opened it: inside was an array of well-organized, shining silver knives in many sizes, each tucked into a velvet-covered slot.

"I'm sure everyone here appreciates your talents," Annie replied as she eyed the knives.

He lifted out one, then another, and moved to the sink, where he carefully cleaned them. Returning to the salad, he positioned the knives in the bowl and quickly crisscrossed the blades, neatly chopping the greens.

"A true chef never goes anywhere without his best tools," he said. "Sort of like a doctor. Or a good mechanic." He smiled again and went to the refrigerator.

"Goat cheese okay with you? It's great with bacon in a breakfast salad."

Annie admitted she'd never heard of a breakfast salad. Maybe they had them in California, but she'd been paying attention to other things. Like work. Which reminded her—she still had a book to finish and another one to start. But first, she really wanted to take a break from writing and use the time to readjust and recharge. Which perhaps was what Rex was doing now, before lunging into starting another restaurant.

"Anything you make will be fabulous," she said. "Though you're right. I wish I'd been here for the Wasabi crab cakes."

Just then the back door opened and in waddled Francine.

Annie's palms flew to her face; her mouth dropped into an unplanned O. She forgot about knives or writing books or even breakfast once she saw the young woman's large, perfectly rounded belly. Resisting the urge to throw her arms around her and dance in circles, Annie merely welled up with tears, scooted toward Francine, and offered a generous hug.

A few minutes later, she and Francine were in the Inn's reading room, which Annie had adopted as her favorite place on the property for solitude, not counting her own little cottage. Shelves on all sides were packed with eclectic choices of books; the room included a corner for comfortable, cushy seating, and a small, handcrafted wooden table where Annie had spent many hours either writing or thinking about writing. She always found contentment there. And now, with Francine seated at the table across from her, it felt even more special.

They each had a plate of quiche, salad, and two warm, mini-butter muffins; a mug of coffee for Annie, a glass of orange juice for Francine.

Annie took a good look at her morning companion. "Wow," she said, "You look terrific. "You're really having a baby, aren't you?"

Francine's short, pixie-cut black hair framed her freshly scrubbed, blushing cheeks and large, soulful eyes, which sparkled with joy. "So I've been told." She rubbed her stomach. "Not to mention that my baby bump now makes a beach ball look like a chickpea." But her comment was said in jest; she no longer showed the look of fear as she had months earlier, back when she'd told Annie that she was afraid. Francine's mother had died after giving birth to Bella—the almost four-year-old little girl whom Earl now referred to as the "Treasure of Chappaquiddick." Once afraid that, she, too, might leave Bella, and now a new baby, motherless, Francine now seemed calmer. Perhaps that was thanks to the love that enveloped her on the island.

Annie laughed. "Are you going to go to Earl and Claire's for dinner tonight?"

"We're planning to."

"And you're still feeling okay?"

"I am. Except little things knock the socks off me now—like going to the Cape yesterday. We had a great time, though. The gallery took twelve of Jonas's paintings—mostly seascapes. The owner loves his use of vibrant colors, even the ones of stormy days. He said it's remarkable how Jonas captures a different feeling with each painting."

Annie knew that Francine's pride in her young husband was as genuine as their feelings for each other. They had conquered their early doubts; the happiness of their small family was now contagious.

"That's wonderful, honey. And what about your new house? Is it ready for the baby?"

Stabbing her fork into the salad greens, she replied, "Not exactly. As you know, I never had a place of my own when Bella was a baby. Taylor's been trying to help, but she never had a newborn in her house, so I don't think she knows what to do, either." Jonas hadn't been raised by his mother but by his grandparents. Like Francine's, his story was long and sad, and provided one more reason for all of Chappaquiddick, if not the entire Vineyard, to be rooting for them.

As Annie savored the quiche, she thought about how she had no experience at motherhood, either, no knowledge of how to outfit a home. When Bella had been left on her doorstep as an infant, Annie relied mostly on Murphy, who offered occasional suggestions from her heavenly place. But this wasn't the time to reveal that information, not even to Francine. No use in having the girl think that Annie had lost her senses out on the West Coast.

"Have you asked Claire?" Annie asked. "She's probably the only one of us who's experienced at this." She didn't mention that John had fathered two baby girls, because she didn't want to be reminded that his ex-wife would be with him on Tuesday.

"I did. But she's busy right now with her garden club."

It didn't seem like Claire to be too busy to get involved with anything, especially when it came to planning for a baby.

Not to mention it was too early in the season for garden club meetings. Wasn't it? But Annie knew there was no point in upsetting Francine by questioning that. Then she had another thought.

"Winnie! Winnie's had more experience with babies than anyone I know. And her daughter-in-law—you know her, right?—well, she's a nurse in the maternity department at the hospital."

"Taylor suggested them. But I know they live up-island, and I didn't want to be a bother . . ."

"Trust me, it won't bother them. Winnie helped me so much with Bella—how could I have forgotten? And as much as I'd love to be your sole support, I really don't have a clue. How about if we drive up to see her tomorrow? The spring blossoms should be gorgeous there. And Bella always has fun at Winnie's."

Francine laughed a quiet laugh. "I still can't believe you don't have a clue. It's so weird to think that when I first came here, I was sure you'd be the perfect person to take care of a baby because you were a famous author. I have no idea why I thought that. But, even though you don't think you know anything, look at all you did for Bella. For us. You saved our lives." Her eyes grew moist. She dabbed them with her napkin, then shook her head. "Sorry for the drama. My pregnancy hormones are going to drive me crazy."

"Enjoy every minute of your emotions. You're entitled to them; being pregnant is a beautiful thing. Or so I've been told."

"You never wanted children?"

In all the time Annie had known Francine, the subject had never come up. Or maybe Annie had become adept at avoiding it. Still, it was a question that she wasn't sure how to answer. "Brian and I were young and thought we had time. Then he was killed in the car accident. My second husband,

Mark, well, as you probably guessed, it was a good thing we didn't have kids." Francine was one of the few people with whom Annie had shared some things about her past with Mark—except about the abortion that she'd had. That was, and would remain, private. Francine had reassured her that not many people wanted to recall experiences that hadn't been their finest moments; perhaps she, too, had something she wanted to keep private.

"Anyway," Annie continued, "after Mark, whenever I felt maternal, I went to my friend Murphy and spent time with her twins." She ran her hands along the rim of the table. "But this isn't about me. It's about you and the lovely baby you're going to have. And the home you're going to make for him— or her." She paused. "You still don't know which?"

From the start, Francine and Jonas announced that they did not want to know the baby's sex, that they wanted to do things the old-fashioned way and be surprised. It caused some havoc for Kevin, who had to find a way to alter the blueprints of the workshop he was converting for their home and turn one of the two bedrooms on the second floor into three—one for Bella, one for the baby, one for mom and dad.

Francine grinned but didn't speak.

"You know!" Annie cried. "Tell me! Tell me!" Then she changed her mind. "Or don't. Maybe you and Jonas want to keep it between yourselves. I understand." She popped half of a mini-muffin into her mouth and tried not to look disappointed.

"Ha ha!" Francine laughed again. "I got you, didn't I? All we are going to share about the baby is that, so far, it's healthy. And, as for paint, we decided on the soft colors of dune grass, beach sand, and the ocean. Jonas is making two murals—one for each of the kids' rooms. Bella, however, has insisted that her mural also has lavender and blue, like the colors from our wedding."

That time, it was Annie who teared up. "I am so happy for you," was all she could say.

Francine hesitated, as if thinking before speaking. "And as soon as you and John are finally married, everyone will be happy for the two of you."

Annie quickly felt her unease return. She finished her coffee, then said, "I'll have a better chance at being happy with him once we're able to spend time together again. I've been gone a long time; part of me still feels like I'm away."

"What do you mean?"

Annie shook her head. "It's nothing, really." She rubbed the back of her neck.

"Is it about his ex-wife?"

The thud landed again in Annie's stomach. "What about her?"

An "uh-oh" look swept over Francine's face. "Um, well, nothing, really. I'm sure it's nothing."

"Francine?" Annie's question came out sounding harsher than she'd intended.

Francine stacked her silverware on her nearly empty plate and rested her hands on the table. "Okay, if I were you, I'd want to know." She drew in a long breath. "I heard Claire tell Earl that—what's her name, Jenn?—was here. Claire was upset. Earl told her if Jenn was up to no good, John wouldn't have been seen in public at the Newes with her. So, like, I said, I'm sure it's nothing." Then she fell quiet. "Is it okay that I told you?"

Forcing a smile, Annie said, "It's fine, Francine. Abigail has a small problem that Jenn's been helping her with. I decided it would be best if I stayed out of it." Her words sounded more confident than she felt.

"Okay, I thought it must be nothing. Well, nothing you had to worry about."

Annie took her napkin from her lap and picked up her dishes. "Right. Well, I do need to worry about other things, like getting my laundry done and getting myself regrouped. Don't tell anyone, but, to be honest, it was nice to be waited on when I was in California." She let out an exaggerated sigh. "But here I am, back in reality, so I'd better get going. I'll give Winnie a call and make sure she'll be around tomorrow and up for a visit from the three of us girls, and possibly four . . . unless the fourth is a boy." She got up, leaned across the table, and kissed the top of Francine's head. "I'll see you later at Earl and Claire's. Maybe in the morning, before we head up to Winnie's, I can come see your beautiful home." Then she left, wondering how much longer she'd have to continue pretending that all was well.

Chapter 6

Annie returned to her cottage with no idea what she wanted to do, other than laundry, for the rest of the day. She started by calling Winnie. But when Winnie's nephew Lucas answered the landline, he said she was on the Cape with some other tribal members working on a joint project with the Mashpee Wampanoags and wouldn't be done for another week. He suggested that Annie try her cell phone. Annie thanked him but said she'd didn't want to interrupt and would wait until Winnie was back.

She returned to the Inn and dumped an armload of clothes into the washer. Then, break or no break, and because working was her perpetual default, Annie returned to her cottage, unpacked her laptop, and set it on the small desk in her writing nook, which looked out on the harbor. She opened the window; the cottage had been closed up for so long, it desperately needed fresh air. Or maybe she was the one who needed it, in order to untangle her thoughts.

She sighed, sat down, and powered on the computer, tapping her feet while it booted up, and for some reason she glanced at her bookcase. The Agatha Christie bust—a gift from Murphy to provide inspiration when Annie had first attempted to write mysteries—stared at her from the top shelf, urging her to start typing. Beneath Agatha, the colorful bindings of books written by others had once silently mocked her, challenging her to believe in herself. But Annie knew it wouldn't be easy to jump from months of adapting her published novels into film scripts, to writing a full-fledged novel from scratch again . . . another of her Museum Girls Mysteries. Which would include a murder or two. Or three.

She'd already written several chapters, but that been . . . when? Months ago. Before she'd gone to L.A. Even before she'd done the six-week book tour in the fall. *Ugh*, she thought. She couldn't recall if she'd liked the story, let alone what direction the plot had been taking.

She wondered if Greg planned to have her adapt this one and the next into scripts, too. That would be nice. Very nice. Of course, she'd have to write the damn books first.

That time she moaned out loud.

Staring at the computer, her creative spirit teased by the partially written file on her home screen, she decided it would be easier to check her in-box first. Maybe typing a few responses to whatever was there would jog her mind back into writing. And off John. And Abigail. And the rest.

There were 431 emails. For God's sake, when was the last time she had checked? She had a vague memory of sitting on the tarmac at LAX, waiting for takeoff, thinking it might be a good time to read emails but deciding she'd rather muse about what a fabulous time she'd had in such a fabulous place. In spite of—or because of—Greg Williams and his purported flattery, the entire experience had been heady. Exhilarating. But, thankfully, as she'd looked out the tiny window of the plane and watched California fade into the distance, Annie had convinced herself that the island was solid and real. The Vineyard was now her past and her present and her future; greater talents than hers had no doubt succumbed to the temptation of Hollywood only to watch their fantasies snap, crackle, pop, and disappear into the darkness as fast as the thunderous flashes of fireworks over Edgartown Harbor on the Fourth of July.

Right now, however, the only thing Annie regretted was not having tackled the emails sooner. Scanning through— never mind replying to—all 431 would take, at best, several days. Certainly way past the time she was expected at Earl and Claire's. Still, Annie continued staring at the screen. Perhaps she did have jet lag, after all.

She decided to scroll through the list and thin out the herd of messages by deleting old headlines from online news out-lets, offers for zero-percent balance transfers, must-have fashions or kitchen gadgets or garden supplies based on her previous purchases from a retail giant. Yes, she decided, ditching junk mail would be far more productive than pretending she was interested in doing work.

Click. Click. Click. The little trash can at the top of the screen quickly gobbled Annie's picks. As was typical, she left unknown names of people alone because those could be legit-imate fan mail, which she always tried to answer. But as she moved through the list, sorting the wheat from the chaff, as her dad would have called it, she nearly blew past another pre-sumed note from a fan until the subject line caught her eye. And abruptly stopped her.

Donna MacNeish, it read.

Donna MacNeish had been Annie's birth mother.

Annie froze; she stared at the screen the way she'd been staring at it when she'd first sat down. Was someone looking for Donna? Someone who hadn't known she'd died?

An ache of loss swelled in Annie's heart. She took a gentle breath, remembering the woman she had grown to love. Then she drew in another breath, that one of gratitude. And she tap-tapped her feet again, forcing her gaze toward the line that showed the sender's name: *Jack Miller.*

An innocuous name, if ever there was one. Perhaps Jack Miller had been an old friend of Donna's—a colleague or a client from Donna's antiques business. But why was he contacting Annie? Not many people had known about their connection. And yet . . .

She checked the date: the email had been sent on March 8, nearly a month before. She rarely remembered to check email when she was busy, and she'd been very busy in California. She'd always felt that if anyone really needed her, they had her cell number to call or text. For Annie, emailing had pretty much gone the way of landlines and typewriters. Except for fan mail, which was forwarded from her website.

She supposed she should call Kevin. After all, Donna had raised him; they'd lived in the same house and had stayed close through his troubles with his first wife and all that followed. But Donna had given her first baby—Annie—up for adoption when she'd been young, unmarried, and alone. It had been years before she'd met her husband, married him, and had Kevin. In the short time Annie had gotten to know her after they were reunited, they'd shared a great deal about their lives. But as far as Annie could recall, Donna had not mentioned a Jack Miller.

Maybe Kevin would remember him.

Before calling her brother (whom she'd stopped referring to as her half brother, because she couldn't imagine that siblings of the same mother and father could be any closer than the two of them were now), she decided she should read the email to be sure it wasn't junk that had snuck through the firewall.

Click.

Dear Annie,
My name is Jack Miller, though I don't know if that
means anything to you. I was married to your birth
mother, Donna, a number of years ago. I am her son
Kevin's father.

Annie made a tiny sound that sounded like a whimper.
She squeezed her eyes shut, then quickly popped them open,
to be sure she wasn't dreaming.

Jack Miller was . . . Kevin's *father*?

If she'd ever heard the name, surely she would have remembered. Her thoughts were skittering like sandpipers on
the beach at Wasque Point, but she went back to reading.

A while ago I read that Donna had been on
Martha's Vineyard. Then I learned that you lived
there, too. I hope it meant you reconnected with her
before she died. I know how much that would have
meant to her.

Annie's eyes grew misty. She blinked back her tears so she
could keep reading.

I also hope that means that you know Kevin. If so,
please tell him I would like to see him again. I'd like
that very much. Thank you.
Sincerely,
Jack Miller

Annie was stunned. She stared, unblinking, her eyes fixed
on the words now on the screen.

Should she ignore the message? Was it a scam? Was Jack
Miller someone who'd known Donna and Kevin . . . someone who thought he could get something now—something

like money? Should she tell Kevin? Or should she reply to the email and dig for more information?

What the heck was she supposed to do?

Breathe, Murphy instructed, so Annie closed her eyes again and did.

A moment later, she decided that she really had to call her brother. This was about him, after all. Not her.

Surprisingly, Taylor answered his phone.

"He's not here," she said. "He forgot his phone. He doesn't take calls when he's at work at the *On Time*, so now he forgets it when he shouldn't. Anyway, I saw it was you, so I answered. So you wouldn't worry."

She was right. Annie would at least have wondered why Kevin hadn't picked up.

Taylor then explained that he was at the Coast Guard Station at Menemsha, watching "some kind of training exercise."

It was nice that her brother was getting so involved with his new interest. "I didn't want anything special," Annie said, not wanting to reveal her true intention. "I only was wondering if you'll be at Earl and Claire's tonight."

"We will. Seven o'clock, right?"

Annie confirmed the time. After they hung up, she sat quietly, rereading the email. She knew she'd feel better if either Donna or Kevin had ever mentioned the name Jack Miller. But they hadn't. Or at least, not that Annie recalled.

Then she remembered the Louis Vuitton trunk in her bedroom, an heirloom Donna had bequeathed to Annie that held Donna's memories. Maybe Annie could peek inside and see if there was something that might show Jack Miller's name—a marriage license? A divorce decree?

Energized by having something to do that legitimized her procrastination about writing, she rounded the corner and rushed into the bedroom, bumping into the garment bag hanging on the back of the door. She stopped to straighten it,

then jerked her hand away, as if it had been singed. This was
not the time to think about what was inside. She snapped
around, remembering her purpose and tromping toward the
trunk, where she retrieved the key and lifted the lid.

She looked inside. It was a shame that Kevin still didn't
want to look at the things that technically were his. Though
he'd only been four when his dad had left, Annie remembered
when Kevin told her he had a few vague memories of him.
One was when the two of them had gone to a Red Sox game,
and his dad bought him a hot dog and a soda. "I thought I'd
died and gone to heaven," she remembered Kevin saying. He
also said his father was a good dad while he was with them,
but that he was gone before Kevin could remember his face.
Or his voice. But in junior high school, Kevin often saved up
cash then skipped school and went to Red Sox games. By
then Donna was working, so he didn't think she knew. He
took the T to Fenway Park and spent all nine innings surveying the crowd, searching for his dad, hoping he'd be there and
that he'd recognize him. His son. But if his father had been
there, they'd never found each other. Annie remembered that
her brother said he'd rationalized the results, or rather the
non-results, by deciding that his dad might have had to move
to Florida for his work, or maybe to London or Timbuktu—
somewhere far away. Otherwise, he would have gone to the
ballpark looking for him.

It was clear that Kevin had felt abandoned, which had
seemed odd to Annie at first, because she was the one who'd
been abandoned, albeit by their mother, and hadn't known
who her father was. But she had been adopted by a couple
named George and Ellen Sutton. And Kevin still had their
mother, while Annie did not.

Unlike Kevin, however, she'd never felt abandoned.
When she'd been old enough to understand the true meaning
of adoption, her dad explained that her birth mother had

known that they—George and Ellen Sutton—were better able to take care of Annie and protect her and give her a good home, and that she must have loved Annie an awful lot to have had the courage to give her to them.

Allowing herself another short bit of self-pity, she resumed her pursuit of the contents of the trunk that pertained to Kevin.

She went straight to the pocket of the inside lid and withdrew the small blue ribbon that she'd seen before: Kevin Mac-Neish. First Place, Dorchester Elementary School, 1986. Annie had no idea why Kevin had received it. However, she did recall that Donna said she'd taken back her maiden name after her divorce and changed Kevin's name to hers. Before that, had their last name been Miller?

Then Annie took out a brochure: Red Sox–Yankees Line-up, June 4, 1990. Along with it was a ticket stub and a hand-written notation that the Sox beat the Yankees, 5–3. Kevin still didn't know that Donna had saved these things, that she'd known he'd gone to Fenway, searching for his dad.

Nestled under the Red Sox items was a photo album. Slowly, Annie opened it; the first page read *Kevin*. No last name was provided. Pictures followed. Shots of Kevin. And his dad. Playing catch. Riding horses on a carousel. Fishing in a small stream using poles that looked as if they had been made of branches from a tree. Kevin and his dad. The man he barely remembered. From the now-grainy, faded color images, Annie tried to determine if the man looked anything like Kevin did today. But aside from the hair color that seemed similar, it was hard to tell.

If only she'd been able to persuade Kevin to explore these treasures. She'd tried on several occasions; so far, he had declined. "Maybe someday," had been his disinterested reply.

She wondered if hearing from his supposed father might be enough to change his mind.

But now, after sifting through every shred of Donna's memories, Annie still didn't have a clue if the man's name was Jack Miller.

Maybe she'd have a chance to talk to Kevin that night after dinner. Weeks had passed since Mr. Miller sent Annie the email; surely he could wait another day.

Claire looked tired. Her pearl-gray eyes were less vibrant, with a slight film of what might be cataracts. Her previously bright white, flyaway hair seemed dry and lackluster. Like Lucy and Kyle, in the short time Annie was gone, the woman had aged.

She did seem happy to see Annie, however, and made a tasty, comfort-food casserole of end-of-the-season scallops, Gruyère cheese, shallots, and cream, topped with rosemary breadcrumbs; she served the dish with butternut squash and wild rice. John and Lucy were there, but not Abigail. Kevin and Taylor and Francine and Jonas and Bella arrived, too. And Earl was there, as it was his house. Everything would have been just as Annie had hoped, except John was subdued.

Kevin, on the other hand, was animated enough for the rest of them. He monopolized much of the conversation with tales he'd heard about Coast Guard at-sea rescues, and how he'd met many of the twenty-four Coasties who worked at Menemsha Station, including Coco, the chocolate Labrador mascot. Earl teased him by asking if he was thinking about enlisting, but Kevin, sounding disappointed, said he'd aged out of that opportunity more than ten years ago.

Every so often, someone asked Annie a question about California, which she answered with guarded enthusiasm. She distributed their gifts, but told Kevin if she'd known he was more interested in the sea than in outer space, she would have bought him a cap from Scripps Institute of Oceanography in San Diego, even though it was a long drive from L.A.

"Or you could have just picked up a WHOI cap in Woods Hole while you were waiting for the boat," Earl chimed in, and everyone laughed, because WHOI was the world-renowned place for oceanography research on the East Coast, while Scripps was the one on the West.

Mostly, Annie watched her brother, who was incredibly relaxed, his cheeks flush either with fun or from the two beers he'd downed along with a heaping share of the casserole. In addition, he seemed content. He and quirky, auburn-maned, Taylor had a congenial marriage; both were eagerly awaiting their new grandchild, Francine and Jonas's baby.

Bella spent a good deal of the evening sitting on Annie's lap, her legs dangling closer to the floor now. She was growing so quickly, this beautiful, loving child with black curly hair; wide, dark eyes that looked like Francine's, but were always on the move; looking, studying, learning. She also had a gift for chatter, which Earl said she probably picked up from him. Studying Bella now, Annie found it hard to imagine how Kevin's father could have abandoned him when he wasn't much older than the precocious girl was now.

Kevin asked Jonas if he'd like to paint out at Menemsha sometime, and said he'd be glad to provide introductions, as if Kevin had lived there all of his forty-six years and was part of the station's operations.

"Speaking of transportation," Lucy said, though they hadn't been, unless she was correlating it to the brief mention of the boat Annie had arrived on, "I have a suggestion for the Inn."

They all fell quiet, and Lucy sat up straight.

"As most of you know, except maybe Bella, I've been taking driver's ed since I got my learner's permit."

Annie vaguely remembered hearing that Lucy had passed her test for the permit sometime in January, not long after Annie had left.

"So . . . I've decided it's high time the Inn had a four-, or even a six-seat golf cart to shuttle people back and forth to the ferry."

The silence lasted another few seconds. Then Earl scratched his whiskers. "Most of our guests bring vehicles over, honey."

"But not everyone. Which gave me another idea. You all know about Mother's Day weekend, and the pink-and-green theme they used to use. Well, I think it would be a perfect time to offer an introductory brunch on the patio overlooking the harbor. And even though I can't get my license until June, I thought we could dress up the cart with pink and green ribbons and not only bring people back and forth to the Inn but give them a full-blown tour of Chappy. First-come, first-served. I could drive the cart if Grandpa comes with me. It would be so much fun. But if they have the dog parade again, I hope it's on Saturday, because Restless will want to get decorated and be in that."

Murmurs murmured; heads nodded.

"And after I get my license in June, I can start a side business for guests—or anyone else—giving them tours of Chappy on my own. Other than Grandpa, who could do a better job? And I can earn money for college."

"After the cart's paid off, of course," Earl said with a loving harrumph. "And the insurance."

"Well, okay," Lucy said. "We can figure a percentage, based on tour sales."

Earl nodded. "If your father agrees, the Vineyard Inn board of directors shall take your idea under advisement and make you an offer." He looked at Kevin, then Annie. "Right?"

"Absolutely," Annie said, as Kevin said, "Sure, absolutely." Francine agreed it might be a nice addition. And John said, "Okay, why not?" His voice was quiet, though, which Annie supposed was understandable.

Thankfully, in addition to the new baby arriving, there now were other things to look forward to: Kevin captaining the ferry; Lucy captaining the golf cart. And the Mother's Day brunch. God, Annie thought, how she loved living on the island. She knew she should remember this moment the next time her thoughts drifted to living in L.A.

The same way she knew she must cut John some slack.

At around eight thirty, there was a knock on the kitchen door, and it turned out to be burly Rex, who was carrying his version of what he said was a California lemon pound cake, though he'd made it with orange zest and orange juice and coated it with a buttery, orangey frosting that he topped with candied orange slices. In the center of the Bundt stood a small plastic palm tree. "I wanted to make an orange tree," he said, "but I ran out of mandarin slices. Anyway, it's in your honor, because we're glad you're back."

"We'll be pleased to eat it as is," Kevin said, and everyone laughed, even John, because Kevin was obviously having such a great time. Too great, Annie decided, to tell him about Jack Miller.

The party broke up fairly early, as Claire said she needed to turn in, and that she'd clean up the kitchen in the morning. Taylor asked Claire if she felt okay—which wasn't unexpected, as Taylor was one of Chappaquiddick's EMTs. Claire simply replied, "I feel like I'm seventy-six," which she was. With that, she said good night, and everyone dispersed.

John and Lucy brought Annie home and John walked her to the cottage door. "Sorry I can't come in tonight," he said, not looking her in the eye as he tucked a lock of her hair behind her ear, as had become a habit—most often when he was handcuffed by his feelings. "I need to bring Lucy home. I don't want to leave the girls alone overnight right now."

Because of Abigail, Annie reminded herself. *It has nothing to do with me.* So she told him she loved him and kissed him good-bye.

★ ★ ★

After John left, Annie went inside and sat in the rocking chair without taking off her jacket. She thought of how it must be hard enough to be a parent when things were going smoothly. But when there was cause for concern . . .

Which reminded her about Jack Miller. And how, no matter who he was, she hated that he might shake Kevin's world when things were going so well. Unless, of course, her brother would be thrilled. Which probably was doubtful.

Snapping on the light, she lit a small fire in the woodstove to take the chill off the night air. She wondered if she should investigate Mr. Miller first. Maybe she could learn if he was harmless. But could she possibly find proof that his search for Kevin was honorable? Or did she think she'd be able to find out if something even more sinister was lurking? In any case, a little up-front vetting might be worth a try. Because Annie was the older sister and wanted to protect her brother. Just as John wanted to protect his daughters—and his parents—the best way he knew how.

Chapter 7

Annie waited until Sunday morning to consult with Google. A decent night's sleep had reinforced her feeling that she needed to stop dwelling on John and Abigail, that she'd thought the girl had detached from her mother, that Jenn's taste in boyfriends had catapulted her daughter back to the Vineyard, apparently the lesser of two detestable locations. But Annie also knew that sometimes, no matter what, "Mom" was the one person a child wanted. She'd seen it happen more than once in her years as a teacher, and often those moms were less capable of mothering than Jenn.

Annie understood that, and yet she still felt . . . rejected.

"Stop it," she blurted out before Murphy had a chance.

Taking a long sip of hot tea, she forced herself to fire up Google and type in *Jack Miller*. In what seemed like half a second, more than half a *billion* Jack Millers, living or dead, were coughed up from the Google bank and onto Annie's screen. She supposed the number could include the world . . . even so, good grief. She limited her search to the United States. Over one hundred million. Which certainly was closer, but it hardly would be possible to search them all. Maybe there was

an outside chance that he was still in Boston . . . which yielded—
click, click—nearly forty million.

Seriously?

Apparently Google didn't care that Annie had a book to
write or that there was an heirloom wedding dress hanging in
the garment bag behind her bedroom door that needed alter-
ing, and a fast-approaching wedding to plan, unless the ex-
wife had intervened with that as well.

She shuddered. Would Jenn honestly try and interfere
with the nuptials? Various scenarios quickly spun in Annie's
mind, all seemingly plausible, all potentially disastrous. Then
she (or Murphy) suggested that she needed to stop being absurd. Certainly John's former wife had been on the island only
to take care of her daughter. And Annie knew what she really
needed was to stop being wrapped up in herself. Such behavior wasn't like her. Or rather, it hadn't been until now.

Getting up from her desk, she pulled the belt on her robe
more tightly around her waist, then wandered into the
kitchen and popped a slice of bread into the toaster. Outside
the window, the sky was easing out of its night shadows, giving way to early-morning, soft Vineyard light. She rubbed the
back of her neck, as if that would help her decide what to do
about Jack Miller. But whenever she leaned toward telling her
brother, she pictured the boy who'd skipped school to go to
the ballpark, where he hoped his dad was looking for him.

Ugh.

The lever on the toaster flicked up; she fussed with a plate,
a knife, and a swab of beach plum jelly that Claire and Lucy
had made last fall.

What if it were you? Murphy's voice suddenly asked. *What
if it had been your dad—before you'd known who he was—who contacted Kevin? Would you have wanted Kevin to keep it from you?*

"No," Annie said, slicing the toast in half. "I'd be wicked

pissed that he hadn't let me decide whether or not I wanted to meet the guy. I'd have a tough time trying to forgive him."

Murphy said no more; she didn't have to.

Annie carried the plate back to the writer's nook, back to her computer. Then, without another thought, she sat down at the desk. She clicked on the REPLY button, which brought up a blank email screen addressed to the mystery man.

Dear Mr. Miller, she typed.

Then she paused, trying to compose an appropriate but succinct message. Why was this so hard? She'd typed millions of words over the years, yet now she couldn't think of one that worked.

Just be kind, Murphy whispered.

Annie sipped her tea again, then continued, the keyboard clicking now almost faster than her thoughts.

> I would like to be able to tell my brother something about you . . . especially since I have no way of knowing if you're who you say you are. Could you please give me some information? Or perhaps an address or, better yet, a phone number so we could speak?
> Thank you.
> Sincerely,
> Annie Sutton

She hit SEND before she had time to change her mind.

Of course, she had no idea if her reply made sense, or if it had been a waste of time. At least if Jack Miller was a con, he might understand that in order to see Kevin, he'd have to go through her.

Finishing her tea and toast, she decided to take a shower. Sunday was brunch day at the Inn, and she really wanted to see the tenants and tell them she was happy to see them and glad to be home. Which would be preferable to sitting and stewing over the latest glitches that were trying to disrupt her life.

They'll disrupt you only if you let them, Murphy said.

Rex was standing at the stove in the kitchen at the Inn, once again doing what he did so well. Which was a surprise.

"Last night after dinner I stayed at Kevin and Taylor's rather than drive back to Aquinnah," he said. "I asked him if you all had thought about giving Francine maternity leave. You know . . . time off now and after the baby comes? We agreed that Claire shouldn't have to take her place . . . there's no need for her to get up early if I can do it. Which I can, because as you know, I have nothing else to do."

Maternity leave? Why on earth hadn't Annie thought of that? She wouldn't have expected Earl to . . . or even Kevin, though he might have had a few females working for him when he had his construction business.

"Rex," she said, "what a wonderful idea. Thank you."

"No thanks needed. It just makes sense. Kevin and I can keep things looking good around here, like Francine does, in between the visits by the cleaners. And Kevin knows how to handle the reservations."

"I can help, too." While Annie was away, Francine had handled it all. But now that Annie was back, she was appalled that she hadn't yet thought about resuming her duties—or giving Francine time off.

Rex laughed. "You have a lot more on your plate right now than I do." He held up an empty plate and waved it for effect.

"Besides," he continued, "like I said before, I don't want to get rusty." He gave her a sly wink as if to say he knew darn well it would take a very long time for his culinary talents to oxidize.

"But it's a long way to travel to and from Aquinnah every day."

"No problem. My sister and brother-in-law offered me their garage apartment. Of course, if you've ever been up there, you'll know I'd never fit."

The first time Annie had seen the apartment, it had been cloaked in heavy, unattractive Victorian décor; when Jonas moved in later, however, he had transformed it into an artist's bachelor space filled with colorful paintings instead of brocade and lace. But Annie had seen enough to know that, yes, the slanted roof and low ceilings would not suit to Rex's ample frame. Not to mention that she wasn't sure he could manage the steep, winding staircase without having to bend his body nearly in half.

"Good point," she said with a smile.

"Anyway," he added, "we decided that if it's all right with you and Earl, I could stay in the room upstairs where Francine and Bella used to be. Until the new mom's back on her working feet."

"Of course it's fine, Rex. It's very generous of you."

He turned to the oven and slid out a baking dish; the air was suddenly permeated with a delectable aroma of nutmeg and cinnamon. "I said it can be my baby gift to her and Jonas. A month before, a month after. Or longer, if I don't have a restaurant of my own by then, 'cuz we'll be in season."

"Sounds great," Annie said, still fixated on the fact that she hadn't thought about giving Francine a break, when she absolutely shouldn't have to keep cooking and running the Inn, being as bulbous as she already was. Or after, when she deserved to spend every minute with her family. "So what can I do to help? Right now?"

"Set the table, if you want."

"I want," she replied. "And I will take over the day-to-day dusting and tidying up around here—there's no need for you to do that. The cleaners are here every week, but you're right, Francine does a good bit of work in between. And my brother has a lot going on now, too. We can save him for when we need an extra pair of hands for heavy lifting."

"You're the manager, so it's your call. But Kevin and I thought you'd be too busy what with writing books and whatever. As for me, I've put out as many feelers as I can for an up-island restaurant that might be for sale; I decided I don't want to start from scratch by building a place." He laughed a hearty laugh. "I'm too old for that." In reality, he wasn't that old; he maybe only had five or six years on Annie.

She collected plates and silverware. "And, as you also said before, when the time and place are right . . ."

"I'll be ready," he said, finishing her thought.

She counted the dishes and utensils. "Are Francine and Jonas coming for brunch?"

He shook his head. "Kevin made an executive decision to call her after he and I talked last night. He told her about the maternity leave; she got wicked excited. Then she said maybe she'll stay in their own little house and that—starting today— she'll make breakfast for Jonas and Bella—until she gets bored. Her words, not mine. She's a sweet kid."

A sweet kid at age twenty-two, Annie thought. And Rex was turning out to be a nice man. Who the heck would have predicted that?

As she carried the tableware into the great room, Annie marveled again at how, after a bumpy start, Rex had melded into the family. For his sake, she hoped he'd find a restaurant before the season started—they would take care of replacing Francine if it happened before then. Between Annie and Claire and Earl and Kevin, there were enough of them to make do until Francine was ready to boot them out of the kitchen.

Breakfast was a feast, not at all like what the year-round tenants and winter renters expected at this time of year. Though Francine always provided delicious, healthy fare, Rex's cooking was five-star. Six, if someone decided there should be such a thing.

After having the chance to catch up with everyone, Annie convinced Rex to let her help him clean up. When all was sparkling again, she retreated to the cottage, hoping to hear from John that he could see her at some point that day. She wanted to ask what she might do for Abigail, how she might be able to help all of them. After all, once they went to Boston and came back, Abigail might need some TLC. From someone besides her mother.

Moving from room to room—well, from the living room to the kitchen, which was really only one room, then into the bedroom, the bath, and the writer's nook, which was all there was to the cottage—Annie didn't know quite where to put herself or what to do. She felt like a teenager waiting to hear if she'd be asked out on a date. At last, she planted herself at the computer and began to type a list of Francine's duties that Annie—or someone—would have to cover for the next couple of months. At first the exercise seemed to offer productive distraction.

Stupidly, however, she'd set her phone in plain sight on the desk. Every thirty seconds or less she checked to see if John had texted or called. As if she wouldn't have heard the alerts; after all, she'd checked the volume several times.

Then she realized she was being foolish again. John was her fiancé. They were going to be married in three weeks. There was nothing stopping her from calling him. Or better yet, going to Edgartown. After all, she had California gifts to deliver to Abigail, which might cheer her up. Besides, it wasn't as if Jenn would be there.

Forgetting to save the document that she'd begun to compose, Annie bolted from the chair as if startled by a crack of lightning in a summer storm. Then, like a villain trying to escape a murderous scene in one of her books, she gathered Abigail's gifts and added a bottle of soothing lavender and vanilla hand cream that she'd picked up for herself. Maybe Abigail would like it. Once in Edgartown, Annie could stop at the Paper Store on the way to the town house and buy a few fashion magazines. Then Abigail would have glossy pages to look at in the neurologist's waiting room instead of trying to focus on the digitized versions on her tablet.

Remembering to wear a jacket this time, Annie was out the door before long and en route to the *On Time*. She didn't expect to see her brother on the ferry. Apparently he was working. His cheeks were pink from the early-spring breeze; his eyes twinkled with delight as he swaggered toward the Jeep.

"Ticket, please," he said.

She laughed. Kevin did, indeed, have a way of making her do that.

"Fine captain you're going to make," she said. "We don't present tickets on the way to Edgartown. Only on the way to Chappy. They're round-trip, remember?"

"I was testing you," he said. "Now put on your hand brake. And turn off your engine."

She complied, as if this were her first trip off Chappaquiddick.

Kevin set the chock blocks under her front wheels. "I'd like to stay and chat," he said, "but I have other customers. Even as a deckhand, I am essential to the operations of this iconic vessel."

Shaking her head, Annie laughed again. She was so happy that her brother was doing well . . . though that might change once he knew about Jack Miller. She pulled out her phone and checked her messages: nothing from the man. Perhaps, indeed, he'd been a con artist. Maybe he was even hoping for money from Kevin's celebrity sister—another twist she hadn't thought of earlier.

Once across the channel, she stopped at the Paper Store, grateful for a nearby parking space, and that copies of both *Vogue* and *Marie Claire* were on the shelf. She then drove two blocks south, four blocks west, and wound up in front of John's place. Abigail's little Beetle was parked in the driveway. But John's SUV wasn't behind it. Maybe it was better that way. She'd be able to spend a few peaceful minutes with Abigail, without her father emitting his moroseness, if that was a word.

Parking the Jeep, Annie grabbed the bags and got out. She walked through the open gate of the white picket fence, passed the small garden that Lucy kept in bloom all summer, and stepped up onto the porch. Because she still didn't feel at ease simply walking in, Annie knocked. She waited to hear the welcoming bark from Restless, followed by the sounds of someone—anyone—approaching the door.

But Annie heard nothing. No barking. No footsteps.

She knocked again. Then she sensed that all was quiet for only one reason: no one, not even the dog, was home.

Standing at the door, bags in hand, she considered searching under the planter for the key. Would John be angry with her for trespassing? She could always say she was worried about Abigail and concerned that no one was around when Annie knew that the girl wasn't well.

Oddly, for a cop, John had yet to invest in one of those

doorbell alert devices that would send a video to his phone and let him know if she was pushing their as-yet-unmentioned boundaries.

Still . . .

And then Annie realized that this, too, was foolish. They'd be married in three weeks. Her soon-to-be stepdaughter was ill. And there Annie was, standing on his porch, acting like a too-proper Victorian lady who once inhabited the garage apartment at Kevin and Taylor's.

Glancing over her shoulder toward the police station, where there did not seem to be any activity, either, she moved to the planter, tipped it up, and retrieved the key, slipping it into the lock and pushing open the door.

"Hello?" she called out just in case.

Again, there was no reply.

She snuck through the living room, into the kitchen, then circled back through the hallway, past the main-floor bath. No one. She came out at the bottom of the stairs that led up to the bedrooms and main bath. She tiptoed up them.

"Hello?" she called again, that time, in a whisper, as if she were Murphy.

It didn't matter; there still was no response.

When she reached the girls' room, the door was ajar. She looked inside; everything was relatively tidy, considering that they were teenagers. Worst of all, both beds had been made. And neither Abigail nor Lucy was there.

Leaving the room, Annie knew there was no point in peeking into John's room, though she did, anyway.

No one.

And no one in the bath.

"For God's sake," she said aloud, "where is everyone?"

But no one answered. Not even the dog.

Chapter 8

*T*he text arrived as John drove off the boat. He should have known it would be from Annie. Or, worse, he should have known to have texted her before they left, to tell her there hadn't been an emergency, but that they were going to Plymouth, though it was only Sunday. He should have known to tell her they'd changed their plans because Abigail wanted to stay at Jenn's tonight and tomorrow, too. That she wanted to be back in her own bed at Jenn's house before they went to Boston.

John knew he should have done those things. The fact that he was a male was not an acceptable excuse, especially for Annie, who soon would be his wife.

He wondered if he should wait until he got to Jenn's to answer Annie. Then he decided he shouldn't be any more stupid than he'd already been. It made him sound as if he were guilty, though he hadn't done a damn thing wrong or anything to feel guilty about.

Abigail was stretched out on the back seat, a blanket wrapped around her, though it was over sixty degrees outside. He longed to put down his window, but he would not.

Lucy was next to him in the passenger seat, air pods plugged into her ears. He couldn't tell if she was listening to music or sleeping.

Restless was on the floor in the back seat, tucked into the well below Abigail, so she could easily reach down and pet him. And so he could quickly spring into action if she needed him.

John wished Annie was with them.

As he turned off Locust Street in Falmouth and went up Palmer Avenue, he decided to stop and fill the gas tank. And text Annie back. That way he could tell her what they were doing. And hope that she'd forgive him for leaving her out. Again.

Chapter 9

By the time she saw John's text, she was on the *On Time* again, and they were docking back on the Chappy side. Annie had already forced herself to pretend that all was fine when her brother took a coupon from her book of tickets and commented, "That was fast."

But now, as she waited for him to finish prepping the ferry for deboarding, she stared at her phone and read:

Sorry. Last minute decision by Abigail to come to Plymouth today. Lucy's with us. Just stopped for gas. Will be in touch.

Plymouth.
Plymouth.
Jenn.

Annie wanted to get out of the Jeep and toss the phone overboard. Instead she bit back her tears, watched her brother remove the chock blocks, set the ramp, and unhook the chain. Then the gate went up and she gave him a limp wave and drove off the boat, a lump in her throat, a knot in her stomach, and tears trying to find a way to escape her eyes.

Instead of going home, she headed for Jeffers Lane, toward the ancient Indian Burial Ground, where Annie often went because it was so peaceful, and God knew she needed a boat-load of peace.

It took only a few minutes to reach the graveyard, though that day it felt longer. But as she finally turned onto the dirt road that led to her contemplative spot, then parked the Jeep and began the short trek up the path, she felt serenity cloak her like a gentle wave at low tide.

So she eased into it.

The small hilltop burial ground was marked by an old split-rail fence dotted with mossy lichen; she went straight to her favorite rock. She sat, facing the best view of Cape Poge that lay below, the sun's rays winking off the slow ripples of water, as if it were being kissed by the spirits of those who had once passed this way.

There weren't many Chappaquiddick Wampanoags still living—the last estimate Annie had read was only three to five hundred. Unlike the Aquinnah tribe, which Winnie belonged to, the Chappaquiddick Wampanoags lived mostly on the mainland of the Vineyard, in other parts of Massachusetts, and in Rhode Island (all of which were the original Wampanoag Nation homelands), and also were scattered in other locations throughout America. She thought about the tribal struggles that went back generations, and how today, with neither land nor federal recognition, the Chappaquiddicks remained a tightly knit group, deeply rooted to their ancestors and to the Wampanoag Nations of Mashpee on Cape Cod and of Aquinnah.

It was calming to think about them now, and about the handful of others who'd once been allowed to be buried there, including John's grandparents, great-grandparents, and great-greats—part of the Lyons clan that had emigrated from England and purchased island land that really had not been their right to purchase. Today, however, tribal members and British interlopers rested together in peace at the burial ground. Thinking about them always made Annie's problems seem inconsequential.

John hadn't shared that part of his family's history with her; Earl had. She wondered if John had been as secretive before he'd become a police officer, holding information "close to the vest," as Earl put it. She started to wonder how—and if—she'd be able to navigate the reticent side of the man who otherwise felt like her ideal mate, just as her phone dinged with an email alert. But though Annie knew there was nothing more important right then than for her to absorb the quiet around her, she also knew that John often emailed instead of texted, especially if what he wanted to say was more private. Maybe he wanted to apologize for his earlier brusqueness.

Pulling her phone from her pocket, she tried to compose herself before clicking on the little icon of the envelope.

When she was ready, she clicked. She didn't expect to see the name Jack Miller on the top line.

She groaned.

Surely, her time at the burial ground would be better spent concentrating on her own mental health than on him, whoever he was.

But she was Annie, notoriously curious.

So she opened the message and she read:

Dear Annie. I will be glad to give you as much information as you want—about me and about Donna and Kevin, as best as I remember them. If you are available, I'd like to come to the island and see you in person. Is there a place we could meet for coffee within walking distance of the ferry in Vineyard Haven? Perhaps tomorrow morning?

He left his phone number in case something prevented him from showing up.

Her initial instinct was to hold him off until she talked to Kevin. But then she remembered all that her brother had been through—how, in addition to having been abandoned by his father, he had to sell his successful business to fund his then wife's long-term care and had dealt with enormous grief and guilt over her circumstances. Like Annie, he'd moved to the island to try and start anew, only to have to watch his beloved mother die. But Kevin had persevered, and he'd done it well. Did Jack Miller have the right to intrude on him now?

Maybe it would be better if Annie met the man first, assessed him in person, and tried to determine what, after all these years, he wanted from his son.

Besides, she decided, she wouldn't feel like doing much else on Monday, except try not to think about John. And Abigail.

Then she remembered she'd told Francine she wanted to see their house. Maybe Annie could go there today. And while she was there, she might be able to covertly gain a little insight on how to handle Kevin's situation that he didn't yet know he had.

"This place is amazing," Annie said as soon as Jonas opened the front door and she stepped into a small foyer that offered a view of the inviting main floor.

"Francine and Bella are upstairs taking naps, but I can give you a tour." He gestured to the kitchen. "You can probably tell what we use this part for."

The kitchen was both attractive and efficient, equipped with the latest stainless-steel appliances, white cabinetry, and a striking, natural stone countertop in shades of gray. They passed through the kitchen to the other side of the peninsula, which Jonas explained would be big enough for four stools once the kids were old enough not to climb up, tip over, and fall off. A small dining area was in front of the peninsula; a tiny study to the left carried a light scent of acrylics on canvas. Jonas said he was working there until they got approval to construct the outbuilding over by the meadow where Jonas could create his wonderful paintings, and Annie could make her handcrafted soap that included island herbs and flowers, and Kevin could store his coveted maintenance equipment.

"I really hope the building commission approves the plans soon," Jonas added with a half smile.

"I expect the odds are in our favor," Annie said, "especially now that you're in the equation. Francine told me that two of your landscapes are now hanging in the town hall." She'd shared the good news in one of their phone conversations over the winter.

Jonas's smile turned into a shy grin. "Yeah, well, no guarantees." Then he turned and led her to the living space. "I call this 'Kevin's living room.' Seeing as how he designed it."

"It's wonderful," Annie replied. And it was. The back wall stretched the full width of the room and was punctuated by floor-to-ceiling windows that mirrored those in the great room at the Inn; they unmasked the same hypnotic view of the harbor and the lighthouse. Another wall showcased a lovely stone fireplace. A sofa and several colorful, unique, yet comfy-looking chairs were arranged in a way that accented a mixed-media collection of oils, pastels, watercolors, and more, none of which were Jonas's, but were the work of other island artists with whom the young couple had become friends through various island galleries.

It was a tasteful, wonderful house for a young family—a startling transformation from the workshop it once had been. Annie tried to imagine that her messy workbench once had been the centerpiece of the space, or that the area around it had been littered with dozens of rectangular molds—the size of small loaves of bread—her stainless-steel cutters and tools and stacks of large trays that she'd filled with the soaps, then set on tall racks that she wheeled outside so that the soaps could cure in the open air.

"Have a seat," Jonas said. "You want tea?"

"The kettle's already on." Francine's voiced lilted from the kitchen area. "You didn't expect me to sleep through a visit from Annie, did you?"

"I didn't hear you come downstairs," Jonas said as he hustled to the kitchen. "You girls go sit. I'll make the tea."

Francine laughed. "He mothers the heck out of me."

"Good!" Annie moved to a living room chair that was upholstered in an ecru-and-mint-green block print. "Your home is fabulous, honey."

Francine joined Annie and sat on the end of the sofa closest to her. "Thanks. If Bella wakes up, I'll take you upstairs so you can see the incredible job Jonas is doing with the murals." She tried to curl her legs under her, then seemed to think better of it. "I'm a whale," she said. "I can't get in any comfortable position."

"Not for much longer."

"Argh. Too long, though. But it won't seem as bad now that you're home."

Jonas presented them with steaming mugs of tea, along with a small plate that held a pile of animal crackers. "Sorry. All the good stuff's at the Inn."

"Which I'm trying not to eat much of," Francine said, "because my ankles swell up if they even smell sugar."

They chatted awhile, as if they hadn't spoken for three months, though they'd talked at least once a week. Francine admitted she was grateful to be on maternity leave . . . though she insisted she'd be available if needed.

"That's not going to happen," Annie said. "Not that any

of us can do all the things you do for the Inn as well as you do them. But, between us, we can at least try not to embarrass ourselves."

"The mark of a true family," Francine said.

Which was when Annie found the opening she'd hoped for. "And as we both know, family isn't necessarily the one we were born into."

"It sure isn't."

Annie took an animal cracker—a giraffe—and examined it. "And like these guys, they come in all shapes and sizes."

Francine's dark eyes fixed on Annie. "What, pray tell, are you trying to get at?"

Popping the cracker into her mouth, Annie quickly chewed and swallowed. "Just some research I'm doing for a book. I thought maybe you could help me. But stop me if you don't want to go there."

"Sounds intriguing."

Annie shrugged. "Maybe. I was thinking of your situation, about how your mother's sister, Marty, is the only blood relation—aside from Bella—that you seem to have left from your mother's side. But what about your father's side? I know that both he and his father have died. But what about your grandmother? Do you know anything about her? Do you remember her . . . or any aunts, uncles, cousins?"

Francine squirmed.

"Honey," Annie said, reaching toward her. "I meant it when I said stop me if you want. I don't want to upset you."

"It doesn't upset me. Honest. It's just that they never really felt like family to me. Don't forget, I was twelve when my father died. He was an only child. A few years ago, my grandfather died. He was a rich man but left us nothing. When my mother and I moved to the Cape, he and my grandmother must have been relieved." She thought for a moment. "Those are interesting questions, though. Not long before Mom had Bella, she told me she'd heard that Gran died, too. I have no idea when. Or how." She shrugged again.

It wasn't the same situation as Kevin's (not even close), but Annie decided it was worth asking the question foremost on her mind.

"What if your grandmother was still alive? What if she contacted you? Would you want to see her again?"

Francine smiled. "You mean, like you did with Donna?"

"Well . . . that was different. I never knew anything about her. I'd never met her."

"Right." She thought for a moment. "I don't know. I don't think I'd see the point. I mean, my memory's pretty vague about those years, but I can truthfully say I've never missed her. I might want to see her again if only so she could see how happy I am, how we didn't need their lousy money. On second thought, I don't think I'd bother. If I've never missed her, that says something, doesn't it?"

"I guess," Annie replied, then decided to change the subject. She didn't want Francine to start asking too many questions . . . she didn't want to slip and say anything connected to Kevin. "But never mind, it was just a random query. It has nothing substantial to contribute to the plot of the story, so I think I'll forget it."

Francine snickered. "Funny, I don't even remember what Gran looked like. Other than she was old."

"Your mother was probably right. That she died."

"Yeah. And I know she didn't like us. One time I overheard my grandfather tell my mother that they'd had 'higher hopes' for their son—my father—than having him wind up with her and me. I believe the word she used was 'saddled' by us."

"Good grief." Annie took another cracker. "Okay, enough.

Here's a question on a nicer topic. Does Bella study each of the animals and try and remember what species they are?"

"Are you kidding? Always. It drives Jonas crazy. He keeps telling her each one is a platypus. She has no idea what a platypus is, but the sound of it makes her giggle. I think it's become a game for her."

Annie laughed and then stood. "Come on. I'll help you up. I really should go get some work done, but I'm not leaving until I see the upstairs. I promise not to wake up Bella."

"I'm not sure either one of us would. Jonas took her for a long walk this morning and she's exhausted."

Treading carefully up each step, Francine led Annie into the nursery to check out Jonas's mural. While Annie was oohing and ahhing over the delightful work, she decided she was glad she'd asked about Francine's grandmother—the words "I've never missed her," said it all. Because Kevin had missed his father. And because of that, maybe he'd want to see him again.

Chapter 10

Annie had no idea why she was wasting time trying to decide what to wear to her meeting with Jack. It wasn't as if she needed to impress him.

Still, she was who she was, and this was her brother's father, or so the man claimed. She settled on a pale aqua denim shirt, jeans and one of the pretty scarves she'd bought for herself at the Huntington Gardens. A white cotton jacket completed her attire, though it wasn't yet summer and her adoptive mother, Ellen Sutton, no doubt would have clucked her tongue to see Annie dressed in white prior to Memorial Day.

They'd agreed to meet at ten thirty at Mocha Mott's on Main Street—right up the hill from where the big boats docked. Jack hadn't said where he was coming from, other than he'd leave his vehicle on the Cape and walk on the ferry. Chances were he wouldn't have traveled too far, unless he was an early riser.

It was her first investigative deduction about what she'd decided to call "the Case of Kevin MacNeish's Father." If she kept pretending she was researching a plot for a novel, the meeting would almost feel harmless.

Before leaving, she checked to see if Rex needed anything

for the Inn from Edgartown. She found him busily cleaning the kitchen—more like scouring the kitchen. He said thanks, but that all was under control. When he added that Kevin was upstairs changing a lightbulb on the staircase if she wanted to check with him, she made a weak excuse and backed out of the room and out the door. The last person Annie wanted to see right then was her brother. She was, however, grateful that, because he was at the Inn, he wouldn't be on duty as an important deckhand. She wasn't sure she'd be able to look him in the eyes without him undoubtedly asking where she was going and what was wrong. Though only half siblings, they had a curious ESPish connection. The kind of intuition that Earl had with John.

Because it was a Monday morning in early April, traffic was light on the road to Vineyard Haven, so Annie arrived at ten o'clock. She parked the Jeep and meandered along Main Street, not wanting to browse through shops or the bookstore and get trapped in conversation with someone she knew.

Staring absently into one of the summer shops, she wondered how Donna would feel about Annie meeting Jack and acting as a "front man" for Kevin. She wished Donna had told her more about her brother's father; Annie only remembered Donna saying that he'd sent a "pittance of child support" for a few years, and that it had trickled off with time. Annie had no reason to believe it wasn't true. Maybe she could use it as a test to prove he was who he said he was. But she'd wait until she had a sense of how the meeting was going. She wouldn't verbally attack the man, even if he'd been a rogue ex-husband and father.

Abandoned, Annie thought, was such an awful word, especially when used in the context of a child. Though Donna hadn't raised her, Annie was grateful that she'd never felt that way. It must have helped that Ellen Sutton hadn't been on her own, trying to support a child.

"If you're waiting for the shop to open, I hope you packed a few meals."

A male voice from behind startled Annie. Then, in the glass, she saw the reflection of a husky man in a Tisbury police uniform. She recognized him as one of John's friends. She turned around.

"Hi, Annie," the officer said. "You do realize the surf shop is closed until Memorial Day, don't you?" His tawny, weathered face crinkled as he smiled.

She looked back at the sign over the door that read: SURF'S UP. She also noticed that the windows she'd been staring into were covered by large sheets of paper, on which the elementary school kids had finger-painted several surfers on their boards atop big ocean waves. Decorating storefronts of seasonal shops was a quaint, fun island tradition.

"Rich," she said, looking back at her visitor, whose name she'd just remembered. Then she laughed. "I'm no surfer. Not even close. I'm afraid I'm only lost in thought."

"Happens to me all the time. How's John? Haven't seen him for a few weeks."

"He's good. Busy. Fewer on staff this time of year, but still there's lots to do. You know how that goes."

"That I do."

Then she saw the big white vessel pulling into the dock at the bottom of the hill. "Excuse me," she said abruptly. "I'm meeting someone. Nice to see you, though. Say hi to Lisa." Lisa was Rich's wife; Annie was glad she'd remembered her name, too.

"Same to John," he called after her as she crossed Main Street and hurried toward the café.

Waving in return, she knew she most likely wouldn't remember to tell John. They'd have other things to talk about. If she ever heard from him again.

★   ★   ★

Annie ordered a latte and picked out a table at the far end of the restaurant that seemed somewhat private. It also had a good view of the front door so she'd be able to see Jack Miller first—though she had no idea how on earth she'd recognize him. She sat, waiting for her coffee, realizing that because she hadn't joined the others at the Inn for breakfast, she was hungry. But her stomach might betray her if she tried to eat.

Gazing around, she hoped she appeared nonchalant, although she was anything but. From the corner of one eye, she spotted a young couple walk in and go to the counter. Half a minute later, an older woman entered. Annie wondered if Jack thought he'd recognize her because he'd seen her photo on the internet. If so, he had no way of knowing that in publicity photos she hardly looked as she did on this ordinary day in this ordinary café on this ordinary, well, almost ordinary, island.

A curl of laughter might have risen from Murphy then if she'd been present.

The door opened again, and a man stood there. His hair was sticking out from under his wool cap, and he was scanning the room, as if looking for someone.

But those were not the things that convinced Annie that he was Kevin's father. What made it clear was that he was a dead ringer for her brother.

She got up and offered a small wave. The man's face came to life, the same way Kevin's did when he was happy.

Jack Miller took off his cap and brushed his hair back with his hand, the way Kevin did, too, except that Jack's hair had a full gray patina, the kind that came with age. He sauntered to her table the same way Kevin sauntered, albeit a little slower.

Annie sat down before her legs grew too weak to keep standing.

He held out his hand; his fingers were somewhat bent, the way Claire's had become from arthritis, though he looked younger.

"Annie," he said without hesitation. "I'd know you anywhere; you look so much like your mother."

She froze. She hadn't expected that. Kevin had mentioned it a couple of times, but . . .

The server arrived with the latte Annie had ordered. *Perfect timing.*

"Would you care to order something, sir?" the server asked him.

He gestured toward Annie's cup. "I'll have one of those."

The server nodded and left. And Jack Miller sat across from Annie.

"So," he said. "Hello."

She responded with a nod. Then she shook her head. "Sorry. You caught me off guard with your comment about Donna." It was a cliché, but it was the best that she could do. She didn't tell him she'd already become weak because of how much he looked like Kevin. *Except the eyes*, she thought now. Jack Miller's eyes were brown. Kevin's were hazel. Just like Donna's. And Annie's.

"How was the crossing?" she managed to ask.

"Not bad for my first time. Even though I'm pushing seventy, I've never been much of a seaman. You probably need to be because you live here."

"I never really thought about it." It was too soon to tell him about Kevin becoming a captain. She supposed she should leave that for her brother to mention, anyway.

"How long have you lived here?"

"A few years."

"Do you like it?"

"Yes. Very much."

"Where did you come from?"

"Boston."

He nodded, as if he would have guessed that.

After Jack asked several more innocuous questions that made it feel that he was quizzing her instead of the other way around, the server returned and set the latte in front of him. He said thank you and waited for her to leave before speaking again.

"So," he said, "what do you think? Am I really Kevin's father? I figured you agreed to meet me so you could give me the once-over and decide whether or not to tell him about me."

He wasn't bossy or off-putting. Instead, he was delightfully engaging. The way that Kevin was.

Annie smiled. "You passed the test the moment you walked in the door. And other things have reinforced it."

He nodded again. He sipped his coffee. He set the tall cup back down. "Okay. But what are we supposed to say to each other now?"

She decided to simply dive into the topic that was on both their minds. "I have no idea what to say. I do know it's nice to meet you. But I feel I have to warn you that Kevin might not be as welcoming. He's always known you abandoned him."

She did not expect that Jack's reaction would be to laugh. Her spine stiffened; she sat up straight.

He set his elbows on the table and held up both hands, palms open. "Please. Allow me to explain. I did not 'abandon' my son. Or his mother. Donna was in love with another man. She told me she was sorry, but that her feelings for the other guy wouldn't go away. Which made it tough to continue with the marriage."

Annie raised her cup but set it back down before she drank. She couldn't imagine that Donna had been unfaithful to him. Or maybe Annie didn't want to believe it.

"I don't know what to say," she said.

"It's okay," he continued. "It was a long, long time ago. It was really hard for me at the time. . . . I loved them both so much. I sent money for a while until she asked me to stop. I think it was hard for her to have any connection to me because she felt guilty, you know? She was a lovely woman, and she said she was trying to be as honest as she could. But it was years before I could feel grateful for that. For not dragging things out and for not making me feel that she'd been using me as a meal ticket when she'd rather have been with him all along. I don't know if they ever ended up together, though I did notice she took back her maiden name."

Annie ran a finger around the rim of her cup. "Donna never married again."

He sighed. "That's too bad."

Hesitating, not sure she wanted the answer, Annie finally asked, "Did you know who the man was?"

"Well, I knew he was married to someone else. She claimed they'd probably never be able to be together but that she couldn't stop loving him. They were star-crossed lovers, I guess." He paused for a breath, then looked into her eyes. "He was your father, Annie."

Chapter 11

Annie had been on the planet long enough to know that feelings came in a multitude of disguises and weren't always rational. Still, aside from a good dose of self-loathing when she was married to her second husband—thanks to Annie playing a role instead of being herself—Murphy, the psychologist (she really had been one, with framed diplomas on the walls of her office), once explained that most of Annie's emotions were typical, based on her age and hormone levels. But Annie never had to endure anything close to the glut of guilt she felt now, thanks to a single latte and an arbitrary meeting that was supposed to help her brother but had wound up hurting her.

Her father had been the reason that Kevin thought he'd been abandoned. No, she hadn't expected that.

After the initial shock, she spent over an hour with Jack Miller, whose company was enjoyable. Perhaps he was like Kevin in even more ways than his physical appearance suggested. And though he hadn't been pushy, he made it clear that he wanted to see his son.

She walked him down to the dock so that he could catch the noon boat back to the Cape.

"It might take me a few days to figure out how to ap-

proach Kevin," she told him. "But I will. I promise." Then
she gave him a quick hug and said she'd be in touch.

All in all, it had seemed surreal.

Fast-walking back up the hill to where she'd parked the
Jeep, her adrenalin in high gear, Annie knew she'd been
launched into overdrive. She knew she couldn't tell Kevin
about Jack until she'd sorted out what had happened. She
wished Murphy were still alive. She wished Winnie wasn't
away. She wished John . . . She laughed. It was interesting that
she'd left John for last. Maybe she thought that women were
better at assessing this kind of thing.

"Please tell me I'm not turning into a reverse sexist," she
muttered to the brick sidewalk beneath her feet.

On the ride back to Chappy, tidbits of the conversation
she longed to have with a friend flitted around like no-see-
ums in July. And though Murphy or Winnie—or John—wasn't
there, at least she could talk to Murphy.

"Can you believe it, Murph? After he and Donna di-
vorced, he married a woman in Vermont who'd been a friend
of a friend. Her husband was killed in the early days of the
Gulf War, leaving her with five young kids. Five! Then she
and Jack had two of their own—a boy and a girl. So he pretty
much raised seven kids with his wife. Anyway, his wife, Estelle—he called her Essie—died a few years ago, so he now
lives with his daughter—I didn't catch her name—and son-in-
law in Yarmouth. On the Cape! On a clear day, I might be
able to see their house from my porch! His daughter and her
husband have three kids; his son's married, too—he lives
somewhere near the Vermont border in upstate New York
and has a boy, too, so Jack had lots of grandkids. But he never
forgot about Kevin. It's incredible."

Murphy wasn't responding, but that wasn't reason for
Annie to stop talking. So her words kept tumbling out, racing
like pigs at the Ag Fair.

"And can you imagine? He said I look like Donna. It felt so strange to hear him say that. So now I only have to figure out how I'm going to tell Kevin about him. My heart wants to believe he'll be really happy to see his dad again and to meet his dad's family, but . . ."

Just past Head of the Pond Road where the alpaca farm was, Annie steered the Jeep onto the dirt shoulder and turned off the ignition. Her heart began galloping. Her chest started to perspire. And her surroundings looked to her as if she were underwater.

A panic attack, she reasoned. *Full blown.*

She closed her eyes and tried to deep-breathe, struggling to slow each inhale, each exhale. It was several minutes before her symptoms eased, leaving her drained of enthusiasm.

With her voice sounding thinner and smaller, she said, "Murphy? Kevin has a whole other family he's never known about. He even has another sister—a half sister, like I am." Her throat swelled, a sign that her body was preparing to cry.

I wondered when you were going to get to that, Murphy finally commented from the passenger seat.

"You figured it out as soon as I said it?"

Murphy laughed her light Irish laugh. *Hardly. I figured it out as soon as he said it. I was right beside you in Mocha Mott's. You really didn't think I'd let you go there on your own, did you?*

Two tears leaked from the corners of Annie's eyes. "You really are my best friend, aren't you?"

Yes. That hasn't changed. But the bigger question right now is, what are you going to tell Kevin?

Annie tapped the steering wheel while she thought. It didn't take long to come up with the answer.

"The truth."

Murphy gave her another few seconds, probably waiting to see if she'd change her mind.

Yes. You are, her friend finally affirmed.

"But will he hate me for meeting Jack?"

We won't know that until you've told him, will we?

"Okay, But will he hate me because my father was the reason . . ."

Stop right there. Kevin is not going to hate you. That whole situation was hardly your fault.

Annie said. "I guess."

No. You know it as well as I do. Just like we both know you'd be miserable if, no matter what the result, you kept all this to yourself.

"Okay," Annie said. "I'll tell him."

Murphy didn't suggest a timeline. In fact, she didn't say anything else. It was clear she had done what she'd been there to do, and now she flitted away.

After another long, steadying breath, Annie started the Jeep. She waited for six or eight wild turkeys to amble across the road before she steered back onto the pavement and headed home.

If nothing else, meeting Jack Miller certainly tempered Annie's earlier fixation with John. And the fact that she still hadn't heard more than that dismissive text from him.

She was no longer worried; she was angry. Was this what her married life would be like? With Annie playing second fiddle to his daughter's mother?

When she pulled into the driveway back at the Inn, she sat for a moment, looking toward the meadow, toward the tall grass that soon would be infused with wildflowers of purple and blue and red and orange. For the moment, it was edged by daffodils—the same yellow blossoms that sat on her kitchen table, thanks to her wonderful brother, who was about to learn he had a really, really big family. She knew she needed to give up her envy, let go of her guilt. Because, deep down, Annie was sure that Kevin had enough love inside him for them all. Including her. She must be sure not to confuse John's excluding her with Kevin's having other siblings. Because, no matter what, Kevin would not exclude her.

She was glad she knew that.

And don't forget it, Murphy's voice suddenly announced, then, just as quickly, was gone again.

Annie got out of the Jeep, and went down to her cottage, feeling lighter, happier. She grabbed the rest of the chicken salad for lunch, followed by half of one of Lucy's cookies. Then she decided to call John. No doubt, he wouldn't answer. But she at least could leave a nice message. She would not be accusatory; she would not sound upset. She would be patient. She would be loving. Which, hopefully, would convey that her only reason for calling was because she cared.

She brought her phone into her writing nook, where she always felt safest, though she had no idea why. As she entered his number, the last thing she expected was for him to pick up.

But he did.

"Hi," he said. He didn't whisper; he made no excuse as to why he hadn't sent up a smoke signal again to let her know that all was okay.

"Hi," Annie replied. "How are things going? How's Abigail?"

"The same. She slept most of the way here."

She noticed he hadn't answered her question about how things were going.

"You must be anxious for tomorrow."

"Yup."

"Are you eating okay?" She knew that when John was stressed, he either overate or did not eat at all.

"We had takeout this afternoon. Chinese."

Perhaps Jenn didn't cook. Or maybe he didn't like her cooking. He did like Chinese food, though, so he must have eaten well.

Annie ran her fingers along the smooth edge of the desk

Kevin had built to perfectly fit the nook. She felt ludicrous. She had no idea what to say next or what to ask.

"How's Lucy?" It was lame, but it was all she could come up with.

"Fine. She's out walking Restless with Jenn and Abigail. Jenn convinced Abigail that some fresh air would do her good."

There was no rational reason for his comment to grab hold of her stomach and wring it the way her mother used to wring out the hand washing before hanging it out on the clothesline. Annie had known that Lucy was there. Restless hadn't been home, so she should have assumed that he went, too. And, of course, Jenn was there. But the thought of all of them to-gether—dog, daughters, mother—made Annie feel she truly was not needed. Or wanted. Restless had always wanted to be near her; he was her shadow whenever she saw him, especially if Lucy wasn't around. She pictured the way he slept in bed with her and John, curled up at their feet, then, during the night, somehow creeping up to the pillows, so that when they woke up, he was planted between them, snoring, yet ready to lap kisses whenever one of them opened their eyes.

But Annie knew that thinking about the dog right now was symbolic of the much larger problem.

"Well . . . ," she said, aching to add something caring and kind, "I only called to let you to know that I'm thinking of you. And that I'll be thinking of you—all of you—tomorrow."

"Thanks," he said.

He didn't say he wanted to hang up, but Annie didn't know what else to say.

"I'll let you go." Her words came out sounding slightly laced with curry. "But please text me or call tomorrow and let me know how things went. And remember I love you."

"I love you, too."

She no longer knew if she believed it.

After disconnecting, she kept sitting at her desk, her head bent now, her hands clasping her temples.

After a while, Annie decided to get back to work. Four days was long enough to ride an emotional roller coaster, wasn't it?

She knew, however, that she couldn't expect the cottage to be the best environment right then to recharge her creative spirit—she needed a place that wouldn't foster self-pity. Even the reading room at the Inn would be too isolating, because everyone there knew not to disturb Annie when her keyboard was clicking. *No*, she thought. She needed to be somewhere more public. Somewhere like . . .

The Community Center, either Murphy or Annie came up with. She had no idea if anyone would be there or if it would be locked, but if nothing else, maybe getting out of her cozy nook would help. She needed to remember that, and that she did have a manuscript to finish sooner than she wished, and another to concoct into a cohesive, publishable mystery.

It shouldn't be difficult. She'd already written almost half of the first one.

Famous last words, Murphy chirped, because she loved dishing out platitudes.

Successfully ignoring her friend, Annie packed up, went outside, and drove to the center in less than five minutes.

Only one car sat in the small, dirt-packed parking area, which meant someone was there. Not a crowd, but at least one person who no doubt had a key and would let her in. Perfect.

The "person" turned out to be Lottie Nelson, who was alone in the office. She wore a pretty, flowered flannel shirt, her graying hair huddled in a topknot, eyeglasses perched low on her nose as she peeked over the frames at her computer. She was busily working.

She stopped typing and looked up. "Annie! Welcome! I heard you were back."

Word flew around the Vineyard in less time than it took the high-speed ferry from Rhode Island to get there in summer.

"Thanks," Annie said. "It's great to be home." The statement had been truer a few days earlier. "But now I'm looking for a place to get some writing done. There's too much distraction at the Inn." It was another white lie she might have to account for someday, but not that day.

"Take your pick from the tables out there." Lottie gestured toward the spacious gathering room. "It's set up for a board meeting, but that's not until six tonight."

"Thanks, Lottie. I'll leave you alone so you can get back to work."

Puffing out her cheeks, Lottie pushed out a whoosh of air. "I'm trying to get a jump on the summer events calendar. Between our growing list of sailing, tennis, rainy-day activities— you know the rest—I wonder if anyone comes here anymore just to relax."

Annie laughed. "Good point. Relaxation is elusive these days. Even you and I laugh at the thought, yet here we are, living in paradise."

"You said it. By the way, how's John's Abigail doing?"

For absolutely no intelligent reason, Annie was surprised. And yet, why was she?

"Abigail?" Annie had no idea what to say or how to say it. She tried to sound noncommittal. "She loves going to school on the Cape. I think she's getting tired, though. Kids today push themselves way too much, don't you think?"

"I heard they've gone to Boston. To see a specialist."

Annie blinked. So much for trying to shield reality. "Did you hear that from Earl or Claire?"

Lottie shook her head. "Neither. Bonnie told me. You know Bonnie. From the post office?"

Right, Annie thought. Bonnie was the name of the woman who worked at the post office and the thrift store, and apparently at the Boys and Girls Club. The woman Annie had just seen on the boat.

"Lottie, would you do me a favor and ask her not to mention it to anyone else? We're trying to keep it from Earl and Claire until there's a diagnosis, if any. You know how much they would worry, which I hope will be needless. But still . . ." She'd intentionally said, "We're trying to keep it from Earl and Claire," as if Annie had any say in the matter. There was no sense airing the rest.

"Oh, Annie, I'm so sorry. I'll be sure to tell Bonnie. I'd better text her because she's so busy these days."

Annie made it a point to smile. "I don't know her well, but she seems like a busy lady."

Dottie laughed. "You could say that. Three jobs, and now she's dating, too. I don't know how that woman finds time to even talk to anyone. Especially since usually she doesn't gossip."

"I wonder who told her about Abigail?" It was more of a question that Annie was asking herself.

"Probably her new boyfriend. He's pretty tight with the family, isn't he?"

"Well," Annie said lightly, trying to mask her cluelessness, "I have no idea who Bonnie's dating. Obviously, I've been away too long."

Lottie laughed. "Maybe I've spoken out of turn about that, too. I assumed everyone knew—it doesn't seem as if they're trying to hide it." She scowled a little, her eyeglasses sliding father down the bridge of her nose as she spoke.

"Come on, Lottie," Annie said with a laugh, "out with it! Who's she dating?"

"Rex. Rex Winsted. Taylor's brother."

Annie turned to stone, as if she were one of the sculptures at Field Gallery in West Tisbury. She had no idea why no one had mentioned that Rex had a lady friend. And yet, why should they? And why should she care? It was a strange coincidence, however, that the woman whose name had eluded Annie when she'd seen her on the boat was the one who was dating Rex. It wasn't a crime; it shouldn't even be a scandal. Rex was single, and it was a good bet Bonnie was, too, or they would have been, as Lottie put it, "trying to hide it." Still, the announcement tipped Annie's scales a little, nudging her off balance, making her realize that a lot had, indeed, happened while she'd been gone.

"Rex," Annie said, "Of course. I thought he seemed happier than he used to be." She emitted a fake laugh, then excused herself so that Lottie could get back to the events calendar and she to her novel. She retreated to the big room, sat down, and stared outside at the grove of scrub oaks and pine trees.

How bizarre were the only words that came to mind. And what made the situation odder was that it seemed Rex had been engaged in spreading rumors. Annie wouldn't have expected that from him. She'd come to believe that he was a good guy who'd simply had a few bad breaks, but not that he was malicious.

But who had told him about Abigail?

And, despite what John had wanted, had Earl and Claire found out, too? Was that why Claire, too, seemed unwell? Was she mentally, physically, exhausted from worry? If so, it would explain why she'd lied to Francine about being too busy with the garden club, which most likely hadn't even met yet this year.

After sitting a few minutes and not opening her laptop, Annie picked up her belongings, returned to the office doorway, and stuck her head back inside.

"Thanks, Lottie," she said, "but I have to go. It turns out I'm needed at the Inn." She had no idea if Dottie believed her; the woman simply waved, told her to come back anytime, and said she hoped all would go well for Abigail.

Annie nodded and left. She wanted to get home and be alone. Again.

Chapter 12

But by the time Annie arrived back at the Inn and saw Rex's old pickup in the driveway, she was no longer bewildered but irked. If he was going to be a regular fixture in their lives, he must learn a few things. Such as, it wasn't cool to share family issues with outsiders unless he'd been told it was okay.

She would talk to him now before putting it off. She stomped into the mudroom, then into the kitchen. But the place was empty; Rex wasn't there.

Deliberately walking slowly to temper her stomping, Annie first checked the laundry room, then cruised the great room, the reception area, the reading room, the media room. No one was around. But when she went back to the reception area at the bottom of the staircase leading up to the guest suites, she heard voices coming from above—none of which belonged to Murphy.

"Now I can take a shower!" a female said with a lilt.

"Yeah, thanks, man." That one was a male.

Then Annie realized the voices came from the elementary school teachers, their year-round tenants who had been with them since the Inn had opened.

"No problem. Happy to help." There was no mistaking the baritone third voice. It was Rex's.

Annie waited for the big man to thunder down the steps. However, he made no more sound than an average-sized person. Perhaps, in order not to disturb the other tenants, he was being courteous. Unlike Annie had been.

"Rex," she said when he came into view. "You're still here."

"Shower drain had a small problem in room five."

"I didn't know you were a plumber."

He stopped one stair up from her and rubbed his large hands together. "When you own a restaurant, you learn to be a fix-it guy or you'll soon be out of business." He stopped rubbing and grinned a kind of puppy-dog grin. "Of course, I went out of business anyway, so I guess there's more to it than that."

Annie returned the grin to acknowledge his self-deprecating humor.

"Thanks. But you could have called Kevin. He usually takes care of that kind of maintenance."

"No need. I was here. Besides, I think he's working on the *On Time*. He's the most devoted deckhand I've ever known." He took the final step and stood in front of her.

"I'm sure you're right." She made a move toward the reading room. "Would you mind coming in here a minute? I'd like to talk with you about something."

He followed her into the room, then flinched when she closed the door after them, as if he just realized that this might be about something serious.

"How did you hear about Abigail?" Annie blurted out.

He folded his arms. "What?"

Annie sighed, went to one of the cushy chairs, and took a seat. "Sit," she said. "Please."

He muscled frame did not fit the barrel shape, so he took a straight chair from the reading table, carried it to where Annie was, and sat.

"Abigail," she said. "John's daughter."

"I know who you mean. His older daughter, right? The blond one. What about her?"

"Who told you she's been . . . sick?"

He scowled. He looked slightly threatening when he scowled, what with his bulk and all.

"And did you tell your girlfriend?"

"What?"

"Bonnie. Your girlfriend. Did you tell her that Abigail's sick?" She thought her question had been clear enough.

"Bonnie Larkin is not my 'girlfriend,' Annie. She's a friend. We go out for dinner sometimes. We hike the Menemsha Hills. Nothing more."

"I wasn't prying, Rex. And that's not why I asked."

He examined his fingernails. "I didn't tell Bonnie anything about Abigail. I don't know anything about Abigail. I didn't know she's sick until you just said it. Even if I did, I wouldn't have told Bonnie. I wouldn't have told anyone. I hate gossip. Especially island gossip."

Foolish wasn't a strong enough word for the way Annie felt. *Embarrassed.* She put her face in her hands, where it seemed to be winding up a lot since she'd been back on the Vineyard.

"I'm so sorry, Rex. It's just that John doesn't want his parents to worry needlessly—or until there's something concrete to tell them. As I'm sure you can guess, the more people who know, the harder it will be to keep it quiet until all the tests are done."

"Excuse me," Rex said. He stood up and went to her. Then he lifted her hands from her face, held them a second, then set them in her lap. He returned to his chair and folded his arms again. "But now that I know something's wrong with John's daughter, can you tell me if it's serious?"

Annie shook her head. "We don't know. Yet." She added a quick correction. "*They* don't know. She's having more tests in Boston tomorrow. We're hoping it's absolutely nothing. Or that it's something that can quickly be fixed."

"Does my sister know?"

"No, Taylor doesn't. Not that I'm aware of. But Lottie at the community center just told me that Bonnie told her and . . . well, that you and Bonnie were dating. So I guess I jumped the gun a bit."

He shrugged. "I've been accused of worse. Sometimes I've even been guilty." He grinned his puppy grin again.

"Oh, Rex, I'm so sorry. The truth is, I'm still trying to re-calibrate my brain from having been gone. And I'm worried about Abigail."

"No problem, Annie. I'm sorry for her. And the whole family."

They sat quietly for a moment, then Rex added, "Maybe Lucy told her. John's other daughter. Didn't she help Bonnie at the Boys and Girls Club?"

Annie now needed to add *stupid* to her list of feelings about herself. She stood up and paced as if she were Kevin, who loved to pace. "You're probably right." Then she had a sudden flashback of being on the boat and Bonnie telling her that Lucy had stopped going to the club. "Too bad she can't keep coming" were her words. "What with everything going on." Before she'd gone back to her car, Bonnie had added, "It's good that you've come home."

Annie ended her pacing. "I think we've nipped it in the bud," she told Rex. "But please don't mention any of this to Bonnie."

He pinched his forefinger and thumb together, then zip-pered them across his mouth in a "my lips are sealed" gesture.

"Thanks. And thanks for accepting my apology." She touched his shoulder on her way out of the room. It felt as firm as concrete—a perfect disguise for the thoughtful man concealed inside.

Annie resisted calling Lucy and telling her what had happened. She was certain Rex was right: Lucy must have told Bonnie that she wanted to spend more time at home to help out Abigail, who was sick. She must also have called her or run into her or something and told her that her sister was going to Boston for tests. It was a simple, logical explanation that Annie could verify if only she picked up the phone and checked with Lucy. But there was no need to add more distress to how Lucy—and everyone—must be feeling right then. Besides, Annie had already made one upsetting call to Plymouth. She didn't need to put herself through that again.

She heated up leftover pizza from three nights before and picked at it for dinner; then she settled into her nook and actually accomplished some writing before going to bed.

But sometime during the night, she was awakened by two loud bangs on her door and someone shouting her name.

Bolting out from under the covers, she ran into the living room and yanked open the door without asking who was there. She didn't need to; she knew Kevin's knock—and his voice.

"Claire's had a stroke," he blurted out. "Taylor's with them. Rex is driving them to the hospital; Fred said he'd bring them across." Fred was no doubt the *On Time* captain on call that night in case of an emergency.

"How bad?" she asked

"Too soon to know."

Annie ran back to the bedroom and threw on yesterday's clothes and a heavy cardigan, grateful that Taylor was an EMT and that she and Kevin lived near Earl and Claire.

"Fred will come back for us," Kevin's voice rambled from the other room.

Grabbing her phone and her purse and tossing a candy mint into her mouth, she closed the door and raced up the hill behind him.

"You want me to drive?" she asked.

His head shook rapidly. "No. I need something to do."

They jumped into his pickup; the engine roared to life.

"Has anyone called John?"

"Earl thought you should be the one to make the call."

"But . . ."

"But I agreed." He ripped down North Neck Road, dust flying in the headlights like tiny moths who most likely had been sleeping, too.

"It's her second stroke." She had no idea if that meant anything.

"I know. But Taylor said once they get to the hospital, and Claire gets a shot of something, it should help minimize the aftereffects."

TPA, Annie remembered from when Claire had her first stroke a few years before. Annie didn't recall what the initials stood for, but she knew the injection worked miracles. "It breaks up the clot," she said now. "If it's caught soon enough."

Kevin's hands remained pasted to the steering even as he drove onto the *On Time* and thanked Captain Fred for the quick response.

Fred nodded from beneath the hood of his yellow slicker. Which was when Annie realized it was raining.

"I want to wait to call until the doctors can tell us more," she said. "Does that make sense?"

"I have no idea. I haven't thought straight since Earl called and woke us up. Do whatever you think is right. But Earl might think it's weird if John doesn't show up."

"He's in Plymouth, Kevin. He's with the girls."

"Oh. So it's not like he can be at the hospital in ten minutes."

The wipers were on now, moving at a fast clip to keep pace with the increasing rain. Kevin drove off the ferry and sped up Dock Street toward lower Main, then zigzagged down South Water, up Davis Lane, across Peases Point Way, back out to where Main Street was going in the right direction toward the hospital.

Annie wrapped her big sweater around her more tightly and sat, shivering.

They rode the rest of the way in silence.

But when Kevin pulled into the parking lot, he turned to his sister. "I really hope she's okay. And that Earl is, too." His tears glistened in the glare of the streetlights that lined the driveway. "She's been so wonderful since Donna died. And Earl . . . God, Annie, Earl's like the father I never had."

He parked the truck and they got out, hurrying to the emergency entrance, while Annie was weighed down by so many emotions that she didn't dare speak.

"They won't let me in yet." Earl stood at one of the big windows in the ER waiting area, twisting his Red Sox cap in his hands, looking out toward the harbor at the big boat that sat quietly in port, awaiting the first trip of the day. He'd once told Annie that one of the boats always stayed overnight on the Vineyard side in case of a disaster. The boats, after all, were the lifeline of the island in ways many people never considered.

Kevin stood on one side of him, Annie on the other, her hand on Earl's shoulder. It was not strong like Rex's; it was small and weak, as if there were no muscles left after seventy-six years of having so many people leaning on him. Literally. Figuratively.

Annie didn't know where Rex had gone, but he wasn't there.

"This is the second one," Earl went on in a whisper. "Annie, you were here for the first."

"I was." It seemed to have happened eons ago. "And she came through it really well, remember?"

Earl just kept focused on the water, as if he hadn't heard her. "Kevin, we're so grateful for your wife's training." Kevin, of course, had nothing to do with Taylor's EMT credentials; Earl might have forgotten that she'd received her credentials at least two decades before the couple had met.

"Me, too," Kevin replied.

By then, all three of them were gazing outside, as if waiting for the boat to turn on its lights so they could walk on. It was easy to see down there, since the hospital lot was nearly empty; most of the staff parked around back.

Then, suddenly, Earl said, "John's in Plymouth, you know."

Annie tried not to react. Not that Earl would have noticed.

"Abigail's sick," Earl continued. "He doesn't think we know. But, Jesus Christ, this is an island." It was all he said, as if it his last comment explained everything.

Kevin looked at Annie. "What's wrong with Abigail?"

She shook her head and said, "She's been tired a lot. So they're doing blood work. That's all." But she held her eyes on Kevin's long enough so he'd be able to tell there was more to the story.

"I think . . . I think it's more than being tired," Earl stammered.

"She'll be fine," Annie said quietly. "And so will Claire." She rested her head against Earl's worn-out shoulder. "You'll see."

"I don't want you to call him yet," Earl said.

"I won't. Not until you say it's okay." She gently squeezed his arm. "How about if we sit down?"

"He shook his head. "No. I'll stay here. But you go ahead if you want."

She did not "want." She could not leave his side. Not the man who was like the father that her brother never had. *Jack Miller*, she thought, was going to have to wait a while longer to meet his son.

Kevin broke away from them as if it were all too much for him to take in. He paced the oversize room. Like so many other large venues on the island, it was too big nine months of the year, but every square foot was needed in-season: June, July, August. Annie recently read that the season now extended into September and October and ramped up again in May. She figured that soon "off-season" would be a misnomer.

Then the familiar *whoosh* of automatic doors opening filled the room—the doors that led to the back rooms where patients were evaluated, tested, monitored. They turned their heads and saw that Kevin was already halfway across the room, moving toward Taylor, who was walking toward them with a woman Annie didn't recognize but assumed was a doctor because she had on a white coat.

Kevin joined them, and the party of three continued to approach Earl, who stood, unmoving, waiting to be brought back to life.

The white-coated woman introduced herself as Dr. Somebody-or-Other, smiled, and said, "Claire is stable now."

She could have said a lot of things: "Claire is in ICU," "Claire is fully paralyzed," "Claire is . . . gone."

Thank God she'd said none of those.

She'd said, "Claire is stable now," and smiled as she said it.

"That's good, right?" either Earl or Kevin—yes, Annie thought, probably Kevin—asked.

The woman nodded. "It means you got her here in time for a lifesaving injection. It means that, while we can only be confident after a little more time, it looks as if she'll pull through with minimal effects, if any. It also means we'd like to continue to monitor her for at least twenty-four hours. Especially because of her history. Would you like to see her now?"

Earl still hadn't moved, other than to turn his head when the doors had whooshed. It was no surprise that, in that moment, his whole body sagged, and he started to sob.

Annie put a hand to her mouth and pressed against it so she wouldn't let out a wail of relief.

Kevin put his arm around Earl and led him to the chairs, but Earl must have muttered something because Kevin changed his mind and steered him toward the lobby at the main entrance, and then her brother and the man who might as well have been his father disappeared around the corner, out of Annie's sight.

Chapter 13

John hadn't slept. How could he? The sofa at Jenn's condo was hugely uncomfortable. Or maybe he was blaming the sofa when his subconscious had decided it would be better not to sleep than to oversleep. It didn't matter that he wasn't the only one there, and that all four of them—no, make that three, because Abigail might not have bothered—had set their alarms.

He stood at the kitchen sink making coffee, eyes drilled on a fancy porcelain tile on the wall, as if it were a window through which he could will the sun to rise, the sky to turn mellow orange, the light of day to dawn.

How he hated being there, in a suburban community of neat, clonelike condominium houses that was too far inland from the water even though it was only a ten- or twelve-minute drive. He knew that even if a window had been there, if he opened it, he would not smell the sea.

At least Jenn had the common sense not to ask him to sleep with her, that she hadn't pulled a stunt like that for sympathy, what with them being the worried parents. He might have left if she'd done that. To be prepared, he'd already Googled "Plymouth, MA, Accommodations" on his phone and found a relatively cheap motel that at least *was down by the water. He didn't think he'd need a reservation, seeing as it was only April.*

"Dad?"

He turned to see his younger daughter combed and cleaned and dressed.

"Abigail doesn't want to go."

He sighed. "I'll go talk to her, honey."

"I don't think it will help."

He walked past Lucy, kissed her cheek, and headed down the hall to the bedroom, feeling heavier than when he wore a bulletproof vest and his gun belt. And more afraid than he did at those infrequent times.

As long as you don't show it, *they'd taught them at the academy.* Never, ever show fear.

It was a technique that, in this situation, seemed to be working on his girls. Maybe even on Annie. Though he probably was kidding himself about her.

Chapter 14

"Absolutely not," Claire squawked while sitting up in her hospital bed, hair sticking up and out, this way and that, her pearl-gray eyes bright and engaged, as if nothing had happened. "You will not tell John about this. You will not tell the girls. They have enough on their minds. Especially today."

"I told you she'd say that," Earl, seated in a chair next to the bed, said to Annie. Annie stood at the foot, facing the patient.

"Don't you think he'd want to know?" she asked.

"It doesn't matter what my son would want. Let him get things sorted out for Abigail. We'll tell him later, when we can all laugh about this nonsense."

The doctor had said she'd been lucky, that it had been only a minor stroke, but it was good they'd brought her there before things might have gotten worse. Which Annie understood to mean, "before Claire had another stroke, that one maybe bigger." Though she didn't completely agree with Claire's decision not to call John, Annie was fairly sure that by the time he was told, his mother would be home and doing great. As if it had been no big deal.

Annie tapped the foot rail. "Okay. Is there anything you'd like me to bring you? A nightgown? Crossword puzzles? Necessities?" It was eight o'clock on Tuesday morning; Claire would not be released until nine o'clock the next day. Technically, her twenty-four-hour stint would be finished around 3 a.m., but apparently no one would be available to release her until nine. She'd already griped about that.

But her voice softened. "Thank you, dear. I'd appreciate anything. Especially clean undies. But the nurse gave me a little toiletry kit, so I don't need any of that."

Annie made a mental note of a few items, including a compact of light blush. Between the white sheets, Claire's white hair, and those lovely pale eyes, she looked rather dreadful. "Ghastly," Annie's grandmother would have called it. The thought of her grandmother reminded her about John's—and of the woman's wedding dress that Annie still hadn't worn, the one Abigail still hadn't restyled to better suit Annie (as had been the plan), and maybe now wouldn't be able to, at least not in the next couple of weeks.

She cleared her throat, as John would have done if he'd been her.

"I'll go to Chappy and come back with a bag for you. Earl? Do you want me to bring you home so you can get some rest?"

Annie and Earl were still by Claire's side, where they'd been for nearly five hours. Once the favorable prognosis had been delivered, Kevin left Annie his truck and went back with Taylor and Rex, who'd been waiting the whole time in the reception area of the main hospital entrance. "Out of the way," Rex had said, as if he still didn't realize he'd become part of Kevin's troops.

"I'll stay," Earl answered. "I want to make sure my wife behaves. You know how she is about hospitals."

Annie smiled. "Okay. I won't be long. But then I'm going to insist that I bring you home. We don't want both of you needing a bed here."

Then she noticed Earl's eyes drifting up to the clock on the wall. "What time is Abigail's appointment? We know she's supposed to have tests after that. But not when they'll get the results."

Annie still didn't know how he and Claire had found out but wasn't sure if she should ask. For all she knew, Jenn had told them. "I think they have to play it by ear," she said. "But they'll probably have answers soon enough." Of course, she had no idea. But she wanted to be positive. For them.

Still clutching his Red Sox cap, which he hadn't let go of since Annie walked into the hospital, he said, "I hope it doesn't take long."

"They have no control over that," Claire said. "In the meantime, maybe she'll get better."

"You've been saying that for weeks. So far, she hasn't."

"If you kids are going to argue," Annie said, "I'll have to stay here and referee. And I really don't want to do that."

Earl lowered his eyes to his cap. "Truce."

"Truce," Claire agreed.

Then Annie couldn't wait any longer. "I hate to ask, but how did you find out about Abigail? The last I heard, John didn't want you to know until it was resolved. He didn't want you to worry. . . ."

Claire laughed. "Are you kidding? We know our son and our granddaughters. We know when something's not right."

"Claire pried it out of Lucy," Earl said.

"You bet your boots I did."

"Only because when it comes to her grandparents, Lucy's an easy mark." Earl laughed, and Claire did, too.

"But John still doesn't know you know?" Annie said.

"Hell no," Earl said, shaking his head.

"We didn't want him to worry," Claire added.

If they weren't so charming, they would be exasperating.

"I'm leaving now," Annie said, "before the two of you drive me crazy." She gave each of them a hug, then left the room and went down the too-familiar corridor, making another mental note to add Claire's good hairbrush to the list of "necessities," before someone mistook her for an aging rock star.

As badly as Annie wanted to check in with John, she decided it would be more prudent to wait, to let him call when he was ready.

After retrieving the items for Claire, returning to the hospital, prodding Earl to come back to Chappy, and arranging for Francine to take Earl's place with Claire—which, after getting past the shock of what happened, the girl was more than happy to do—Annie got back to work on her manuscript. The sooner she was done, the better her chances were of being able to avoid starting the next one until summer was over. That way she could tend to the Inn and try to find time to make more boutique soaps for the artisan fairs in the fall. Oh, and perhaps she'd get married on April 23. And perhaps she'd be able to help Abigail, if help was warranted. Or wanted.

But she refused to dwell on those things. So she sat at her desk and powered up her laptop, determined to get to work. Which she would have done, if an email from Jack Miller hadn't popped up in her in-box.

"This is not a good time," she whined at the screen.

But Annie often wasn't good at listening to herself.

Hello Annie, the email began. **It was so nice to meet you yesterday.**

Yesterday? Had that been only yesterday?

I know you said it might take a few days before you
told Kevin about me, and I'm not trying to push you.
But I am eager to see my son again. From everything
you told me, Donna did a wonderful job raising him,
which I believe. She was a remarkable woman. I'll try
not to pester you. Believe me when I say I am
already grateful for the time you gave me and for
getting to meet you—Donna's daughter.
    Hope to hear from you soon—
    Jack

She looked away from the computer. Outside, a tiny
house finch was perched on a branch of a scrub pine, its rosy-
red face turned toward her. It was a common bird, not a majestic one like an osprey with its breathtaking five-foot
wingspan or an inquisitive snowy owl that always looked as if
it had something important to say. Instead, the little house
finch and its brothers and sisters were regular visitors to the
Inn, part of the family.

Annie sighed. She wondered if Murphy had planted the
bird there to remind her that Kevin needed to be a priority,
too, and that she really did need to tell him about Jack. Earl
and Claire and John and all of them could do the dance of trying to protect one another, but Annie wasn't sure that was always the most sensible approach, especially within families.
People were still individuals and had a right to know whatever
might be important for their lives. And as much as Kevin said
Earl was like a father to him, the truth was, Earl was not his father. Jack Miller was. And Jack was alive and presumably well
and living on the opposite side of the sound, only a few nauti-
cal miles away.

And though Annie had no way of knowing if Kevin
would want to see his father again, or if Donna would have

welcomed the idea, Kevin did have the right to know that Jack wanted to see him.

So, before diving into her work, Annie picked up her phone, called her brother and updated him on Claire. Then she invited herself to Kevin and Taylor's for dinner. While she was there, she supposed she might as well tell Taylor about Abigail. Because everyone else seemed to know. Everyone but Francine and Jonas. Annie knew that at some point she should tell them, now that Earl and Claire knew. She wouldn't want Francine to feel left out, because that feeling sucked.

The early evening was cold for April, with a strong island breeze that ruffled the still-naked trees whose buds hadn't yet burst out their green leaves. On the way to Kevin and Taylor's, Annie thought about how she was happy that she'd finally been able to get back into her manuscript in spite of so many thoughts buzzing in her head like honeybees at Sweet Everything Farm in Chilmark. She wondered again if this book, and the next, also would be "picked up by Hollywood," as the saying went, and if they'd want her on the scriptwriting team again. She wasn't sure how she felt about that, since right now her world felt more complex than any plot twists she could imagine. She was, however, proud that she didn't feel guilty about not yet responding to Jack's email. Maybe she could send him hopeful news later that night. Or maybe she'd suggest that Kevin email him directly, so that she could stay out of it, where she belonged, with one less plot twist to have to worry about.

Taylor greeted her at the back door of the Cape-style, gray-shingled house.

"Claire's still doing well?" she asked.

Annie nodded. "Yes. Francine spent all afternoon with her and gave me a positive report. Earl went back to relieve her, and I haven't heard otherwise, so I assume she's on the right track. Thanks to you, Taylor."

Taylor waved it off and motioned Annie inside. "Just glad all is well."

Annie had only been inside Kevin and Taylor's house a few times; typically, they all converged at Earl and Claire's. Even on Annie's first Christmas Eve on the island, she'd gone there, and Taylor showed up. At the time, Annie hadn't yet met Donna, and Kevin would come later. But that first Christmas Eve was when she'd met John. She tried not to laugh now when she remembered she'd thought that Taylor and John were a couple. She never told him that.

As she moved into the kitchen now, Murphy chuckled in her ear. They both now knew that such a coupling would have been a disaster: two headstrong people, each needing to be in charge.

"Wine?" Taylor asked while Annie slipped out of her jacket.

"Sure. What can I do to help?"

"Nothing. Table's already set."

Annie tucked her hair behind her ears as if she were anxious. She was. "Where's my brother?"

A shuffling of feet followed a distant rustling of paper as Kevin emerged from the living room area wearing the faux deerskin slippers Taylor had given him for Christmas. Kevin had never been a hunter but decided that the fake stuff was both warm and animal friendly.

He was holding a copy of the *Gazette* now, one of the island's two newspapers, available online and still in print.

"There's an article here about the upcoming Mother's Day extravaganza," he announced. "Maybe you and John should postpone your date for a couple of weeks and get married at the lighthouse. Maybe the town politicos will let you dress it up in pink and green ribbons—didn't Lucy say they did that one year? If nothing else, the wedding might be good publicity for your TV series. And don't laugh. I'm only half kidding."

"You, little brother, are absurd. Do you really think John would want to do that?"

"No," he said, setting the paper down. "But the weekend festivities should be fun. There'll be goings-on all over town. And it's for a good cause. Profits go to kids' scholarships."

Taylor handed her a glass of red wine. "You could always sell your soaps at your wedding reception." She had finally developed a sense of humor, such as it was. Maybe some of Kevin's had rubbed off on her.

"Now, now," Kevin said. "There's no need for sarcasm." He went to the refrigerator, took out a beer, cracked it open.

Taylor winked at Annie, then pulled dishes from the cabinet. "Chowder and salad for dinner. You two might as well sit at the table while I get it together. I figured you've got something on your mind, Annie. Or you wouldn't have asked to come over. You can go in the living room if whatever it is isn't my business."

No matter which side of her personality Taylor chose to show, at least everyone always knew where they stood with her. It was a fact that Annie was getting used to.

"Here's fine." Annie didn't think Kevin would mind, and she did not want Taylor to feel snubbed. Or that Annie was keeping a secret from her.

They sat at the table. Annie sipped her wine, knowing she was expected to deliver a statement.

"Kevin," she began. She drew in a long breath, said a quick prayer to Donna that this was the right thing to do and another to Murphy for support. "The other day, I had a very strange email. I wasn't sure what to do about it. But here I am."

She fully expected Taylor to tell her to quit stalling and spit it out.

"I'm listening," Kevin said as he placed the *Gazette* next to him and took a swig from the beer bottle.

"I can't think of a way to say this, other than to just . . . say it."

"Uh-huh."

Taylor stopped clattering dishes and pans.

Annie fidgeted with the cloth napkin at her place. "It was from someone who said he knows you. And that he'd like to get in touch with you."

Kevin laughed. "And why's that a big deal? I have nothing to hide. From anyone. No matter who. What's his name?"

Annie hadn't wanted tears to come to her eyes. But, looking at her innocent, sweet brother, a man who was happily content to drink a beer in an old house where he seemed comfortable and enjoyed schlepping around in fake deerskin slippers and catching up on the island news while reading the newspaper the old-fashioned way, she did not want to upset the life that he had now. She really, really did not. No matter how nice Jack Miller was.

"Annie?" Kevin asked. Then he leaned forward, elbows on the table, as if beginning to understand that this might be important.

"Give her a minute," Taylor barked. "She'll come out with it sooner or later."

Taylor was right.

So Annie took another deep breath, looked at her brother, and said, "The email was from Jack Miller, Kevin. Your father."

Chapter 15

Silence.

Annie didn't know if it lasted five seconds or five minutes, but the dead air seemed to linger for an eternity. Like when the police had come to her old Boston apartment and told her that her first husband, Brian, had been killed in a car accident, and the world, Annie's world, completely stopped revolving, her breath had stopped breathing, her body felt as if it had turned to stone.

She wondered if those things were happening to her brother now.

"Kevin?" she asked, because enough time had passed.

He glanced over at the newspaper, as if trying to deflect his reaction.

"Surprised it's not in the *Gazette*," he said. "'Cuz that should certainly be newsworthy. Front page, even."

If Taylor had picked up a slice of Kevin's sense of humor, maybe he'd absorbed some of her sharpness. Right then, however, Taylor seemed to have nothing to say.

At that moment, someone knocked on the back door. And Rex walked in, carrying a covered dish.

"Evening, all!" he said.

Taylor spun to her brother, then back to Annie. "I forgot to mention I invited him."

Which meant it wasn't a good time to continue their discussion.

"Did you make something good?" Kevin asked as he stood. "'Cuz all we have is chowder and salad." He seemed his usual bright and cheerful self. Or at least he might have seemed that way to anyone but Annie. Or maybe Taylor. But his shoulders were stiff, and his head wasn't moving, so Annie would have bet that his body had gone rigid, the way hers once felt as if it had turned to stone.

It also appeared that Kevin was grateful for the distraction. Annie knew a lot about the power of that.

"Lemon drizzle cake," Rex replied. Then he patted his stomach. "After that orange cake, which I thought came out pretty good, I decided to try and keep things light, so I'm ready for the season of T-shirts and shorts."

Kevin laughed a little too loudly.

A plasticized conversation followed about calories and fat content and how easy it was to rack up few pounds over the winter, when chances to exercise were minimal, even on the Vineyard, which was known for its trails and ancient pathways that could be enjoyed year-round if one had a puff parka and a good pair of hiking boots. Kevin said gaining weight must not have been a problem for Annie over the winter, what with her having been in the sunshine, nibbling on avocados and sucking oranges. Annie said that anyone might think that was true, though most of the time she sat in an office . . . and blah-blah-blah. Small talk. Empty-headed chatter.

The synthetic-speak went on for the next several minutes, if anyone was keeping track of the time.

Kevin offered Rex a beer, which he accepted.

Taylor stirred the chowder.

And Annie was thinking that if she had to sit there another

second, playing the role of someone who was saying one thing while her mind was riveted to another, she would jump up and start shouting. Maybe she'd even start shaking all over, the way the Shakers had done in the eighteenth and nineteenth centuries, as if a higher authority were urging Annie to talk about what really mattered.

"So, Claire's okay?" Rex suddenly asked, which was the most sensible thing any of them had vocalized since he'd let himself inside.

"She is," Taylor replied. "No aftereffects. No paralysis."

"Good, good," he said, nodding.

"Not like the first time, right, Annie?" Kevin said as he shuffled back to the table and swigged his beer again.

"Kevin . . . ?" she asked, hoping to get him to say something, anything about Jack Miller, in spite of his in-law being present.

He seemed to know what she meant, because he shrugged. Which didn't reveal what he was thinking. Or feeling. Except that he did not want to discuss it.

Rex set the cake on the counter and joined them at the table. He tried to squeeze in behind Annie.

"No," Kevin said, "don't sit there. Take my place."

Silence again.

"Kevin . . ." It was Taylor who addressed him.

He forced a smile. Not plastic, more like putty. Silly Putty, Annie remembered from when she'd been a kid, that sticky, beige, malleable stuff that she loved to press against the cartoons in the Sunday newspaper, peel off, then hold up to a mirror to read the jokes.

"For the first time in my life," Kevin finally said, "I believe the beer isn't agreeing with me. I think I'll go lie down while the rest of you feast. Save me a slice of that cake, though. I'm sure I'll feel up to it later."

With that, he shuffled out of the kitchen, down the hallway to the first-floor bedroom. Before disappearing from sight, he called, "Enjoy your meals!" Then his footsteps scuffed away, their sound fading like the engines of planes passing overhead on their way to New York or Boston.

After explaining to Rex that Kevin had been terribly upset about Claire having the stroke—which Annie knew was true, though she suspected his weird reaction to her mention of Jack Miller was more the culprit now—Annie glided back into the conversation about Claire and told Rex what had happened when Claire had her first one several summers before and everyone had been rightfully alarmed. She'd collapsed during the garden tour in Edgartown, landed in the Atwaters' hollyhocks, and was rescued by a couple of tourists. Obviously, Claire had survived but had needed extensive rehab, which she hated doing because she said it was humiliating to have young, physically fit physical therapists stand around and watch her old body try to do things it no longer could.

At last, the chowder was hot and Taylor swiftly served it. She had not commented on Kevin's behavior—in fact, she hadn't said a word since he'd left them. Rex didn't say whether or not he noticed the shift in his sister's disposition, and Annie happily dived into the chowder, grateful to have something to do other than talk.

They seemed to eat fast, as if there was somewhere else they'd all rather be. When the time came for cake, Annie said she'd like to wait a few minutes, then she asked Taylor if it was okay if she checked on Kevin.

"Go," Taylor said. "We'll save you a big piece of lemon whatever-it-is." With her auburn mane tightened in a severe ponytail, her topaz eyes looked catlike and cautious, and her face overall was stiff with restraint. It was obvious that her husband's distress over Jack Miller hadn't escaped her.

It wasn't until Annie was halfway down the hall that she realized she'd never seen the bedroom where Kevin and Taylor slept, had never ventured beyond the first-floor bathroom. She expected that, in addition to two bedrooms on that floor, upstairs, there most likely were two more, each with the single bumped-out dormer that was visible from the driveway. They might or might not have shared a small bath. She'd never asked, though she knew that Francine and Jonas had lived there together before Rex had thundered his way back to the island.

She found only one bedroom on the first floor, but it was a large space that would have spanned the depth of the house from front to back except for a large bath and another door to what Annie supposed was a walk-in closet. Around the room, various configurations of old wooden furniture seemed to be situated in the same places where they'd been for decades; on the outside wall, white eyelet curtains hung at two windows, and at two more at the front. The walls were papered with a print of cabbage roses that must have been left over from Taylor's mother. "Mother" was the only name Annie had ever heard her called. Though Mother was long gone now, her wallpaper remained, and most likely her furnishings, too, including a bed with a spindled maple frame. A bureau, a chest of drawers, and two nightstands further displayed the out-of-date provenance. Annie half smiled as she thought of the many families who had not been outwardly traditional yet often remained surrounded by the nostalgia of their childhoods. But, as with the cabbage roses, some things were just old, the only exceptions being several nice paintings of vibrant Vineyard landscapes that looked like Jonas's work.

Kevin was flat on his back on top of what looked like a handmade quilt on top of the spindled bed. Because they'd just passed into Daylight Saving Time, Annie could see her brother in the twilight, so there was no need to turn on a light.

If he was crying, he would not have wanted to be in the spotlight.

But Kevin wasn't crying. His eyes were open, vacant. She knew he must have heard her coming, but he did not acknowledge her.

Standing next to the bed, Annie quietly said, "I know it's upsetting, Kevin, but it doesn't have to be. Maybe Donna would be happy for you."

He hesitated and then snorted. "No offense, but that's kind of doubtful. I'm sure she'd be pissed to know that the man who walked out on us, leaving her to raise me alone, has suddenly reappeared now that she's gone . . . now that she can't confront him face-to-face and tell him to go to hell."

This wasn't the right time for Annie to mention the memorabilia that Donna had saved of Kevin and his dad. Not when he was so clear about his feelings.

"You can't be sure of that. You don't really know what happened between them."

"Oh, I'm pretty sure. I'm pretty sure that was her I heard lots of times, crying at night when she thought I was asleep."

It wasn't Annie's place to say he might be wrong, that Donna might have been crying because she missed Annie's father, not Jack. No, it wasn't her place to tell him that Jack Miller had a very different story from the one Donna had told Kevin. But still . . .

She spotted a small chair in the corner. It had been upholstered—no doubt decades earlier—in cabbage roses that didn't quite match those on the wallpaper. A "ladies' boudoir chair," Donna might have called it, as she'd been an expert antiques dealer. Annie went to it and sat. She folded her hands and twisted her fingers as if she were knitting. She waited for him to speak again. But he did not.

So, after a few minutes, Annie said, "I met him."

Kevin bolted upright on the bed; a pillow covered with a white-ruffled sham skydived to the floor. "What?"

In the dim light, she felt his eyes blazing.

"I tried to talk to you about it. But you were so busy. Then I decided maybe it would be better if I ran interference. If I vetted him to determine if he was worthy of seeing my brother."

His gaze penetrated her, twin hazel laser beams boring into hers. "Where? When?"

"Mocha Mott's. Yesterday."

"That rat bastard's *here*? On the island?"

She gulped on the words that he'd chosen. She knew then that she'd made a mistake. She spoke again, that time with caution. "He lives on the Cape. He only came over to meet me." She held back on saying that he lived with his daughter and her family. *One thing at a time*, she thought.

Kevin got off the bed, his indentation carved into what must be one of those pillow-top things that Annie detested because they made her shoulders ache. At some point recently, he and Taylor must have replaced the original coil mattress.

"Jesus," he said. Then he started to pace. "What am I supposed to do with this little piece of news? I suppose you want me to be elated."

She wasn't sure what kind of reaction she'd expected; she should have realized it would be this. On several occasions when they'd been sitting in a restaurant and her brother became nervous, angry, or agitated, his legs tended to bounce up and down, shaking the table and everything on it. Pacing was his second-favorite nervous reaction.

She decided it was better to watch him pace than to feel the earth quaking.

"Kevin, of course I want you to be happy," she said. "But

the truth is, I have no agenda. This is your decision. Yours alone. All I can tell you is that he seemed sincere. Actually, he seemed nice. But I'm not in your shoes." She glanced at his feet. "Nor am I in those godawful slippers that you insist are so comfortable." She hoped that would produce a short laugh out of him. It did not.

She stood up. "Do with the news whatever you want," she said softly. "But know that I love you and I only want the best for you. No matter what you decide." She wanted to hug him but feared he'd turn away; he also tended to reject affection when he was upset.

So Annie left the room and returned to the kitchen. She joined Taylor and Rex at the table and accepted a sliver of lemon drizzle cake, hoping she'd done what she needed to do.

At eleven thirty, John called.

Annie was asleep, but she'd left her phone on in case she was needed at the Inn or if anything happened with Claire. At least, that's what she tried telling herself, when she knew very well it was because she hoped to hear from John.

She shook off the night and answered.

"Hey," he said, his voice low and sounding tired.

"Hey, yourself." She was awake enough to know not to act upset that he hadn't called sooner. And to remember not to mention his mother's stroke. "How are you?"

"Okay."

It was hard for Annie to think of him in any way other than the strong, strapping, Detective Sergeant John Lyons, the guy who could be counted on to rise to any occasion at any hour of the day or night; the guy who was able to take control of the most horrific situations and resolve them with peace and order.

"How did it go?" she asked. She hoped he was home—*home* being in Edgartown, not in that other house on the mainland. She hoped that the girls were in their beds with Restless nearby, and that John was sitting on the sofa, his feet up on the coffee table, holding a beer, barely drinking it. John tended to open more bottles than he finished.

"It was a long day," he said. "She had a bad reaction to one of the tests. That was the hardest part, at least for me. Anyway, they're keeping her overnight to finish up testing to-morrow."

Which Annie knew meant there were no results as of yet. And that chances were, John wasn't where she had hoped he would be.

"How is she now?"

"Asleep. I'm in the day room. I'll sleep here tonight. They wheeled an extra bed into her room." He paused. "I didn't want to leave her."

Annie remembered that feeling. She had spent several days—and nights—at her mother's bedside, waiting, waiting, waiting for her vigil to be over, waiting for her mother to die. When she finally did, the result was not relief but loss. Huge, hole-in-the-gut loss that she hadn't anticipated. But Annie had only been thirty, was already a widow, and had lost her dad, too.

Abigail isn't dying, she reminded herself, and wished Murphy were there to agree.

"She'll be happy you're in the room," Annie said, not wanting to ask if Lucy was there, too, because she didn't want to know if Jenn was. She wondered if some emotions ever stopped being childlike. Childish.

"Lucy went back to Plymouth with Jenn. Restless is there. . . ."

Annie closed her eyes. She was glad they weren't on Face-Time.

Then he said, "I miss you. I feel like you're still three thousand miles away."

It was, of course, exactly what Annie-the-child needed to hear. But John was the one who needed her more. To be supportive. To be the adult.

She pushed back the comforter, sat up, and turned on the lamp on the nightstand. "I'm right here," she said with what she hoped was a soothing voice. "I'm less than an hour away."

"Not counting the boat," he said with a laugh that was small, but good to hear.

"No one ever counts the boat time. It's one of the first things your dad taught me." She wished she hadn't mentioned Earl. She hoped it didn't trigger John to ask if his parents were okay.

"I hope I can come home tomorrow," he said.

"Me, too. But you're where you need to be right now, John. And I'm right here whenever you need to talk. I left my phone on tonight. And I'll leave it on every night until you're back in bed. Beside me." It was good that he could not see her tears. "I love you," she added.

"I love you, too." He went quiet a moment, then said, "I guess I'd better go. Time to return to my role as a dad."

"It's not a role, John. It's who you are. And you're a wonderful one."

Providing moral support was exhausting. After they hung up, Annie got up, slipped into her robe, and went to the kitchen to make tea. While the kettle was heating, she leaned against the counter, her back to the window, her gaze mindlessly floating around the living room–kitchen. As often as Annie had been called on to be supportive for whomever or whenever, she'd been on the receiving end plenty of times. Even when Murphy had been sick, her friend had known that Annie, too, needed support.

"It shouldn't be called 'moral support,'" Murphy had said when she was in her bed, her hairless head wrapped in a tur-

ban, her blue eyes as bright as ever. "It should be called '*morale*
support.' We're here to boost each other's morale. Not our
morals. We already know that in past years our morals were
often questionable. Who wants to revisit that?"

She'd made Annie laugh, as Murphy always had.

Over time, Annie had learned to treasure good memories,
to know that while they couldn't make difficult times easier,
they made them easier to endure.

The kettle whistled.

Annie removed it from the burner and turned off the gas.
Then she went back to the bedroom, took off her robe, and
climbed back under the comforter, knowing that when the
time came to be strong for anyone who needed her—John,
Kevin, Claire, whomever—Annie would do her best to provide *morale* support. Until then, she needed to stop worrying
and go back to sleep.

Chapter 16

Claire was doing fine and would, indeed, be released from the hospital Wednesday morning. When Earl called to tell Annie the news, he added that the doctor had recommended a few days of rest—both for his wife and for him.

Annie offered to drive him to pick her up, but he said Kevin had that covered.

Of course he did, Annie thought. Distraction—there was that family trait again—was far more appealing than wondering whether or not he should be elated that his real father was trying to see him.

Deciding to put her own skills to good use, Annie dismissed a notion to do any writing and instead enlisted Francine to go with her to Earl and Claire's. Together they could change the bedsheets and have lunch ready for when the couple returned . . . and for when Annie hoped to be able to tell if Kevin had processed all that she'd told him.

She also reminded herself that helping others was a good kind of busy, as she'd be using her hands for something other than typing or, rather, trying to type with so much on her mind. As important, Annie knew that going to Earl and Claire's with Francine would mean she'd have Francine beside her to share cheerful chitchat about Claire's quick recovery and, of course, about the soon-to-be new baby.

All of which was why, after putting fresh linens on Claire and Earl's bed, Annie was in Claire's kitchen now with a very pregnant, very happy, very glowing Francine.

They decided to make seared garlic-and-ginger salmon (one of Claire's favorites) with riced cauliflower and an arugula salad, and to make extra because Annie hoped that Kevin would join them. If anyone wanted dessert, she'd brought a hunk of Rex's lemon cake left over from the night before that Taylor had insisted she take.

Finally, as Annie and Francine were finishing the lunch preparations, Kevin's pickup pulled into the driveway. Annie watched from the doorway as they all got out. The men stood on either side of Claire, something she seemed to grouse at for a moment, then she at last conceded and allowed them to loop their arms around hers. Once Claire was safely inside, however, Kevin mumbled something about needing to help Taylor. He did not acknowledge Annie or even look her in the eye. As she watched him walk away, she realized he hadn't even turned off the ignition. He'd seen her Jeep parked in the driveway, of course; he must have known she was inside. And, apparently, he wanted no part of being around his sister, the traitor in the family.

He was still angry.

There was no other explanation.

Francine looked at Annie with curiosity. She knew Kevin well; she must have sensed that something wasn't right.

Annie bit back her disappointment, smiled a fake smile (she'd become good at manufacturing those), and waited on her fiancé's mother with as much loving kindness as she could muster.

They stayed a short while after lunch until Claire announced she was eager for a nap. Earl said he'd turn on the

TV and watch whatever the heck people found entertaining on a Wednesday afternoon. Annie made sure to tell them John had called and said all was well, but that they'd run out of time before finishing Abigail's tests. It hinted of a white lie, but Annie didn't care. Right then, it was more important that Earl and Claire were okay.

After the older generation went to their respective respite spots, Annie and Francine cleaned up the kitchen, then quietly left. Annie had barely backed out of the driveway when Francine looked over at her.

"Do you want to tell me, or am I going to have to read your mind?"

Annie knew that later she'd rationalize why she decided to tell Francine about Jack Miller. Right then, however, she simply needed a friend. With Murphy who-knew-where and Winnie long gone off-island, that left Annie with one option: the girl sitting beside her, her jacket unbuttoned, unable to close around her precious, bulbous belly, her large, soulful eyes sincere with wanting to help. Annie knew that Francine would be every bit as compassionate and as comforting as Murphy or Winnie. And that though Francine still was young, she had a whole lot of wisdom, thanks to having had to grow up too soon.

So Annie cracked the window on her side of the Jeep because it was a sunny day and she thought that the clean spring air might help her keep her equilibrium.

She inhaled. Exhaled. Then she sat up straight within the confines of her seat belt.

"Remember the other day when I asked how you'd feel if you learned your grandmother was still alive and wanted to see you?"

Francine laughed. "All I kept thinking was that you have a pretty wild imagination."

A half smile was the best Annie could manage. "From what you said, your grandmother's dead, so I don't think we have to worry about her. And we don't have to worry about you. Because your family's right here now. All of us. Except your aunt and uncle, of course. But they're in Minneapolis."

"And they plan to come for a visit this summer to see the baby. But what the heck are you getting at? Do you know something about my family that I don't?"

It had been a stupid way to introduce the topic. "No, no!" Annie cried. "Not you. This isn't about you, honey."

"Well, good. But something's bugging you, and don't tell me it's not. If it isn't about me, it must be about your brother."

Annie nodded. "You noticed."

Francine's eyes seemed to grow even larger. "That he avoided us? Of course I did." She paused for a few seconds, then said, "Oh, no. Please don't tell me that his ex-wife wants him back. . . ."

Shaking her head, Annie replied, "It's worse." She inhaled, exhaled again. "It's his father, Francine. Kevin's father wants to meet him."

Francine let out a whistle. Then she rubbed her belly as if it would calm her as well as her baby. "Details, please."

So Annie spilled the rest of the story, about how Kevin had thought his father had abandoned Donna and him when he was only four. How he'd thought Jack Miller wanted nothing to do with him. And how Jack had emailed Annie. And how she'd met him. And then told Kevin.

"Yikes," Francine said when Annie finally stopped to take another breath. "You're right. That's way worse than me possibly finding out that my dead grandmother's still alive."

Annie had no idea how to respond to that, so she kept on track. "I tried to do the right thing. But now my brother's angry with me. I'm afraid he won't get past this. Not for a long time." She paused. "When he's upset, he holds in his emotions. It's like he's afraid if he lets them out, he'll explode or something."

Nodding, Francine said, "I know. It's like he's not impulsive. I thought that was a good thing."

"I used to think so, too. But I don't like that he's avoiding me."

"He'll come around. You know that. But what about— what's his name, Jack? How did you leave it with him?"

"I said it might take a few days."

"And you saw him Monday?"

"Yes."

"Well, it's only Wednesday. I'd say you have until the end of the week to get Kevin to talk to you again. And maybe you can convince him that his father isn't such a bad guy. Or at least that he deserves a second chance."

Annie steered onto North Neck Road and considered Francine's words. It was true, Kevin wasn't impulsive. He was patient. He needed to think things through. He had far more patience than Annie ever had; she absolutely had not inherited that particular branch of their family tree.

"Geez," Francine added then. "An awful lot is going on around here."

Annie smiled again, but that time it was genuine. "But you and that baby of yours are the best news of all. I'm counting on both of you to keep the rest of us going until . . . well, for a long time."

"There's another big piece of happy news," Francine said as she shifted on the seat.

"What? Tell me! I need all the happy news that I can get."

"You're home," she said quietly. "It was a long winter without you."

Then, just as Annie glanced toward her to thank her for

saying that, Francine pressed a hand more firmly against her belly and winced.

"Oh, God," Annie said, abruptly pulling to the roadside, and automatically reaching for her purse to get her phone. It wasn't there. Not the purse. And not the phone. She'd been juggling bags with lunch food and must have left them at home. She stopped the Jeep. "Are you okay?"

Francine laughed her wonderful laugh again. "I'm fine."

Annie rested her hand on Francine's arm. "Are you sure?"

The young mother laughed again. "It's just a small cramp. The doctor said it's probably nothing. I called just before we left." She smiled a big smile. "You really need to stop worrying about everyone, Annie."

Annie knew Francine was right. She needed to leave others and their problems alone and get back to her life. If someone needed her, they'd find her. In the meantime, she should focus on her work. She patted Francine's arm. "Thanks, honey," she said. At least she could let Francine know she appreciated her concern, despite the fact that Annie had no clue how she would, or could, stop worrying.

She steered the Jeep back onto the road and headed toward the Inn in search of some peace and quiet that might help her relax, though she supposed there was a fat chance of that.

It turned out she was right. Because after she parked in the clamshell lot, said good-bye to Francine, and had gone into the cottage, she saw her purse on the kitchen counter. Groping for her phone, she quickly came up with it and saw there was a recent call from California. And though he hadn't left a message, she recognized the number.

It was after four o'clock—probably not the best time for Annie to call her literary agent in New York. But if there was an agent as attentive as Louise, Annie hadn't met her.

"Annie Sutton. As I live and breathe."

"Louise. I'm so glad you're there."

"I'd rather say I'm strolling the Champs-Elysées, but, no, I'm sitting at my desk. Have you finished the manuscript? Please don't tell me you called to say your wedding's been postponed."

Annie suddenly regretted making the call.

"Not quite done with the manuscript," she replied, then bit her lower lip. "As for the wedding . . . one of John's daughters has been ill. They're in Boston seeing specialists right now. We're waiting for test results and trying to stay positive. About Abigail. And the wedding."

"How old is she?" Trish asked.

"Eighteen. Almost nineteen."

"Huh. Oh, dear. It could be lots of things."

"I know. But we're staying optimistic. But it's not really why I called. I wondered if you have any idea why Greg Williams called me today?"

"He did? Well, well. So tell me. Why did he call?"

"I don't know. That's why I asked you. I was at Earl and Claire's. I didn't have my phone. . . ."

"He didn't leave a message?"

"No."

"Why don't people leave messages anymore?" Louise sniveled.

"I have no idea about that, either. I guess because they think you'll see their name and you should just call them back."

"But you didn't."

"No. I wondered if . . ."

"If I knew why he'd called."

"Right."

"I don't. So maybe you should go right to the source? It's not too late to call L.A. Unless, of course, he's the one on the

Champs-Elysées. In which case it's ten o'clock at night, so he'll most likely be at dinner."

Annie never ceased being amused by Louise's offbeat wit, which was always light enough not to be taken seriously.

"Then I'd better hang up now so I can catch him before the crème brûlée's served."

"Good idea. And let me know how you make out."

They hung up.

Annie smoothed her seersucker shirt, as if it could have had a wrinkle, then she combed her hair. Not that she thought Greg might see her, but if she felt better put together—a lot to ask of a quick smooth and a comb—she knew she'd sound more confident. She supposed she could have changed her clothes, but that might be over the top. Even for her.

But she shouldn't have bothered doing anything, as his phone went straight to voice mail. Unlike the wizard of Hollywood had done, Annie left a message.

That evening, while Annie sat at her computer, diligently working on the manuscript that Louise had unintentionally (or not) reminded her needed to be finished, the phone rang. It was too late for Greg to be returning her call if he was in Paris. But not if he was in L.A.

She checked her phone. It wasn't Greg.

"Hey," John said when she answered.

"Hi," she said, trying to make room in her brain for him while hoping that the scene that she was working on wouldn't sink into a lost train of thought. "How did today go?"

"It could have been better."

Then she remembered that one of her characters needed to find a dead body in her fictitious museum. The victim was a man, sitting on a bench in the courtyard, slumped into the begonias, an antique silver letter opener from their Prince Albert collection sticking out of his neck.

Scribbling the words *begonias,* P. *Albert,* and *neck,* Annie hoped she'd remembered what they meant. Of course, she'd dreamed up the bit about the begonias, thanks to having her memory jogged about Claire's having collapsed in the Atwater's hollyhocks years earlier.

"Any test results?" She tapped her pen onto the pad and tried to sound sincere, though the make-believe world she'd been creating in her mind still whirled around the museum courtyard.

Then John made an odd, howling sound like one from a crying, dying animal. And Annie's creativity completely shut down.

"John?" she asked, dropping her pen.

"She has MS, Annie," he managed to say. "My girl has multiple sclerosis."

Chapter 17

It was too much to take in. It was too much to believe. And it was too damned much to try and be a strong, supportive father, a man who could show his daughter—make that his daughters—that he was, would always be, their hero who could make everything right.

It was too much to ask of any man.

Especially when he, Detective Sergeant John Lyons, keeper of the people of picturesque Edgartown on the magical island of Martha's Vineyard, couldn't do a goddamn thing to make this go away.

It was bad enough he was sitting on the front screen porch of the three-bedroom, two-bath ranch in a quiet neighborhood, where he'd escaped in order to call Annie.

The porch was nice. Along with the whole house, he'd bought it, paid for it, and handed it over to Jenn in their divorce. He'd done that so his girls would have a decent place to live when they were at their mother's. When she started high school, Abigail had wanted to live on the mainland, too, in civilization, she'd whined.

Lucy, God love her, wanted no part of that. She was an islander through and through, the way he was, the way generations of the Lyons family had been.

But sickness wasn't something that ran in either side of his family, so John didn't know how his ancestors would have felt if they'd been diagnosed with something that needed treatment, something that could become debilitating. Something like pediatric multiple sclerosis, a label that the doctor had diagnosed but said the word pediatric was both flexible and iffy, given Abigail's age, because most MS patients were considered to have adult MS if they were over eighteen. He said it didn't make a lot of difference, though, because all patients had bouts of relapses and remissions. Times when they had symptoms like fatigue and weakness, vertigo and blurred vision, all of which Abigail had now.

The doctor gave them a laundry list of other symptoms that Abigail might or might not develop, but John had been listening while in his own state of fatigue and weakness, which had begun when he'd been sitting in the waiting room, trying to make civil small talk with his ex while Abigail was being tested.

At that point, it had been hours since they'd arrived at the hospital. They'd moved into the doctor's office, though John didn't remember having left the waiting area. Jenn sat next to him again; she was tapping every word the man said onto her iPad because, as Lucy often said, her mother was a control freak.

There were treatments, the doctor continued. But there was no cure. But Abigail wasn't going to die. A huge weight lifted from John then, though some of it returned when the doctor said that her level of disability couldn't be predicted.

Disability, John thought now. Like people with crutches and walkers and wheelchairs. Blue-and-white tags for rearview car windows. Monthly government checks if they weren't able to work. If they could not be part of the world. If they couldn't become a fashion designer as Abigail had dreamed.

The cold dampness of early April made it too soon to be sitting on the porch; he held a bottle of beer that might help warm him up, but he'd only had one or two quick swigs. Still, it was easier to be out there than inside, where later that night he'd be sleeping on a sofa that had too many pillows and cushions that were too soft, as if they were *made of marshmallows. Jenn had picked it out because it was going to be in her house. He'd paid for the sofa, too.*

He wondered how Annie would feel if she knew about that, if she knew about all the money he had spent to make his ex-wife's life more comfortable even though she was the one who had walked out.

Restless let out a bark as he jumped from his prone position at John's feet. He was focused across the lawn, on alert, notifying the whole damn town that an SUV had pulled into the driveway of the look-alike three-bed, two-bath.

John reached out and scratched Restless behind the floppy ears. Since they'd been back from Boston, the dog had mostly stayed at Abigail's side. Until John had gone out to the porch and the dog had followed him, as if he knew that John was hurting, too, and needed watching over.

Both man and dog observed—though John had much less interest—as a woman got out on the passenger side. She was toting a few bags that looked to be from Shaw's or Market Basket. Then the garage door rumbled up and the driver edged the SUV into the space while the woman crossed the lawn toward the front door. She glanced over to Jenn's, spotted John, and waved. He managed to lift his hand and return the greeting. He might have met her once, but did not know her name.

He wondered if she and her husband had kids and, if so, if they were healthy.

Multiple sclerosis, the doctor's words echoed in his mind again, followed by a tight grip around his gut.

Then he heard the front door open behind him; Restless slipped from his touch, his attentions now diverted.

"Dad?" It was Lucy, who'd been acting like a trouper, though John figured she was as scared as the rest of them. "Mom said dinner's ready."

They'd picked up fish and chips on the way back from Boston, so the food only needed heating up. Not that anyone was hungry. Still, *the time it took to get the table set, drinks poured, and the reheating accomplished had given him the chance to duck outside and call Annie. He wished she was there. He wished she could be with him. He didn't think he'd told her that.*

Muffling a sigh, he stood up and went to the door. If Lucy still had her ponytail, he'd have given it a playful tug. But his younger daughter was too grown up for that now, so he merely patted her shoulder and followed her into the house, trying his damnedest to act as if everything would be fine.

Chapter 18

John had asked Annie not to tell Earl and Claire—or anyone. He said he'd be home on the weekend and would talk to his parents face-to-face. Annie wondered if Claire would tell him about her stroke before or after. Or, more likely, not for a very long time. Not after she learned her granddaughter's diagnosis.

Moving from the living room to her bedroom, Annie grabbed the quilt her mother had made as a wedding gift for Annie's first marriage—what felt like a century ago—and that had remained one of her favorite possessions. Her mother had used squares of fabric left over from Annie's childhood, dresses and skirts that Ellen Sutton had lovingly made: polished cotton Sunday dresses, pleated wool skirts for school, even the buttercup-colored satin gown Annie had worn to the eighth-grade semi-formal dance and afterward spilled a chocolate frappé on at Brigham's. Over the years, the quilt had served Annie well: in times of stress, malaise, or confusion over where life would take her next. Right then, as she stretched out on the bed and pulled the quilt over her, she felt all three of those emotions, perhaps mostly confusion.

What was she supposed to do with the latest news? As tempted as she was to Google every imaginable keyword that would lead her to information on multiple sclerosis, Annie didn't dare. She didn't want to get caught up in trying to be a doctor; she didn't want to read anything negative or, actually, anything at all. She had to remember that Abigail was John and Jenn's daughter, not hers. She had to tell herself she was merely an outsider, a bystander.

A disenfranchised griever, Murphy suddenly reminded her of the term psychologists used when someone who wasn't technically a family member had lost someone they loved, or feared they would lose them. In this case, Annie was someone who felt she needed to stay out of sight. Hide in a closet. Or under the bed. The same bed where she and the father of the ill child had made love so many times. The fact that they were supposed to be getting married did not seem to matter. Annie was detached. Disenfranchised.

Her gaze wandered from the mattress to the back of her bedroom door, where John's grandmother's wedding dress hung, still awaiting its reincarnation.

She'd been looking forward to that.

Right then, however, she would prefer to throw something at it. A ceramic mug, perhaps one of her favorites from Morning Glory Farm. Better yet, the bust of Agatha Christie that stood on the bookcase. Yes, she thought, Agatha was hefty enough to do some real damage to that ugly creation— with the big shoulder pads and heavy, tufted bodice—that Claire expected Annie to wear.

"Are the gods trying to tell us that John and I aren't supposed to get married?" she asked Murphy, who might or might not be paying attention to the latest twist in the drama called Annie's life.

I have no idea. They don't consult me on these matters.

"Very funny." At least her friend had been listening.

It wasn't meant to be funny. I know you're hurting, Annie.

Tears lodged in her throat instead of in her eyes. "I really am, Murph. Abigail was finally headed in a good direction. She was excited about her future."

It might not have to change, you know. She might have to adapt a little, shift things around from time to time. But her goals don't have to change.

Annie sighed. "I'm not sure she'll have the strength for that. I hardly know her. Not the way I know Lucy."

You'll have lots of time to get to know her.

"Sure. If I ever stop feeling sorry for myself, too." She turned onto her side and toyed with a corner of the quilt, trying to rid herself of her feelings of guilt that she was putting her own misery before Abigail's. After all, the girl must be suffering more than Annie could imagine. And, yes, Abigail still was a girl, barely into adulthood, too young to have to deal with this enormous obstacle dropped smack in the middle of the path toward her future.

Running her fingers over the scraps of polished cotton and plaid wool, Annie wished she could remember how childhood had felt, when all things seemed happy, when she lived in a house that was safe and loving. Well, there were those weeks when her mom had disappeared, but even then Annie and her dad had managed okay. And when her mom returned, they'd picked up where they'd left off, creating a bubble of "normalcy" around Annie again, which, at the time, she'd believed in. Just as they'd intended.

But before she could completely immerse herself in her sorrow, there was a loud knock on her front door. Two knocks, actually.

Kevin sat at the table, facing her.

"It's late," Annie said, sipping the tea that she made for them. Though she would have preferred to cry out, "Go away!"

she couldn't do that to her brother. Maybe she felt sorry for him, too.

"If I promise to be good, my wife lets me go out after dark."

His quirky sense of humor had returned, which was comforting. Because right then, Annie wasn't strong enough for him to be angry with her. *Life is too short and too damn complicated*, she thought. There wasn't time to take anyone, any day, for granted. Even a long-lost father. And though she wanted to ask if he'd forgiven her for bulldozing into his business with neither his permission nor his knowledge, instead, Annie started to cry.

He reached across the table and grasped her hands. "Hey. It's okay. I know you were only trying to help. . . ."

She shook her head, pulled her hands away, and grabbed a tissue, which she used to cover her eyes. She wanted to speak but couldn't.

"I'm not upset with you," he continued. "I'm upset with *him*. That he tracked you down 'cuz he was too chicken to come straight to me. . . ."

Annie loved John. She loved his daughters and his parents. She loved the friends she'd made on the Vineyard. But Kevin was her real family; they shared the same mother. They also shared each other's joys and each other's heartaches. And for that, she'd always be grateful that he'd come into her life.

She wished she could tell him about Abigail. But she feared if she opened her mouth to talk, the entire story would come gushing out. Which meant she'd break John's trust not to tell anyone yet. But Kevin wasn't just anyone. Still, he hadn't shown up at her door to hear about Abigail. Or John. Or Annie's problems. Not when the issue about his father loomed.

Nonetheless, she raised her head, blinked back more tears. Then, with her lower lip threatening to quiver again, she quickly said, "Abigail has MS, Kevin. And I have no idea what to do."

He looked at her. Stunned.

So Annie told him the whole story.

And Kevin listened. He was great at that. Especially since it had nothing to do with him, or with his rat bastard of a father.

When she was finished, her brother stood up. He stuffed his hands into the pockets of his jeans, and he paced.

"God, Annie," he said.

They continued that way for a few minutes, Annie staring at her tea, Kevin doing circles around the braided run in her small living room.

"You can't tell anyone," she said, but had no idea if he heard her.

He finally stopped pacing and said, "Is she real sick?"

"I think her symptoms have been scary. Now that they know what it is . . . now that they know there's a treatment . . ."

"But no cure?"

"No. No cure. Not yet."

"So she'll have times when she's . . . not well? And times when she is?"

"Apparently. Yes."

"When I had my business, I had a guy who had it. He did pretty well, but at one point he had to leave. Not because he was having a tough time keeping up, but because he never knew when he'd relapse. Working on construction was too risky."

Annie nodded.

He returned to the chair at the table, took a drink of his tea, which must have been cold by then.

"God, Annie," he said again. "The poor kid."

Which went without saying.

"So what's the next step?" he asked.

She sighed, glad that she'd stopped crying for the moment.

"John is coming home this weekend. I don't know if the girls will be with him. He's going to tell his parents. Which is why he doesn't want anyone to know until after he has."

Kevin paused, set down his mug. "Oh, man, they already knew there was a problem, but this? This is going to . . ." He stopped. "Oh, God. What if Claire has another stroke?"

"I'm going to stay positive. Besides, I believe that not knowing is sometimes more stressful than learning the truth, don't you? It's so easy to speculate the absolute worst when no one's told you what the real problem is. I do know that Claire gathers a whole lot of strength when the people she loves need her to." Annie prayed that she'd be able to do that, too.

"What about John? Is he okay?"

Annie wanted to tell her brother that she didn't want to talk about John. But that would be self-serving again. "He'll be fine. It's Abigail we need to think about the most."

Kevin nodded and let out a rush of air. Then he got up again, went to her refrigerator, and helped himself to a small bottle of flavored seltzer. He studied the label as if he'd expected the contents to be beer.

"Could you use a little good news?" He leaned back against the counter, unscrewed the cap, and took a long drink.

"Always," she said, and attempted a smile.

"This is going to come as a surprise, but I decided you're right. I want to meet my father. I need to give him a chance to explain. Or I'll go to my grave thinking that he was a jerk. Which maybe he is. But at least if I find out for myself, then I'll be sure."

No, she thought. She had definitely not expected to hear that.

Her smile became genuine. "Did you decide this right now? As a way to cheer me up?"

"Not really."

"Liar."

He smiled.

She got up, went to him, and hugged him. "Thanks, brother."

"Anytime. But will I sound like a two-year-old if I ask you to come with me?"

"Yes. But I wouldn't miss it for the world."

After Kevin left, Annie sat at her computer and composed an email to Jack.

Yes, Kevin would like to meet him. Would it be possible for him to come back to the island? They could meet at Mocha Mott's. And she hoped he didn't mind, but she would be with him.

She sent the email and went to bed, not bothering to wash out her mug or put the empty seltzer bottle into the recycling bin, but trying to be happy that at least one thing seemed to be going right.

The next morning, Annie told herself she'd slept well (she hadn't), and that she was hungry (she wasn't). But along with light makeup to help mask the dark circles under her eyes, she put on what she hoped was a good game face that implied "Everything is fine. Nothing to see here."

By the time she plodded into the kitchen at the Inn, Rex was loading the dishwasher with the after-breakfast dishes. She'd apparently lost track of time, her troubled mind having gotten in the way.

"Looks like I'm late," she said.

"We'll be sure to dock your pay," came the reply.

Annie loved that most people around her had quick wits and good senses of humor. She'd decided it was due to the unpolluted island air, especially now that spring was warming it up. But though Rex had been witty, he didn't seem particularly happy. Maybe he hadn't slept well, either. Or maybe he'd argued with Bonnie over the fact that she'd spread the news about Abigail and that he'd been accused of it. Right then, however, Annie decided not to ask. She had enough to think about.

"Got leftovers?" she asked.

"I can fix eggs Benedict, if you want."

As much as she loved Rex's cuisine, the image of eggs now bubbled in her stomach. "Sounds great, but on second thought, maybe I'll just have toast. The days are ticking down before I have to fit into my wedding dress."

She had no idea why she'd said that. She only knew she was grateful that all he did was smile, nod, and say, "In that case, help yourself to fresh rosemary bread in the bread box. I made it before sunrise."

Stopping herself from asking why he'd been up so early, she carved off a slice of bread, stuck it in the toaster, and heated water for tea.

"Any word on John's daughter?" Rex asked.

"I talked with him last night. She's doing okay."

He nodded and went back to loading the dishwasher. Annie hoped he knew that if there was something she could tell, she would tell it.

"Call me selfish," she said, "but I hope you don't find a restaurant for a while. You're spoiling our tenants, and they deserve to be."

He closed the dishwasher door and wiped his hands on a linen towel. "Funny you should mention it. Yesterday I heard of a place on South Water that's about to go up for sale."

There were several reactions Annie could have had, but being glad for Rex, whom she still did not know well, wasn't one of them. Not now. Not when his leaving would interfere with the running of the Inn in what promised to be another busy season. And would be one more thing she'd have to handle.

So she only said, "A prime Edgartown location, for sure. It must be nice. But expensive."

"Don't know. Probably."

She buttered her toast, poured her tea. "I'm sorry, Rex. That was insensitive. I've got a lot on my mind right now, which is a lousy excuse for being rude."

His bald head nodded. "No problem."

Annie ate and drank in silence. Then she thanked him for being there and said she was going to check to see how the room reservations for summer were coming along. And she slinked out of the kitchen. She didn't want Rex to think she didn't care about his happiness, but she knew that, at the time, she didn't. And she rarely did a great job at pretending.

Annoyed with herself for being a jerk, she moved through the great room and into the reception area. She stopped at the front desk—an antique that had belonged to Earl's grandfather and, like his ancestors, had been on Chappaquiddick for as long as anyone remembered. It was crafted of vintage, gleaming walnut, with nooks, crannies, pigeonholes, and, most important, a center drawer that now concealed a laptop so the Old World charm wouldn't be blighted by a visual of technology. The laptop was essential; the software was automatically linked to the Inn's calendar where up-to-the-minute room availabilities were visible, so guests could instantly book a room online.

She unlocked the drawer, removed the laptop, and powered it up, just as her text alert beeped. She hoped it wasn't Greg, as she didn't feel like knowing what was going on with him, either. Pulling her phone out of her pocket, Annie glanced down and saw that the text was from Lucy.

Everything is so messed up, the girl had typed. **I want to come home.** She'd added three crying emojis.

And Annie's heart broke just a little . . . and then a little more, crumbling one bit at a time, leaving tiny anthills on her soul.

Touching the words on the screen, as if that somehow could soothe Lucy, Annie knew there was nothing she could do. She was not there to help; she would not be there to help. So she moved into the reading room and closed the door behind her. She sat in one of the comfortable chairs, buried her face in her hands, and cried as if she'd finally grasped the realization that nothing ever would be as it had been before.

Nothing.

Nothing at all.

Chapter 19

Annie had no idea when John would be back on the island. "Over the weekend" gave him latitude, so she knew she couldn't hold him to a day or time. Nor did she have an inkling as to whether he'd want her to go with him to Earl and Claire's to tell them the diagnosis.

Which was all the more reason she was thankful that after she'd composed herself and returned a gif of a big hug to Lucy, Annie heard an email alert. And though she still had dozens of the 431 left to peruse, the latest one was welcome: it was from Jack Miller. Perhaps somehow, like Kevin, he'd known that Annie needed some shoring up.

Click-click.

Hello, Annie. I was thrilled to read your message. You didn't mention when I can meet him. Maybe tomorrow? As I'm sure you can tell, I'm anxious. If not tomorrow, Saturday? Thanks for your patience with me. Jack.

She smiled. It was endearing that he'd confessed he was anxious. Kevin no doubt would be anxious, too, though he might not admit it. Perhaps, along with so-called wisdom, the ability to fess up to vulnerability came with age.

Then she realized she and Kevin hadn't talked about a date for the meeting. He wanted her to go with him, but how could she go today—or tomorrow—when John might be coming home? Shouldn't her fiancé take precedence over her brother?

Of course he should.

But the fact was, she didn't know when John was coming home. For all she knew, it could be tomorrow. Or Saturday. Or Sunday. In the meantime, she'd hate to put off father and son until after that. Maybe, like Jack, Annie was anxious. And maybe she really, really needed a reason to feel good. Because everything had been so screwed up since she'd come back from California.

California. The thought of which reminded her she hadn't yet heard back from Greg. Maybe he was tied up. Or maybe he'd changed his mind about whatever he'd wanted to say to her.

Maybe it was just as well.

Looking out the front window of the Inn, Annie watched as a robin dug into the ground, no doubt seeking a worm to bring back to her nest. Annie didn't remember when the baby-blue eggs hatched: mid-April seemed early, but the temperatures were milder on the island than they'd been in Boston, not that Annie had ever seen baby robins in the city.

She pulled her gaze back to her phone and wondered why she was procrastinating. It's not as if she were a mother bird needing to nurture her babies. Or maybe she was.

With that less than ingenious insight, she let out a soft laugh and texted Kevin.

Need a day and time for Jack. How about tomorrow?

She sent the message, closed the laptop, and returned it to the desk. Then she went to the wide staircase that led up to the bedrooms and sat on the second step. She glanced down at her phone, thinking Kevin would answer right away. While she waited, she clicked back to Lucy's plea.

Everything is so messed up. I want to come home.

Her heart crumbled again.

If Kevin could meet Jack tomorrow, they could get it over with. And Annie could go back to obsessing about John and Abigail. And Lucy. And Earl and Claire, and how upset they'd be when they heard the news.

She lowered the phone to her side and gazed out the side-lights of the door. Kevin and Earl had designed—and, for the most part, built—such a magnificent, peaceful-looking, peaceful-feeling Inn, it did not appear as if anything unsettling could happen inside. She wondered if any of their summer guests had a clue how hard life on the island sometimes was, and that, sooner or later, Vineyard magic wasn't quite what it seemed. Islanders were, after all, just regular people, struggling to get through their days and weeks and years like so many others who lived in a less glamorous place.

The text alert went off.

Ferry duty tomorrow. Can he do Saturday morning?

She said she'd set it up with Jack and get back to him with the time.

Then she stood up, moved closer to the window, and looked outside again. The plump robin was gone. No doubt back to her little nest, where new life, new hope was beginning.

Annie only wished she knew if a cycle of life was beginning—or ending—for her.

The rest of the day, Annie struggled with her writing, with one eye flicking back and forth to her phone, waiting to hear something, anything, from John. Even though she knew it was only Thursday, she also kept checking the clock, as it synced with arrival times for the big boats, in case he came home early. But long past dark, when the last boat, the nine thirty, had crossed over from Woods Hole, Annie gave up waiting and went to bed.

Friday morning, Jack emailed to say he could take the same boat he'd taken earlier in the week and meet them at the coffee shop just before ten thirty Saturday morning. Annie was pleased to think she had something to do besides side-glancing at her phone every two seconds.

She also had an email from her editor, Trish, asking her to be in touch on Monday because she needed an update on her progress of the novel. Maybe the meeting with Kevin and Jack Miller would be a happy, animated reunion and get Annie's endorphins so fully charged she'd return to her desk and write and write and write so that she wouldn't have to fib when she responded to Trish and she'd be finished before summer.

Unfortunately, Friday became a carbon copy of Thursday, with Annie spending hours pretending to be productive yet accomplishing little for the literary world. And without any more contact from John.

But at eleven o'clock that night, her phone rang.

"Annie Sutton. It's really you."

As she pulled herself from a sleepy fog, it took a moment before she recognized the throaty, Hollywood voice. She also realized she'd dozed off while sitting on the rocking chair, a half-empty glass of wine by her side. She quickly checked caller ID to be sure she was correct.

"Greg," she said.

"You remembered. I'm impressed."

"Your area code gave you away." *As did your name*, she thought, but didn't mention it in case he took the fact that he was on her contact list as something significant.

"I know it's late on the East Coast, Annie, and I'm sorry to bother you. But something's come up."

She couldn't tell if the "something" was good or bad. If they'd decided to trash the series, wouldn't Louise or Trish have known first? Oh, God, was that the real reason Trish wanted to talk on Monday?

You're such a negative Nellie, Murphy whispered.

Annie smiled. "Something important?" she asked Greg.

"One of your scriptwriting teammates—Cerise—is moving back to Canada. She's from Vancouver, if you didn't know. But now her mother's ill and needs her help. I tried to get her to work remotely, but she said she'll be too busy. She also has a nephew with cystic fibrosis that her mom was a caregiver for, so Cerise will have to help out with him, too."

Wow. He sure had unpacked a lot of information. "Oh, Greg, I'm so sorry to hear it. She's so nice. And such fun." Cerise was in her forties and wore neon-colored clothes and alternated her hair color between pink, blue, and purple. She also had an infectious sense of humor. She'd moved to L.A. some two decades ago and had told Annie that she never wanted to leave.

"She'll be missed," he said. "What's more, I'm left with a big hole in my team of writers."

So . . . Annie had the feeling he wasn't calling only to convey sad news.

"And . . . ?" she asked.

"Well, I know you liked being here."

And there it was. "Yes. It was great."

A sigh whooshed through the cross-country, satellite connection. "Are you going to make me get down on one knee and beg, like the guy who gave you that rather attractive diamond ring?"

Annie's gaze shot down to her left hand, to the marquis-cut diamond in the platinum setting on her ring finger. The diamond had belonged to John's grandmother—his mother's mother, not the grandmother whose wedding dress, like Annie, was still hanging in wait. John had the diamond reset so that it was surrounded by smaller ones; he'd surprised her with it as a symbol of how much he loved her.

Her stomach turned inside out now, if stomachs could do that.

"You're asking me to work for you—remotely?"

"No. I want you to move to California. I gave Cerise the remote option because I'd hoped the situation in Canada would be temporary. She said it won't. But I think you could tell how much better a team works out here when they're together in the same room, when the ideas shoot from one of you to another, the energy building and building until it propagates a masterpiece. Well, a TV series, anyway."

At least Greg wasn't deluded into thinking what they did was of life-or-death importance.

"I can't," Annie replied. "I live on the Vineyard, Greg. My life is here. My family is here."

"What about a test run? Another three months? Or six?"

Clearly, he'd been thinking about this.

"I will pay you handsomely," he added.

"You already have." She was reminded that she'd made

a commitment to herself that once the money started to come in from the series, she'd make a substantial donation to Martha's Vineyard Community Services. She wanted to do something to help the people of the island . . . and another Hollywood paycheck would be a fabulous addition. But if Annie was gone from the island for another three months or six . . . if she left John, left Kevin, and the rest . . . what if she decided not to come back?

"Are you talking about me writing scripts for my next books? Or for someone else's?"

"Either. Both. I need help. Will you at least think about it? Your work and your work ethic are so perfect for our company . . ." Well over sixty, maybe older, Greg was, indeed, a veteran flatterer.

"First of all, it's almost midnight. Even if I were to 'think it over'—and I'm not saying I will—this is hardly a good time of day to think about anything except sleeping."

"Got it," he replied. "But I'll need a quick answer because there's lots of work on the table. I have other options, of course, but you're my first choice. So once the sun rises, I expect you'll do some serious thinking and get back to me. Monday at the latest. Then I'll contact your agent and talk salary."

"But Greg . . ." Annie began, but he said good night and disconnected.

Saturday morning, Kevin was at her door at eight thirty, as if it would take two hours to get to Vineyard Haven instead of maybe thirty or so minutes at this time of year. And, after tossing and turning the night before until she finally fell asleep, Annie hadn't yet had a chance to do any "serious thinking" about Greg's offer. Let alone come up with an answer.

Instead, she rushed to finish dressing and run out the door.

"We need a plan," her brother said when, a few minutes later, he steered his pickup onto the *On Time* like a pro, which, Annie supposed, he really would be as soon as his application was accepted by Boston.

"A plan for what?"

He huffed. "For what I'm supposed to say to my father—though I never thought those last two words would come out of my mouth again."

She patted his knee. "Kevin, brother, we don't need a plan. Just remember that chances are, this isn't easy for him, either. Just be your kind self, okay?"

His eyes rotated toward her, then back to the ramp as he rolled the truck off the ferry and onto Dock Street. They passed the sleek black sculpture of the whale's tail that appeared to be diving into the earth, then they headed up the slope, into the maze of one-way streets in the village. Once they reached the triangle, Kevin bore right. He'd apparently decided to take the longer way, which people tended to do if they wanted either to see the ocean or procrastinate. Because Kevin saw the ocean every day, the first reason was doubtful.

Gazing out the window and across Vineyard Sound, Annie saw the strip of earth that was Cape Cod, less than ten miles away "as the seagull flies," Earl liked to say. The water between the landmasses was deep aqua in color, a little bit winter, a little bit summer. On the island side of the water, topping the low sand dunes, wild plants of beach roses had begun to green; once the branches had fully leafed, buds of pretty pink or white flowers would appear, along with tiny thorns.

Kind of like life, Murphy whispered to her. *Part soothing, part painful.*

Because of the enormity of what Kevin and Annie were

about to do, she wished she could share Murphy's comment, but, as with Francine, she would not. Especially when he was about to see his father. She'd also decided not to remind her brother about the childhood mementos and photos of him and Jack waiting in the Vuitton trunk.

"Maybe I should start by telling him I'm going to be a Coast-Guard–certified captain of a seagoing vessel," Kevin said.

She laughed. "You don't need to try and impress him."

He grumbled something incoherent, then said, "Knowing me, I'll probably only tell him things I think he'll want to hear. If I start doing that, you have my permission to kick me under the table."

"Oh, good," she replied. "Finally, I have your permission to kick you."

"Ha ha," he replied, his tone flat.

"But I have to warn you, I'll also take you up on that if I hear you get nasty to him. Like if you call him a rat bastard."

Kevin made no comment.

Annie adjusted herself on the seat and considered reminding him to be himself. Instead she decided to let him work through his anxiety in his own way, because she knew that sometimes being supportive meant being quiet, not offering advice, whether solicited or not.

They arrived at the small café before Jack did and sat next to each other, facing the door, on the same side of the table. Kevin said he knew it was weird, but that he'd be more comfortable with them the two of them facing Jack. And the door, so he could see Jack before Jack saw him.

Annie didn't mention that she'd sat in the same place on Monday, and for the same reason.

Kevin studied the chalkboard on the wall behind the

counter and perused the daily specials. Then he started shaking his right leg, which, of course, made the table quiver.

She pressed her hand on the table. "I'll make a deal with you," she said. "I won't tell you that when you shake your leg it drives me crazy, and I'll agree it's okay for you keep doing it if you must. All I ask in return is that you stop it when Jack comes in. Aside from the fact it will no doubt annoy him, too, it will slop our lattes all over the place."

Her brother looked at her as if he had no idea what she was talking about. Then he smiled. "Taylor hates it, too. But I hardly know when I'm doing it."

"Fine. So I'm not alone. But do we have a deal?"

"As long as you elbow me if I start doing it."

"Or I'll kick you under the table. Ever since you brought it up, I've been relishing the opportunity. Now, tell me what you want to drink or eat, and I'll go order it."

He asked for a regular coffee with cream and whatever kind of muffin they had. And he stopped shaking his leg.

"No," Annie said, as she stood to go to the counter, "please. Keep shaking. Get it out of your system before he gets here." She smiled, and that time he laughed.

"I keep thinking maybe he won't show up," he said. "Which would make my life easier."

"He'll be here."

"You don't know him like I do."

Annie didn't remind him that he had not seen his father in forty years, so he hardly "knew" him at all.

As the minutes seemed to tick by slowly, Kevin returned to jitterbugging the table. The number of people in the café had grown in fitting with it being a Saturday morning. Islanders were either out doing errands or grabbing a quick breakfast before the ten forty-five boat they needed to catch to go shopping in Falmouth. Unfortunately, with so many people came loud conversation. Annie wanted to ask Kevin if he thought they should go somewhere quieter; she supposed they could walk up to the Vineyard Haven Library; maybe Amy, the director, would let them sit in the program room if it wasn't in use.

But at 10:22, just as Annie was about to offer her suggestion, she spotted Jack Miller outside on the sidewalk as he passed the blue MOCHA MOTT'S GOOD COFFEE sign, with its cartoonish logo of a toothy character. Jack's stride was determined, much like Kevin's.

"He's here," Annie said.

Kevin went rigid, his eyes drilled on the door. He stopped shaking his leg; he also might have stopped breathing.

The glass door opened; Jack walked inside and scanned the room. Annie stood up and waved. He gave her a quick nod, paused for a contemplative second, then approached them.

She nudged Kevin to stand, but he didn't move. She hoped he wasn't making a statement of silence.

"Annie," Jack said over the din, "good to see you again." He reached out and offered his hand.

His palm was a little damp, and possibly trembling.

"The crowd should thin out once the ten forty-five starts boarding," Annie said. She had no idea if that was true, but she wanted to say something as they shook hands. "Kevin?" she asked.

His eyes never left Jack, but his expression revealed no emotion. He gestured for the man to sit. It was obvious he did not want a hug.

"Kevin," Jack said as he sat. His eyes looked tired, as if he hadn't slept. Annie hoped he hadn't had second thoughts about the meeting.

Kevin nodded, which was no surprise. After all, he wasn't

going to say, "Hi, Dad. How've you been for the past forty years?"

Annie was determined not to try to control the conversation. She toyed with her mug of latte and let the men sit in their discomfort for as long as they needed.

Finally, Kevin spoke. "So you found me."

Jack put his elbows on the table and pressed his fingers together. "The truth is, I found Annie. I recognized her picture because she looks like your mother. And I recognized her name."

Kevin sat back in his chair and folded his arms. Annie would have bet he wanted to shake his leg.

"Then I looked up Donna's name and saw that she passed away. I'm sorry, Kevin. She was a wonderful woman."

Annie wasn't sure that Jack should have mentioned Donna so soon. She hadn't warned him that Kevin might get defensive. At least she'd been right about the crowd thinning out, so if her brother caused a scene, fewer people would be there to bear witness.

Jack lowered his voice. "I saw your name in her obituary. And Annie's. It said you both live here on the island. It didn't take much effort to find an email address for Annie. Her picture's everywhere. She's a real celebrity. A famous author." He gave a light snort. "And to think I once was convinced that the internet would bring on the end of the world."

If he was joking, Kevin wasn't buying it.

Annie stood up. "Excuse me, but can I get you some coffee, Jack? It looks like the waitstaff is still busy." She decided to blame the waitstaff rather than admit that she wished she could be anywhere else right then than at the table, waiting for Kevin to say that he was going to be a captain of the *On Time*. Unless he'd changed his mind and intended to tell his father what he really thought of him.

Jack said whatever Kevin had would be fine.

So she moved to the counter, grateful to be away from them. She was amazed that Jack was able to keep his cool. For all of Kevin's nervous chatter about his father on the way there, she was curious as to why he was simply sitting and staring at the man. Maybe by the time she returned, they'd be engaged in conversation, and she could slip out the door and let them get reacquainted without her hovering. Maybe her presence was making her brother self-conscious.

While waiting in line, as badly as she wanted to look over her shoulder and see what was, or was not, going on, she continued to face forward. And to remind herself that she had no idea what it must feel like to be Kevin right then. Or ever. Like many people, he'd had a lot of tough breaks, most of which had not been his fault. How he managed to sustain a usually cheerful disposition was an enigma to Annie. She doubted that she could have maintained his "chin up" spirit for as long as he had.

By the time it was her turn to order, Annie was having second thoughts about encouraging the reunion. She only hoped her brother wouldn't blame her if things went awry.

But it's his right to know, she thought, not sure whom she was trying to persuade.

When the latte was ready, she included a sizable tip because she didn't want to wait for change. She turned and headed back to the table, keeping her eyes focused on not spilling what was swaying in the mug. But as she reached the table and shifted her attention to her brother, she realized he was alone.

"Where's Jack?" she asked, a queasiness rising inside her.

Kevin stood, picked up his napkin and mug, and headed to the trash bin and the buckets for used dishes. He stayed there, hands in the pockets of his jeans, clearly waiting for

Annie. She got the message. She went to the self-cleanup area, dumped out the coffee, and followed him out the door.

"So?" she asked quietly as they walked along Main Street toward his pickup. "What happened? Where did he go?"

He zipped his light jacket against the breeze that was rolling up now from the harbor. His pace quickened; Annie rushed to keep up.

"Kevin?"

He stopped abruptly, turned to her, and raised the collar of his jacket. "That man," he said steadily, "is not my father."

Chapter 20

Annie knew that her brother had at least one tender memory of his dad—the time he'd taken Kevin to watch the Red Sox play. Beyond that, she didn't know much. Perhaps over time, Kevin's fond thoughts of that game had faded, shrouded by other, not-so-nice memories. Maybe Donna and Jack had argued often, and their raised voices had frightened the small boy. And those recollections, combined with watching his mother struggle to be a good single parent, made it easier for Kevin to believe that Jack had abandoned them. Him.

The deduction made sense to Annie. But on their way back to Chappy, she knew it wasn't the right time to ask. So, instead, she thought about fathers. In particular, hers.

As an adopted kid, she'd grown up not knowing who her birth father was, what he looked like, what he did for a living, if he would have let her go to the senior prom when she was a freshman—unlike Bob Sutton, who did not. Those things had seemed important when she was in her teens and seeking a grown-up identity. It had been triggered one day at her friend Stacy's house.

"You're just like your father!" Stacy's mother shouted after Stacy stormed into her bedroom room and slammed the door, leaving Annie standing in the hall with her friend's teary-eyed mother. Then the mother stormed off, too, but in another direction, slamming another door. Annie made her way outside and walked home, thinking about Stacy being "just like" her father, and wondering if Annie was "just like" hers. Whoever he was.

Would she recognize him on the street? In the market? In the waiting room at the dentist's office when she went for a cleaning?

Would her real father walk up to her one day and say, "Excuse me, I can't help but notice that you're just like me"?

Even at age fifteen, she'd known she was being ridiculous. But Annie's imagination was already rooted in making up stories, the seeds of which, she supposed—as Kevin accelerated along the roundabout, causing her to grip the dashboard as if she were on the ferry in a storm—might have been planted by a subconscious desire to know who her birth parents were.

But Kevin had known his father, albeit briefly. The memorabilia and the photos in the Vuitton trunk of a smiling little boy—the fact that he still recalled the hot dog and ice cream his dad bought for him at Fenway—indicated that he'd loved him. And, yes, the man had left when Kevin was four years old—but was that too young for him to have a clear memory? Or was his perception clouded by not having known the truth?

A few years before, Annie asked Kevin about the day his dad left.

"It wasn't a day," he told her at the Newes over drinks—hers wine, his beer—on a wintry afternoon that was too gloomy for either of them to feel like working. With wood crackling in the old colonial pub, glowing with warmth as it had done for nearly three centuries, Annie engaged her brother in conversation about his childhood.

"It was more like days, weeks, months, for all I know. My dad was a salesman of home cleaning products, not a door-to-door guy like those from the fifties and sixties, but one who traveled from corporate office to corporate office around the country, hawking his company's wares to stores that were big-box and small-box and boxes in between. He pitched larger places to take on the line of products with private labels so customers thought they'd produced them; he told smaller places that his company's national advertising meant the products would fly off their shelves. But he was gone a lot. And then he just never came home." Which Kevin had taken to mean that Jack had abandoned them.

As they pulled onto the *On Time* now to head over to Chappy, Kevin unbuckled his seat belt. "I have to talk to Larry about the weekend schedule." Larry was the captain on duty.

Annie nodded, but once the door was closed she let out a small cry of exasperation. It wasn't her place to tell her brother what had really happened. It wasn't her place, and yet . . . and yet it seemed bizarre that he was so determined to believe that Jack wasn't his father. How was that possible? Kevin resembled the man . . . and Jack's story jibed with what Donna had told her. And what Annie's birth father had confirmed in a letter she saw after Donna died.

But now, Annie wondered if she should investigate Jack further. Because until Kevin had the right information, he'd be cheated out of knowing the kind of man his dad really was. And Annie would forever feel guilty that her birth father—inadvertently—had stolen Kevin's father from a four-year-old little boy.

When he dropped her off at the Inn, Kevin barely said good-bye.

But as Annie walked down toward her cottage, she spotted Francine's car in the clamshell parking lot. Because a few minutes with Francine and little Bella were a sure cure for the self-pitying blues, Annie changed direction and went toward the house. But when she knocked on the door, there was no response. Perhaps the three of them had gone somewhere together.

Annie thought about going up-island to Winnie's, but her friend would have just arrived home from the tribal meeting; she deserved a breather before being barraged with Annie's drama. *Make that dramas, plural*, she reminded herself, because Greg's offer had now been added to Annie's troubling pile of "stuff." It wouldn't be fair to dump it all on her friend.

So, instead of sharing her troubles, Annie considered going into the Inn to look for Rex. Then again, other than asking how the hunt for a restaurant was going, and if he'd heard anything more about the place on South Water Street, she wouldn't have much to say. And the truth was, Annie still wasn't really interested.

She thought about going to Earl and Claire's to see how Claire was doing, but Annie knew her mood might alert them that she knew something about Abigail that they didn't yet know.

She refused to think about Greg again, because that decision was too big to make and was the last thing she felt capable of doing.

So Annie decided to do what she did best when she needed to untangle her feelings: she got into her Jeep, turned on the ignition, and made her way to the ancient Chappaquiddick Wampanoag burial ground, where the silence of the sky and the view of Cape Pogue and the sea beyond had listened to so many of her secrets.

It took only a few minutes to get there.

* * *

After parking the Jeep on the side of the road, Annie trudged up the sandy path that was edged by tall sea grass, which kept the small cemetery well hidden.

She was greeted by her favorite sight: the sun flickering off the blue water below, as if it were nighttime and the twinkling were from thousands of fireflies.

The second thing she noticed was the figure of a man hunched in front of a gravestone. He seemed to be crying. And, dear God, it was Earl.

Without considering that he might want to be alone, she rushed over and crouched beside him.

"Earl? What's wrong? Has something happened?"

He looked at her, unashamed of his tears.

"Annie," he said. "Oh, Annie, it's all my fault."

That's when she realized he was kneeling in front of a grave that belonged to someone named Martha, born January 14, 1943, died March 20, 1955. And that the marker was in the section where several Lyons family members had been laid to rest.

"What's your fault?" Annie asked gently.

He wiped his eyes with a thick gardening glove. Small clippings of seagrass surrounded him; he must have been tidying the family plots.

"This is Martha," he said, nodding to the stone. "Not many people remember her now. She died when she was twelve. She was my sister."

Annie was surprised. "I didn't know you had a sister."

He nodded and teared up again.

It was hard to imagine that Earl would have knowingly brought harm to anyone; maybe there'd been an accident that he'd been part of. Annie quickly calculated that in 1955, Earl would have been too young to have been driving a car. Or a pickup.

"I'm sorry, Earl. But I can't imagine how it could have been your fault."

Shaking his head, he said, "No. Not Martha. It's my fault about Abigail."

And then a few pieces began to fall into place. "Was Martha sick?"

He wiped his eyes again. "She had MS, just like Abigail, which, by now, I know you know. Martha also had a heart condition. I guess that was the real reason she died. But I should have told John about the MS part. John should have known."

Though Annie suspected that, yes, for Earl to be so upset, Martha must have had multiple sclerosis, she was slower to grasp how he'd found out about Abigail's diagnosis. And how he knew that Annie knew.

"You talked to John?" she asked, her voice cracking a little.

"He came to the house this morning." He looked over at Annie. "I thought you would have been with him."

She didn't know what direction to look in or which words to cobble together. "I . . . I didn't know what boat they'd be on. I had something to do with Kevin, and I wanted to take care of it before . . ." Then she knew her excuse didn't matter because Earl was staring back at the grave marker and didn't seem to be listening.

"Martha was a pretty girl," he said. "And smart. But she was sickly."

"I didn't know MS was genetic."

"I don't know if it is. Claire said even if it is, it wouldn't have mattered if John had known. For one thing, John wanted kids. For another, Martha was born with a heart defect. Thank God John's girls don't have that. I don't even know if the two things were connected. But if I'd told John, maybe when Jenn got pregnant she could have had some kind of test . . ."

Annie was glad his words trailed off then, because she did not want to hear about John's ex-wife's pregnancy.

"How did Claire take the news?" she asked.

"Better than me. She told me to stop overreacting. Well, Abigail is her granddaughter, too. But Martha wasn't her sister."

Annie reached over and touched his arm. "I'm so sorry, Earl. Tell me more about Martha. What was she like?"

He sputtered, then said, "I'd like to say she was sweet. But the truth is, she was a royal pain in my arse."

Leave it to Earl to be honest.

"So you weren't close?"

He picked at a blade of grass. "Like I said, she was smart. 'Smarty-pants,' I called her. When they gave her a wheelchair, I told her if she didn't stop being mean to me, I'd push her off this hill and she'd wind up in the water and no one would find her for months or maybe years."

"Did she believe you?"

"No. She knew me better. We fought a lot, that's for sure. But she was my sister."

Then, as he grabbed another blade of grass, his body tipped backward, and he wound up on his rump.

"Jumpin' Jehoshaphat!" he cried out. "How am I supposed to get up? Did the good Lord forget how old I am?"

Despite the situation, they both laughed.

"Come on," Annie said as she stood up, "I'll give you a hoist." She bent down and slid her arms under his shoulders. "On the count of three . . ."

They managed to get Earl to his feet, tears still in his eyes. "What a godawful day," he muttered.

"I agree. Where's your truck?"

"At the community center. After John left, I wanted to go to Edgartown to talk to him in private. To tell him about Martha without Claire around. But I got as far as the community center when I got . . . upset. Too upset to drive. So I parked and walked here. To have a word with my sister."

They went out to the road while he talked.

"Is Claire alone?" she asked.

"Nope. I called Taylor to come by for a while."

"Good. I'll drive you home. I can pick you up later or to-morrow, if you want, and bring you to get your truck."

"Kevin can do it," Earl said. "He lives closer."

"Okay," Annie said, not wanting to think about Kevin then, either, but she supposed it would be better than dwelling on John. That he hadn't called to say they were home. Or that he didn't want her with him when he gave his parents the news. Annie would have gone with him, even if it meant leaving Kevin alone to meet Jack Miller. After all, John was going to be her husband; she, his wife.

But as things stood now, it was obvious that Annie was slipping from his world.

Chapter 21

When Annie got back to the cottage, she sat at her desk and opened her computer to check her in-box, mostly because she didn't know what else to do or where the heck to put herself. She didn't expect to see a message from her agent.

Call as soon as you get this.

Annie propped her elbows on the desk and rubbed the back of her neck. She didn't want to talk to Louise right then. She didn't want to talk to anyone but John. Louise, however, wasn't typically given to urgency. Or to contacting Annie on a Saturday afternoon. So Greg must have decided not to wait until Annie made her decision before calling her agent.

If she wasn't mentally spent, she might have been angry.

Composing herself, Annie reached for her phone. "Hey, Louise. What's up?"

Louise laughed, which she also did not often do. "Production is officially underway for your Museum Girls series. As is a fat chunk of your overall payment, which is en route to your Martha's Vineyard Bank account. It no doubt will be recorded Monday."

Surprise. It wasn't about Greg.

Annie was flummoxed. Taken off guard. She couldn't re-member the exact amount due her once production had begun. She supposed she'd be hard-pressed to remember de-tails about much of anything at that moment. She also recalled that, though she'd told Louise that Greg had called her, she hadn't updated her about the conversation.

"Hello?" Louise asked. "I must have missed hearing your outburst of enthusiasm."

"Sorry. I've got lots going on here. But, yes, this is good news."

"And what about Greg? Did you talk to him yet?"

Finally, the question she'd rather not have heard. "I did."

"And?"

Annie took a deep breath, then summarized his offer.

When she finished, Louise had one word: "Wow."

"Wow, indeed."

"I take it you haven't made a decision?"

"No. But I don't know how it's possible. I live on the Vineyard. The man I was going to marry just found out that one of his daughters has MS, so I'm not even sure if he still wants to marry me. And I convinced my brother to meet the man I thought was his birth father, but apparently is not. So, no, I have not had a chance to consider whether or not I should pull up all the stakes I've planted here on what once was a peaceful island and move to sunny L.A."

The silence that followed lasted only a few seconds.

"Since you put it that way," Louise said, "it doesn't seem like you have much of a choice. I mean, why wouldn't you want to start over in a fabulous place with a fabulous new ca-reer?"

Annie bit her lip and tried not to smile. "Maybe because I no longer have the wardrobe for it?"

Louise laughed. "Nobody does, Annie. But you're a writer,

not an actor. All you really need are a few basic outfits and lots of flashy jewelry."

"Don't forget footwear. These days I'm into sneakers and hiking boots. I only have one pair of black heels. And they're about four inches lower than stilettos."

"All kidding aside, I think you'll be well able to afford a whole new wardrobe. Or ten, if you want."

Annie looked out the window at the quiet harbor. "That's the problem," she said quietly. "I don't know what I want."

"The decision must be yours and yours alone. But don't let that man's charm bully you into making a decision you may regret."

At first Annie thought Louise was talking about John. Until she realized Louise had met John only once and would hardly have called him a bully.

"Greg Williams can't bully me. I'm too old to have stars in my eyes." Which probably wasn't totally true, but she wanted to think otherwise.

"One more thing to consider," her agent added. "Your books. You're still under contract for the one you're doing now, and another. And publishers frown upon authors who ditch them for what might erroneously be perceived as a better opportunity."

Point taken.

They talked a while longer, with Annie promising she'd decide soon. But when they finally hung up, instead of pouring a glass of wine, settling in her rocking chair, and doing some serious thinking, Annie closed her in-box and, once again, Googled pediatric multiple sclerosis. Because, in spite of John's strange behavior, that was what mattered to her most.

John didn't call until after nine o'clock that night. By then she'd found information that offered both helpful and hopeful treatments and prognoses for Abigail. Unfortunately, the notes from website after website became redundant. Rather than get overwhelmed, Annie decided to get back to work on her book. If she took Greg up on his offer, at least she'd be breaking only half of her two-book contract. Or maybe she'd be able to get the second one written in her spare time when she wasn't on the patio nibbling avocados and sucking oranges, as Kevin had put it.

When the phone rang, John's photo popped up. She'd taken it at South Beach a couple of summers before on a rare afternoon when they'd both taken time off from work while the island was still thick with tourists. Annie loved how relaxed John looked in his "surfer swim trunks," as Lucy called her dad's black shorts that nearly reached his knees and had yellow stripes around his lean stomach. His chest and arms and calves were so finely tuned that he looked almost as if he were still in his thirties: clearly the result of him staying in police-officer shape. "Detective Sergeant," he often corrected her with one of his heart-melting smiles.

"Hi," she said as she connected. "I ran into your father. He said you made it. And that you told them."

He paused, then said, "Yeah. It was right up there on the list of things you never want to have to tell your parents."

There was no point in mentioning she wished she had been there with him. "Your mom handled it okay?"

"She's a rock."

Apparently no one had told him that Claire—the rock—had had another stroke.

"How's Abigail?"

"Scared. Like the rest of us."

"John, I've been doing some research . . ."

"Research won't change things, Annie. We have a great team of doctors. We're listening to them. Not to Google."

A thousand bees stung her.

"I know you mean well," he added, too late.

"Can . . . can I see her tomorrow?"

The silence was so long, she thought he had hung up. "John?"

He cleared his throat. "I'm really sorry, Annie. But Abigail didn't go with me to my parents. She stayed in Plymouth."

Annie supposed that was understandable. "Well, can I see you?" It seemed like a foolish question to be asking her fiancé, but there it was.

"Um . . ." he began, and before he took his next breath, Annie felt an ache in her heart, as if it knew what was coming next. "I'm not on the island anymore. I went right from Chappy back to the boat. They squeezed me onto the *Katama*."

The *Katama*, Annie knew, shouldn't be confused with the section of Edgartown out toward South Beach that had become increasingly popular in the past years. The *Katama* John referred to was technically the M/V *Katama*, an aging yet rugged open freight boat that hauled trucks back and forth to the Vineyard with surprising reliability. Even when issues occurred—a failed generator, a snapped deck hatch—everyone forgave her. All of which Annie could not believe she was thinking about, as if she were researching "ferries of Martha's Vineyard" instead of talking with the man she was supposed to marry very soon.

"So . . . you're back in Plymouth?"

Silence again.

"I've decided to take some time off work. I hope you'll agree that we should postpone the wedding—again. There just isn't time . . ." He stammered a little. "Anyway," he continued, "Lucy wants to stay here, too. With Abigail. My girls need me, Annie. I hope you understand."

And that, Annie knew, was definitely that.

She sat on her bed, wondering if she should burn the wedding dress that Mabel Lyons had been married in, in all its ugly splendor. Mabel Lyons had been Earl's mother. And also the mother of Martha Lyons, the twelve-year-old girl whose body had been laid to rest in the Wampanoag burial ground on Chappaquiddick back when only a handful of folks of European ancestry had been allowed in. The girl who'd had multiple sclerosis in an era when treatments for heart disease and support systems for chronic conditions no doubt had been limited.

She wanted to scream. For Abigail.

For John.

For herself.

Knock it off. It was Murphy, of course, showing up at the right time.

"I know," Annie replied. "I stink at this. I'm supposed to be a woman who plows ahead, overcomes adversity. A freaking martyr."

Murphy laughed. *Don't go that far. You're human, not superhuman. And with being human comes disappointment. Depression. The same way humans can be joyful. Even elated.*

"I thought by now I had evolved beyond that."

Why? Because you've had three or four traumas in your life? Please. Look around. I'll bet you know a dozen people whose lives have been tougher than yours.

Annie didn't need to look around. She knew Murphy was right.

She sighed and closed her eyes. "Oh, Murph, what would I do without you?"

Lucky for both of us, you don't have that problem.

Annie laughed. Laughter, she supposed, was healthier than burning the wedding dress. And better for the environment.

"Annie? Are you alone?"

The voice was soft, feminine. For a moment, Annie wasn't sure if she'd dreamed up that one, too. Maybe it was Ellen

Sutton, the mother who had raised her. Or maybe it was Donna. Riding in from the heavens on Murphy's coattails.

"Annie?"

She blinked. And realized the voice was Francine's.

"Oh," she said, quickly sitting up. "Hi. I didn't hear you." She shook herself back to reality and went into the living room.

Francine stood there, her bubble of a belly eclipsing her petite body to the point where she resembled a far-fetched skit on *Saturday Night Live.*

"I'm sorry. I knocked, but you didn't answer. I saw your car here but not John's, so I was . . ."

"Worried about me?" Annie smiled. "Come here. Give me a hug. The best way that baby will let you."

The hug was endearing for its intention, if not its awkward maneuvers. And Annie felt better already.

"Sit," Annie said. "Tea?"

"Sure. Decaf, if you have it. The baby's been doing enough gymnastics on his own. Or her own."

Annie smiled, put the kettle on, and took out two bags of chamomile. It was getting late; maybe the tea would help prevent her from having a sleepless night, ha ha.

"Is that why you're still awake?" Annie asked. "Baby gymnastics?"

Francine shook her head. "No. I know about Abigail. About her diagnosis. Lucy sent me a text."

"Ah . . . and she asked you to come and check up on me."

Because Francine was innately shy, she lowered her head. "Well . . . yes."

Annie walked to the rocker where Francine now sat. She reached out and lifted the young woman's chin. "Thank you. It means a lot to me that you're here."

A tender smile emerged.

The teakettle whistled.

Annie went back in the kitchen and tended to the tea. It seemed as if she'd been doing a lot of that since she'd been home.

"How's Lucy?" Annie asked. "I know she's not a fan of being in Plymouth."

"She's worried. Not only about her sister but also because John told her you're going to postpone the wedding."

Happy to have something to do with her hands, Annie dunked tea bags and arranged a few shortbread cookies on a small plate.

"It doesn't feel like the right time to celebrate," Annie said. "We're disappointed, but the focus needs to be on Abigail now." Her voice sounded steady and very mature. Not at all like she was feeling. Or that she'd made up the explanation on the spot.

"Bull," Francine replied. "It sucks, Annie. It all sucks."

Annie laughed. "Yes. That's a better way of putting it." She picked up the plate and started toward the table when Francine spoke again.

"And Lucy's going to miss the prom. So there's lots of what you called 'disappointment' all around."

Annie stopped. And frowned. "But the prom's not until May, right? Surely Abigail will understand if Lucy is here for that. It will be her first prom and she really likes Kyle. And her dress! She loves her dress." Claire had made Lucy's powder-blue dress for what should have been Annie and John's wedding on Christmas Eve. She'd designed it so that the overlay of silver sparkles could be removed to transform it from less wedding to more high school prom.

She set the plate of shortbread on the table.

"Lucy doesn't want to leave Abigail. Not for any reason," Francine said. "Those were her words. For now, she plans to finish her sophomore year remotely. She said that, if needed, her father can pull a few strings to make it happen."

For two sisters who'd rarely gotten along—Abigail was like her mother, while Lucy was a clone of her dad, which John once told Annie explained a lot about who got along with whom and why—Annie thought it was odd that Lucy wanted to stay. But in addition to having John's personality, Lucy also had his heart. So despite all the ways in which Abigail, who was three years older, had bullied her throughout their childhood, it wasn't surprising that Lucy would be loyal. It was more surprising that John would "pull a few strings," as he'd always avoided doing anything that might look as if he were using his police officer status for special privileges.

She fixed the tea, brought it to the table. Francine waddled the six or eight steps over and joined her.

"I'm sorry, Annie. I assumed John told you that."

"Let's just say that in spite of all the incredible communication skills he employs on the job, he doesn't have a clue how to use them in his life." She pressed her lips together and forced a grin.

Francine sipped her tea. She studied the mug, then her gaze dropped to her belly. Annie recognized it as a mark of avoidance. She had, after all, known Francine for several years, and they'd come through some tough times together.

"What else?" Annie asked.

While rubbing her belly, Francine slowly raised her head. "Well . . . it's just that if he didn't tell you about Lucy wanting to stay, he might not have told you the rest."

"The rest of what? He said he was taking some time off from work. . . ."

And then Annie knew that the A-bomb or the H-bomb or whatever bomb had the power to blow up her whole world was about to drop right there in her cozy little cottage on Martha's Vineyard. *Smithereens*, was the word that popped into her mind. John was going to blow Annie's world to *smithereens*.

"Do you have more definitive information as to how much time is a 'some'?"

Francine tried, but failed, to look nonchalant. "For a while, I guess. Lucy said he'll be there until Abigail's situation is under control. It could be a week or two . . . or it could be . . ."

"Months?" Annie asked, though she supposed that Francine didn't know for certain, any more than John, Abigail, or Lucy possibly could right now. Or *Jenn*, Annie reminded herself. The ex-wife, the mother, with whom the father and daughters—who had been living compatibly (or almost compatibly) as a trio on the island—were now living. Jenn. On the mainland. Where Annie was not allowed to intrude. Because they were a family, after all.

She bit off a small piece of a cookie, then spat it on her napkin. She didn't dare chew and swallow a morsel of anything. Not then. Maybe never again.

Chapter 22

It was a good bet Annie hated him now. Or at least, that's what John believed as he headed on foot to the corner store in Plymouth to get the print edition of the Sunday New York Times, *though he probably wouldn't read it. When he was off duty, he still liked to spread the paper out on the kitchen table, one section at a time, the way he and his dad had done when he was young and still living at home. His friend and co-cop (as they called one another) Detective Lincoln Butterfield once said you could tell someone's personality by which section of the* Sunday Times *they read first.*

John liked the first section first. The news. Good, bad, whatever. Bring it on, *he'd always thought.*

Linc read the financial section. Which was probably why he'd squirreled away more money than John had.

Annie read the Book Review. *Of course, she did.*

Annie.

God, he thought now as he walked through the neighborhood that had vans and SUVs parked in the double-wide driveways and ranch houses like Jenn's squeezed too close together, what the hell was he going to do about Annie?

He couldn't think about having a wedding.

He couldn't think about Annie moving into his town house; there would be too much upheaval. Hell, he didn't even know yet when he'd be able to go back to the island.

And, to be honest with himself, he couldn't even think about seeing Annie face-to-face. Not only because he was hanging on for dear life, trying to be strong with the family he already had, but also because she might ask if he had slept with Jenn. And John couldn't lie to Annie. Nor could he tell her the truth, that, yes, last night they'd slept in the same bed. They had not had sex, but they'd held each other and silently cried. Their firstborn was sick. Wasn't that reason enough to want physical comfort?

So, no, he couldn't see Annie. Because even he would not have believed the truth.

He wondered what Linc would say about what that revealed about John's personality. And if it meant there was no hope for John and Annie as a married couple.

Pulling his sunglasses from his shirt pocket, John slipped them on. There was no point in having the neighbors see the indestructible detective father crying like a wuss.

Chapter 23

When Annie woke up, it was Sunday. She was surprised she'd slept at all. As she sat in the rocker drinking yet another cup of tea, she was grateful that it wasn't yet summer, when guests would be combing, prowling, gathering all over the grounds. She wasn't ready for socializing. Not to mention that if she took Greg up on his job offer, she wouldn't even be here. Perhaps ever again.

Was that what she wanted?

Right now, it felt as if it was.

She waited for Murphy to ask if Annie thought running away was a good long-term solution. But no sage advice arrived. With Annie's luck, this was one of those times when her old friend was going to compel Annie to unravel this latest mess on her own.

Damn.

Greg asked if he'd have to get down on one knee and beg "like the guy who gave you that rather attractive diamond ring." Greg's proposal hadn't been for marriage (he was already married, and not Annie's type anyway), but it was for a commitment. A chance to change her life. Again.

Glancing down at her ring, Annie remembered the afternoon a few days before Christmas when John surprised her
with it. They'd been shopping for gifts, mostly for Abigail and
Lucy, and wound up at the Town Bar and Grill for lunch.

He'd ordered champagne.

After the server poured, John raised a glass. "To us."

They clinked.

And then he reached into his pocket and took out a
small box.

"For you," he said. "Merry Christmas."

She laughed. "It isn't Christmas yet."

He smiled, his beguiling eyes lit up like the brightest stars
in the night sky over Chappaquiddick.

The box was wrapped in glossy red paper and tied with a
white satin bow. She undid the ribbon and removed the
wrapping. A leather cube stared back at her, the kind that jewelry—nice jewelry—came in. She looked at him again, smiled
quizzically, and then opened it. Inside was the most magnificent ring she'd ever seen. She sucked in her breath.

"Will you marry me?" he asked.

It was a lovely joke, as their wedding was already sched-
uled for Christmas Eve.

But things hadn't gone according to their plan. In the
months since then, a lot had happened. A lot of good. And not
so good. Somehow, they'd navigated everything. Until now.

If she left the Vineyard, what would she miss out on?

Francine's baby, of course. And watching Bella become a
big sister.

She'd miss out on taking pictures of Lucy and Kyle dressed
up for the prom (if they made it to the prom); she'd miss being
at Lucy's graduation (again, if Lucy showed up). Worst of all,
Annie would hate not knowing what direction Lucy's life
took.

Nor would she know how Abigail would deal with whatever disabilities she might incur, while still pursuing her dreams. *Call me silly*, Annie thought, *but I think she'll find a way.*

And yet, Annie would not know for sure.

Above all, she would hate not being near her brother, even though he wasn't speaking to her.

She'd miss Earl and Claire. Even Taylor. And it would have been fun to see if Rex ever got his restaurant that he undoubtedly would turn into an unequivocal success.

She'd miss Winnie and her wisdom and her wonderful clan. And she'd miss learning about the island and its ways and the community she'd come to love. Every day, it seemed Annie learned something new about this place, her home.

She didn't know if she'd miss John. Maybe she would, once the pain subsided.

But, in truth, Annie would miss their tenants and the summers when she met so many nice people who were guests at the Inn.

She'd miss the traffic and the crowds and trying to get reservations for dinner. She'd miss the rousing energy.

She'd stay in touch for a while, but then she'd get busy and her island family would get busy, and soon months, then maybe years, would pass. The way it often was with high school girls who pinkie-swore that they'd stay in touch, then barely recognized each other at their twenty-fifth reunion.

Maybe Annie needed to come up with a time line, as if she were plotting one of her novels. She supposed she could accept Greg's offer if she didn't need to go there right away. Maybe she could ask if she could hold off for two months. That way, she could stay on the Vineyard a little while longer. She could finish the manuscript she was working on. She would get to hold Francine's baby and see Lucy in her prom dress, maybe even help Abigail if the girl came back to the island. And two months should provide enough time to determine whether she and John would be together—or not.

Yes, she thought. A two-month waiting period seemed like enough time for her to decide where she wanted or, rather, needed to be. If Greg wanted her that badly, it should be a reasonable request. In the meantime, Annie could concentrate on making memories. Including Mother's Day weekend, an event that might help move the Inn in a new direction—one that would succeed with or without her.

Francine would be able to take on a more active role once the baby came and she was back on her feet. Soon she'd have enough college credits for her degree and was already better qualified to run an Inn than Annie, who hadn't really been qualified at all. And Earl would still be around. And Kevin. And others (like Rex) who might be available to pitch in if needed. Maybe it would also be a good time to give Francine a share of Annie's percentage of the Inn's profits.

Yes, it seemed right.

It felt right.

First, however, Annie needed some quiet time, a few hours to sit with her idea and embrace it. A good way to do that was to go to Winnie's. Not to share her drama or ask for advice but solely to be in her friend's presence. Hopefully, Winnie was had recuperated from the Cape and would welcome a visitor.

But in order to avoid another disappointment, Annie decided not to call ahead. She simply got into her Jeep and headed toward the *On Time*. If Winnie wasn't home, someone usually was, as her clan all lived together in a big, rambling house. In times of trouble, none of them had left the island. They'd stuck together. They had stayed.

But Annie wasn't Winnie. Which was why she already knew that the first thing Monday morning, Pacific Daylight Time, she would call Greg. Before she chickened out.

★ ★ ★

"I'm so glad you're here!" Annie exclaimed when she saw her friend puttering in her large, intentionally untended yard that displayed a palette of wildflowers: blue, purple, yellow, white—the names of which Winnie knew well, though Annie only remembered the ones whose blossoms she blended into her handcrafted soaps—lavender violets, with their soft candy scents; sunny cowslips, with their lemony aroma; and many more.

She would miss making her soaps.

"And I say the same to you, my friend," Winnie said as she offered a comforting hug. "How does it feel to return to a more gentle life?"

Gentle was not a word Winnie would have used if she had known what had transpired over the last several days.

Annie's nonresponse and no doubt wide-eyed expression must have given that away, because Winnie took her by the arm and guided her into the pottery studio.

"We can talk in here," she said. "The house has too many Sunday-morning people with big ears and unsolicited opinions. But I expect you know what that's like." Tall and square, Winnie wore her hair in a long, gray braid that seemed to have grown grayer; it snaked from behind her neck, over her shoulder, and down one of her ample breasts. Her skin had the rich patina of copper, making her white teeth radiant whenever she smiled, as she did now.

They sat on threadbare, overstuffed chairs that Winnie had picked up on the side of the road years earlier. Though her clan teased her about them, she said that, like her, the chairs had had a long, hopefully useful life but weren't yet ready to call it quits. They were by the door, close to the kiln that filled the space with welcome warmth from the chilly up-island breeze. She mentioned that she was in the process of firing her trademark pottery soup bowls in striations of burnished reds, soft golds, and white mochas, the shades of the Vineyard's historic Gay Head Cliffs.

"It's been a long time, my friend," Winnie said.

Annie returned the smile. "Too long. California was stressful in some ways, but also exhilarating. Being able to walk on the beach or through the Huntington Gardens in January were wonderful treats."

Winnie nodded, waiting for more.

Taking a deep breath, Annie paused, then exhaled. "And now I'm home. Where everything's a mess." She realized she'd just quoted Lucy's text message.

And then the drama gushed out exactly as she hadn't wanted, as if an eave had split during a spring storm, and her words cascaded out too fast, too forceful, too many.

She told Winnie things she couldn't bear to tell anyone else—how she was angry about Abigail's illness, for Abigail, for Lucy, for Earl and Claire, and for herself. She told her about John's detachment, and how she'd accumulated an embarrassingly high amount of self-pity over the whole situation.

Throughout her rant, Winnie never, not once, injected a word. More surprisingly, Annie had not shed a tear, as if her anger had eclipsed the empathy she once had for others

When she was finished, they sat a moment longer before Winnie spoke.

"So," she said, her tone low and soothing, "I hope you know that everything you said is an accurate description of being human."

Annie sat with her hands folded, her gaze dropping to the colorful, handwoven rug that covered the packed-earth floor. She wondered if Winnie had been conferring with Murphy.

They talked a while longer about Abigail, about multiple sclerosis. About the difficulties Abigail might need to confront, and how she might want a strong support system. Just thinking about it was exhausting.

Annie fell silent for a moment, then said, "And there's more, Winnie. It's about Kevin." She spilled out that story, too, ending it with the coup de grâce that he insisted Jack Miller was not his father. "So I'm angry with Kevin, too. Because he still has a biological parent on planet earth, and it's like he doesn't want to believe it." She paused. She swallowed. "I'd give anything to be able to see my parents again."

"Wow," Winnie said. "What makes Kevin think it isn't him?"

So Annie filled her in on the rest, ending with Jack's claim that Donna had been in love with another man, something Donna had never told Kevin.

"And I feel guilty because that man was my father," she continued. "If I'd never been in the picture, Jack would not have left them. Which may be part of why Kevin's angry, too. Because Jack probably told him." After that, Annie was drained, spent.

Winnie shifted her bulk on the weathered chair. "You sure are burdened with a lot of guilt, my friend."

Looking back to Winnie's calming face, Annie forced a smile. "Which is why I drove up here today. Not only to see you, but also because I felt safe to share all these disasters with you. Which I knew if I didn't share soon, I'd explode."

Winnie pondered Annie's words. Then she said, "Kevin's situation might at least have a solution. When he said the man wasn't his father, did he believe it was someone posing as him?"

"I guess."

Winnie shrugged. "You met him. What do you think?"

"Kevin resembles him . . . mostly in their build and the way they walk. And Jack's face looked familiar to me." She asked herself, if she'd had no expectations, if she'd only seen a man—a stranger—would she still have thought he looked familiar? "I suppose it's possible that I thought I saw similarities because I wanted it to be Jack. For Kevin's sake. But why would a seventy-year-old man do that?"

"Money?"

Annie laughed. "Well, Kevin has none of that left."

"But you do. Or at least the perception that you do is out there in the world. You said he found out that you're a writer. Maybe he thought he'd found a benefactor."

On further thought, Annie shook her head. "No. I clearly remember when I saw Jack in the doorway, I instantly thought he was a dead ringer for Kevin. Besides, Winnie, a simple DNA test would provide the truth."

Winnie nodded slowly. "Yes, it would. But if I were you, I'd investigate the man a little more before you brought that up. You know things about him now. Maybe you can find more on the internet before you discount your brother's reaction."

Then she added, "Now, tell me more about California. Was it everything you hoped it would be?"

California. Good grief. Annie had barely touched on that, hadn't even mentioned the job offer or her decision. She'd save that for another time, when her brain cells weren't so crowded. Right now, she had something more important to do.

After prying herself from the safety of Winnie's world, Annie drove back to Edgartown, her mission to learn as much as possible about Jack Miller foremost on her mind. But when she arrived at the queue for the *On Time* . . . well, if she had a choice of running into anyone, she would not have picked her brother. But there was Kevin on the ferry, standing outside the captain's booth, watching Larry, who was at the helm. Or whatever it was called.

They were piloting the craft into the dock.

Annie jammed on her brakes. Then she cranked her wheels, drove a few feet, reversed, and repeated it all three times before succeeding in making a U-turn on narrow Daggett Street and pretending that she didn't know that it was one-way. If Kevin had watched her motor vehicle gymnastics and commented on them later, she'd make up a story about having forgotten something essential at the store. Not that she needed to worry about his commenting on anything.

Once out on North Water, she headed north toward the Harbor View Hotel, then meandered around the side streets, moving slowly, acting like a conscientious driver rather than an unbalanced woman who shouldn't be behind the wheel of a car. Checking her watch, she noticed it was almost one o'clock; she decided she could research Jack Miller as easily at the library as she could at home. Winnie was right: now that Annie knew more about him, an internet search might yield better results. Besides, a research trip had a more viable purpose than killing time until Kevin's shift ended, whenever that might be. So she headed toward the library, where she knew they offered access to in-depth databases and articles from newspaper morgues. Things she couldn't get on her computer or her phone.

Although the one library in Edgartown was open on Sundays during the summer, it was not summer yet.

"Grrr," she mumbled as she saw that the parking lot was empty and the lights in the building were turned off. She yanked the steering wheel, trying for another U-turn, but then stopped, turned off the ignition, and assessed her choices.

Then she saw that both the West Tisbury and Vineyard Haven libraries were open on Sundays year-round. She'd passed the West Tisbury one only minutes ago. Did she really want to do back in that direction, or should she drive all the way to Vineyard Haven?

Seriously? Murphy asked. *It takes, what, fifteen minutes from here? Remember how long it used to take us to drive from your house to Filene's Basement?*

Murphy was right. An hour or more slogging through city traffic—riding the gauntlet, they used to call it—was always worth the trip if they wanted a new dress or shoes or whatever.

Fixing her gaze on the red-brick, multiwindowed library wing that housed the children's department, Annie decided to gather her thoughts. She pulled out her notebook and jotted down some notes.

Jack Miller.
From: Yarmouth. And Vermont.
Age: 69–70.
Wife: Estelle. Died 2020ish?

Staring at the page, she knew it wasn't much to go on. But Google had performed wonders with fewer details.

She set down the book and pen and restarted the Jeep. But as she began to back out of the lot, she nearly collided with a pickup truck that was pulling in. A woman was behind the wheel; a pile of thick auburn hair was pinned loosely atop her head.

Annie stopped the Jeep and got out and approached the vehicle.

"Hey, Taylor," she said to her sister-in-law. "Fancy meeting you here. But it's closed. It's Sunday."

Taylor grimaced. "I forgot."

"Hi, Ammie," came a small voice from the back.

Shielding her eyes against the sun's glare, Annie saw Bella safely strapped into her child's seat.

"Bella, honey! You're with Grandma Taylor!" She hoped she didn't sound taken aback, but Taylor didn't often entertain the child. Typically she was engaged in her caretaking duties during the day, every day. Maybe that had changed while Annie was away. God knew, a lot of things had.

"Mommy's going to have a baby!" Bella cried a happy cry.

"I know! Isn't it wonderful?" Annie responded, trying to peek around the auburn mass to see Bella more clearly.

"She means now," Taylor said. "They think Francine's in labor. Jonas took her to the hospital."

Annie felt her face freeze.

"*Now?*"

Taylor glanced at her watch. "They left about forty minutes ago."

"Oh, God," Annie said. "I've got to get over there. Are you okay to watch Bella?"

"I would have been fine if the library was open. But, yes, I believe we can handle it, can't we, Little Miss?"

In the back seat, Bella giggled.

For some childish reason, Annie felt a pang of jealousy.

"Okay, I'll get over there and let you know what's happening." She fast-walked to the Jeep, then stopped and quickly spun around. "West Tisbury Library is open. So is Vineyard Haven." She waved, jumped back into her vehicle, and waited impatiently for Taylor to leave so that she could get the heck out of the lot and to the hospital in Oak Bluffs.

Chapter 24

It was a false alarm.

By the time Annie made it to the hospital, what had seemed to Francine like contractions had abruptly stopped.

"I feel like an idiot," Francine said from the bed in the emergency room.

Jonas had pulled up a chair and was sitting beside her, holding her hand.

"The doctor said it's not uncommon," Jonas told Annie. "Especially with the first baby." But whereas Francine looked tired, Jonas looked baffled.

"I'm sorry the news dragged you all the way here," Francine said.

"Nonsense. I was in Edgartown. I ran into your mother, Jonas. She told me you were here—actually, it was Bella who told me."

"Did she say, 'Mommy's going to have a baby'?" Jonas asked.

"Those were her exact words."

"In the past couple of days she's been saying that to everyone," Francine said with a grin. "This morning, I started to wonder if she has psychic powers."

Annie laughed. "Maybe. Or maybe she's just excited." She hoisted her pocketbook up onto her shoulder. "Are you going to stay here just in case?" she asked.

"Only for a couple of hours so I can rest. Apparently I'm not even close to having this kid." Her words were laced with sarcasm, but she wore a tender smile of disappointment.

"Come on, Frannie," Jonas said, "the doctor said you're fine, and not to forget that, technically, you're not due for almost another month."

She sighed. "Right."

Annie tried not to show concern. "I'm sure the doctor knows what he's talking about, honey." As badly as she wanted to ask Jonas if he wanted her to stay with Francine so he could leave, Annie knew better. Not only were they the ones about to become parents, but they also were right-and-proper (as Claire would say) husband and wife. Still, Annie had what she thought was a great idea.

"Hey," she said, "would you feel more at ease if you could stay on this side of Chappy for few days? John and the girls are in Plymouth. Even Restless is with them. I'm sure John wouldn't mind if you want to stay at the town house. Even though it doesn't sound like anything's going to happen anytime soon, being closer to the hospital might help you sleep better. What do you think?"

"Frannie?" Jonas asked.

Annie loved that he'd begun calling Francine by that nickname. Like the way Bella called Annie "Ammie." Nicknames shared between two people always seemed genuinely loving.

She realized that was something else she was going to miss if she took Greg up on his offer.

But Francine shook her head. "No. But thanks, Annie. I don't want to take over their space, especially now. They might want to come back on the spur of the moment, which would be awkward. Besides, Taylor told me she's delivered nine babies in her career as an EMT when they couldn't get off Chappy fast enough."

"Okay, but think of that as a plan B. And remember you can always change your mind." She had no idea how John would feel about it, but right then, Annie didn't care. "In the meantime, if you need anything, let me know, okay? I'll be in the area a while." She wasn't going to tell them that she was avoiding Kevin or that she intended to dig up as much information as she could on his long-lost father.

They said their good-byes and Annie went out to the parking lot, partly sad for Francine because she was so eager yet uncomfortable, and partly relieved, because Annie didn't think she'd be able to focus on the new baby, what with everything else bouncing around inside her, as if she were the one almost ready to give birth.

Rationalizing that, because it was practically a straight shot with far less traffic (meaning almost none), Taylor would have chosen to drive due west from Edgartown and bring Bella to the West Tisbury Library, Annie guided the Jeep over the drawbridge and into Vineyard Haven. She passed the small shops tightly lining both sides of Main Street, and that time she enjoyed going slowly and checking out the storefronts that were in the midst of being painted, complete with shiny new shingles and sparkling windows. It was the delightful spring dance of getting ready for tourist season.

Up the small hill, the shops were replaced by equally close-set homes, some of which were more than a century old. When Annie reached the library, she turned onto the side street to park. Which was where she saw Taylor's pickup squeezed into a spot.

Annie stopped and cursed under her breath. She didn't

feel like driving all the way to West Tisbury. So she decided to go home. If Kevin chose not to speak to her, that was his problem, not hers.

Still, she went the back way, because it would take longer. Maybe by the time she reached the ferry, her brother would be off duty.

Annie hadn't needed to worry. By the time she reached the Chappy ferry, Captain Larry had turned "the reins," as Kevin called them, over to Joe Nelson. And Kevin was nowhere in sight.

She drove the rest of the way to the Inn in peace, grateful that when she arrived, though a few vehicles were in the lot, Kevin's pickup wasn't one of them. But nor did the vehicles look like any that belonged to the tenants. Wanting at least to show her face to whomever might be around, she went into the big kitchen before going down the small slope to her cottage.

No one was there.

She walked into the great room; no one was there, either. The massive room with the soaring ceiling, enormous stone fireplace, dining room on one end, and living space on the other felt hollow. Empty. Abandoned, the way that Kevin felt when he'd been four years old; the way he apparently still felt. Perhaps the vehicles in the lot belonged to off-season tourists who'd parked there to walk along the beach. Word might have spread that if nonpaying guests used the path that led down to the water, the owners of the Vineyard Inn would turn a neighborly *blind eye*—a wonderful old term that Annie once learned had been coined in the late seventeenth century.

Moving through the great room, she decided that, as long as she was there, she should go to the reception area and check on any added upcoming summer rentals. But as she reached the antique desk where the computer was stored, she heard soft boom-boom sounds coming from the media room. Maybe a couple of the tenants were having a rousing video game match. Annie loved it when one of them took advantage of the amenities.

Intending to step inside and offer a simple hello, she walked past the reading room toward the sound. But the figure seated in the special gamer's chair wasn't one of the tenants. Even from behind, she could tell that it was Rex.

She howled.

He lifted his hands from the controls, rotated in the chair, and gave Annie a mortified smile.

"You caught me," he said.

"I wouldn't have known you were here if you'd put on the headphones."

"I only planned to be here a couple of minutes." He stood up and stretched his *Tyrannosaurus rex* body.

"How'd that work out?"

He yawned and glanced at his watch. "I've been here over an hour."

"Wow. You must have needed a break."

"I wish. It was more like I need something constructive to do. I appreciate that you're letting me help out here, but I need a job. Something that involves more of my brain."

"And your talents," Annie said. "No word on the place on South Water?"

"Nope."

She nodded. "Stay positive."

He turned off the electronics. "They opened for the season last week, just in time for the Easter crowd. I almost went to check it out, but I'm not big on dining alone. Unless it's in my own place." He tried to smile again, but that time was not successful.

"Are they open tonight?"

"Yup. Weekends only until Memorial Day."

"If you're free tonight, I'd be happy to go with you," Annie said, surprising herself. "John's off island, Francine will probably be resting, and my brother isn't speaking to me. Frankly, I could use a night out with good conversation and no agenda."

"Seriously?"

"Sure. It'll do us both good. My treat." And she meant what she'd said; she had no agenda.

He looked down at his jeans and denim shirt. "Guess I'd better change out of my designer chef's outfit. What time?"

"Seven?" It seemed to have become the go-to dinner time for the mismatched family she belonged to.

"Sure. I'll meet you here at quarter till." He rotated the chair back to the game. "Which gives me plenty of time to get to the next level."

Annie laughed again, then said, "Wait. I noticed a couple of strange vehicles in our lot. Any idea whose they are?"

"Town planners. They're in the meadow, checking out the land where you want the new outbuilding to go."

She thanked him but didn't mention that the outbuilding was the doing of Kevin and Jonas, not hers. After all, she didn't know now if she'd ever use it, if she'd ever make soap again.

Annie spent the rest of the afternoon feeling oddly recharged. Rather than waste time scavenger-hunting for information on Jack Miller, she decided her energy would be better spent working on her manuscript. Whether or not Greg accepted Annie's counterproposal, it would please Trish, her editor, to know that Annie wouldn't drop the ball on her novel-writing career—at least, not yet. Louise and Trish had been a dynamic duo from the beginning of Annie's career, without whom her books no doubt would never have achieved as much notoriety. Or been as lucrative. She made a quick note to contact MV Community Services and let them know that a check would arrive soon. No matter what happened with her California decision, she'd continue to honor her commitment to help Vineyard families. At least for a while.

Aware that her wardrobe would, indeed, need a major reset if she left the island, she dressed in plain black pants, her lone pair of dress shoes, and a pale blue cable-knit camisole and matching cardigan that she'd bought on a rare whim on Rodeo Drive. The only jewelry she added was a pair of silver earrings, though she still wore the platinum, three-diamond engagement ring that she wasn't yet ready to remove. If she ran into any of John's friends, she didn't want to stir up questions or turmoil. It was too soon for that.

At fifteen minutes before seven, Rex knocked on her door.

"You look like a dashing restaurant entrepreneur," Annie said, acknowledging his white shirt, burgundy tie, and black pants.

"Good. Then no one on the island will recognize me."

So far, the evening seemed to have the makings of good fun.

Because his old, rusty truck (he'd bought it for next to nothing and said it was worth every cent he paid) was in the shop, he borrowed Kevin's pickup; Rex told him he had plans in Edgartown but did not mention Annie. "I didn't want him to think I was sucking up to the boss."

She laughed a little nervously. If her brother learned that she and Rex were dining out together, he might jump to far-fetched conclusions. But at least it meant he wouldn't be working at the ferry and was home.

Eight minutes later, they arrived at the Lord James, which was about one-third full. It was a lovely space, with windows overlooking the harbor, a reflection of the melon-colored sunset illuminating the banks of Chappaquiddick on the opposite side. The restaurant was on the south, not the north, side of the *On Time*, so they couldn't see the Inn from there. Thankfully, Francine had texted a couple of hours before to say that she and Jonas were home, so someone was on the property in case of an emergency. She didn't note that the emergency might be hers, which reassured Annie that Francine wasn't anxious about what lay ahead for her.

"It's a few weeks early for the best stripers," Rex told Annie after they'd perused the menu. "If you want fish, I recommend the halibut or the cod."

She closed her menu and set it down. "I shall defer to a professional chef to choose something wonderful. I'm not fussy."

"Ah!" He rubbed his bald head as if feigning frustration. "The choices could use some updating. Right now, they're all boring, so it's tough to pick." Then he set his forehead in concentration. After a few moments, he selected grilled cod with onion butter for Annie and pan-seared halibut for himself. "It's easier to tell the quality of the restaurant if the food isn't disguised with too many sauces."

Naturally, he was a pure foodie, a perfectionist.

She waited until their wine arrived before settling back in her chair and asking what he thought of the décor. With its dark wood walls and furnishings, and oil paintings of clipper ships on the walls, it was a nicely done re-creation of how Annie imagined the Vineyard had looked in the past.

"Like the menu," he commented, "it's out of date. There's a way to have island charm without looking like it was decorated by a bunch of old guys."

She smiled. "Such as?"

"First, I'd capitalize on the view. The way you've done at the Inn. They've got three walls with harbor views here. They need to make it work for them! Ceiling-to-floor windows. A major expanse of the water so patrons will feel like they own one of those boats. Or yachts, depending on which month it is."

Annie couldn't disagree.

"And I'd do the walls in light colors. Maybe not white, but a soft green or blue, even creamy sand, something that would blend with the outside. And comfortable chairs, for God's sake. If you want patrons to spend a couple of hours here, you shouldn't give them wooden chairs without upholstering the seats. It's easy enough to have some kind of faux leather that's durable and easy to clean. And padded."

Then he asked Annie if she'd had a favorite restaurant when she'd lived in Boston. And, for over an hour, while enjoying their dinners, they talked about food and restaurants and how to make sure patrons had a reason to return.

"So," Annie said when she'd nearly cleaned her plate, "do you want to reverse your initial impression about the food?"

Rex wiped his mouth with his napkin. "Partly, yes. The food was well cooked; the presentation was excellent. The chef could have been a little more creative, but I'd hire him as a sous. Which he might be, anyway, once the season starts. All in all, though, a decent job." He laughed. "It feels strange to be reviewing a restaurant where my worst criticism has to do with the décor."

"Sounds like you're ready to buy. To make it your own. With those walls of windows."

He drained his wineglass. "Yeah, it would be nice. But my dad would have called it a pipe dream."

"Seriously? But you've proved yourself, Rex. And it's not like you're twentysomething anymore."

He chortled. "Tell me about it. But the truth is, I don't have enough capital. If I rented out the cabin for the summer, maybe I could convince Taylor and Kevin to let me live at their house until things were up and running. For all I know, there's an apartment upstairs here, which would work nicely." He turned his wineglass in small circles, as if swirling a newly poured vintage. "I could scrape together enough for a down payment if the bank would negotiate with me. But . . . " His voice trailed off as he set the glass on the table and huffed. "No. It's a pipe dream because I don't have the money. And no way to earn enough unless I can buy a restaurant. One of life's great dichotomies, right? You need money to make money."

Annie glanced around the room. It wasn't hard to imagine what Rex had envisioned. "It sounds like you need an investor," she said.

"Or another line of work." He pushed back his chair. "Besides, I'd be lucky to get a license for a food truck. Forget about one to sell alcohol again, especially in a richy-rich tourist place like this where it would be essential in summer." He nodded toward her empty plate. "Do you want dessert?"

"I'm afraid the sous-chef filled me up."

"Me, too." His smile was smaller than before. "Time to get back to reality. But I enjoyed this evening, Annie. Thanks for suggesting it."

She didn't know if he'd regret it later, if she'd prodded him to risk sharing a dream that he wouldn't be able to attain.

At least she'd been able to feel almost normal again, not like a woman who was buying time, waiting to see if her prince would ever ride back into town.

With both Kevin's and Rex's dilemmas logjamming her thoughts, trying, but not quite succeeding, to smother her anguish about John and Abigail, Annie could not get to sleep. So she got out of bed and wrapped her robe around her. While a mug of tea was brewing, she took a cinnamon bun out of the freezer, nuked it, then booted up her computer. Her senses might not be alert enough to go back to her writing, but maybe it was a good time to learn something about Kevin's father.

She glanced at the notebook she'd used in the library parking lot. Then she typed his name in Google's lovely search engine, followed by his age and Yarmouth, MA.

Nothing. Only a *Did you mean Jack Miller Yarmouth Port MA?*

She was certain he'd said Yarmouth. And as far as Annie knew, there were several Yarmouths: South, West, Port, and plain old Yarmouth—all of which were sprinkled from Cape Cod Bay on the north side to Nantucket Sound on the south. Colonial New England had been, on occasion, mapped out in a questionable way.

She checked Yarmouth Port anyway. But the Jack Miller there was only forty-seven. Which not only wouldn't be him, but couldn't be his son, either. For one thing, it would have made him older than Kevin. And Jack had clearly said his *daughter* was the one on the Cape, along with her family.

Deleting Yarmouth, Annie typed in "Vermont," where he'd lived when he and Estelle had been married. But, according to Google, over thirty million Jack Millers were there. Which must have been a technological miracle, as there weren't quite 650,000 people in the whole state.

She began to scroll the millions of options when she had a better idea. One she should have thought of first. She typed in *Estelle Miller. Vermont. Obit.*

"Ha!" she said when a short string of obituaries surfaced.

The first one was dated two years earlier. So she opened it quickly.

Estelle Mae Miller, daughter of the late . . .

Annie skipped the first part.

. . . widow of Captain Ralph Jordan, USMC, killed in action during the Gulf War; beloved wife of Benjamin Miller of this town . . .

"What?" Annie shrieked. Who the heck was Benjamin Miller? Was it possible that his nickname was Jack? Or was it a typo? It didn't seem likely, yet the obituary did seem to be about Jack's wife, Estelle. Essie, he had called her.

Annie continued to read.

. . . mother of seven children . . .

It didn't say which ones had belonged to Captain Ralph and which ones were Benjamin's.

But it did feel absurd. Yet she must have been Jack's wife. Everything but the first name of the husband who'd survived her seemed to fit.

Scanning through the children's list, Annie thought she might find the name of the daughter who lived on the Cape. But the article didn't note where the children lived. Then Annie remembered Jack said he and Essie had "a son and a daughter"—in that order. So there was a good chance the son had come first, followed by the daughter, which would mean she was the younger of the two, and the youngest of the seven kids. So her name would be the last one mentioned.

Donna Lee Chapman.

Annie tried to gulp but suddenly she couldn't swallow. *Donna.* Had he named his daughter after the woman he'd claimed to love so much? Annie and Kevin's mother? Had he married another woman though he still loved the first? Which would have been weirdly similar to what Donna had done?

She sat there for a while, staring at the screen, hesitating to make another move, as if finding Donna Lee Chapman would be encroaching even more on Kevin's personal life. And yet Annie couldn't help herself. After all, Donna Lee wasn't exactly Kevin's sister. She was his *half* sister, just as Annie was.

But who the heck was Benjamin?

Chapter 25

After a few more minutes in a state of near catatonia, Annie felt ready to continue. So she did an in-depth search for Donna Lee.

According to the first article she found, Donna Lee Chapman, indeed, had become a Cape Cod resident, as Jack had said. She'd married a man named Bruce and had three children, also as Jack claimed. She'd also been arrested for possession of a Class A substance. Twice. He hadn't mentioned that.

Annie couldn't find a follow-up account of conviction or incarceration, but there was an obituary.

An obituary?

Her heart beat a little faster.

She held her breath.

And clicked on the obit.

Donna Lee (Miller) Chapman, age thirty-six, daughter of Benjamin—there was that name again—Miller and the late Estelle Miller of Vermont. No cause of death was listed. That was a year and a half ago. After her mother had died.

"Oh, God, Murphy," Annie whispered. "Did you see this?"

Yup. I've been reading over your shoulder now. Very sad.

"No kidding. A young mother . . . with three probably small kids. Very sad for sure."

The world has gotten awfully strange since I left.

Annie didn't have the time to get into a discussion about that.

"Hey. Wait," she said instead. "Do you know if Jack is really Kevin's father?"

No. As I've told you before, they don't let me in on everything.

Annie looked around the room, hoping no one had come in and was listening to her one-sided conversation. When she was certain she was alone (in the physical sense, anyway), she asked, "Well . . . isn't there someone you can ask?"

I haven't been here long enough. Besides, I can't be sure, but I might still be on probation.

"But . . ."

No buts. Keep digging around. First, though, go back to bed.

Annie was convinced that her best friend loved to irritate her.

Before doing as she was told, Annie had one more search in mind: she Googled the name Bruce Chapman in Yarmouth. The only mentions were in Donna Lee's obituary and a veterinarian in Hyannis, whose tiny photo on the website made him look as old as Earl. Which didn't seem right. And Annie didn't know the names of the kids, so she couldn't look them up on social media.

It felt like a dead end.

So she went to bed wondering what in God's name was happening. Where on earth Bruce Chapman was. Where the children were. And why on earth Kevin's father—if he was Kevin's father—had lied. Because it didn't seem plausible that a name like Jack was a nickname for Benjamin.

Or was Kevin right—that the man who she'd thought resembled her brother wasn't his father at all? Could Benjamin Miller have had a brother? If that was the case, why wouldn't Jack call himself Benjamin? Ben? Benny?

But a bigger question was, if Jack was an imposter looking for money, weren't there easier ways today for people to make money?

"Argh," she said to herself that time. "Do what Murphy said and go to bed."

So she did.

Monday morning, Annie was surprised that she'd slept through the night. She'd dreamed that John had called, that he'd told her Abigail had been misdiagnosed, that she would be fine, and they'd be home on the noon boat. In her dream she knew that her world would start revolving in the right direction again, and she'd be saved from calling Greg and making what might be a huge mistake.

But even in the middle of the dream, she sensed it wasn't real. Still, she felt heartbroken when she woke up.

She showered and dressed, tossing on a white fleece and jeans, hoping to ward off the chill of the rainy morning that was capped by a thick gray sky, a harbinger of an ugly, damp day.

Skipping breakfast at the Inn again, she made tea, sat down at her computer, turned on the desk lamp, and stared at the screen. She was done googling people she didn't know. And she wasn't in the mood to be creative. Most of all, it was too early in L.A. to call Greg. So she logged in to online banking, checked her account balance, and saw that the funds from Louise had been deposited. She started to forward the money to Martha's Vineyard Community Services, then stopped. A trip to their office in Oak Bluffs might offer a happy diversion. And maybe she could learn more about how her contribution was going to help, which might provide a needed poke for her to make the call to Greg—a call that could wind up generating more money than Annie needed. Her dad once said that the best way to conquer the blues was to reach out and help a stranger. Which would be great, because, right then, Annie did not feel able to help anyone she knew and loved.

Sooner or later, she supposed it was bound to happen: Kevin was at the *On Time,* working alongside Captain Larry. Thanks to the rain, Annie kept the windows up and merely gave him a quick wave. She hoped he couldn't read her expression; he might be able to tell that now she was the one who didn't want to talk with him. Not until she knew more about Jack, though right now, she had no idea how that was going to happen.

Thank God, it wasn't long before she was off the little ferry and made it to MV Community Services. The environment was friendly and camplike, with a cluster of small, one- and two-story, gray-shingled buildings nestled among pine trees and white birches, and connected by wooden walkways, worn pathways, and wheelchair ramps. Annie parked the Jeep, pulled up the hood of her rain jacket, and darted inside to the development office.

A young woman sat behind a desk; she had smooth, dark skin that hinted of a Latina-European blend, and she wore a pretty pink sweater that accentuated her jet-black hair and chestnut-colored eyes. She reminded Annie a little of Francine.

"Good morning," Annie said. "I'd like to speak with the development officer. If possible."

The young woman introduced herself as Brenda. She glanced at the phone on her desk and got up. She was tall; she stood eye to eye with Annie, who was a head taller than petite Francine.

"I'm sorry, but Barbara just took a phone call. She might not be too long, but can someone else help you?"

Annie smiled. "I'll wait."

"Are you Annie Sutton?" Brenda called after her. "The writer?"

"Guilty."

Brenda laughed. "Guilty. What a perfect a word for a mystery author to say."

With a quick blink, Annie said with a laugh, "You're very perceptive. I honestly never thought of that."

"Well, it's perfect. And I've read all of your books."

It was always difficult to know how to respond to a fan, so Annie was grateful when the office phone rang and Brenda excused herself. Taking a look around, Annie spotted a brochure from a small table; a quick scan showed a list of services that the agency provided. Aside from the operation of the fabulous Chicken Alley Thrift Shop in Vineyard Haven, Annie hadn't known the depth of what the organization offered, or that it provided support services for all ages and situations, from seniors and veterans to youth and families, with programs and one-on-one assistance available island-wide. Her father would have approved.

When Annie was in the fourth grade, her dad taught her the value of giving. On the Sunday night before Christmas, she went with him on his favorite mission to give anonymous gifts to their Boston neighbors in need. The act was in conjunction with a local charity, but Annie knew her dad slipped extra goodies into each sack—coloring books, crayons, and small toys for kids; oranges and cheese and summer sausages for the families; new white socks and warm mittens for all. He even brought a few new clothes for a boy in Annie's class. But it wasn't until Annie moved to the Vineyard that she realized the importance of giving. Which was why, when she'd learned that "Hollywood" money would be forthcoming, she set up a private foundation and named it the George Sutton Foundation. It would never be able to compete with the Rockefellers or the Fords or Bill and Melinda Gates, but that wasn't the point. It was her small way of helping, and of honoring the memory of her dad.

"Ms. Sutton?"

Setting down the brochure, Annie smiled.

"Barbara?" she asked to a woman now standing before her. "Please, call me Annie." Then, filled with her dad's never-fading love, she followed the woman into the development office.

Funny, Annie thought, as she dodged the teeming rain and climbed back into her Jeep, but George Sutton had been right. Finding ways to help strangers in need was a wonderful way to stop thinking about oneself.

Before Annie left, Barbara had asked if she'd be willing to have a photo taken with their CEO.

"We have many donors who don't want the publicity, but for those who are willing, it helps bring attention to our cause," she said.

Though Annie didn't usually like giving people a window into her personal life, if it helped them gain more exposure to their needs, she was all for it. Besides, it appeared that no matter what she did or did not do, if anyone wanted to find her, or just find out about her, these days they easily could. Jack Miller had already proved that.

She agreed, and they were quickly joined by the CEO, who also was a woman.

No one seemed to mind Annie's fleece-and-jeans attire.

"It helps prove that you're regular people," the CEO said. "One of us."

They posed in the reception room in front of a nice grouping of pictures of island social gatherings. Barbara said they typically took donor photos outside, but the weather was definitely not cooperating. Then, holding up her phone, she snapped a quick image. Nothing fancy. Which also felt right to Annie.

She drove back to Edgartown with a smile, despite the fact that, in addition to the rain, the wind was doing its typical swirl around the perimeter of the island, as if the land were the center of a pinwheel, powered by an unending circular motion. When Annie first moved there, she'd been startled by the squalls and gusts and breezes. Now she tended not to notice them as much. Especially when there was something more important on her mind, like now, when she'd just handed over a check for five figures and told Barbara she hoped there would be more to come. They agreed that the money would go to whatever services currently needed it the most.

Buoyed by unexpected, happy emotions that, after many years of personal struggle, she was now able to give something to others, Annie didn't head toward the *On Time* but instead went down Summer Street. Which led directly to John's. It felt like a good time to believe in their future, to remember that he really existed, that he was still in her life, and she in his. That this was only a rough patch that they could overcome at some point. Together.

Then she remembered she had to call Greg.

With the three-hour time difference, he could wait.

The town house was, of course, deserted. The windows were dark, the drapes were pulled; it was as if when the people inside had left, they knew they might not return for a long while. The rocking chairs were missing from the porch; the window boxes showed only a few green leaves of daffodils, with no yellow blooms. Maybe Lucy hadn't watered them since they'd sprouted, which must have been around the time Abigail had begun sleeping so much.

Pulling into the driveway, Annie parked behind Abigail's little VW Beetle. She stared at the yellow, igloo-like roof of the car. Then, without warning, Annie's mood slid into despair. It no longer seemed to matter how many people her windfall would help or that her dad would have been proud of her charitable commitment. Not when she couldn't help the ones she loved. Especially Abigail. Unless Abigail wanted to come back and take advantage of the island's caring services, which were designed to protect their own.

"Reality in a nutshell," the counselor had said. "When someone's life changes, we try to make the adjustment a little easier."

Annie looked back at the lonely town house and realized then that she'd been crying.

Sometimes even the bleakest things can change for the better, Murphy suddenly said. *But it's hard to see the good until it gets around to showing up.*

The thought was appreciated.

Wiping her tears, Annie whispered a small good-bye to the town house. Then she backed out to the street and went down the hill to the *On Time,* forgetting that Kevin might still be there. Which he was.

She pulled onto the ferry and he set the chocks under her tires. Then he knocked on the driver's-side window.

Annie lowered it and handed him her coupon book.

He tore one off, returned it, and unexpectedly bent to look her in the eyes.

"I thought you'd want to know that Earl and Claire are going to Plymouth tomorrow morning," he said. "Claire wants to see Abigail. I'm going to take them, so Earl doesn't have to drive. I'm not sure how long we'll be gone."

That seemed to be all he wanted to say.

Annie thanked him for letting her know. She was about to ask if they could talk later that day, but he walked away to tend to a truck behind her that was boarding.

Chapter 26

For a million reasons, Annie wanted to scream. Instead, as soon as she made it back to the Inn, she marched through the relentless storm and went to check on Francine. It was a sure way to be cheered up.

"Ammie!" Bella greeted her at the front door.

Hanging her wet jacket from the doorknob, Annie finger-combed her hair, then stooped down to fluff Bella's shining curls. "Hi, sweetie," she said, and planted butterfly kisses up Bella's arm.

The little girl giggled.

"Where's Mommy?"

"Sweeping."

"I'm not *sweep*ing," Francine announced from across the room. "I was *sleep*ing."

"Sorry," Annie said with a little laugh. "I'm just checking to see how you're doing."

Francine's pixie face surfaced above the opposite side of a sofa cushion. "Thanks. And you didn't disturb me. It's really, really hard to sleep when you have a well-meaning caregiver buzzing around," she said, gesturing toward the four-year-old.

"Mommy! I'm your nurse! Wemember? At the hospital I learned how to fwuff your pillows so you feel better?"

"And you are doing a wonderful job." After a couple of tries, Francine negotiated with her body to sit up. She let out a long sigh and rubbed her belly. "I was really hoping it had been time. I'm so tired of hauling this critter around."

"I'm afraid you'll still be doing that after he—or she—is born."

"At least I can put him—or her—in the crib or do a hand-off to Jonas and catch a break." She waddled over and offered Annie tea.

"No, thanks. But while I'm here, maybe your nurse could use my assistance?"

"Bella?" Francine asked. "Can Annie help you do something?"

The little girl scratched her head as if she'd seen someone do that when pondering.

"Can you paint pictures?" she asked Annie.

Annie laughed. "Not nice ones. That's your daddy's job." Jonas was, of course, "Daddy" to Francine, just as Francine was "Mommy." Someday, Bella would be told the circuitous truth.

"He's not quite finished with the murals," Francine said. "Featherstone asked him to teach a watercolor class for a couple of weeks. The timing is lousy, but I thought he should take advantage of being around other people. Who knows how long we'll be cooped up in a few weeks?"

Annie nodded. "You look like you're the one who could use tea."

Francine nodded. "Something herbal without caffeine? In the cabinet to the left of the sink?"

Bella pattered behind Annie's footsteps into the kitchen area.

Walking no more than eighteen or twenty feet to the table, Francine sat down and panted as if she'd run a marathon. "I've been trying to get the nursery finished. I still have no clue what I'm doing."

"Have you checked online?"

"About a million websites. 'How to prepare for your baby.' 'What you need to do before baby arrives.' 'Must-haves for baby.' It's enough to bring on false labor. Oh, wait. I already had that."

Annie laughed. "Did you talk with Claire?" A pang of guilt reminded her that she hadn't mentioned Francine's woes to Winnie or asked for baby advice.

"I did. She was a big help, but I'm still not sure what I'm doing." She gave a half smile. "As wonderful as your mother-in-law is, it's been a long time since she had a baby."

Annie didn't mention that Claire wasn't yet her mother-in-law, because that would make her think about John, and she didn't want to do that again. Nor did she want to think about when Abigail and Lucy had been babies. Yanking off the top of a tea tin, she wasn't sure how to deflect Francine. Especially since Annie had been the one to bring up Claire's name.

"She told me she helped set up the nursery for Abigail," Francine continued. "But by the time Lucy came along, things between her and Jenn had changed . . . and, oh, God, Annie. I'm sorry. That was the last thing I should have brought up, right?"

Shaking her head, Annie said, "No, honey, it's fine. Do you know that Kevin's taking Earl and Claire to Plymouth?"

Francine bit her lip. "No."

"I think they'll feel better once they've seen Abigail. They've both been so worried."

Bella scrambled up onto Francine's crowded lap; Francine

put an arm around her to keep her from falling. "I can't imagine what all of them are going through."

"Neither can I." Then Annie decided there must be happier things to talk about. "Hey, I had dinner with Rex last night," she announced a little too loudly.

Francine blinked. "Seriously? Like a date?"

Annie let out a laugh. "Hardly! He's been working hard. I wanted to treat him to a meal. If I were half the cook he was—or half the cook anyone was—I would have cooked for him. But we went to the Lord James in Edgartown."

Francine whistled. "Fancy. Are you sure it wasn't a date?"

Picking up a tea bag, Annie pretended to toss it at her. "Yes, I am sure. We talked about his future plans. He'd like to open a restaurant, you know."

"Yeah, he told me. I hope he waits until off-season."

"Well," Annie said, "it might not happen at all. But it would be a big investment for him to get the kind of place he wants. And then there's all that licensing nonsense."

"To sell booze?"

"Yes."

"I learned about that in my restaurant management class. The professor said it's often the trickiest part of opening a new establishment, because sometimes it's based on who you know and where you want to open. That kind of stupid stuff. But he also said if a buyer takes on an existing place and the license is part of the deal, it makes things easier. Rex knows enough people on the island . . . doesn't he? He grew up here, right? Well, he might get it done even faster if he looks for one for sale. Unless . . ."—Francine scrunched her eyes, trying to look sinister—"unless our Rex has been a bad boy. According to my professor, that sort of thing takes the cards off the table." She paused, then offered a little smirk. "Was he a bad boy last night?"

"Francine! Stop!"

"Fwancine! Top!" Bella echoed.

Francine laughed. "Sorry. I'm in a weird mood today. Hormones, probably. But, kidding aside, didn't I hear that he wasn't the most likable kid when he was growing up?"

"That was ages ago, honey, and I don't think it amounted to much. And *no*, he was not a 'bad boy' last night. It was business." She handed her a mug full of tea. "Sheesh. I can't wait for your baby to come so you'll get back to being your rational self."

"Don't blame everything on him," Francine said, patting her belly.

"Did you say *him*? As in the baby? As in it's a *boy*?" Annie couldn't help teasing her back.

"Did I say that out loud?"

Then Annie realized it had not been a joke. Tears sprang to her eyes, and she raced around the counter to give Francine a hug. Then Bella joined in, squealing in a singsong voice, "Oh, boy! Oh, boy!"

Annie felt happy again, the brief intermission her senses had taken in John's driveway now shoved far back in her mind, where they belonged.

After promising not to tell what Francine had (intentionally?) let slip to "a single living soul" (especially Jonas, who thought it might be bad luck to reveal the gender secret), Annie pulled on her still-wet jacket, left Francine, Bella, and the almost baby boy, and crossed the puddle-soaked grass toward her home, smiling all the way. A boy! A nice little brother for Bella, the way Kevin was Annie's. They probably would squabble over meaningless things once in a while, the way Annie and Kevin did—well, until now. But "now" wasn't so meaningless. The thought of which made her vow to stop the nonsense as soon as he came back from Plymouth.

And how she wished she could help Francine with the planning. But Annie knew less about babies than Claire did. Or less than Francine, who, except for the couple of weeks that Bella had been with Annie, had figured it out all by herself. And done it nicely.

Stepping into her cottage and sliding out of her rain jacket again, Annie decided it was sweet that Francine had told her it was going to be a boy. If they hadn't been talking about Rex . . . and if Francine hadn't brought up his "bad *boy*" reputation, Annie might not have known until ahead of time.

Her thoughts flipped back to Rex.

Bad boy, indeed. Last night, Rex had been everything but. Which was good, because Annie didn't know what she would have done if things had gone otherwise. The fact that they were becoming friends was plenty enough for her. And he had a girlfriend, anyway. What was her name again?

Then, from out of nowhere—*Nowhere? Really?* Murphy seemed to say—Annie came up with an idea that people whose brains weren't as clogged as hers might have landed on sooner.

It was a great idea. She thought.

Annie liked Rex. He was a nice man, doing his best to reinvent his life. She was glad that her first impression of him—a tough, mysterious, sizable, and scary guy who seemed to enjoy hanging out in the darkness—had been wrong. And, in spite of Francine's playful suggestion, he must not have been a bad boy when he'd been in Boston because he'd owned a multi-starred restaurant that served liquor. As for when he'd been a Vineyard boy, well, chasing squirrels to steal their acorns hardly would have warranted a rap sheet.

Which was why, now that Annie had delivered the check to MV Community Services, and Francine had unknowingly shown her that reasons to be joyful really could be around any corner, Annie wanted to talk to Rex again. The idea that she'd come up with could help his dream take root and could give her another positive project to pack into her life. And it might offer a way to keep her island family in her future, no matter where she lived.

Annie didn't know if John would approve; it only mattered that she did. Besides, John had left her out of decisions she thought he should have shared . . . Wait, she commanded herself. Do not go there again.

My sentiments exactly, Murphy chimed in.

With a chuckle and swagger, Annie snatched a dry jacket from the closet, bolted back out the door, and trudged through the rain up to the Inn.

"There you are."

Having shaken off the raindrops, Annie had dumped her jacket in the laundry room and found Rex back in his familiar denim shirt, this time wearing rubber gloves and holding a bottle of disinfectant. He was cleaning the lavatory on the main floor at the Inn.

"Yup, here I am. Doing what most women would love to see me doing."

Annie had nearly forgotten she'd offered to do some of the unpopular chores with the cleaners on a lighter schedule. She silently swore to change that, starting tomorrow.

"Put the bottle down and peel off those gloves. I'll meet you in the reading room." She spun around and no doubt left him puzzled.

Then she stopped at the reception desk, plucked a pen and a notepad that was inscribed with the Vineyard Inn logo, then moved into the reading room. She pulled out both chairs at the table and noted that they were amply padded, which Rex must have approved of when he'd first seen the room.

She sat in one chair and clicked the pen a few times.

He arrived in less than a minute, accompanied by a faint aroma of bleach.

"Sit," she said, nodding to the chair across from her.

He sat.

"I feel like I've been sent to the principal's office," he said.

"You've had experience with that, have you?"

He laughed. "Some. Yes."

She smiled. "Not this time." She liked that he had the ability to laugh at himself, at his past mistakes. It had taken years for her to learn how to do that.

"I have a proposition for you."

His eyebrows shot up. "Oh, my. What will Detective Sergeant Lyons think of that?"

Shaking her head, she rolled her eyes the way that Lucy often did. "The detective sergeant will get over it. It's not that kind of proposition. But I'm serious about this, Rex. It's about your future."

He paused, his demeanor transmuting from that of a mischievous kid to one of a somber adult.

"What about it?"

"The Lord James has a great reputation and you couldn't find a better location. I'd like to invest in it with you. You said you could scrape together a down payment. I'd like to match whatever you can come up with. And maybe add more if it would make the difference between a yea or nay from the bank. All above board, Rex. Perfectly legal. We'll draw up documents. I'll be an investor, nothing more. If you want to buy me out at some point and are able to, that would be fine."

He stared at her as if he'd never seen her, as if she were a total stranger. It reminded Annie of the old TV show her dad often mentioned, where a guy named Michael Anthony showed up at a seemingly random person's door and handed over a check for a million dollars.

"I'm serious, Rex. You're an incredible chef and a native islander. Last night I could envision everything you talked about, from the way you'd renovate the place to the way you'd have it decorated and mostly that you'd update the food selections. I don't know much about the restaurant business, but when I was married to my second husband, we traveled a lot and ate in a lot of places. He was in the financial business—sort of—so we usually ate in top-of-the-line establishments." She didn't add that he had been a jerk with a penchant for a flamboyant lifestyle. Or that she'd willingly worn blinders.

She clicked her pen again.

"Jesus, Annie," Rex said.

"Hey," she said, trying to take the edge off, "we're family, right? My half brother is married to your sister. I have no idea how that plays out on genealogy charts, like maybe you're my half brother-in-law or something. And I'm now in a position to have more money than I probably deserve, just because streaming services are taking advantage of the current wave of people who crave new series in order to binge lots of episodes when they have time." She ran a hand through her hair again. It was still damp. "And I have no idea why I just explained all that when you probably already know. Anyway, please think about it. I've decided to give away a lot of what I'm being paid to charity. But I also want to invest in a worthy business. And I would consider your restaurant more than worthy." She hadn't thought about the "investing" aspect until now, but Rex didn't need to know that.

He rubbed his face with his hands. Annie hoped he didn't have traces of bleach on them.

"Annie," he said softly, "you have no idea how much I appreciate your offer. But I can't accept it. I'm sorry." He pushed back the chair and stood.

She jumped up from her chair and grabbed his wrist without intending to. "Rex. Please . . . this is not the time to play a 'macho man' role. The truth is, I'm not even sure how much longer I'll be a year-round resident. But please don't tell anyone I said that. Maybe helping you get situated is one more way I can contribute to this island that's been so good to me."

He stared at her. Then he shrugged. "I really hope you don't leave, Annie. But, honestly, I'm not playing at anything. I thought I made it clear last night that I can't get a liquor license again. And there's no point for me to have even the greatest restaurant without one."

She eased her grip from him. "But why, Rex? You had one in Boston, didn't you? Was it in someone else's name?"

His face flushed; his eyes—a topaz color, the same hue but slightly darker than Taylor's—turned from Annie's.

"Can't we leave it alone? Will you just let me thank you for your generous offer and decline it with regrets? It won't work for me, Annie. I'm sorry, but it won't."

With that, he gave her a sad smile and left the room.

And Annie wasn't sure if she should feel embarrassed for herself or sorry for him.

Chapter 27

John was a grown man. Yet he couldn't help but tear up Tuesday morning when his mother hugged him and then his dad did, too. His mother had to leave the room. But his dad cried along with him and didn't seem uncomfortable to do so.

"Thanks for bringing them, man," he said to Kevin after Earl went to join Claire in Abigail's room.

"I'm so sorry, John," Kevin said, clapping him lightly on the back. "Abigail will be okay, though. Annie told me it's treatable."

John nodded. "The part that's tough is it'll be a roller coaster. And she won't be able to predict when her remissions will come and go. Maybe she'll be able to sense when things are moving in that direction . . . but not for a while, I guess. . . ."

Kevin shook his head. "Poor kid."

"I know she could have something much worse. Either of my girls could. And yet . . ." He stepped away from Kevin, went to the window, and looked across the street at the neighbor's house, where nothing seemed to be happening. It was probably a regular day for the family and the kids. A day they were taking for granted, because that's what people did. Didn't they?

Hadn't he?

"How's Annie?" he asked.

"Okay," Kevin replied. "Upset. About Abigail."

"About a lot of things, I bet."

"Mostly Abigail."

Turning back to him, John said. "I don't know when I can come back to the island. Abigail wants to stay here, which is the best solution while she's having treatment. I think her doctor on the Vineyard would be able to handle it, but she wants to be with her mother. And I don't know what the hell to do, Kevin. I should be able to leave her here . . . but I can't. Not now. And I don't know when."

"I think my sister will understand."

"I don't know why she would. I'm the one who kept pushing her to get married in the first place."

"John, you had no idea something like this was going to happen."

Walking to the recliner that Jenn said she'd bought a long time ago so that he'd have somewhere comfortable to sit when he came to visit (which he hadn't done often and not at all since Abigail had moved back to the Vineyard to live with her sister and him), he dropped onto the seat and let out what felt like all the air stored up in his lungs.

"I just don't know what the hell to do," he said again.

Then Lucy came bouncing around the corner, followed by Restless, who entered yapping, apparently having just figured out that another new person was there. Lucy hugged Kevin, and Restless nearly knocked him over with his wagging.

And John closed his eyes, grateful that his family was there, even though they were minus one. The one he didn't know what the hell to do with. Or without.

Chapter 28

It was back to square one for Annie. Back to being happy for Francine and excited for the future baby; happy for being able to contribute some funds to island families; happy that her work apparently had been deemed successful by people she did not know but who mattered a lot to Annie—her readers.

She was not happy about Abigail's situation. Or about the way John had excluded her. Dismissed her, actually.

She was not happy that Kevin was avoiding her, as if it were her fault that Jack Miller hadn't fit the bill, though Annie still had no hint as to what was behind that.

Nor was Annie happy that Rex had turned down her generous offer.

John. Kevin. Rex. It seemed that the men of her generation and in her current orbit had moved to a different planet. A different galaxy. A different universe.

Deciding she might as well keep going while she was on such a dubious roll, once back in her cottage she pulled out her phone and, without hesitating, called Greg.

His real voice, not his voice mail, answered.

"Ms. Sutton," he said. "This is a nice surprise. I hope."

She squared her shoulders and smiled, even though he couldn't see her.

"That depends on whether or not you're open to negotiating."

"You want more money? Shouldn't I be talking with your agent about that?"

"Absolutely. Louise would never forgive me if I tried to do that on my own. But, no, it isn't about money. It's about . . . well, time."

"Time for what?"

"To rearrange my life. So I can do the best possible job for you without totally screwing up other things that matter to me."

"Details, please."

So Annie outlined what she'd been thinking: two months for her to stay on the Vineyard and finish the manuscript she owed her publisher. She did not mention Francine's baby, Lucy's prom, or maybe helping Abigail. She did not mention wanting time to see if she and John would be together— or not.

"And then what?" Greg asked.

"And then I'll come out there. Work for you full-time. I'd really like to arrange the test run that you mentioned— another three months. So we can be sure I'll fit."

"I changed my mind on that. You were just here for three months. I already know you fit. Make it six months, and I'll consider giving you your two-month delay."

"Six months," she said, her thoughts starting to churn. Would that be enough time for things to settle down with John? Or would there ever be enough time? She bit her lip and tried to face reality. "What about the bungalow? Would I be able to stay there?" The production company used the bungalow for visiting writers, camera people, actors, or whomever required housing.

He paused. "I'd have to consider that in your salary negotiations. In the meantime, is there any chance if during your two-month delay you could do something remotely if I run into a jam? Maybe writing, maybe editing?"

"Hard to say. It would depend on how complicated it is. I still have to finish my manuscript for my publisher." She had no idea if he'd agree or if he was wavering. She suspected that men like Greg were adept at playing games; he hadn't come this far in such a ruthless business without having cutthroat skills.

He didn't answer right away. She allowed him the silence, not knowing if it was a tactic or a genuine need to think.

"Contact your agent," he finally said. "Tell her I'll be in touch tomorrow so we can draw up your contract."

"And I'll get the two months?"

"As long as you give me six once you're here."

Annie squeezed her eyes shut. "Deal," she heard herself say.

That night, she emailed Louise the details. Then, with her adrenaline unabated, she wrote a couple of thousand more words on her manuscript. She fell asleep at the desk just as the sky began to lighten on the horizon; the last thing she remembered was that she'd stirred, unkinked her neck, and gone to bed while still in her clothes.

And now the sun beamed through her windows; it was past noon.

She was making breakfast when she was interrupted by a call from Louise, who already had heard from Greg.

"You're serious about this?" her agent asked.

"I am. I'm not going to sever ties here—not completely, at least not yet—but I need a new challenge, Louise. I need to take charge of me again. The two-month window gives me plenty of time to finish the manuscript. And don't worry about the second one. I'll get it done. You know I will."

"As long as you're sure, I'll get right on it."

"I'm sure."

"And I'll get you the best deal possible."

"I know you will."

They talked another minute, then hung up. And Annie was left smiling. She'd been home less than two weeks, and already had grown weary of what felt like standing on her head.

She knew she couldn't change things for or with John. But their future was too cloudy; she needed to move forward and deal with whatever came of that. In the meantime, she couldn't sit idle, getting too involved with other people's lives in order to keep busy. Yes, she thought, this might be the best decision.

She did, however, need to deal with Kevin. Her brother was important; she hoped he felt the same way about her.

Maybe the one you need to deal with is Jack Miller, not Kevin, Murphy blurted out, as if she'd been there all along, which she probably had. It was like her not to comment on a subject until she saw that Annie had come to a concrete decision of her own.

"Why should I deal with Jack?" Annie asked. "The man lied to me. To us. His daughter's dead. She might have been wrapped up in drugs. She left three kids and a husband. So Jack was probably after money all along. Maybe for his daughter's kids, which might give him the only bit of credit I can muster. Still, if that's what he was doing, lying wasn't a great way to open the conversation."

Maybe the one you need to deal with is Jack Miller, not Kevin, Murphy repeated, as if she were an old vinyl record stuck in a groove.

Annie wanted to yell at her to stop being a smart-ass, but she knew that she could ill afford to alienate another person. Not that Murphy was a person. Well, not anymore. Not really.

"So what am I supposed to do? I can't exactly hop on a boat, go over to the Cape, hunt for Jack Miller, and then stalk him until he confesses. I have no clue where he is. He didn't give me an address; and even Google has half a billion of them." She gulped her tea. "Besides, what would be the point? Kevin's pretty clear that he wants nothing to do with him. I need to respect that. Don't I?"

Maybe the one you need to deal with . . .

"Shut. Up." Annie said, no longer caring if she hurt her long-dead friend's feelings. She stomped out of the kitchen, went into the bathroom, and cranked on the shower, as if Murphy couldn't have followed her, flapping a finger in Annie's face like a nun in the parochial school Murphy had attended back when discipline often was that simple. And that effective.

But with hot water bombarding her skin, Annie had another thought. Wherever Jack Miller was, he must have access to a computer. Or a tablet. He had sent her a few emails, hadn't he?

She dried off and dressed in haste. Then she returned to her computer. It wasn't until she called up his email address that Annie realized that more than three days had passed since she and Kevin had met him at Mocha Mott's. And that since then, Jack hadn't asked to see him again.

Raising her hands above the keyboard, she composed a few brief words in her tired head. Then she typed:

Jack—or whatever your name is—
You lied to us. I'd like to know why. If you told my
brother, he's not sharing the info with me. If you
didn't, then you owe both of us an explanation.
Including the truth about your daughter. And whatever else you lied about.
Annie

She clicked on SEND without a second thought.

And then there were two knocks on her front door.
Kevin's knocks.

"You're back," Annie said when she opened the door.

"I am. It's a family thing, you know? *Their* family, not
mine. And Earl and Claire wanted to stay a couple of days."

She nodded. As close as all of them were—Annie, Kevin,
Earl, Claire, John, and the girls—things felt different now.
Kevin was right: Earl, Claire, John, the girls, and, yes, she sup-
posed Jenn, too, were the family. The biological one.

A lump formed halfway down her throat.

"Come in," she said. "You want something to eat?"

"I'll have a beer if you have one. And then I'll apologize
for being such a jerk."

"You can apologize first if you want. Get it over with?"

"I thought I might need liquid courage. How I reacted
was kind of a big deal."

"No, Kevin. Your reaction wasn't a big deal. You had
every right to be upset. What is a big deal is what *John* is
doing. Part of me understands all the reasons why he's cut me
out of what is, without a doubt, the most critical, serious, gut-
wrenching thing that's ever happened to him—certainly to his
daughter—and I'm trying to be compassionate. But, no. The
way he's done it really hurts. A lot. I haven't even heard from

him since Friday. We're canceling the wedding. Oh, wait. He said 'postponing.' Somehow, I have a feeling it will be canceled, not postponed."

That's when Annie broke down and cried.

And Kevin stepped closer to her and circled his arms around her.

"I'm so sorry, Annie. Jesus. What a bloody mess. And you've been going through this every minute since you came back, and then I stepped in and made your life even worse. I'm sorry. I'm so sorry."

They stood there a few minutes until her crying started to abate. Then he kissed the top of her head.

"So, will I ever get that beer or what?"

She pulled away from him, wiped her eyes, and laughed. "You're an idiot," she said.

"I know. And I'm good at it."

With at least one drama on the way to being resolved, Annie went to the refrigerator and took out two beers. She typically would have chosen a glass of wine for herself, but right then sharing beers seemed friendlier. More like the thing a brother and sister would do after they'd argued. Not that Annie had experience with that.

"To getting over our first real sibling fight," she said.

They sat at the table. They clinked bottles. They drank.

"Sorry you were rewarded with the brunt of my meltdown," she said. "I guess I've been holding it in."

"No problem. I hold stuff in, too, you know."

She laughed. "Yes, I do believe I know that." Then she hesitated. "Kevin? I only have one question. You never explained if you meant that Jack Miller was not your father because he wasn't how you'd remembered him . . . or because you didn't think it really *was* him. That he was an imposter."

He stared at her. "We're going to have this conversation after I apologized and witnessed your meltdown, too?"

"Yes. Sorry. I need to know."

He sighed but didn't seem angry. "I don't know, Annie. Maybe it was some of both. I kept thinking he was too short to be him."

"Kevin, the last time you saw him, you were only four. If he seemed shorter now, it's probably because you're taller."

He laughed, then shrugged.

Picking at the label on the bottle, she lowered her eyes and said, "I don't know if this will help, but he lied to us."

Kevin paused one of those pauses that probably took only two or three seconds but seemed to last an hour. Lately Annie had enough of those to last a lifetime.

"What?" he finally asked.

"The woman Jack said is his daughter isn't in Yarmouth anymore. She died. She had some substance-abuse issues. Class A. The big stuff. Anyway, she died when she was thirty-six."

Annie waited for him to digest the information.

"And there's something else," she added. "Do you remember if Jack's first name was Benjamin?"

Her brother's face morphed into an instant frown.

"Huh?" he asked.

Annie saw no reason to repeat it. She knew that he had heard her.

"No," he said. "His name was Jonathan. But everyone called him Jack. Except Mom. Sometimes Donna called him Jonathan, like if she was pissed at him. I remember that because she mentioned him from time to time. And not in a good way. Not the way he wants us to believe."

He stood up and paced the room. "How'd you come up with 'Benjamin'? And the rest?"

"Google. I found his wife's obituary. And his daughter's. If either of them was really his. Anyway, the wife left a husband, Benjamin; the daughter left a father, Benjamin. I have no idea if we'll ever learn the truth, but just before you got here, I sent him an email in which I sounded pretty irritated. Because I am."

He returned to the table and sat, his initial eruption slightly eased.

Cocking a half smile, he said, "What'd you say in the email?"

Annie sighed. "I told him we know he lied to us about his daughter. And that I don't know what he told you, but I want to know whatever else he lied about."

"Ha! You are amazing, sister."

"Yeah, well, there's a chance we'll never hear from him again."

"I would be fine with that. I really would. And, no, he didn't tell me anything except that he didn't abandon me. Which was when I told him to leave. So he left."

She got up, moved her beer in front of him, and went to pour a glass of wine. "Okay then. I won't send him another snarky email. If he sends me one, I'll tell you, but you don't have to act on it. I'm done sticking my nose into other people's business."

Including Rex Winsted's, she thought. Though she had considered it, she decided in that moment not to try and dig into his background in search of reasons that he might not be able to get a liquor license. Prying could be too hurtful to others. And she refused to drag anyone else into her web of suffering for the sake of trying to take her mind off John.

Besides, in two short months, things were going to look a lot less bleak for her.

Kevin stayed an hour, then went on his way. After all, Taylor most likely was waiting for details on how things had gone in Plymouth.

With the weight of other people's situations slowly lifting

from her shoulders, Annie was determined to focus on the present. She decided to work on her manuscript for an hour or so, then walk up to the Inn and find things that needed doing: washing linens, windows, dishes, whatever.

Soon she became entrenched in her work, fully aware that this day, this hour, she was doing the kind of writing she loved most: creating narratives for novels. She hoped that wasn't a bad sign. For as much as she'd had fun working with others on the film scripts, the passion had not been the same. Maybe someday it would be. But right now, her novels felt more personal; her characters, more real. Like so many other things, she'd have to wait and see. And give the rest a chance.

Then Annie remembered that her books had had always felt real to Lucy, too. Lucy loved keeping up with Annie's creations, always asking questions about why a character had done or not done something, and how Annie was going to get him or her out of the jam she'd put them in. Lucy also loved grilling her about where her ideas came from, how she did her research, and if she invented characters that were like any real people on the island.

Lucy. One of the few names that could break Annie's current concentration.

And why wouldn't it? Her last text had been so sad, so unsettling. Annie started to wonder how Abigail's illness was going to affect her sister. After all, Annie knew from experience that when a family member or close friend was sick or had died, at first those closest to them were too busy trying to keep things going, trying to make appointments, arrangements, whatever was needed, with no time left to address their reactions. Often those came later, much the way her meltdown over John had surfaced days after he announced they should postpone the wedding. Maybe the delay was nature's way of helping people tamp down the shock. She hoped that wasn't going to happen to Lucy over Abigail's condition.

That's when Annie decided to send Lucy a text. Not to pry. Not to intrude. Just to let Lucy know that she cared about her very much and was concerned for her as well as for Abigail.

Because, with or without John, Annie did love the girl.

Chapter 29

Hey, girl, Annie texted Lucy. Checking to see how you're doing. Because I'm thinking about you.

She closed with an emoji of a shimmering pink heart, because pink had been Lucy's favorite color when she was younger.

After a few minutes, when there was no reply, Annie stood up and stretched. She felt good about having reached out to her; Lucy would know she had, and that was all that mattered.

With about an hour of daylight left, she grabbed her phone and jacket and left to walk down to the beach, determined to add its beauty and its peace to her bank of island memories. When she was halfway down the sandy path, her phone rang. It was Lucy.

Annie stopped. And smiled.

"Lucy! I hope I didn't take you from anything."

"Nope. I snuck out to the porch so I could hear your voice."

Though Annie had been trying to be meaningfully stoic, another small piece of her heart crumbled away.

"It's good to hear your voice, too. Are you okay?"

"Mmm, yeah, I guess. Grandma and Grandpa are here, but you probably know that."

"I do. How's that going?"

"Good. I think it's easier with them here. Except Grandma took over the kitchen and my mom's not happy about that. I'm trying to stay out of the way."

"Sounds like a good choice. Two people in any kitchen can be risky." A thought of Rex brushed against her mind unexpectedly, urging her to learn why he'd been so quick to squelch his dream.

She shook it off and asked how Abigail was feeling.

"Better, I guess. She started taking some medication with a name I can't pronounce. This morning she said she feels like she has the flu, but the doctor said it's a common side effect and will go away. But she's not as tired as she was on the island. I think she likes being here. With Mom. And Dad, too, of course."

Dad. Right. He was there, too.

Taking a few steps, Annie turned her attention to the tall beach grass that, like the trees, was starting to green up for summer.

"And are you still planning to stay until she goes into remission?"

"I think so. Yeah. I'm sorry about Mother's Day weekend, though. We would have had a good time."

Annie felt her jaw stiffen. "There's always next year."

"Sure." Her voice went unusually soft, as if she didn't think she'd be there next year, either.

"You're not still worried about your sister, are you? Now that they have a diagnosis and know what to do . . ." Annie picked up her steps again and made it down to the water. The tide was coming in; the waves dampened the shoreline, each small white crest of foam breaking with rhythmic precision.

Then, on the other side of the connection, Annie heard an

unfamiliar voice call out to Lucy. No doubt it was Jenn. Annie gnawed her lower lip and dug the toes of her sneakers into the sand.

"Do you have to go, dear?" she asked.

"Yeah," Lucy replied. "Are you at the water? I can hear the waves."

"I am. I'm looking for sea glass. It's not as much fun without you, though."

At which point, Lucy might have started to cry, but Annie could not be sure. Then she heard the same voice call out again.

"I have to go," Lucy said, and quickly hung up.

And Annie dropped onto the sand, looked out to the sea, and wondered why life had to be so godawful sometimes.

She didn't work that night. But in the morning, knowing that she needed to stick to her plan, Annie went up to the Inn just as breakfast ended. Rex gave her a few scraps of blueberry waffles and homemade yogurt, and she announced that the first thing on her agenda was to thoroughly clean the books and the bookshelves in the reading room—unless there was something else he thought she should tackle instead.

"It's a great idea," he said. "Dusting books is more of a woman's job than a man's, don't you think?"

It was a moment before she realized he'd been joking.

"Very funny," she replied. She ate while Rex busily cleaned up the kitchen. Lucy had reminded her that Mother's Day was coming soon; now that Annie was back in her brother's good graces, she wondered if he'd help distribute some of her soap to the shops in town. The idea for brunch probably should be scrubbed, but at least she could let people know she was still part of the community and still wanted to share in its Mother's Day celebration.

However, she didn't know how much soap was left from

last year, and whether it would be enough to set up small displays in a few shops in Edgartown. She remembered Kevin had said that when he was working on Francine and Jonas's house, he'd had to do the carpentry in the garage that wasn't heated. He also said he'd stowed her soaps and supplies in the storage room at the Inn.

Before she finished her breakfast, she brought her dishes to the sink, quickly thanked Rex, and said she'd start the dusting right after she did something else.

He laughed.

She made a face, then went to the first-floor storage room to prowl.

It was spacious, with lots of shelving, cabinets, a couple of tables, and a whole lot of what looked like . . . junk. There was, however, hardly an inch to move. She squeezed her way to her wooden molds and long stainless steel trays that were neatly stacked on her drying racks; someone—no doubt Kevin—had spread a tarp across the top to keep the dust off. In one corner, plastic tubs were piled high; Annie assumed they held her remnants from the Christmas in Edgartown Holiday Fair. She doubted that much was left; she calculated how long it would take to make more and allow the bars to cure before the slicing, wrapping, packing could be done. The timing for Mother's Day would be next to impossible.

Then she recalled that at least one tub, maybe two, held an ample supply of seconds—those that had been chipped or scraped during the soapmaking process. She wondered if a "scratch and dent" sale would at least give her some credit for participation.

Thinking all those thoughts while wriggling around the obstacle course in the room, Annie stepped on a mound of boxes in order to reach one of the tubs. But as she grabbed the edge of the tub and pulled, the boxes beneath her collapsed, the lid popped off the tub, and bars of soap shot up, down, and out, in what looked like a thousand directions.

She soft-landed on a pile of tarps and swore under her breath.

"Need a hand?" Rex stood in the hall, peering into the storage room.

She sighed a heavy sigh. "That would be helpful. Thanks."

Twisting her body to jostle around the boxes once again, she miraculously wound up in the hall, standing next to Rex.

"I want to figure out if I have enough soap to bring into town for Mother's Day weekend."

He laughed. "I thought Mother's Day was a day, not an entire weekend."

Right, Annie thought. He hadn't been back on the island long enough to learn that, in his lengthy absence, the Board of Trade had expanded Mother's Day into an extravaganza. And he'd missed the part of her homecoming dinner when Lucy had brought up the subject.

"Wait," Annie thought as a lightbulb of an idea switched on over her head. "We'd talked about offering a Mother's Day brunch on Sunday morning of that weekend and Lucy giving golf cart tours of Chappy. But with Claire and Lucy away, and Francine, well, she'll no doubt be unavailable . . . would you be game?"

"You mean to do a public thing? For people other than the tenants?"

"Sure. Why not? You could show off your culinary skills to the world again. Or, at least, to the Vineyard." She also realized it might reassure him that there were no hard feelings about his turning down her offer to help fund the Lord James. And it would be nice to include him, as they couldn't afford to lose Rex right then.

"The dining room table only seats twelve."

"Okay, so there won't be room for the whole island. But we'd thought about serving on the patio as well. We can set up more tables and let the guests choose which location they'd prefer when they make their reservations."

"We might need a special permit because you'll be selling food."

"We can let Earl take care of that when he gets back. It will help his mind focus on . . . other things."

"Will you have a tent on the patio?"

"Why not?" she repeated, a sense of being happy again starting to take hold.

He sighed. "I can go to Tilton's and check out the tent rentals. Man, you work me to death at this place."

"I know. But you're strong. You can take it. Now"—she pointed back into the storage room—"if you can reach those totes and stack them in front, I'll go through them later. As well as the ones I trashed all over the floor. And as for you, you'll also have to come up with a menu. Which you'd better get working on so we can take out ads in the papers and post on our website and social media. In the meantime, it will be fun to get on board. We need to lighten up around here, don't you think?"

And maybe by then, if Lucy wanted to be part of the fun, she would come home. At least for the weekend. After all, the whole thing had been her idea.

Annie wondered why she hadn't thought of it sooner.

Before getting carried away (a favorite term of her mother's, as in "Don't get carried away, young lady," whenever Annie wanted to try something new—a sport, a role in the drama club's spring play, a hobby like writing), she knew it was time to find out if what she was planning was feasible. So after Rex had moved the totes within her reach, Annie dismissed him with honors. Then she went into the reception area. Pausing for a bit, she ran her hand over the smooth surface of the front desk; she wondered if Earl's sister, Martha, had ever sat there at the Lyons family heirloom doing homework or writing letters before she'd gotten sick, before they'd known about her illnesses.

Annie closed her eyes. This was not the time to think of unfortunate Martha or even Abigail.

Instead, she reached into the all-important center drawer where the laptop was concealed. She took it out and checked the calendar. And she really, really wished that the first thing she saw hadn't been April 23. Her wedding date.

Setting her jaw, she refused to get emotional; she highlighted the notation and hit the delete key. Done. Gone. April 23 was now available for . . . whatever.

Her stomach tightened, and then her throat, both of which were followed by a strong desire to return the laptop to its hiding place and leave the Inn in tears. Instead, she took a slow, steadying breath and metaphorically *hoisted her bra straps*—a favorite saying of Murphy's from long ago. She then returned to her mission.

As expected, no other events were on the schedule from now until Mother's Day weekend, except, coincidentally—and luckily—the professional cleaners would be there the Thursday before.

Hooray. Perhaps it was a sign from the chamber of commerce gods.

Next, Annie did due diligence by calling a member of the Board of Trade to make sure it wasn't too late to take part.

"Absolutely not!" came the enthusiastic reply. "But you'll need to email us your details by the end of this week, so we can include the Inn in the brochure, online, and, of course, in the press releases to the media. And we can help you take care of the permit, if you want help. Your kitchen is already approved to serve food, correct?"

"Food but not liquor."

"So you won't be able to serve alcohol. Will that be a problem?"

She had a quick thought of Rex and his dilemma. There was no time to try and conquer that now. "No, we'll simply alert people to that when they make reservations."

"And you can get the details to me by the end of the week?"

She said that she could. And that it would be great if they could handle the additional permit. She didn't add that it would be easier than to wait until Earl returned. Then she agreed to gather the details for the promotions by the end of the week.

Hardy har har, a familiar Murphy belly laugh seemed to echo through reception area.

Annie chose to ignore her friend.

After saying "Thank you" profusely, and then hanging up, Annie then took the laptop to the reading room. Sitting at the table adorned with her favorite lamp—a green-glass-shaded, brass-based replica of those in the Boston Public Library—she knew that before getting carried away (thank you, Ellen Sutton), she'd have to make a list. Subject. Needs. Assigned To. Cost. Completed.

The menu would be easy, because that would be Rex's job, and Annie had no doubt he'd carry it off without a glitch.

Servers would be more difficult, as it was still the off-season. She'd check with the tenants, but she'd bet that those in the restaurant business, either full- or part-time, would already be booked. She'd need to confer with Rex about that. Maybe she could contact MV Community Services and ask if they knew of anyone who might be interested in earning some extra cash.

While Rex went to check out available tents, maybe he could reserve linens, too. There were some cloths left over from their grand opening, but they should have newer ones.

Now that she and Kevin were speaking again, she'd put him in charge of seeing if they could borrow tables from the Chappy Community Center.

Annie assigned herself to handle the flowers and table settings, as well as small giveaways if she didn't have enough of her boutique soaps.

She would also take care of the ads and getting the information to the Board of Trade. If only Restless wasn't in Plymouth, Lucy could have dressed him up in pink and green. Even if there wasn't a dog parade, they could snap a photo of him in costume, under the sign at the Inn. "Kids and dogs attract attention," an advertising guru once told Annie when they'd been on a date and she was between husbands one and two. It was a lousy date, as his ego was as big as the Hancock Tower, but at least she remembered his little gem of wisdom, for whatever it was worth.

Thinking of Restless, of course, made her think of Lucy. And her fabulous idea of a golf cart tour of Chappaquiddick as an add-on to the brunch, with rides first come, first served. But it wouldn't be right to ask someone else—Jonas? Maybe Earl?—to do the honors.

What about Lucy's boyfriend? Murphy asked. *What's his name?*

"Kyle," Annie whispered. She stared at the screen, fingers poised above the keyboard.

He's getting gypped out of the prom. Maybe he'd like to do this for her. You know how sweet young love can be.

"Yes, I do," Annie said, happy that she wasn't too old to remember being sixteen, wearing her first bikini on South Beach in the summer, seeing Brian for the first time. It was a magical beginning to a magical dozen years, though they didn't know it wouldn't last longer than that.

"I'll have to ask her if she'd mind, though."

Whatever. It's just a suggestion.

Of course, Murphy's "suggestions" usually were perfect, especially since she'd relocated to the other side.

Printing out her list, Annie closed the laptop and returned it to the desk. Before she went forward with the plans, she needed to talk to Kevin. She assumed he'd be elated; he'd high-fived Lucy's golf-cart service announcement, and he'd once proposed making the place available for weddings and special events. So far, only one wedding had taken place there, and the other one had just been deleted from the calendar.

Quickly rerouting her thoughts back to Mother's Day, Annie sensed that the brunch would be a big success. Until she headed out the door to go to Kevin's, and nearly crashed into Jack Miller.

Chapter 30

"What are you doing here?" Annie snipped, as if he were a burglar in the night instead of Kevin's supposed father. It was a sunny day; he was dressed in a white shirt, black pants, and a black sport coat, as if he were going to a wedding or was a maître d'. She stopped herself from snarling that if he was looking for money, he could come back on Mother's Day and they'd employ him from ten to two.

"I came to see you. And to see my son." At least he wasn't trying to bribe her with a bouquet of flowers.

She stood on one foot, then the other. She wanted to ask how he'd found her, but then she remembered Google and their charming maps.

"Anything you have to say I think should wait until my brother hears it first. Frankly, I shouldn't be involved at all. It's between the two of you."

He nodded, as if he understood. "Is he around? He lives here, doesn't he?"

She supposed he could have told her how nice the property was, how the location was incredible and that the Inn looked welcoming. Perhaps he didn't want to give the impression that he needed cash, after all. Which also might be why he was dressed as nicely as he was.

"No," she said, "Kevin doesn't live here."

"Oh. The website said—"

"That he's an owner of the Inn. So am I. So is one of our friends. But, no, Kevin doesn't live here." She wasn't about to tell him that her brother and his wife did live on Chappaquiddick, about a mile and a quarter southeast—by the way blue herons flew—from where they were standing now. Let Kevin be the one to do that. If he wanted.

"Can you call him? Tell him I'm here if he has the time to talk? He didn't . . . um, he didn't give me his cell number."

Jack Miller—or whatever his name was—was a quiet man who spoke softly, yet clearly. He was not bombastic as Annie had known some men to be, and did not seem interested in taking control. Those things, and the fact that he didn't even have his son's phone number, were what made Annie suddenly feel sad. Sorry for him, she guessed. Especially if it turned out that he, indeed, had been the man who'd married Donna MacNeish when other men might have turned from her once they learned she'd had a baby out of wedlock and still loved the baby's father.

If any of that was true.

Annie took her phone out of her pocket and called Kevin.

"Jack Miller's here," she said. "At the Inn. He'd like to speak with you if you have the time."

She was glad that Jack had looked away, down toward the harbor and the lighthouse, so he wouldn't be able to tell that her face was trying to pretend all was well, that Kevin hadn't just growled, "Jesus. What's he doing here?"

She didn't answer because she'd already told him.

Then her brother expelled a moan of air. "Jesus," he said again. "I've been doing yard work. Give me a few minutes to get cleaned up, then I'll be there."

"Okay," she said, knowing that at least he wouldn't show up in a white shirt and black pants that matched Jack Miller's because she doubted Kevin owned them. "Text me when you get here. I'll give him a tour of the grounds while we wait."

Though Annie hadn't intended to do that, being outside in the fresh air might help her head stay clear and stop her from feeling she had to sit and converse about things she'd rather not converse about, such as showing him her cottage and telling him it was where Donna had chosen to live out her final days. No matter how many lies the man had told, if he was Kevin's father, he didn't need to hear that. Unless he wanted to.

By the time Kevin arrived, they'd scoped out pretty much every square inch of the three-acre parcel. Although Jack had said he'd been a salesman most of his career, he asked a lot of smart questions about the building and the impact that the Inn had on Chappy's infrastructure. Annie couldn't give him detailed answers but she knew that Kevin would love to. If he didn't chase him off the property and down to the *On Time* first.

Kevin's text said he was on the patio, so, with a heap of gratitude, Annie led Jack from the meadow where she'd given him a half-baked explanation of the outbuilding they wanted to build and where she'd run out of ways to kill more time.

The men didn't greet each other as if they were old friends. Annie took a step back and suggested that the two of them go into the reading room, where they could close the door and talk privately.

Kevin tossed her a pleading glance and said, "I was hoping that you'd join us."

Because Kevin was her brother and she loved him . . . and because she felt that this encounter was her fault . . . she followed the man who was dressed up in black and white, and

Kevin, who wore clean jeans and a dark blue, long-sleeved Henley shirt from the Black Dog that Annie supposed was new because she'd never seen it on him.

They declined her offer of tea or beer, which was how Annie knew her brother must be nervous. It also was a bad sign, as she knew that sipping was a good way for Kevin to keep occupied whenever he was trying to think of what to say next. And it was better than shaking the damn table with his jumpy leg.

She suggested that they sit in the comfortable chairs, away from the table, while she took one of the straight ones.

"Needless to say, I'm surprised to see you," Kevin blurted out.

"I have a few things to explain."

"Yes. You do."

Annie watched the words bounce back and forth between them; she could almost see them printed in the air, as if they were subtitles on a foreign film.

She folded her hands in her lap and tried to pay attention.

"Starting with your name," Kevin continued. "What is it . . . exactly?"

Jack sighed. "Benjamin Miller," he replied. "Benjamin Jonathan Miller."

That took Annie by surprise.

But Kevin didn't blink.

"Why is my middle name Raymond?"

She had no idea why her brother had asked him that.

"Raymond was your grandfather's name. My father's."

Kevin's face sagged a little then, as if he thought he'd caught Jack in a lie but hadn't.

"Why?" Jack asked. "Did your mother tell you my name was Raymond?"

Kevin's eyes were downcast. "No. I always knew your name was Jack. And I knew sometimes she called you Jonathan."

Jack's mouth turned up on one side. "When she was mad at me."

"Yeah. Why didn't she call you Benjamin? Or Ben?"

"No one did. That was my father's middle name. He was nicknamed R. B. Your grandparents called me B. J. But I put a stop to that when that wholesale club place started outside of Boston. I didn't want people to compare me to discount food or tires."

Kevin lifted his head and almost smiled. Then he turned somber again. "What's the deal with my sister? And do I really have a brother? Or is he dead, too?"

The corners of Jack's eyes squinted, as if someone had pinched them. He glanced over at Annie, as if wanting her to intervene, as if she knew any more than Kevin did about his supposed siblings.

"Your brother's name is Donald. He and his wife live in a small town outside Saratoga Springs, New York. His wife's family is in politics. Donald has a good job at the state house. But I don't see him very often. Let's say our likes and dislikes have a hard time crossing the aisle."

Annie understood what Jack meant. She'd had several friends whose families had been torn apart thanks to red and blue tides that had ceased ebbing and flowing together.

"Anyway," Jack continued, "Donald will be forty this year—he's not that much younger than you, Kevin. Donna Lee was the baby. She died when she was thirty-six."

Kevin's attitude seemed to have changed from being on high alert to listening attentively.

"Was it an overdose?"

Jack pressed his lips together and nodded. "Her husband—
Bob Chapman—well, he went through a lot with her. I guess
she picked up the habit after their third child was born. She'd
had a lot of tearing in her insides, which gave her a lot of pain.
She got hooked on opioids. You've probably heard a story or
two about how that goes."

Both Kevin and Annie nodded.

Then, as his eyes grew misty, Jack added, "When she was
young, she was a sweet girl. A lot like her mother, Essie." He
shrugged. "Who knows why these things happen."

"I'm sorry," Annie said, and then Kevin followed suit.

"I came down to the Cape to help Bob out with the kids.
He's a veterinarian; he works at his father's animal hospital,
but his father just retired and moved to Florida."

Annie held back from suggesting that they update the animal hospital's website.

"So . . . ," Jack continued, "with young Bob's dad gone,
he and I decided to keep the family together, keep the kids in
their house, you know? We're like a sitcom—two men, one
of them a geezer, that's me—trying to raise three little ones,
all of them girls." He chuckled the way Earl often chuckled.
Then he shook his head. "We're doing okay, though. They're
good girls. Cute as buttons. The oldest one misses her mom;
the middle one only remembers a few things about her; the
little one, well, she didn't get to know her."

Annie held back tears. She suspected that Kevin did, too.

Then Jack stood up. "So now you know the truth. I don't
expect you to want to get to know me better, or anything like
that. I only wanted to see you again, Kevin. But now I'm glad
you know what really happened. That I only left you and
Donna because she was still in love with Annie's dad."

Annie stiffened. She hadn't shared that with her brother.
But by the way Kevin nodded, Annie suddenly realized that
Jack had given him those details just before Kevin booted him

out of Mocha Mott's. Because he didn't believe him. Or because he didn't want to. She also knew that Kevin hadn't told her because he didn't want to upset her.

Families can be pretty weird, can't they? Murphy whispered in her ear.

"Will you come to my house for dinner?" Kevin asked Jack abruptly as he, too, stood up. "I'd like you to meet my wife."

Jack checked his watch. "Another time? I need to get back to the boat and drive home to Yarmouth before it gets too dark. My old eyes have one hell of a time seeing once the sun's gone down."

Kevin smiled. "I'll take you to the boat. I've got a half shift at the *On Time*, but I can get you to Vineyard Haven first."

"Thanks, that would be great," Jack replied. "I didn't mind taking the bus to Edgartown, though. It gave me a chance to see some of the island."

"Well, now you'll get to ride in an authentic island pickup." He turned to Annie. "You want to come with us?"

"No," she said. "You two go along. I've got lots to do here."

She hugged Kevin and then Jack. As they left, she heard Kevin say, "Did I tell you I've been training to be a captain of the *On Time*? Any day now, I hope to hear that I've been accepted . . ."

Once the men were out the door, Annie smiled through happy tears; gazing out the window, she watched as they crossed the grass, walking with an identical gait toward the driveway. While she watched, she half wondered what in God's name had just happened, and why it was that just when one had given up on people and on life, things like this really could occur to restore one's faith in something, no matter what, or whom, it was.

★   ★   ★

Rex settled on lobster eggs Benedict as the main entrée, and scrambled tofu with avocado and roasted veggies as a vegan offering. He added breakfast sausage (both pork and plant-based), pancakes (walnut and blueberry), cranberry scones, salads, and a host of other selections, including light desserts. He suggested that they serve the main course, and then let the patrons select the side dishes and desserts from a buffet table.

Of course, Annie couldn't take in all of Rex's ideas after what had just happened between Kevin and Jack. She was too dazed to see her brother so ecstatic. She was too amazed that they'd been reunited, right there at the Vineyard Inn. Kevin's life might change because of it, but Annie was determined not to worry. Especially since Jack hadn't alluded to needing money. Not once. And chances were that Bob Chapman made a good living as a vet.

With her smile not yet waning, she said to Rex, "Whatever you want will be magnificent. As for me, I've made a list." She held up the sheet of paper that she'd just printed out. "What do you think about flowers for the table?"

"Pink tulips," he said without hesitation. "Pink flowers, green leaves. Even though they no longer use it as a theme, pink and green make a nice color combination. Perfect for Mother's Day. And we should have the flowers delivered a few days before so they start to wilt before Sunday. Tulips are so much nicer when they arc down a little than when they're standing up, trying to pretend that they're daffodils."

Annie laughed. "Okay. "I'll give Donaroma's a call. How many?"

"A dozen for each of the eight tables we can set up on the patio. Another two for the dining table in the great room, and three or four more dozen in case of emergency."

"Emergency?"

"Yeah. Like if too many people show up and we need to set up a couple of extra tables on the lawn. Or if some of the blossoms keel over and fall off. And let's add some white lilacs for a little fragrance. In case the pancakes burn."

"Were you a party planner in a former life?" she asked.

"When you own a restaurant . . . ," he began.

"You probably need to know a little about many things." She laughed again as she finished his sentence.

"Exactly," he replied.

Annie had begun to understand that though Rex resembled a wrestler with a big baritone voice, and in addition to being a fix-it man, he had a softer side that he wasn't afraid to show. He also had a clever wit.

She wondered if Jack Miller liked to joke the way that Kevin did. But one thing Annie knew: Her first impression about how much Jack and Kevin looked like each other had not been wrong.

"I'd better check to make sure we have enough place settings," she said. "We talked about doing events a while ago, but I'm not sure we're equipped well enough. How many do you think we'll need?"

He leaned against the counter and folded his large arms across his chest. "Depends on how you want to do this."

"What do you mean?"

"The reservations. Buffets can be better to do in groups at a time . . . like a ten o'clock sitting, an eleven thirty, a one o'clock, whatever you want."

"I have absolutely no idea. What does your professional gut tell you?"

"Because this is a maiden voyage for the Inn, my professional gut, as you call it, thinks we should limit it to a first seating at ten, a second at noon. Then everyone will have time to relax and enjoy the food and the surroundings. And it will give us plenty of time in the kitchen to keep things under control. In other words, I think it'll work better if we don't get carried away."

Pressing her lips together, Annie held back from asking Rex if he'd ever known Ellen Sutton.

"I agree. I also know I'd better get my brother involved before we go any further." She looked back at her paper. "I've probably forgotten a lot of things. If Kevin's available tomorrow, maybe we can meet here and go over everything." She'd also love to have the chance to talk to him about Jack while the conversation was still fresh in her brother's mind.

Rex nodded. "Tell him I'll throw some lunch together for us. I think better when I'm cooking. And though I might not have been the one who planned every detail of a party, it's safe to say that I know how to feed a crowd."

"I have no doubt. And, best of all, if anything goes wrong, at least our guests will have a terrific view." She looked out the expanse of windows down to the harbor and the lighthouse. And for the millionth time since she'd moved to the island, Annie felt at peace. To be able to live in this magical place where even the worst problems had a way of never seeming quite as bad.

She wondered if she'd still feel the same after being gone six months.

She quickly pushed the thought away because, right then, she needed to call Lucy again. This time, she'd ask how she would feel if Kyle—or Earl or Jonas—took her place driving the golf cart as a tour guide of Chappaquiddick.

Chapter 31

Lucy picked up on the first ring.

"Good timing," she said. "Restless and I are out walking. What's up?"

Annie had gone back to her cottage so she could be alone when she and Lucy talked. It was more difficult to fake sounding upbeat when others in the room probably knew that "upbeat" was not how she felt about the situation in Plymouth. "How's that sweet little guy doing?"

"It's weird. Most of the time, he won't leave Abigail's side. It's like he knows she's sick."

"Dogs are amazing that way."

"Yeah, well, I remember when he liked me better."

"Lucy!"

"Just kidding. I wouldn't want to be my sister right now, even if it meant getting my dog back."

"He still loves you."

"I know. He tells me all the time."

Annie smiled. "Speaking of love . . . You know that we all love you very much and miss you very much, don't you?"

"Yeah. But I have a feeling you're about to tell me bad news."

"It's not bad news, honey. In fact, I think it's wonderful. And I—we—have you to thank."

"For what?"

"For the idea to get the Inn on board for Mother's Day weekend. We've decided to have a Mother's Day brunch. Like you suggested."

Lucy paused. "Really?"

"Really. Rex is working on a fabulous menu, and I'm trying to figure out the details. I'm dragging Kevin into it, too." Suddenly, Annie wasn't certain she should ask Lucy about the golf cart tours. With everything else going on in the girl's life, the last thing Annie wanted was to make her feel left out. There was too much of that going around these days.

"Oh, wow," Lucy finally said. "That's ridiculous! In a good way. I sure wish I was there to help."

"Me, too. But if you have any thoughts about how we can make it successful, we can use them."

"What about the golf cart tours? Are you going to do them without me?"

Annie forced another smile. "It was a great idea, honey. But I don't have a clue how to do them without you. Besides, we only have a few weeks. And we don't have a golf cart. Or a driver. Maybe we should hold off on that until next year."

If Murphy were there, she might accuse Annie of reverse psychology or, at the least, of a warped kind of bait-and-switch.

"Not necessarily," Lucy said. "Maybe I can come home for it."

Annie hadn't expected that. "Oh, honey, that would be wonderful! But I wouldn't want Abigail to feel like you're trying to get away from her because you'd rather be having fun."

"Well . . . I think she'd be okay with it. We're sleeping in the same room, so we've had a bunch of late-night talks."

At first, Annie was touched to think the sisters were growing closer. Then a hopeful thought zapped her better senses: Lucy once told her that Jenn's house had three bedrooms . . . so John and Jenn must not be sleeping together. The relief it brought, however, was short-lived; just as quickly she remembered that Earl and Claire were there, so of course the girls would have to double up. She sucked in a breath. She really didn't want to think about the bedroom arrangements in Plymouth.

She forced herself not to groan or even sigh.

"Well, I need to get the information to the Board of Trade this week. And put the ads together. And, as I said, we don't have a golf cart. So we'd have to pull this together fast."

"My dad knows a guy at the links. Maybe you could borrow—or rent—one of theirs. A six-seater, don't you think? You'd need to ask, like, right now though, 'cuz, Mother's Day or not, it'll be a weekend in May, and you know how that goes."

The "links," Annie knew, meant the Royal and Ancient Chappaquiddick Links, the nine-hole, uniquely enchanting golf course that had begun in the late 1800s and had been run by the same family ever since.

"Oh, my gosh," she said, "I hadn't thought of that. See why it's so good to have you around?" As soon as she said it, she realized she shouldn't have. She already knew that Lucy would rather be there.

"Like I said, maybe I can come. Just for the weekend?"

"Don't worry. We'll put it in the ads, and if you can't get here, we'll just say our driver had to go off-island."

"I could ask Kyle for you, but with it being Mother's Day . . ."

"Right. He would be busy."

"Or Grandpa could drive them around. He might like that. And I think they'll be back home in a couple of days."

Annie didn't mention that she'd already thought of Kyle,

Earl, and Jonas, too. But with Earl's long-standing family history on Chappaquiddick, he'd be the most fitting candidate. And, Lucy was right, he might like doing it.

"You're a genius," Annie said. "And a gem. Thank you, thank you, for being in my life, Lucy Lyons."

"Argh!" Lucy growled.

"I was being nice."

"Ha! It's not that. Restless just pooped on somebody's lawn and the guy is three feet away, weeding his garden. Gotta go clean up the mess." Lucy rang off before she had a chance to hear Annie laughing.

Kevin had agreed to come to lunch; luckily, he wasn't on the schedule as a deckhand until later in the day. Taylor came with him and they sat with Annie at the island in the kitchen, watching Rex whip up lunch: a stew of lentils, sweet potatoes, and fresh greens. He'd also dug slices of Francine's eleven-grain, homemade bread out of the freezer and thawed them; he said he'd heat and serve them with a dish of olive oil, garlic, and herbs.

Kevin said he had to stop his tongue from hanging out of his mouth. He was in high spirits; it was good to see him being himself again.

"I really like the idea of Mother's Day brunch," he said, his eyes glued to Rex's spoons and knives, which were swiftly working away. "Maybe I should invite Jack and his grandkids. It might give them a nice chance to honor the memory of their mother. Even though the little one can't possibly remember her."

Apparently, father and son had bonded when Kevin took him to the boat. Which would account for her brother's joy.

The brunch-planning meeting was lively, and it felt good to laugh together again, to work together on something positive.

Halfway through the meal, Taylor asked, "What about music?"

"Music?" It hadn't occurred to Annie to have music.

"Okay. I suppose the good news is that you must not have thought Mother's Day brunch would be appropriate for a marimba band." Taylor was, of course, referring to Harlin, one of the Inn's year-round tenants for a couple of years, whose band had played on the patio for the Inn's grand opening and at a few other outdoor events.

"You're right, but it doesn't matter. Harlin bought a house on the Cape last year, so he's no longer around."

"I think what she's asking," Kevin interrupted, "is if you'd like her to play."

"The cello? Would you? Oh, yes, Taylor. That would be terrific." Annie was surprised she hadn't thought of it. After all, she always felt better when she and her sister-in-law were on the same side of anything.

Taylor nodded. "And it would be proper, right?"

"Very much so. Thank you."

"Not to mention she comes cheap," Kevin added. "I talked her into playing for her supper and nothing more."

"Will you settle for payment in the form of leftovers from brunch?" Rex asked.

"As long as you're the one doing the cooking."

"Guaranteed. What's also guaranteed is that I won't be making supper after feeding a hundred or more people."

"A hundred or more?" Annie squeaked. "Guess I'd better get going on the ads."

For a couple of hours, she had a wonderful time, as the four of them brainstormed possibilities and probabilities and her things-to-do list started to take shape. Best of all, she did not think about John. Not once.

★   ★   ★

The nights were the hardest. During the day, Annie was good at pretending: after all, it was what she did for a living. Making up people, making up stories, making up a plot that would be resolved around page three hundred. For years she'd felt that life was better when she could spend her days dreaming up everything about it.

But the nights on Chappy were very dark. And despite the fact that the grounds of the Inn were filled with honest-to-goodness people—all the bedrooms were occupied with tenants; Rex had taken up residency in Francine and Bella's old room; and Francine, Jonas, and Bella were in the house next door, a mere sixty or seventy steps away—Annie felt very much alone.

So, after the group disbanded and she'd spent the remainder of the day writing ad copy and sorting out details, she sat in her rocking chair, holding a glass of wine that she barely touched. Her thoughts drifted to California. And how and when she was going to tell everyone her plans.

She did not regret her decision to go, though it was hard to grasp that she'd be leaving by mid-June. It was nice to think that she'd be back by Christmas. If she came back at all.

But she'd be in an environment where everyone was a transplant from somewhere else—Chicago, Dallas, even Muncie, Indiana, and other cities and towns Annie had barely heard of. Like Cerise, most of them had lived in L.A. for several years. They worked closely with a man that everyone called Bobster, who drove a vintage Thunderbird convertible, a former Broadway playwright who claimed to be over sixty though he didn't look a minute over forty. He said it was thanks to the sun, but Cerise informed her it was more likely thanks to plastic surgery, because the sun was hasher on the skin than clouds were. She also said that, no matter what the old song said, it sometimes did rain in Southern California, and when it did, it poured.

Also on their team were two young people in their late thirties: he was a computer network specialist and a transgender male; the other was a lesbian whose background was in agritourism but had lost her job after a northern California fire. The youngest of the group was a twenty-seven-year-old former beauty queen who was an expert at hip-hop culture.

They were an eclectic, congenial group, mostly because they had something in common that each of them cherished: a love of storytelling. Annie recognized that the potpourri of their ages was not a coincidence, because each of them unquestionably brought different viewpoints and experiences to the brainstorming table. Not since moving to the Vineyard had Annie felt that she'd found people she totally connected to. The big difference, of course, was that these people were writers. Just like her. She would miss Cerise, but chances were, if Annie left after her six-month stint, Greg could easily replace her, no matter what he said.

The bungalow would make it worth signing the contract to go. Situated above the foothills, it was high enough for Annie to glimpse the Pacific Ocean when the air was clear. The view of the water was different, though, as it made her feel backward. It reminded her of a friend in Boston whose apartment was identical to hers, except the floor plan was reversed; whenever Annie visited, she stayed put in her chair out of fear that if she got up, she might bump into a wall if she needed to use the bathroom.

But feeling that the ocean was backward was the only negative thing Annie could come up with now about going back to California.

On Annie's last day there, Cerise had insisted on driving her to the airport in her pink-and-silver Smart car. As Annie waited on the terrace for Cerise to arrive, the soft scent of California wild roses—*Rosa californica*, Bobster had explained— lingered in the air, as if offering to sneak into her suitcase and go home with her. She thought about how her time there had been fulfilling in ways she hadn't expected.

Perhaps it was due to the people and the work—all of which she'd found rewarding.

Perhaps the sunshine was more energizing than rainy Vineyard days.

So maybe it was inevitable that right then, sitting alone in the Chappaquiddick darkness, Annie began to wonder why she'd ever come back.

You know what they say about the grass always being greener . . . , Murphy interrupted.

"But maybe it is, Murph," Annie answered. "Maybe sometimes it really is."

Silence followed.

Then Annie wondered if the biggest reason she'd been California-dreaming was because John was dumping her.

"There," she said to her old pal as she raised her glass and took a gulp. "I'm finally acknowledging that's what's happened. The main reason for it—Abigail—is sadly legitimate. Even forgivable. And yet the bottom line is, I *am* being dumped. Left at the altar that was never meant to be for me."

And though she expected to hear Murphy tell her she was being silly, her friend did not comply.

The silence said it all.

The next morning—Friday, day seven since she'd spoken with John—Annie pushed down the dark side of her emotions and went into action again, this time checking to determine if she had enough leftover soaps to sell on Mother's Day weekend, or if she should pan the idea as nice but hardly doable. Her mission, however, was interrupted when she went into the kitchen and saw not Rex but Francine, who spun around to greet Annie and bumped her with her belly.

"Sorry," Francine said. "These days, I seem to do that whenever I see someone."

"Maybe we should make a sign to hang around your neck that says, 'Beware: Baby on Board.'"

"Ha ha," she responded with a note of despair.

"Why are you here, anyway?" Annie asked. "The Inn is off-limits to you. For now."

"We ran out of sugar?"

"Funny. But not very believable."

Francine sighed. "Okay. I'm bored. I sleep more than Bella does. Jonas says it's too early for him to start doing his *plein air* spring landscapes, so when he's not teaching at Featherstone, he takes Bella on little trips around the island—exploring nature trails, collecting sea glass and wampum on the beaches, showing up at every event for kids that the libraries offer. All the libraries, not just Edgartown. He says he wants to keep the house quiet for me. Which is wonderful. But, like I said, I'm bored."

"Your husband is a very nice man. Thoughtful and kind." Annie didn't add that there were many women who would long for a husband like that, because she had a feeling that Francine already knew.

A sigh came again. "I know. I'm lucky. But it doesn't mean I'm not bored."

Annie planted her hands on her hips. "Okay. As long as you've made the grave error in judgment to leave your cozy nest, I'll put you to work." She told her about their plans for Mother's Day weekend.

"Oh!" Francine exclaimed, clapping her hands, "This is awesome! What can I do? How can I help?"

Annie laughed. "Honey, I'm afraid you're going to be a little indisposed in a few weeks. That little fella is due right before the festivities, so you'll be in the midst of your own festivities."

A frown pinched Francine's brow. "But I can help with the planning, can't I?"

Not wanting to hurt her feelings, Annie smiled and replied, "Absolutely. And you can start by coming with me to the storage room. I don't know how much soap is left, but there's no time to make more. So if there's not enough, I can cross 'selling soap' off my to-do list."

"Lead the way," Francine said, and slowly followed. "Are you going to donate the proceeds to Community Services again?"

"If there's enough to make it worthwhile."

"I can bake bread. You can sell that."

Annie laughed. "Okay. But only if you let me pay for the ingredients."

"Deal. As it is, in order to get everything for the baby, I'm going to have to rob a bank. Or convince Jonas to do it."

"Bonnie and Clyde of Martha's Vineyard. Somehow, that doesn't have a ring to it. And please remember that if you need anything for the baby, anything at all . . ." She reached the storage room and waited for Francine to catch up.

"Thanks, Annie. But, like I've said before, Jonas and I want to do this on our own."

"As long as you know I'm here, and I have plenty of money right now. And, speaking of saying things before . . . do I have to I tell you again that you'll be otherwise engaged on Mother's Day than baking bread?"

Francine caught up to Annie. "I can make the loaves ahead and freeze them. And I can make a few of Lucy's recipes like walnut-and-fig, cranberry-and-orange—those kinds of breads—ahead of time and freeze them, too." Where Francine was known for her wonderful herb breads, Lucy liked creating the sweet ones, because she claimed that she hated kneading and waiting for the dough to rise.

"You are unstoppable, aren't you?"

"Everything I do I've learned from you."

With that, they both laughed, and Annie opened the door to the small room.

"Okay, but right now, here's what we'll do. Rex already moved the totes to the front of this mess. I'll slide one carton out at a time; you can poke through it and tell me what's in there. Everything got so crazy after the Christmas Fair, I can't remember how I left things."

Stepping into the closet, Annie moved the closest tote, which was lighter than she'd hoped, and set it at Francine's feet. "Wait here. I'll get a chair so you don't have to keep bending up and down."

As she started to walk away, Francine called out, "Stop. Are these the only ones left from the Fair?" She had lifted off the lid and was staring inside.

"I don't know. I guess." She went back and saw that there were fewer than a dozen bars inside. There was another dozen that she'd spilled on the floor earlier, but their corners were no doubt dented, so they'd be seconds now.

The next tote revealed an equally small amount.

"Where are the rest?" Francine asked.

Annie picked through a few bars; some had lost much of their scent. "What 'rest'?"

"The ones for the rooms."

Annie had forgotten about the cases of soap in the upstairs linen closet. When opening the Inn, they'd decided on a couple of traditions: one was to give every in-season guest a loaf of Francine's homemade herb bread to take home; the other was that every guest bathroom would have a fresh bar of one of Annie's soaps for guests to either use there or take with them. They'd kept an inventory of those soaps upstairs, along with other seasonal supplies. And they were well preserved in airtight containers with lids that did not arbitrarily pop off.

"You really are a genius," Annie said. She made tracks from the storage closet and went directly toward the hall that connected to the staircase that led up to the guest rooms. Her pace was quick, as if the soaps might disappear if she didn't hurry.

"Wait for me!" Francine called, trudging after Annie.

Annie slowed her pace and waited, because she wouldn't want Francine to give birth in the hall. That would be a distraction she could live well without.

Chapter 32

John knew that when his parents left for home, he should go with them. He knew he should go back to Annie, back to his job, back to the people of Edgartown who were depending on him.

But his daughter was depending on him, too.

Of course, she'd already told him to leave. She reminded him that she was going to be fine, and that she'd lived in her mother's house all through high school, and that she was comfortable enough there. She told him that her mother really was a good mother, even if she wasn't perfect.

"But who is?" Abigail had added with a smile.

At least she was smiling now.

He sat on the porch. It was lunchtime again, though John wasn't sure what day it was. Thursday, maybe. Or Friday. He only knew that it was lunchtime because his mother was bustling in the kitchen and it wasn't yet dusk and his stomach told him he was hungry. His dad had taken Jenn and Lucy to the supermarket, saying that Claire wouldn't rest until she knew that by the time they left the next day, the cupboards would be full and the freezer would be stuffed with a whole bunch of meals that she planned to make and pack this after-noon, so that, after she and Earl were gone, no one would have to worry about eating.

It was his mom's way, John knew.

At least Jenn hadn't put up a stink about it.

As for John, his back ached from sleeping on the sofa. He wondered if, after his parents left, it would be right for him to ask Lucy to keep sleeping in the other bedroom with Abigail so that he could have the third one for himself. It was going to be either that or, with his back now totally wrecked from the sofa, he'd have to sleep in Jenn's bed, which he did not want to do. He knew that emotions could create a perilous situation, and John hated the idea of having regrets.

He knew he should call Annie again. But he was afraid. Afraid to hear the letdown in her voice again.

Rubbing his stomach, he tried to convince himself that the pangs he felt really were from hunger and not because what he really wanted was to throw up.

Chapter 33

That afternoon, Kevin arranged to borrow enough tables and chairs from the community center so that they'd be set for Mother's Day. Annie needed to figure out what to do about linens: she chose white cloths rather than pink or green, because white would be more versatile for future occasions. She left a note for Rex to order the number and sizes of linens that they'd need when he went to Vineyard Haven to check out the different tents.

Annie also decided they should have white cloth chair covers that could be tied with pink and green bows. She added "call bridal consultant" to her list, because she knew there was no way she could "dress" the chairs herself and have them look professional.

Sitting in the reading room, she finished the media ad about their event and sent it to the newspapers as well as to the Board of Trade so that the information could be included in their promotional efforts. She'd added the tour of Chappy because she had faith that Earl would be able to secure a golf cart, if not from Royal and Ancient Links, then from another golf course, especially because Annie would remind him it had been Lucy's idea. They'd worry later about who was going to drive it.

Annie realized, however, that she did need to go to Granite and buy pink and green ribbon for the soaps that she and Francine had found right where Francine had said they'd be. There were dozens of them, which was great. However, they were only wrapped in white beeswax paper with a round sticker that read *Soaps by Sutton,* and noted the kind of soap each was—*Beach Roses and Cream, Buttercup Balm, Violets and Honey.* Annie had kept the packaging simple and less costly for the bars that went into the guest rooms; netting and ribbon were reserved for those she offered for sale at the seasonal festivals. While at Granite, she'd also pick up extra packaging materials; once the details of the Mother's Day events were under control, she might make more soap for the upcoming summer. Even though she doubted she'd have time between finishing her book and packing for California.

Best of all, keeping busy helped her mood stay elevated. And whenever her eyes drifted down to the diamond on her hand, she didn't feel as bad as she had yesterday or the day before. She didn't even worry about when the time would come for her to take it off and give it to Claire, who, after all, had been its rightful heir until Annie came along. She'd return Mabel Lyons's wedding dress at the same time—which would be easier.

Annie was so calm, in fact, that when her phone rang, she didn't hesitate to answer it with a smile. It was even nicer when she heard Louise's voice on the line.

"Is this a bad time?" her agent asked. She sounded stressed, which wasn't like her. Usually, Annie's editor was the worrier, the one perpetually under pressure and uptight. Not Louise, despite the fact that both women cycloned through the publishing world of Manhattan.

"What's up?" Annie replied with guarded anticipation.

"The network bigwigs hate the last two film treatments you did out there. They said they're not up to par with the earlier ones." "Out there," of course, meant California, home of the veritable sunshine, the soft-scented *Rosa californica*, and the backward views of the ocean.

"Wait," Annie said because she was pretty sure this wasn't a dream. "What are you talking about?"

"Exactly what I said. They hate them. The last two you did. They claim that neither plot has the same layers of interest as the others, and that the characters became too kitschy for prime time."

Annie knew that if she were talking on an old-fashioned phone that had a cord, she would be curling her fingers through the coils now.

"I don't understand."

"It's simple: they rejected them."

Her throat constricted; a light throbbing started in her temples. It always had amazed her how the body could respond so quickly, well before the mind had a chance to process what was being said or to know what to do about it.

"But . . . I wrote them with Cerise. And Bobster. And the others. The same team I did the first ones with." They had done six scripts in all. The first four were approved while she'd still been there.

When Louise made no comment, Annie asked, "So now what?"

"Go back to the drawing board. Start over. Do it yourself. You know your characters better than any of those people they had you working with. And you need to jump on it: they need the rewrites in two weeks."

She rubbed her temples, then her forehead. Two weeks bumped right up to Mother's Day weekend. "I'll do my best. You spoke to Greg about this?"

"He's the one who called. He said he went to bat for you.

After which he reminded me that, though he's the head of his production company, he has no control over the network people. They're the bosses. I'll email you a copy of the notes he took when he met with them. They have some specifics that might help you understand what they think are flaws."

"What about . . . what about the new contract?"

Louise paused for an earsplitting second. Then she said, "He suggested we hold off on it until they approve your rewrites. He said he'd be foolish to bring in a writer whose work the network said has lost its spark. Though you were part of a team, the series is based on your books. And your name is listed as head writer. Sorry, Annie. That's show business."

After they hung up, Annie squeezed her eyes shut. She didn't move from the beautiful reading room, aware that she was in a painful stupor. Could she really turn two film scripts around within two weeks? How long would it take before she heard that those, too, were rejected? And if Greg's offer was off the table now, what was she supposed to do with what had suddenly become her totally unsettled life?

"Hello?" The greeting was delivered as a question.

Annie opened her eyes. And saw Rex standing in the doorway.

"Is everything okay?" he asked. "I wasn't eavesdropping, but I couldn't help but hear your end of the conversation . . ."

She shook her head. "Just some writing business. I need to make some revisions to a couple of the TV scripts. For the good people of Hollywood."

"Revisions. Ugh. I don't know what they entail, but it sounded awful."

Annie didn't know how to answer. Until now, everyone in the industry—both in New York and Hollywood—had loved everything she'd written.

He shuffled a little, as if trying to decide what to say next. "I came to find you to see if you needed anything from Edgartown. I'm going over later to pick up ingredients so I can test the recipes I want to make for the brunch. Then I'm going to Vineyard Haven. Might as well not wait to check out the tents and get the linens squared away."

Annie nodded like the robot she'd suddenly become. "I'm all set for now, but thanks." She didn't mention the netting and the ribbon; she'd have to pick those out herself.

Rex paused another moment. "If it's any consolation," he said, "I know what it feels like to be trashed by people who don't even know you."

Taylor's brother was a nice man. Unlike Rex, Annie knew she was going to have a hard time letting go of her dreams: first, to marry John, and then to be a scriptwriter. But if she couldn't marry John and wouldn't be welcome in California, would she do what Rex had done—pull in her tail and pretend to be happy when her world had spiraled into a nosedive? Hadn't she already had to do that too many times?

Rex said he'd check back later. He left before she could ask what his secret was to hoisting his bra straps. And why he had been trashed. Was it about his restaurant? The place that earned all those Michelin stars? And if he had been "trashed" during the pandemic, when everyone was suffering in one way or another, who could have been so insensitive?

And why in God's name was Annie thinking about Rex when she should be tackling her own new set of problems?

Because sometimes you're better at solving other people's issues than at helping Annie Sutton, Murphy said.

She was right, of course. But whenever Annie helped others, didn't that help her see her own life with less apprehension? If Murphy were still a therapist with a real couch and all, she'd have a field day with that epiphany for sure. But, psychoanalysis aside (there clearly was no time for that), was there some way she could help Rex without his knowing it?

Then she remembered something Francine had said: ". . . in order to get everything for the baby, I'm going to have to rob a bank."

Which sparked a deeper question. If Rex had, as he said, been "trashed" by people who didn't even know him, why? And had it contributed to his inability to get another liquor license?

With her Mother's Day list tucked safely in her pocket, Annie left the Inn and went back to her cottage, where she booted up her computer, and promptly Googled *Reginald Winsted, Boston.* She stared at the screen while waiting: It took only three seconds for her eyes to widen, her mouth to drop open, and a wave of shock to wash over her as if a high tide had surged.

Boston Restaurateur Sentenced for Money Laundering

Annie gasped. The headline was bold and startling; the article was brief. She quickly checked the date: a full two years before the pandemic had begun. She steadied herself. Then she began to read.

> Reginald "Rex" Winsted, owner and head chef at the former Cedar Hollow, a popular restaurant and bar in the Back Bay, was sentenced to five to seven years for money laundering over $200,000 after having changed his plea to guilty in Suffolk County Superior Court. Winsted will serve his term at MCI-Norfolk.

There were more details, but Annie only skimmed them. Her mind, instead, was racing with questions: Was it true? Or had someone set him up? Even worse, if word about this spread around the island, would it harm the reputation of the Inn—*her* Inn, Kevin and Earl's Inn—if he was working there?

She got up from the computer, went into the kitchen, and put the kettle on, hoping the activity would help her think straight. The only thing she knew was, it probably was the reason that Rex couldn't get the liquor license: He wouldn't be allowed.

Pulling out a tea bag and a mug, she tapped her fingertips on the countertop while waiting for the water to boil. She knew she needed to address this but did not know how. First, she must tell Kevin. Maybe they should talk to Earl when he got home tomorrow, though he had more important things on his mind than to be dragged into this. Besides, she supposed there was a chance that Earl already knew. Did Taylor? She was Rex's sister, after all. Maybe Annie should leave everyone but Kevin out of it for now. Together, they could decide what, if anything, to do about it.

But if, in order to protect the Inn's reputation, they fired Rex, what about Mother's Day brunch? Was it too late to pull the ads and the Board of Trade promotions? What excuse could Annie give? She couldn't blame it on Abigail's being sick. It wasn't true, and it wouldn't be fair to her.

"Argh!" she groaned.

No kidding. Thankfully, Murphy had shown up at a convenient time.

"What am I supposed to do?" Annie pleaded.

Don't ask me. This wasn't on my radar.

"But it could be damaging to the Inn."

It could.

"You're not helping."

Sorry. I guess I have to think about it. Maybe you should talk to Kevin first.

It wasn't much, but at least she'd reinforced what Annie thought.

"I will. Right now."

Fishing through her purse, Annie pulled out her cell. But Kevin didn't answer. Had he said anything about working at the *On Time*? Well . . . she had to go to Edgartown for ribbon, didn't she?

Just as Annie was heading out the door, Francine was there, tablet in hand, making notes.

"I figured out how I can make at least a dozen loaves of bread and still have them be fresh for Mother's Day if I'm 'otherwise engaged,' as you so aptly put it. And I can make another dozen of Lucy's recipes."

Raising her hands and brushing back her hair, Annie smiled and tried to look composed. "I have to run to Granite. Come with me. You can give me details on the way, and I'll decide if it will be too much for you."

"Sometimes you're no fun at all," Francine said as she shuffled back to her house to get her purse.

Annie decided it would be good to have Francine with her now; if Kevin was working, Francine's presence would stop Annie from blurting out Rex's story right there on the ferry, where other people might hear. Instead she'd say she needed him to stop by her cottage on his way home.

Yes, she thought. It was good that Francine was with her.

But it wasn't until they were in the Jeep, heading to the pier, that Annie realized Francine looked a little pale.

"If I prepare the dough and let it rise once, I can freeze it, then you—or someone—can let it thaw and rise a second time . . ."

"Are you tired, honey?" Annie interrupted.

Francine closed her eyes. "A little," she said quietly.

"Only a little?"

It took a moment for an answer.

That time, she said, "I think I might be in labor."

Annie stopped herself from saying, "Oh, no, not again," because that would not be helpful, and even more, because the girl did look uncomfortable. And maybe in pain.

"Honey? What do you want to do?"

"I don't know, but I'm glad we're going off Chappy. I really don't want to have this baby in my kitchen with only my mother-in-law to help."

Annie had known Francine long enough to know that, in spite of her earlier announcement that Taylor's midwifery skills were a fallback birthing plan, she would much prefer to be at the hospital. Annie also knew that Francine had been anxious about the aftermath.

"Okay, then, we'll get you there," Annie said, trying to sound calm. "If you want to keep chattering, telling me how to bake frozen bread dough, or how to put a diaper on a baby for all I care, that's fine. Otherwise, we can talk about what might lie ahead if you are, in fact, in labor now." She forced a laugh.

"I've already had one false alarm. I'm going to feel ridiculous if this is another."

"Let's face it, honey, sooner or later, your little boy is going to join us."

Francine merely nodded and stared out the windshield at the road.

North Neck Road wasn't much more than a wide dirt path made worse in the spring by puddles that now filled up nature's potholes. Annie was glad when they made it onto the pavement that was a straight shot to the ferry.

"Did you call Jonas?"

"No. He took Bella up-island today. There's a public event at the tribal center; Winnie asked if Bella would want to go. Taylor went with them. I forgot about that."

"All the better for us to be at the hospital, then."

Twisting on the seat, Francine stretching out her seat belt to relieve the pressure on her belly. "Oh, boy," she said. "Please remind me I'm not due for two and a half more weeks. Or, better yet, remind him." She pointed to her stomach.

Annie kept her eyes on the road but leaned toward Francine's lap. "You heard your mother. Two and a half more weeks, remember?" Then she forced another laugh, grateful that Francine was too preoccupied to have noticed that Annie's palms were sweating on the steering wheel.

When they reached the dock, after what felt like the longest trip from the Inn to the ferry known to woman or man, Annie was happy to see Kevin's pickup in the lot.

"Look," she said, pointing toward his truck, "Kevin's working. One more person on your team."

Francine didn't answer but gave Annie a weak grin.

"With Taylor unavailable, I'll call the EMTs," Annie continued as she wheeled into the queue lane. At least she was first in line. Which helped make up for the fact that the *On Time* was putt-putting across the harbor and only halfway toward Edgartown, on the opposite side. "They'll send an ambulance to the dock. It'll be waiting for us when we get across. And they'll let the hospital know."

Francine shook her head. Francine nodded. Francine clearly did not know what to do.

"I think I'll do that," Annie said, fishing into her purse that she'd thrown onto the console. Thank God for 911.

Just as she succeeded in reporting the emergency, a rust-bucket old pickup pulled in behind her in line. *Crap*, Annie thought, it was Rex.

One of the most crucial moments of Annie's life, and surely the most crucial for Francine's, and the one man Annie didn't want to see right then was going to be present. Reginald Winsted. The money launderer.

She was wondering how to avoid him, just as Francine began to pant.

Chapter 34

Kevin signaled toward the Jeep to board.

"He's coming," Francine said between pants.

"I see him." She steered the Jeep onto the ferry.

"Not Kevin. The baby." She unhooked her seatbelt and doubled over as much as possible, what with the baby in the way. Or on the way. Or both.

Annie pivoted toward her passenger. *"Now? Honey, are you sure?"* She knew that she was speaking in italics but couldn't help it.

Francine panted.

Kevin set the chocks in front of the tires of the Jeep but walked past them without looking inside. He was busy waving Rex onto the ferry.

Scanning the *On Time*, Annie didn't see the captain. Only Kevin. *Oh, God*, she wondered, did that mean they'd be delayed?

A rattling motion behind them told her that Rex was boarding.

Kevin leaned into the driver's side of Rex's rust bucket, as if he had something important to tell him.

Annie blew her horn.

In the mirror, she saw her brother jump.

She rolled down her window and waved—frantically—beckoning him to come.

He realized what she meant, smart brother that he was.

"Where's the captain?" she shouted more loudly than necessary. "We've got to get across. The baby's coming!"

He crouched down and peered inside. "Francine?"

Pant. Pant.

"Jesus," Kevin said, and quickly stood. "*I'm* the captain."

"No, you're not."

"Yes, I am. I got my license yesterday. It was waiting when I got home from the Inn. Jesus, it's my first day. Captain Larry just handed the controls over to me. Leo was going to be my deckhand, but he got tied up . . ."

"Kevin! Shut up! Just get us across. The ambulance will be there."

"Jesus," he said again, then jogged past Rex to the back of the ferry, where he quickly lowered the gate and did whatever else he needed to do.

In Annie's rearview mirror, she saw him signal Rex to get out of the pickup.

Great, Annie thought, gripping the steering wheel harder. *A baby's life was now in the hands of a novice captain and an ex-con.*

"Everything's going to be fine, honey," she told Francine. Or maybe she needed to hear it for herself.

Suddenly Rex was at the passenger door.

Against her better judgment, Annie unlocked it from her door panel. And the *On Time*'s engine began to rumble.

"Come on, Francine," Rex said softly. "Let's get you in the backseat. I bet you'll be more comfortable lying down, right?"

Annie got out to do something—she had no idea what—

just as Kevin thrust the ferry's gearshift forward. She jerked backward and forward, grabbing the door handle and hanging on.

On the other side of the Jeep, she noticed that Rex had taken off his jacket and draped it around Francine. He opened the backdoor and helped Francine get in.

"By any chance, do you have a blanket?" he called across the roof of the Jeep to Annie.

She nodded. She kept one in the back for when Bella was with her and might want a nap.

"Can you get it?" Rex nodded toward the back.

She scurried to the back, grabbed the blanket, dashed around, and handed it off.

By then Francine was on her back, her sweater rolled up, her belly exposed. Her knees were pulled up. Rex covered her with the blanket then squatted down. Annie wanted to ask if he knew what he was doing, but so far, it looked as if he knew way more than she did.

"He's crowning," Rex said, his voice steady, calm. "Okay, little lady," he said to Francine. "Stop pushing, okay? *Do not* push. Relax. And do your breathing. Did you learn how to do that?"

Francine murmured something.

"Good." He turned back to Annie. "This baby's ready to pop."

The *On Time* jerked a little, as if hitting a wave.

"The ambulance will be at the dock . . ." She glanced toward Edgartown but did not see flashing red lights.

Rex, however, shook his head. "No time to wait."

"What can I do? Should I go on the other side and hold her head or her shoulders or something?"

"I can hear you," Francine groaned. "And, yes, I would like that."

"No," Rex said." It's not a good idea to open the door. Not with the northeast breeze."

"Oh." Annie felt slightly dumb for not realizing that.

"Tell your brother to dock as gently as possible," Rex said. "And to keep the gate down. We don't need any gawkers."

Annie started to move.

"But first," he added, "take off your shirt."

"Excuse me?"

"It's white. It's soft. I'm going to need it."

When she'd tossed on her long-sleeved, white T-shirt that morning, little did Annie know what its purpose would be. She ripped off her jacket, then her shirt. Then she put her jacket back on and zipped. That's when she noticed that Rex, too, had removed his T-shirt. And that he'd spread it on the seat under Francine.

She handed him hers.

"Linens," he said. "They're in a trash bag on the front seat of my truck. I grabbed a few samples for Tilton's. So I was sure about the sizes.

Ingenious Rex. He must have found the linens that they'd used at the grand opening.

"And get my knife case," he added. "It's under the linens." Like a good chef, Rex always had his black case close at hand.

"Anything else?"

"Sure. Hot water, if you have any." He laughed. "We're surrounded by water we can't use. Go figure."

Go figure, indeed, Annie thought but didn't say. Instead, she looked out to the harbor. They were nearing the Edgartown shore. Thank God. Then she reached into the front seat and grabbed the stainless-steel water bottle that she'd filled the day before. "It's not hot, but it's fairly fresh."

"I'll take it."

Then Annie couldn't hold back any longer.

"Rex," she said with a smile for Francine to see, "have you done this before?"

"Nope. But I've had medical training. Mostly for giving the Heimlich. But when you're in the restaurant business, you need to be versatile."

Apparently he wasn't kidding when he'd given her that pitch before.

Francine yelped and grabbed onto her belly.

Rex scooted in more closely and held her knees. "Breathe. Relax. You got this, girl."

Annie darted around the vehicle and up to the control booth. "Rex said to dock gently and keep the gate down. The baby's coming fast."

"Jesus," Kevin whispered, his eyes glued on the dock ahead. "Are you okay to do this?"

"My license says so."

She bit her lower lip. "I only meant that . . ."

"That it's my first time? And that I might be a little nervous?"

"Well. Yes."

He rubbed his head and gave her a quick smile. "Hell yes, I'm nervous. But don't tell Francine."

She nodded, his smile reassuring her that this would be fine. That *they* would be fine.

"Any chance you have bottled water?" she asked.

"In the corner." He gestured with his chin, his gaze steady on the dock.

She bent down, wriggled around his legs, and pulled out two half-gallon water bottles. "You're a lifesaver," she said.

"Yeah, well, we'll see about that when I land this thing. Hang on for the bump."

"Wait! No! Can you stop docking until . . . oh, man, Kevin, I don't know. But I think she's really close . . ."

He looked at the controls. "Okay, I'll try to idle this thing. But the current's almost five knots. . . ."

"Just do your best, brother. That's what Rex is doing." She touched his cheek and kissed it.

Then she scampered back to the passenger side of the Jeep. Rex's broad shoulders now filled the space between her and Francine and blocked Annie's vision. And muted Francine's sounds.

Until . . .

A wild moan filtered through the glass.

Then silence.

Followed by the gentle cry of a newborn baby.

Then the sounds of two adults laughing.

Annie opened the passenger door opposite the breeze and climbed onto the seat. She quickly flipped down the lid of the glove compartment and grabbed the bottle of hand sanitizer. The kind she'd gone nowhere without since the pandemic had begun. And which Earl had kindly replaced with a fresh one.

She pivoted on the seat; she blinked. And let out a huge *"Awww."* For there was the baby, all pink and wriggly, a bit icky, but gorgeous, with a thick mop of dark hair, just like Francine's, and clearly, a healthy set of lungs. To top it off, he was wrapped in Annie's long-sleeved white tee.

Laughing and crying, Annie handed Rex the sanitizer.

"It's a boy," Francine said, as if Annie didn't already know.

"He's beautiful, honey." Annie reached between the seats and smoothed Francine's damp hair. "You were wonderful. You made it look easy."

"I was afraid if I made too much noise, Rex would give up on me."

He laughed, rolled up some of the soiled linens. "Not possible. But don't get too carried away. . . . As I recall from the manual, we've still got some work to do."

So Annie kept Francine busy until the placenta appeared. Rex wrapped it in a clean linen tablecloth. "I have no idea if the EMTs want this, but better safe than . . . not."

Then Kevin appeared on the driver's side.

"Kevin!" Annie shrieked. "Who's driving the boat?"

He smiled. She realized how badly she'd missed that smile over the past few days. "We docked. I figured it was okay, 'cuz it's not like I couldn't hear what was going on, what with all the moaning and fussing and a baby crying."

"See for yourself," Annie said as she hugged him. "It's a boy."

He leaned inside and peered over the seat. "Wow. He's a beaut. Looks just like his mom."

Then everyone started to cry.

Francine was the first to regain control. "Will someone please call my husband?"

Annie laughed and pulled out her phone.

"Oh," Kevin said, "I almost forgot. The EMTs are here. They want to know if they should come aboard."

Annie wanted to kiss her brother again for getting his cargo safely across the channel. As for Rex, she was ashamed that she had doubted him. And she wanted to kiss him, too, for doing the toughest task of all.

But Rex was busy talking to Kevin. "Tell them to bring a stretcher. And a couple more blankets."

As for Francine, she was studying the sweet face of the little baby that she was holding in her arms. And she didn't say a word.

Words, Annie knew, weren't always needed.

Chapter 35

Annie followed the ambulance to the hospital.

Rex continued on to Tilton's; he said Francine should be with her family now. Annie failed to convince him that, like her, he was now an honorary member.

Kevin stayed on the *On Time* because, technically, his shift had just started and wouldn't be over until over until eight o'clock. His parting words were that he would never have believed his first solo ninety-second trip on the Chappy Ferry could be so . . . eventful.

Once Jonas and Taylor arrived at the hospital, and Annie was assured that Francine was as healthy and fine as the adorable baby boy, she headed home. When she reached Edgartown, she skipped going to Granite for the ribbon; there would be plenty of time for that. For now, she wanted to bask in the thrill of the day. But as she arrived at the *On Time*, she realized she should call Earl and Claire. And Lucy. She did not want to call John; the others could tell him. She didn't want her good mood to plummet.

As she boarded the ferry, her brother's welcoming smile sparked another idea.

"Everything okay?" he asked when he collected her ticket.

"It's fabulous. Jonas is thrilled. So is your wife. Do I call you Gramps from now on?"

"Sure, why not? Bella already does. Sometimes it's 'Grandpa Kevin.' That started while you were away."

Annie felt a small pang that she'd been gone a long time. And that in two months, she'd be going away for a longer time. Unless she changed her mind. She wondered—not for the first time—that if she'd been there when Abigail first showed symptoms, things with John might have turned out differently.

She rubbed her neck, dismissed her thoughts, and smiled back at her brother.

"So . . . I'm really glad we're friends again," she said.

"We never were not."

"Yes, we were. When I overstepped a giant boundary."

"Well, it's true you did that. But all's well that ends well, right?"

She nodded. "And now my brother has become Shakespeare. Would you at least reassure me I'm right in thinking that things between you and Jack are okay now?"

"You're right. They are."

"And you're not upset about the part of my father . . . and Donna?"

He laughed. "I am not. Now please drive forward, ma'am. There are vehicles behind you."

Annie suspected it wasn't the last time they'd talk about Jack Miller. Which would be fine with her.

Then she leaned out her window. "Wait!" she cried. "Will you call Earl? Tell them about the baby? In case Francine didn't call them yet?"

"No. I don't have my phone."

So Annie tossed him hers, because she really wanted him to have the pleasure.

Once back at the Inn, she went into the reading room and straight to the cabinet where Bella's toys were stored. A large sheet of paper and a few big crayons were all she needed. Setting the paper on the island in the kitchen, she printed big block letters:

IT'S A BOY!
6 lbs., 8 ozs.
Born Wed. afternoon
on the
CHAPPAQUIDDICK FERRY
To FRANCINE & JONAS
All are doing well
No name yet —stay tuned!

She added some colorful squiggles and things she tried to make look like balloons. Then she found a roll of tape and stuck her grand announcement on the refrigerator door, where everyone would be sure to see it.

Stepping back, she critiqued her work: It was without frills or pretention—a true hallmark of the Vineyard way of doing things. When she'd been in California and was on the phone with Lucy before everything happened with Abigail, Lucy talked about having a baby shower for Francine. Maybe they should have a surprise shower after the Mother's Day weekend but before the Inn opened to tourists for the season on Memorial Day weekend. And in case Annie was busy getting ready to leave again. But first she supposed she should check the calendar.

For no particular reason, she didn't take the shortcut but

went the long way through the great room. Since Annie had been home, whenever she'd come into the Inn, she either went into the kitchen or snuck down the back hallway to the reading room. She'd hardly been in the great room.

But now she stopped for a moment to admire the serene yet majestic feeling that the room evoked, from the broad, floor-to-ceiling windows that framed the impressive vista of the harbor and the lighthouse to the tall, slate fireplace that scaled the two-story wall. She and John were supposed to have been married in front of that fireplace.

She stood, staring at the backdrop of the wedding that apparently had not been meant to be. At least this time, there was no need to cancel arrangements; they'd planned to wait until she was back on the Vineyard to make them. All they'd done was pick the date; one week from today.

Clutching the tape in one hand and the crayons in the other, Annie sat in one of the oversized, comfy sea glass–colored chairs and stared into the fireplace, her vision quickly veiled with tears she didn't want. She half expected Murphy to say, *It's really okay to cry sometimes.*

Annie loved John, she really did. They were too old to have babies the way Francine and Jonas were. And yet they were going to be a family, a real-life, forever family. Marrying John was going to make up for all that she had missed, with his daughters and his parents, all of whom she loved, too. She'd felt like Cinderella finally finding her perfect prince, despite the fact that they were both over fifty, a little gray, and slightly tarnished by age and experience.

But now . . .

Then Annie heard lively commotion from the kitchen. At first she thought Rex was talking to someone; her stomach tightened. She didn't know how relaxed she'd be able to be around him now, not since she'd learned what she had learned.

Money laundering.

Prison.

She needed to talk to Kevin. Pronto.

But would he agree . . . or would he say that she was med-
dling again?

Ugh, she thought. She considered ducking out of the great
room, then sneaking through the reception area and out the
front door. Until she realized that neither voice belonged to
Rex; two of the year-round tenants must have come in the
back door and seen the sign about the baby.

Annie wiped her eyes, stood up, and left the great room,
knowing that if she could chat about the baby, her joy would
return. And that, once again, she could shoo her demons
away. At least for a little while.

She did not expect the encounter to launch a new idea of
how to address the issue about Rex.

The husband and wife schoolteachers—Marty and Ronni
Amanti—were the tenants who had screeched and giggled
when they'd read the birth announcement. And when Annie
told them the whole story about how it had happened on
Kevin's first trip across as captain, and how Rex happened to
be there with linens and his chef's knives and a half-working
knowledge of how to birth a baby, and how Annie had found
water and her hand sanitizer left over from the pandemic—
well, the couple nearly capsized from wide-eyed amazement.

They agreed that they were sorry they'd missed out on
helping. As Annie sat with them at the kitchen island, their
lively banter moved from the latest high-stakes drama to other
times when the tenants had become part of the action. And
Annie was again reminded how fortunate she and Kevin and
Earl had been that the people living at the Vineyard Inn
treated it as their home, and the staff as family.

Like with the patience and unwavering support they showed

in the beginning, when skeletal remains were found on the beach and threatened to shut down the Inn before it could open.

Or the time when Simon Anderson—a world-famous journalist, celebrity du jour—was about to arrive and they'd pitched in and spit-shined the Inn, then later, pulled together to help determine if Simon had shot one of their own.

And when one of the treasured family had gone missing and the tenants had pitched in, scouring the grounds day and night, first on foot, then on snowmobiles until the answer was found.

Marty and Ronni agreed that they'd been through some crazy, scary times, but the best part was that they'd all worked together with a common goal.

Even in the less dramatic situations, they'd helped out.

It was a touching conversation, but for Annie it triggered a possible solution about Rex: Maybe Simon Anderson could help. Simon wasn't just the former Boston local TV news guy who'd skyrocketed to fame and caused a memorable fracas at the Inn; he'd also become a friend. And he would have nothing to lose or gain. Best of all, Annie knew she could trust Simon to keep this between them.

Excusing herself, she moved into the reception area, unplugged and removed the laptop, and carried it and the land-line into the library and closed the door behind her. She sat down at the table and scrolled through the Inn's past reservations until she found Simon's phone number. She called. And left a message on his voice mail.

Then she googled the information she'd found about Rex again. Just as she was wondering how it could be possible for the man who'd gone to prison for money laundering to be the same man who, only hours earlier, had delivered a baby on a moving raft of a ferry, Simon returned her call.

"Annie!" he said. "My wife and I were talking about you

just the other day. Are you back on the island from the land of make-believe?"

"I am," she replied. "And it was a great experience." Which was true. It was also true that the network hated two of the scripts, her future plans were now in jeopardy, and she had two weeks to prove herself. But there was no reason to bore Simon with that. "But a whole lot has happened since I've been home. I was hoping you might be able to help figure something out."

Leaving out the parts about John and Abigail, leaving out the joy of Francine's baby's arrival, Annie gave him the rundown on Rex Winsted, a man who had come back to Chappy in the fall, had owned a fabulous restaurant in Boston, and was a master chef. Then she added that he'd said, in spite of wanting to open a restaurant on the island, he probably couldn't get a liquor license. Which had sent her to secretly cruising the internet—mostly because she wondered if something in his background would be detrimental to the reputation of the Inn, as he'd taken over managing their kitchen for a while.

"In the process of my research, I found out he'd spent time in jail for money laundering."

Simon had the dignity not to indicate whether he was shocked. No doubt he'd seen and heard about a lot of good guys, bad guys, and those in between.

"I've been told that when he was growing up on the island," Annie continued, "Rex was a scrapper, but not a criminal. Since he's come back, he seems like an upstanding citizen. But I'm concerned that if our tenants find out about his past . . . or if it shows up on yelp.com or one of those tourism sites, well, I don't know what it could mean. Of all people, you know how quickly bad news travels. So I wondered if you might have some advice. What with your penchant for investigating the dark side of life." She laughed; so did Simon.

"I'm not sure what you want, Annie. Do you want me to find out if this could hurt you legally? Or do you want to know something about his jail time?"

"I think I'd like to start with finding out what was behind the money laundering. Something about the story doesn't feel right to me. One of the articles said he was sentenced to five to seven years. But based on the dates between the article and when he arrived back on Chappy, he was in jail only a little more than three years. Wouldn't he have served more time if he'd really been guilty?"

"I have no idea. What I do know is that money laundering is a felony. So, yes, he probably can forget getting a liquor license. But I have a friend who'll know. And I don't know what to say about telling your tenants. Maybe my friend can help with that, too. Would that work for you?"

She told him she'd be forever grateful, and whenever he could manage to bring his wife to the Inn for a weekend, a lovely room would be on the house. She didn't mention that she might not be there.

"And there's one more thing," she added. "Rex is my brother's brother-in-law. Kevin is married to Rex's sister."

"Oh. So no pressure on me, then," Simon replied, with a lighthearted chuckle.

After they hung up, Annie felt much better. She decided to go back to the hospital and visit the little baby and find out if he had a name yet. And on the way, she'd get her phone back from her brother.

"Reginald Kevin Flanagan," Francine announced. "After my two saviors."

Annie knew she'd never been great at masking her emotions. So, instead of revealing how she felt about the baby being christened with Rex-the-criminal's name, she pretended to sneeze. Which gave her a few seconds to try to regain her composure.

Francine and Jonas laughed.

At least Taylor had taken Bella home. Taylor was much sharper than she usually let on, and, in addition to probably having the skills to recognize a fake sneeze when she heard one, if she also knew about Rex's past, she'd be sensitive to anything that mentioned her brother, the famous restaurateur who'd lost everything, thanks to a bit of money laundering. Yikes.

"We're going to call him Reggie," Jonas added. "My uncle Rex got the first-name slot seeing as how he was at the helm of the delivery, while Kevin received a well-deserved honorable mention because he was at the helm of the ship that brought my wife and child to safety."

He was being corny, which Annie found endearing.

At least they didn't name him Helm. Murphy came from out of nowhere and whispered in Annie's ear.

"I'm sure they'll both be very honored," Annie said, wearing what she hoped was a loving expression.

"If he'd been a girl, we would have named her Annie Claire," Francine said.

The little tears that had formed earlier threatened to leak from Annie's eyes again.

"All I did was sprint around the deck, getting things for Rex."

Francine smiled and shook her head.

And Annie prayed that they'd never find out about what the original Reginald had been doing in Boston not long before he'd become a hero.

"The doctor wants to keep me here for twenty-four hours," Francine said. "It's only because of the 'unusual conditions' of where Reggie was born."

"What was so unusual?" Annie asked. "Because the water

was choppy in the harbor? Or the fact that my brother was making his maiden voyage as a captain? Or that your doctor isn't a doctor but a chef?"

They all laughed, which felt amazingly great. There were few things as soothing as family laughing together.

The moment was cut short, however, when Annie's phone vibrated. It was Simon.

Aware of a need to maintain her smile, Annie excused herself and stepped out of the room and far down the hospital corridor.

"I got voicemail at the Inn, so I hung up and tried your cell," Simon said.

"You're not only smart but fast," Annie replied.

"Ha ha. I was only fast because it's all in who you know. This time, I knew the right one. I have a friend who remembered Rex's case. He wasn't involved, but he often went to your guy's restaurant. He said that Rex first pleaded not guilty. He claimed his girlfriend did the books, and he didn't know anything about any money laundering."

"That makes sense to me," Annie said.

"Wait. There's more. Right before the trial, he changed his plea to guilty. Which was why he went to jail."

She frowned. "Why'd he do that?"

"Don't know. But you were right; he only did three years. The good news is that if getting a license is important to him, my friend might be able to get the conviction expunged."

"Seriously? Does that mean he won't have a record?"

"Yup."

"I wouldn't think that was possible. Money laundering seems so . . . serious."

"Not if it's considered a misdemeanor. Rex pleaded guilty, but there was no concrete evidence that he was the one

who'd done the finagling or that he'd used the money for personal gain."

"How strange."

"Well, the prosecutors proved it was laundered through
his restaurant, so he was convicted on that and his plea. But if
he wants to go through the process to get it expunged, my
friend can help. He'll even charge the family discount rate."

"Wow. You must really want that weekend here with
your wife."

"Yes. We need a break."

Annie laughed. "Just give me the dates when you're
ready." In the worst-case scenario of Annie being gone, they
could at least put them in her cottage, where Simon had been
before.

"I'll do that. In the meantime, talk this over with Rex. My
friend said his best bet is that Winsted was covering up for
somebody else."

"You really are an investigative journalist."

"I try."

Chapter 36

Saturday morning, Annie waited until the tenants would be done with breakfast and Rex would be alone, cleaning the kitchen. She texted and asked him to stop by her cottage when he was done. She said she had something to show him. She didn't care that it was a white lie.

He responded: Things to do. 11:00 ok?

She agreed, then went to her desk. Sooner or later she'd have to start working on film treatment revisions, unless she wanted to get fired before she even saw a contract. Or worse, she'd have to pay back part of the money she'd already earned for the work. Most of which she'd already given to Community Services.

She did a quick search and found the files for the scripts.

She read through them. Twice. She couldn't figure out what was wrong; why they thought the writing was different from the scripts that they'd accepted.

Was it her fault? Had she become so sidetracked since she'd been back on the Vineyard that she couldn't recognize the work wasn't up to par? Maybe she'd lost interest.

Still, Annie prided herself on her work, so she settled in

and began to rewrite. Then deleted. Then tried again. And again. And still she didn't know what she was doing.

At ten past eleven, Rex's burly self arrived at her door. She was grateful for the interruption until she remembered why he'd come.

He'd brought a bottle of champagne to celebrate the baby.

She wished he hadn't done that. It would make the conversation more difficult. But she welcomed him inside and found two flutes while he undid the cork. Then they sat in her small living area, Annie in the rocker, Rex filling the small sofa.

"So," she said, "nice work yesterday."

He chuckled. "My sister told me they're naming him after Kevin and me."

"That they are. And you get top billing."

"Reggie," he said, chuckling again. "As far as I know, there's not a kid in the world named after me. I guess there's a first time for everything, right?"

"Absolutely." She could tell by his lingering smile that he was pleased.

He shifted his frame and lifted his glass. "Cheers to Reginald Kevin."

Annie copied his form, wishing she didn't feel so awkward, her unspoken words poised perfectly still, like a seagull on a beach, praying that a careless tourist would leave some crumbs of food.

Then Rex launched into a review of the drama on the little ferry, while Annie let him do most of the talking. She hoped it would help him get it out of his system so that they could move on to the real reason he was there. When he finally added that he'd been able to get all the linens he thought they'd need for the brunch, Annie knew that it was time.

"Rex." She intentionally took on a somber tone. "There's

something else we need to talk about. And I'm going to come straight to the point."

He shifted again, his bulk clearly too large for the sofa, for the room.

"I know you were in prison."

He lowered his bald head; he studied the champagne flute. "Not going to deny it."

"I also know there's more to the story. I'm concerned that our tenants—or one of our guests—might find out, and that it could come back to haunt us all. So I'd rather hear what really happened straight from you."

After waiting a moment, the big man nodded. "I didn't do it. Hell. I wouldn't even have known how."

"But you pleaded guilty."

He paused again, either trying to buy some time to make up a story or to summon up courage to recall the scene he'd hoped he'd left behind. "I guess it's better for you to know the truth than for me to keep worrying that sooner or later the grapevine on the Vineyard is going to find out. To be honest, I've been worried about it since before I decided to come back. But I had nowhere else to go." He set the glass on the end table and folded his arms.

"Her name was Raejean."

A woman, Annie thought. Of course.

"We lived together. She did the books. When the cops took me away in handcuffs, they locked up the restaurant. They posted a sign that said, 'Closed until further notice.' I had no idea what was going on. I thought maybe Raejean made a mistake when she filed our taxes or something. I was sure that the 'raid,' as one of the cops called it, would get resolved in an hour or so, and I'd be back in time for the dinner crowd. It was a Friday. Our busiest night." He unlatched his arms, tented his fingers, and tapped his thumbs together. "Man, was I wrong."

Annie waited a moment, then asked, "What happened next?" She was fairly sure that, so far, he was telling the truth.

"Long story short, I was fingerprinted, interrogated, and locked up until my hearing. I had a good attorney, one of my regular customers. I said I wasn't guilty. And I honestly wasn't worried. They let me out on bail. I went home. But Raejean wasn't there. Her stuff was gone. All of it. I remember I sat on the couch and had no idea what to do. It took a long time to sink in that maybe she had something to do with the whole mess. I didn't know how or why. We'd been together seven years. I trusted her, so I stayed out of the financial end of things. Stupid me."

If anyone knew what it felt like to be taken advantage of by someone they trusted, someone they thought they loved, it was Annie. She'd been through the emotional wringer with husband number two, though she didn't wind up in prison, for a while she was panicked by the possibility that he'd done something illegal that might come back on her.

"Finally, I called Rae," Rex continued. "She didn't answer her phone. I spent a couple more days on the couch. I called something like seventeen times. Finally, she got back to me. I asked her what the hell was going on."

He puffed out his cheeks, let out the air.

"'Oh, Rexy,' Raejean whined. She used to call me Rexy. 'Sexy Rexy.'" He guffawed. "Anyway, like I said, she whined. Said she was sorry. Said she screwed up but that she didn't 'mean to.' Then she said she'd wanted to tell the cops everything but she couldn't. When I asked her why, she said, 'Because I'm pregnant, Rexy. I'm having our baby.'" He paused, as if to let that shred of news sink in.

"Oh, God," Annie cried, though she hadn't meant to say it out loud.

"I couldn't let her go to jail," he continued, his voice lower, sadder. "How could I? She was pregnant. With my baby."

The air in the living room grew heavier with each thing he said.

"So I changed my plea to guilty. I still didn't know any details. I only knew my kid wasn't going to be born in Framingham. That's where the women's prison is—the oldest one in the whole damn country for females that's still in operation. Not that you need to know that stupid fact."

After a moment, Annie asked, "Did she tell you why she packed up and left? Or where she went?"

"She went to her sister's," he snorted. "She said she was afraid the cops would find her. Later I realized she must have been afraid that I'd rat her out. Which, of course, made no sense, because in the beginning, I didn't think she was guilty of anything, either. But by the time she told me, it didn't matter where she was. As long as she and our baby were safe, I wanted to leave her out of it."

Annie suspected there was more to the story, so she sat as still as possible and let him keep talking.

"A few months after I was convicted, my lawyer ran into Raejean. She didn't look pregnant. When he asked her about it, she laughed. And she walked away."

Annie hadn't expected that. "She wasn't pregnant?"

He shrugged. "Turned out it was doubtful that she ever was. But I couldn't prove she lied to me, so I kept my mouth shut and did the time. The truth is, I was exhausted. Too exhausted to do anything except stay in my cell and behave. Which I guess helped my attorney get me out in three years instead of the five to seven I'd been sentenced to."

Chances were, he'd been not only exhausted but incredibly hurt. Annie knew that was often an especially tough emotion for men to admit. Maybe even tougher than serving time in prison.

She stood up, went to the sofa, and sat on the small coffee table in front of him. Then she reached for his hands and let her fingers be swallowed by his.

"I'm so sorry, Rex. What a terrible experience."

He lowered his head again.

She pulled his hands toward her and was about to hug his entire body when John walked in the door.

He could have pivoted on the heels of his shiny black boots and stormed out of the cottage. Annie wouldn't have blamed him. Instead, her fiancé—if he was still that—stood stock-still, not physically filling the space as much as Rex did but exuding a more intimidating stance with his rigid posture and steely eyes. John had enough police training and experience to know how to do that effectively.

"John." Rex was the first to speak. He did not stand; perhaps it was a learned role of "you can't bully me" that he'd perfected over the years. Or maybe he was just tired from having spilled his confession.

But they were two men. Each with a penchant for an unspoken agenda.

"I didn't expect to see you today," Annie said, and stood up, because one of them had to shatter the spell.

"Obviously," John said.

Rex laughed. "Hell, man, knock it off. You have no idea what today's been like."

John's glare didn't ease. "No, I don't. Why don't you tell me, Annie?"

"Stop being ridiculous," she said. "Both of you." She turned to Rex. "Would you mind leaving, Rex? I'll check in with you later."

He nodded and heaved himself up off the sofa.

John stepped aside to let him pass.

Once Rex was gone, John shoved his hands in the pockets of his jeans.

"Sorry if I interrupted." He was, of course, being sarcastic. It was a side of him he didn't often show, mostly because he had to work hard at being that way. He seemed to have forgotten that Annie knew him well, and knew that about him.

"Francine had her baby yesterday," she said.

"I know. I was bringing my parents back. I heard the ambulance call when we were on the boat."

Seriously? He'd come back yesterday? Heat flared in her cheeks. She did not want to argue . . . and yet . . .

She picked up the champagne glasses and brought them to the sink. He had no right to act angry with her because Rex was in the cottage when he'd been home since yesterday and hadn't even called. She didn't even know if that last thought made any sense.

"How's Abigail?" she asked, trying to stay calm.

"Not too bad."

She turned back to see him moving his body as if stretching his back. Maybe he was trying to decide whether to sit down.

She walked over to him. "John. Can we stop this nonsense?"

His pearl-gray eyes studied her. "No offense, Annie, but I don't call it nonsense when I walk in here and see . . ."

"And see what? Me trying to comfort someone who had a powerfully emotional day yesterday and it's only now catching up to him?"

John scowled. "So he delivered a baby. Now he's superman. I wouldn't have thought it was a reason for a grown man to cry."

She took hold of his arm. "Stop it. Stop trying to use Rex to cover up your stupidity for not having called me since you've been home."

He stepped away from her and moved over to the table. Then he stopped and hesitated, as if he weren't sure if he was going to stay.

"Annie . . . ," he started slowly.

And that's when she knew. He'd arrived at her cottage without knowing Rex would be there. And it didn't seem as if he were stopping by to tell her how his daughter was or how much he had missed Annie or how he was happy to see her. It also didn't seem as if he'd showed up to reschedule their wedding plans.

She placed a hand on her stomach, waiting for the thud that she knew was on its way.

"I have to go back to Plymouth. I have to stay with my family for a while. Until Abigail is squared away. Until she's through the worst of this initial stuff and we figure out where we'll all go from here."

She stared at him. When he said that he'd stay until "we figure out where we'll all go from here," Annie couldn't tell if he'd said "where" to mean where they would live. Here or there. The Vineyard or Plymouth. John's house. Or his ex-wife's. With his family. She also didn't know if the "all" included her.

"I'm sorry," he said. "I came back with my parents so I could tell you. Face-to-face. In person. You know."

Yes, she knew. She also knew there was no point in mentioning again that he'd already been there a full day.

Her legs grew weak. She pulled out a chair and sat at the table. She wondered if this was anything close to how Rex had felt when he'd learned that Raejean had betrayed him.

"I love you," John added. "But sometimes it's not enough, is it?"

He sounded like an old weepy song. She wondered what percentage of recorded hits had been about broken hearts.

"So, are you and Jenn back . . . together?"

The clock over the sink must have ticked for several more seconds, but Annie didn't hear it.

"Please, Annie. Don't make this harder on me than it already is."

Harder on *him*? He was the one abandoning ship. She was the one who'd be left on the island to explain to everyone why he'd left, why he wasn't coming back, and that, no, there definitely wouldn't be a wedding. But Annie could not say those things because John was the one with a child who was sick.

Sometimes when we're hurting, we have to hurt other people, Murphy said. *It's called life. And it sucks.*

That it did.

So Annie knew she couldn't get angry, she couldn't get mean. At least not to John. He was doing the best he could. And she did love him. Part of the reason was that he was who he was. Strong. Steady. A dependable port in a storm.

But he was in a lot of pain now. And it didn't look as if Annie was the right one to help him. So, one more time, she needed to hoist up those bra straps.

She struggled for a breath. "Maybe you should leave now," she managed to say.

He checked his watch.

"Yeah, I need to pack more stuff for Abigail. And Lucy."

And for you, Annie wanted to add, but did not. It was clear he hadn't brought Earl and Claire back to the Vineyard simply to give Annie his news face-to-face. In person. He'd also come back to pack up his island life and ship it to the other side of the sound. The mainland. The real world.

He went to the door. He opened it, stepped outside, then quietly closed it behind him.

And Annie stayed seated, waiting to feel something other than numb.

Chapter 37

At least no one else stopped by to see her. Those who knew what had happened—Earl, Claire, maybe even Francine and Jonas, and who knew who else—left Annie alone for the remainder of the day. Until seven o'clock, when Kevin called. Not texted, but called.

"Taylor wants to know if you'll have dinner with us tomorrow," he said gently.

She sighed. "I take it you know."

"Yup. And we won't talk about it unless you want to. All I'm going to say is it's a hell of a thing to have happen after yesterday was so amazing. And I'm sorry. And call me anytime if you want to talk. Or if you just want to hang out."

She let out a soft laugh. "I thought you weren't going to talk about it."

"Sorry, can't help it. I'm worried about you."

"It's okay, Kevin. I'm okay. Or I will be. And thank Taylor for the invitation. I'll be there tomorrow. What can I bring?"

"Your patience. Because she's taken about a million pictures of Reggie already and she's going to bore you to death."

"Sounds perfect."

They rang off. There had been no need to ask what time she should arrive: seven o'clock, as always. Vineyard dinner time.

Then Annie realized she was still sitting at her table, wondering what to do next. The late-day sun crept through the window; she decided that some fresh air would be good. She grabbed a jacket, her purse, and her phone, then went out to her Jeep. Within minutes, she arrived at Dyke Bridge, having forgone her favorite spot at the burial ground because she didn't want to be reminded of Earl's sister, Martha.

Yes, she thought as she got out of the Jeep and walked toward the small bridge, it was better that she'd gone there than to the cemetery.

As frequently happened off-season, no one was around. For which Annie was glad.

She sat on a large rock by the water's edge, looking north to the quiet lagoon, a thin strip of water that connected Cape Poge Bay to Poucha Pond. Small pebbles mixed in with scallop shells that must have been opened by seagulls blanketed the sand. As the water lap-lapped the small shoreline, something in the sky caught her attention: an osprey, one of the once-threatened species of large, soaring birds that had found their home on the island.

Like I did, she thought.

Black and white with touches of brown on its underside, the giant bird appeared to halt midair. It cocked its wings and arced them, stared briefly at the lagoon below, then plunged—feetfirst. Faster and with more precision than an Olympic diver, it broke the surface of the water; seconds later it emerged, grasping a stunned fish in its bill. Carrying its treasure, the bird tipped its five-foot wingspan, as if it were an airplane preparing to land. Then, with senses as keen as those of a barn owl at night, it landed on the nest of sticks and twigs that it had built on a wooden platform atop an old telephone pole—one of dozens of accommodations that had been planted on the island years ago in the hope that the ospreys would find them. They had, and they thrived, their numbers multiplying each year.

Earl, of course, had told Annie all that.

And now, as she sat, she watched. She waited for something to happen that she could not see: fledglings, perhaps. Or maybe not yet. Earl had also said that mama ospreys usually lay three eggs, and that incubation lasts just over a month.

Since Annie had moved to the Vineyard, Earl had taught her so much, including how to adapt to the many ways of the island, its people, and its traditions. Everything that blended to provide its rhythms. She reminded herself that she hadn't come there looking for love; she'd longed to find a community where she would feel that she belonged. John had been an unexpected bonus. So why should the fact that he'd chosen to leave his home—and her—cause Annie to do something foolish, like move to California? It was true that Southern California had flowers that bloomed year-round, and sun that shone almost every day, but the whole time Annie had been there, had she really been comfortable? Or had she been aware that she was only another curious visitor like so many who graced Martha's Vineyard in summer?

Still, it was a chance to have a six-month break, plenty of time to get her bearings back. Unless she'd messed it up by writing two lousy scripts.

If she sat on the rock at the tip of the lagoon until the sun went down, Annie supposed her answer would be the same: heartbreak or not, like the osprey, the island was where Annie had come to roost. It was simply where she fit.

Which might explain why, after nearly a full week, she'd yet to finish the revisions to the scripts. But she wouldn't give in yet. It was too soon; she was too raw.

Accepting that sometimes the best decision was a non-decision, she returned to her Jeep and took her phone from her purse. Then she called Kevin and asked if they could switch tomorrow's dinner to the Inn, where they'd have enough room for Earl and Claire and Francine and Jonas and Bella and Reggie, too. And Rex, if he wanted to come. After all, their little mismatched family had something big to celebrate: a new fledgling who'd been born in a very special place.

"I'll get over it," Annie told Francine the next morning when she went to see the baby, who was still as cute as when he'd been snuggled in her T-shirt on the *On Time*. They were upstairs in Reggie's beautifully painted room; Francine sat in a child-sized chair upholstered in lavender that Annie had brought in from Bella's room; Annie was in an antique rocking chair that she'd bought for Francine; it was almost exactly like the one that was a fixture in her cottage, the comfortable seat where she'd rocked Bella endlessly during the weeks when Francine had chosen Annie to be Bella's guardian.

It was nice that Francine let Annie hold the baby and gently rock him while he slept, his tiny baby breaths in sync with the movement of the chair.

"Of course you'll get over it," Francine said. "But probably not today."

"Or tomorrow. But I have plenty to keep me busy. I have some work to do, and, more important, I'm going to be whatever help I can with this precious little boy."

"And will you be his godmother?" Francine asked.

The rocker didn't miss a beat. "What?"

Francine shrugged. "I know that Jonas and I aren't churchgoers, but, believe it or not, we were both raised Catholic. We'd like Reggie to be baptized in the church. And Bella, too, since my mother died before that could happen. Anyway, Jonas and I were talking about it, and we'd really like it if you were both Reggie and Bella's godmother. If you wouldn't mind."

Annie's eyes filled with tears. "Mind? I would be honored, honey."

"Thank you. That means a lot."

"It means a lot to me, too."

Then Francine hesitated. "Do you think Kevin would agree to be their godfather?"

Annie smiled and wiped her tears. "Well, you'll have to ask him. But I think we both know he'll jump at the chance."

"Will Earl and Claire be hurt that we didn't pick them? They've done so much for us, right from the beginning, but . . . well, they're older and . . ."

"And nothing, honey. They'll still be here for you and Jonas and the kids no matter what. They might even be grateful not to have one more responsibility, especially now with Abigail . . ." She stopped herself from finishing the sentence, because Annie had vowed to limit her mentions of that part of the family, as she was no longer part of them.

"We thought about that, too," Francine said, her voice quieter, respectful for both Annie and Abigail. Perhaps more than the rest of Kevin's troops, Francine was well aware that life could, and often did, change in a heartbeat.

Then she offered Annie one of her sweet smiles. "We'd like to get it done before the season starts, but after Mother's Day, if you're still planning to do the brunch. What with Lucy gone and now with me . . . well, I have no idea if I'll still be able to make some bread, but I'm going to try."

Despite the unexpected, six-pound, eight-ounce arrival, Annie knew that some decisions still needed to be made, that things needed to get done. But she also knew she was good at that.

"We're already committed to the Board of Trade. But let's talk about it tonight at dinner, okay? And see if everyone's still up for a big event." Between then and now, she'd have to make a couple of phone calls and have another talk with Rex, which, she hoped, would not be interrupted. Maybe later that night, she'd call Lucy and let her know their plans. Or maybe it would be easier on both of them if Annie just left her alone.

Besides, there were other things she needed to do.

That afternoon, Annie had a meeting with a man she didn't know: Jim Bennett. He said he was from Manhattan, that he and his wife had moved to the island thirty years earlier, but their kids were back in the city and wanted their parents near them.

"The truth is, we're getting too old for the hustle of the island," he said as he ran his hardworking hands through his thinning white hair. "Whoever thought there'd be more hustle on an island like the Vineyard than on the island of Manhattan?"

Annie smiled. They sat across from each other at a solid oak table; her shoulder grazed one of the large windows that looked out to the harbor; one of the old clipper ship paintings hung on the wall behind Mr. Bennett. The Lord James, lovely as it had been, would be a magnificent restaurant property with some updating and freshening up.

She expressed her interest in buying the place.

She tried not to wince when he announced his starting price.

Between her donation to Community Services of a large chunk of cash and Hollywood now holding her feet to the fire over the scripts, Annie couldn't be sure what was going to happen next. Or if the riches they'd once proposed would disappear like surf spray in a breeze.

Still . . . Annie had faith in Rex. And she'd talked to Simon's attorney friend before she'd come to the Lord James. The man had said there was a "better than good chance" he could get Rex's record expunged, but that it would take several months.

Could Annie keep everyone and everything afloat till then?

She squared her shoulders now. Of course she could. Because after all her years of struggling, she'd learned that when she set her mind to something, she was capable of making it happen.

She thought she got that kind of strength from her dad. Or from Donna. Maybe both.

Before leaving the restaurant, she shook hands with Mr. Bennett. And Annie walked back to the *On Time* feeling happy. And enthusiastic.

Now all she had to do was talk Rex into accepting her offer.

Dinner at the Inn was set for five thirty, between baby-Reggie feedings. Taylor had insisted on making one of Kevin's favorites and what Rex had called their mother's signature dish: shepherd's pie, served with a simple green salad and store-bought dinner rolls. Annie didn't mention that, like Kevin, it had also been her favorite meal when she was a girl. She loved all the good feelings her only living blood relative brought into her life.

That day, however, Kevin was late. Everyone had already gathered at the Inn, including Rex, who'd finally finished puttering around the kitchen that had become his domain while Francine was in absentia. She wasn't absent that night, though; with Jonas and their brood, they now took up an entire end of the long dining table.

Earl and Claire sat on one side; opposite them, places had been set for Taylor and Kevin and Rex, who had claimed the chair closest to the baby in order to admire his wiggly, gurgly namesake who was wearing an adorable T-shirt that was far too big for him and read: VINEYARD BORN. It was pink, but

Earl explained it was the only one in the Main Street shop, and, for Pete's sake, he hadn't had much notice.

Then Taylor appeared in the doorway from the kitchen, wiping her hands on the oversize apron that might have fit Rex. Across the bib, in giant blue letters, it read: EAT. I MADE ENOUGH FOR AN ARMY. Earl had seen that one in the same shop, too, and hadn't been able to resist.

It was nice to think that a little lightness was returning in the family.

"Kevin called," Taylor said. "He got held up at the *On Time*. Nettie Reynolds fell and broke her hip, so the ambulance jumped the line."

Everyone nodded; they knew that emergency services took precedence over any other vehicle trying to come to Chappy.

Annie wanted to ask if Kevin had been on captaining duty or if he'd been somewhere else. Come to think of it, she hadn't seen him all day. She looked around and noticed that everyone at the table suddenly was busy doing something: Jonas was straightening Bella's high chair; Francine was fussing with the baby, while Rex was asking her something or other; Claire was rearranging her silverware, and Earl was examining his fingernails. When Annie glanced back to the kitchen doorway, Taylor had disappeared.

So Annie sat. And waited.

In less than five minutes, she heard the back door open, and Kevin's voice bellowed in from the kitchen.

"Is everybody here?" he asked.

Murmurs and impatient sighs of "Yes," echoed all around. Annie knew if Lucy had been there, she would have rolled her eyes.

Then Kevin came into the dining room, followed by Taylor.

Annie didn't understand why they were making such a big production out of a shepherd's pie with family, until an unexpected guest trickled in behind him.

"Everyone," Kevin said, "this is my dad. Jack Miller."

Annie held back a bucket of emotions that swelled up inside her. She stood up and gave Jack a welcoming hug.

"I'm so happy to see you again," she said.

"It's not that I didn't want to tell you earlier that he'd be here," Kevin said to his sister, "but sometimes surprises are more fun. And I thought everyone might like to meet him before he shows up on Mother's Day."

After giving Kevin a playful swat, she hugged him, too.

Then chairs were shuffled to make room for the guest. And everyone started firing questions at Jack, who was, after all, the new kid on the block. The best one came from Bella, who, after determining that Jack was Kevin's father the way Jonas was hers, asked "Mr. Jack" if Kevin had been a nice little boy the way her new brother was. So Jack did some fast talking, which seemed to satisfy the little girl for a minute until she asked if Kevin had been as nice a baby as she had been. So Annie reiterated the story of how Bella had shown up on her doorstep in the middle of a blizzard at Christmastime. Of course, everyone there, except for Jack, already knew the story, but Bella always seemed to relish the retelling.

Taylor waited until the stories about Jack and Kevin and Annie and Bella had finished and the happy banter that followed settled down before bringing in the shepherd's pie, to everyone's applause.

"Rex, maybe you should change the Mother's Day menu to this!" Jonas exclaimed.

Rex said it was a great idea, and that, by the way, he had an announcement, too.

"Does everyone know the Lord James restaurant?" he asked.

Yeses and sures were shared, except by Jack, who nonetheless seemed to be enjoying the frivolity.

"Well, thanks to an investor . . . ," he winked at Annie, "it's going to be mine now. Shall I put my sister's signature dish on that menu, too?"

Stunned silence was followed by another barrage of questions.

"We'll do Mother's Day weekend as planned," he said. "But I hope the owners of the Inn will consider giving up the notion of doing weddings and banquets and send the group events over to my place instead."

"And I," Annie joined in, "think it would be great fun to provide each of our summer guests with a coupon for a free dinner at the Lord James."

Rex then explained he wasn't going to change the restaurant's name. "It's so well known, why screw up a good thing?"

The rest of the evening went by so fast and was filled with so much chatter and laughter that Annie nearly forgot about John. It did, however, help her feel that maybe she'd be able to heal sooner, and better, than she would have expected. She was, after all, in the perfect place and with the perfect people who would enable that. For the next two months.

Epilogue

Annie was amazed that when Mother's Day rolled around, they were ready. Within a day of the notice of the brunch being posted in the media, online, and with the Board of Trade, all the reservations were filled. And now the tables—both on the patio and in the dining room—were resplendent with centerpieces of pink tulips and hydrangeas with green floral accents. There were pink long-stemmed roses for the ladies, and pink-and-green bows on the backs of the chairs that were covered with white linen, as if this truly were a celebration.

A week before, right up to the deadline, Annie had submitted her revisions of the scripts because meeting her obligations was important to her. She still hadn't heard back from Louise or Greg; she still wasn't sure which coast she'd be living on in another month.

For now, she focused on the day.

Kevin had made an extra space for a special outdoor table for five: Jack, his son-in-law, and Jack's grandchildren—three little girls whom Bella quickly befriended. Jack said that though the children's mother was gone, he wanted his granddaughters to honor and remember her. So Kevin had not been wrong.

Francine greeted the guests and brought them to their tables; Bella handed them the menus on which Jonas had painted a view of the harbor from the Inn. He had also made an attractive sign for a side table where Francine's breads and Annie's soaps were sold out by the time the first wave of guests were seated.

Earl and Jonas had picked up two six-seater golf carts from the Royal and Ancient Links; the golf course had just received brand-new carts, so the two they'd offered up were the older models. Annie and Claire laughed when they watched the men decorate the carts in pink and green ribbon. Annie was glad that Claire looked healthy again.

Taylor was on the patio, playing her cello, dressed in white, having forgone the pastels. She said she didn't want to be confused with a centerpiece.

Rex was hustling in the kitchen; Annie went inside and directed the servers, a group of clients from Community Services who were volunteering. Annie suspected they might have been recipients of part of her donation. And all the Inn's tenants had donated their time as the cleanup crew, even Charlie, who worked for the Steamship Authority and lived at the Inn during the week but went home to Fall River on weekends. This weekend his wife and kids were also at the Inn for the special day.

Just as the first round of appetizers were delivered, Annie stood in the kitchen window, surveying what they'd managed to put together. The ladies were dressed in lovely pre-summer dresses; the men in shirts with collars, some even wearing ties and sports jackets. It was a gala event, indeed, accentuated by the spectacular weather that featured not only a sunny sky but also a gentle Vineyard breeze, which was showcased by white sailboats in the harbor.

You didn't think I'd let your Mother's Day be anything but wonderful, did you? It was Murphy, of course. Always by Annie's side.

She decided to meander among the outside tables to be sure people had everything they needed, but as she stepped outside, she heard a barking dog.

Oh, no! she thought. They couldn't have a dog burst onto the lawn, disrupting the brunch and the tables and do God knew what kind of damage.

Pulling up the hem of her long pink skirt, she trotted down the steps, then sped around the corner to fend off the commotion. She did not expect that the dog would be Restless—dressed up in pink-and-green finery, and playing with Earl.

Nor did Annie expect that standing next to the dog, holding his leash tightly, was Lucy.

Annie's mouth fell open as if she were one of the old men catching a quick nap on the porch at the Chilmark General Store in summer. Her teeth sank into her lower lip as she tried to hold back tears.

Lucy smiled. "I came to live up to my promise. I'm here to give the golf-cart tours. That is, if I'm not too late. And if you'll have me."

Annie stooped and scratched behind Restless's ears to give herself a chance to try to hold back her emotions. When that didn't work, she stood up, unashamedly letting tears run down both cheeks. She gave Lucy a big, big hug. And with every second that she stood there, Annie felt a million pounds of stress slowly evaporate; she hadn't realized how much had been weighing her down. Silly her.

"Before you ask, I'm alone," Lucy said quietly.

"No, you're not. You brought my favorite canine." Annie

pulled away with a smile; she straightened Lucy's braid of copper hair. It was shorter than it had been before her haircut, but it looked as if she intended to grow it long again. For some reason, that pleased Annie.

"The truth is," Lucy said, "I wanted to come because it's Mother's Day. And you've been more like a mother to me than anyone else."

Annie was speechless. Her heart warmed in a way she'd never known.

"Even more," Lucy continued, "I'm not going back. I love my parents and I love my sister, and I'll be there when they need me. But I'm moving in with Gramma and Grandpa. The island is my home. And you're a humongous part of it."

"And it's okay with your dad?"

Then it was Lucy's eyes that filled with tears. "It was his idea," she said. "He told me he didn't want you to be alone."

Just then the air reverberated with happy applause. Perhaps it was for Taylor's lovely cello music or maybe for the shepherd's pie that Rex had added to the menu, in honor of their mother.

Perhaps it was for Francine, the newest of mothers.

Lucy bent down to adjust Restless's bow in case the applause had been for him.

Maybe Murphy started it, because, God knew, she loved a good party.

Wherever it had originated, or for whatever reason, Annie decided, then and there, that if the revised scripts were accepted, and if the offer was still open, she was going to sign the contract to go back to California. Though the Vineyard and its people were what she loved the most, she needed a break. And Annie needed to give John one, too. As long as she stayed there, he'd worry that she was waiting for him. And too much a part of her would be.

But she was not afraid of making changes, big or small.

Like starting a good story, she always loved not knowing what was up ahead.

And she could be home for Christmas. But she wouldn't promise that.

The hardest thing would be telling everyone. Especially Lucy.

I'll be here, Murphy said.

Lucy stood up and laughed. "Where else would you go?"

Bewildered and a bit suspicious, Annie asked, "What?"

"I heard you say that you'd be here. I asked where else you'd go."

She didn't know if she should laugh or cry. Instead Annie put her arm around Lucy and held her close, safe in the knowledge that Murphy would look after her while Annie was away.

Acknowledgments

Many thanks to the amazing crew who keep the dependable Chappaquiddick Ferry running year-round in tip-top shape, and especially to those who shared their time and knowledge with me about its overall operation. I am embarrassed to say that, prior to this, I had no idea that every captain must have an extensive background of operating certified watercraft and has to pass a comprehensive course, a series of written exams, and medical and drug tests to meet U.S. Coast Guard requirements essential for the *On Time*.

Thanks also to Janice Donaroma of Donaroma's Nursery, Landscaping, and Floral Design. Janice was the initiator of Edgartown's original Pink and Green Weekend, for the background and insight into the elaborate and fun Mother's Day weekend celebration, and she provided me with many wonderful stories about the event.

And to Barbara Bellissimo, vice president of development, marketing, and communications for Martha's Vineyard Community Services, thank you for your time and insight about the terrific services provided to islanders through its many diverse programs. Most of all, thanks for explaining the importance of ongoing donor support, both financial and as volunteers. The organization is truly a critical part of the heart of the Vineyard.

Don't miss the first book in Jean Stone's heartwarming
Vineyard series . . .

A VINEYARD CHRISTMAS

In the midst of a Christmas blizzard: A baby on the doorstep.

It's taken a long time and a little heartache, but Annie Sutton is finally following her dream of living on Martha's Vineyard. She fell in love with the island's singular beauty while
using it as a setting for two of her novels. In her cozy rented
cottage on Chappaquiddick, she's settling in for her first Vineyard winter—complete with a fierce nor'easter on the way,
forecast to bring high winds and deep snow. But the blizzard
also brings something unexpected to Annie's front porch: a
basket, encircled by a ribbon, containing a baby girl. The note
reads: "I named her Bella, after my grandmother. Please help
her, because I can't."

Adopted as a child, Annie is grateful for wonderful parents
who raised her as their own. Yet she also hopes to spare little
Bella the feelings of abandonment that still haunt her. And so,
rather than take the baby to the police, Annie decides to keep
her and try to find the birth mother, giving her a chance to
change her mind.

But it's not easy keeping a secret in a close-knit, island
community, especially amid the bustle of Christmas. Before
the holiday ends, there will be revelations, rekindled hope,
and proof that families—the ones we are born into and the
ones we claim for ourselves—are the gifts that truly matter . . .

Available from Kensington Publishing Corp. wherever books are sold.

Chapter 1

The turnout was better than Annie had expected. It was, after all, a bitter, see-your-breath kind of morning, with a brisk December wind whirling around Vineyard Sound. But sunshine was vibrant against a bright blue sky, painting a perfect backdrop for the evergreens and colorful lights that decked the lampposts along Main Street, the storefronts, the town hall. Around the village, the traditional Christmas in Edgartown celebration was underway: on her walk to the elementary school gymnasium, Annie had witnessed the beloved parade of quick-stepping marching bands; mismatched, decorative pickup trucks; and a Coast Guard lifeboat perched atop a flatbed trailer that carried Santa himself, who waved and shouted "Ho ho ho!" while tossing candy canes into the cheering curbside throngs.

The atmosphere inside the gym was equally festive as "Jingle Bells" and "Joy to the World" scratched through the ancient PA system. Browsers and shoppers yakked in high-pitched voices and jostled around one another—many were armed with reusable bags silk-screened with the names of island markets, banks, insurance agents. By day's end, the bags would no doubt bulge with knitted scarves, island jewelry, specialty chocolates, and, hopefully, one or two of Annie's handcrafted soaps.

From her station behind a table under a basketball hoop, Annie wore a hesitant smile. The Holiday Crafts Fair had been open less than an hour, but she'd already sold seven bath-sized bars and a three-pack of hand-shaped balls she called "scoops" because each was the size of a scoop of sweet ice cream. Her cash pouch now held fifty-two dollars—not bad for her first endeavor in making boutique soaps by using wildflowers and herbs that grew right there on Martha's Vineyard.

But as happy as the earnings made her, Annie mused that fifty-two dollars was hardly a sign she should quit her day job. Then a middle-aged woman in jeans, an old peacoat, and a felt hat with a yellow bird crocheted on the brim approached the table. *An islander*, Annie knew. A year-rounder, like Annie was now. She'd seen her somewhere in town—the post office, the movies, the library. With the days growing shorter and colder and the streets less cluttered with tourists, faces were becoming familiar. The woman in the peacoat examined Annie's wares, which were wrapped in pastel netting and tied with coordinating ribbon: pink for beach roses and cream; yellow for buttercup balm; lavender for violets and honey.

At the far end of the table, a young woman sniffed a scoop of fox grape and sunflower oil: Annie had gathered the buds, then added the oil for velvety smoothness, the way her teacher, Winnie Lathrop, had showed her.

"How much?" the young woman asked as she adjusted a basket on the crook of her arm. It was a big handwoven basket, the kind Annie's aunt had used to hold skeins of yarn. This one, however, held a sleeping infant, snugly wrapped in a thick fleece blanket.

Annie smiled again, the ambiance and the people almost warming her spirit and her mood. "Four dollars. Ten dollars for a three-pack of mixed scents."

The young woman, who looked barely out of her teens, had short, pixie-ish chestnut hair and sad, soulful eyes that were large and dark and looked veiled with sorrow. She set down the scoop, readjusted the basket. Then she picked up a piece of cranberry and aloe oil soap that was tied with red ribbon. She did not speak again.

Wincing at the snub, Annie wondered if she'd ever learn not to take the actions of strangers personally. "As hard as it is for us to believe, not everyone will love you or your work," her old college pal, her best-friend-forever, Murphy, had once told her after a tepid review of one of Annie's books. "Forget about them. They're pond scum anyway."

"Annie Sutton!"

Startled to hear her name, she quickly spun back to the present. Only a few people knew she now lived on the island; fewer knew who she was or that she had a backlist of best-selling mystery novels. She turned from the ill-mannered young woman and politely asked, "Yes?"

The caller's hair was as silver as the foil bells made by the first-graders that the custodian had hung from the gymnasium rafters. She wore a smart wool coat that fit her nicely—a Calvin Klein or Michael Kors. Her well-manicured fingernails were painted red and matched her lipstick; her purse might have been a Birkin bag—a real one, not a knockoff. She'd most likely arrived that morning on the *Grey Lady*, the special "holiday shopping" ferry that had come from Cape Cod straight into Edgartown for the festive weekend.

"You're Annie Sutton? The writer?"

Annie's cheeks turned the same shade as her beach roses and cream. "Guilty." An often-rehearsed, engaging grin sprang to her mouth. She hoped it was convincing.

The woman's eyes grazed the table. "And now you're a soap maker?"

"Just a hobby."

"Well, goodness, I hope so. When's your next book coming out?"

That, Annie wanted to reply, *is a good question.* But she could hardly say she was reassessing her life, that she had lost her inspiration to write, that she was now on a healing sabbatical. If the news ever went viral, Trish—her patient, yet perfectionist editor—would never forgive her. "Soon," she said, aware that several browsers at her table had shifted their focus from her products onto her, and that other shoppers were drifting her way. In her peripheral vision, she noticed that the young mother remained standing, silent, her head slightly cocked, as if she were listening. "Actually," Annie continued, shaking off silly discomfort, "I'm still working on it. It's the first book in a new mystery series."

"Well, hurry up. Your readers are dying to read it!" The woman put a hand to her mouth and giggled. "Yes, we're *dying* to read your next mystery. That's a pun. Get it?"

Annie nodded and said she did.

The woman picked up nine three-bar sets and plunked them down in front of Annie without checking the scents. "I'll take these. The ladies in my book group will adore them. Will you sign the labels?" She juggled her big purse and pulled out a credit card.

Annie had pierced a small hole for the ribbon on each oval-shaped paper label, which had an illustration of the island, the name of the flowers or herbs she had added, and a frilly typeface that read: *Soaps by Sutton.* There was no blank space for a signature. Embarrassed, she turned over each label and penned: *Happy Holidays! Annie Sutton.* It had not occurred to her that Annie-the-soap-maker would be "outed" at the fair, that she'd be asked to dish out her autograph.

"I love your books, too!" another voice called out. "Will you sign a bar of soap for me?"

"Me, too?"

"Me, three?"

The requests shot out from a line now swollen with reusable bag–toting patrons.

"Do you live on the Vineyard?" another voice hollered.

Annie sat up straighter on the metal folding chair. "I moved here at the end of the summer," she replied, summoning full celebrity persona now, the one she'd cultivated at Murphy's insistence.

"Did you buy a house?"

"No, I'm renting a guesthouse—a cottage—over on Chappaquiddick."

"I love Chappy!" someone else cried. "Whereabouts are you?"

"North Neck Road." She cleared her throat and spoke loudly and pleasantly, as if she were at a book reading.

"Does your new book take place here?"

"Is it an autobiography?"

"A murder mystery?" a different voice cried. "That would be a terrible autobiography!"

The crowd tittered, then another woman asked, "Will you be finished with it soon?"

The chattering rushed at her, the voices drowning out the PA system's "Jingle Bells." Annie remembered a time, not long ago, when she'd prayed to have a few fans of her books. *Be careful what you wish for*, she reminded herself, trying to keep her rising anxiety at bay. She forced a laugh, rang up another sale, signed another autograph, and sadly wished that this day were done. "My first book was the closest I've come to writing about my life. That was hard enough."

"Was that the one where your character was adopted?"

"Yes," she said, then collected more dollars, signed more labels. "It was before I started writing mysteries; I can assure you that no one in my life has been murdered!" Not that she would have minded learning that her ex-husband had met his demise.

The crowd laughed along with her, except for the girl with the sad, soulful eyes, who simply wandered away.

If this were an ordinary off-season Saturday night, Annie might have stopped at the Newes for a bowl of chowder and a glass of chardonnay on her way back to Chappy. But the 275-year-old, brick-walled, fireplaced pub would be packed with the weekend wave of merry, but tired, shoppers—mostly women with their friends, having lots of fun. She would hate being alone.

With the fair finally over, she stepped outside, took a long breath of the crisp night air, and willed herself to feel, if not completely happy, then at least content: there was no good reason not to. Yesterday, Earl Lyons—the white-haired, robust caretaker for the estate where she rented the cottage—had loaded four cartons of her soap into his pickup truck, driven onto the small ferry over from Chappy, and helped set up her table at the fair. He'd said he'd be glad to come back if she needed any leftovers hauled home. But now, carrying a single bag that held only a handful of unsold soaps and a fat envelope of cash and receipts, Annie decided to walk. Maybe the exercise would help her figure out if she'd found a new trade, after all—and help her shed what was beginning to feel like a dose of Christmas blues.

She put on her alpaca mittens ("The warmest you'll ever find," Earl had advised when he'd offered helpful hints about the island), then pulled the matching knit hat over her straight, silver-black hair that barely skimmed her shoulders. Though the night air was calm, the trek to the boat would be chilly, and the crossing downright cold: the miniature ferry that navigated the 527-foot channel from Edgartown to Chappy offered no shelter for passengers, only a three-sided glass cubicle where the captain stood. More like a motorized raft than an actual boat, the one running that winter was called the *On Time II* and only held three vehicles, or an SUV and a UPS truck, or some other meager configuration. Benches that hugged the sides could seat up to twelve walk-ons, though Annie hadn't seen that many people on the boat since tourism predictably had plummeted after Columbus Day weekend. A slightly larger *On Time III* crisscrossed the *II* in season, but was in dry dock now, taking its turn for maintenance, getting prepped for the next onslaught in the spring. There was no sign of an *On Time I*, though surely it once had existed.

Leaving the school grounds, she walked on past the new library to the fire station, where their original cast-iron bell, circa 1832, was displayed on the lawn. Like much of the village, the bell was decorated with hundreds of enchanting holiday lights.

She turned onto Peases Point Way, then crossed the street to avoid the graveyard, something Murphy would have found ridiculous.

Annie sighed. God, how she missed her best friend. She knew that the loss, the grief, were at the core of her glum spirits. Murphy once said: "Men can come and go in life, but best friends last forever." At the time, Murphy's hand had been clutching the stem of a glass of pinot noir, having come over after calling Annie at midnight with a rare need to escape from her "workaholic husband" and her "rambunctious boys." The two of them had smiled, clinked glasses, and taken another sip, neither of them having any idea how suddenly and sharply cancer would snap the "forever" of their bond.

Peases Point Way connected to Cooke Street, where Annie took a right and headed toward the harbor. But at South Summer Street, she changed her mind and turned left instead. She passed the eighteenth-century, gray-shingled building that had once been a poorhouse, but where the *Vineyard Gazette* had been located for over a century now. On the opposite side of the

narrow street was the gracious, stately Charlotte Inn, known for
its old-world charm. Annie jaywalked across the road, climbed
the three front stairs, and stepped into the foyer.

A woman in a sleek black dress stood at the mahogany reception desk.

"I know the terrace isn't open in winter," Annie said, "but
may I sit at a table if I only want wine?" She pulled off her hat
and shook out her hair.

"Are you alone, or will someone join you?"

"It's just me," Annie replied, keeping her tone carefully
neutral. The woman was just doing her job, she reminded herself. *She isn't mocking me for the fact that I'm alone.*

They moved into a candlelit room that was filled with din-
ers who were conversing in intimate tones. Then, as if guided
by the universe—or, more likely, Murphy—the hostess led
Annie to a small table that had a view of the terrace. Annie
thanked her, sat down, and gazed out at the redbrick courtyard.
The wrought iron tables were gone, as were the navy umbrel-
las, which, early last summer, had shaded Annie and Murphy as
they'd whiled away a sunny day. They'd been wearing flowered sundresses and open-toed sandals that showed off fresh
pedicures. The sunlight had brought out the red in Murphy's
shoulder-length hair. As usual, they'd shared plucky conversation about some things that mattered and many more that
didn't. It had been a celebratory weekend, a girls' getaway to
mark their fiftieth birthdays—Annie's had been in February;
Murphy's, in April.

And now, on this December evening, Annie ordered a Chambord Cosmopolitan instead of her usual chardonnay. She and Murphy had sipped Cosmos that afternoon—Murphy claimed that
vodka dressed up with Chambord and orange liqueur showed
more enthusiasm than wine. "We made it to fifty; we deserve
to live a little," she'd declared. A full-time behavioral therapist,

the mother of twin boys (the rambunctious ones), and the wife of a well-respected Boston surgeon (the workaholic), Murphy prided herself on maintaining a positive attitude and mostly agreeable relationships with her family, friends, and an assortment of alcoholic beverages.

"If I drink this, I'll get drunk," Annie had said. "You know I can't drink the way you do."

Murphy asked the waitress to bring Annie more cranberry juice on the side. "Now," she said, turning back to her friend, "tell me about your next book."

Annie sighed. "I'm struggling with it. It's about two women who work in a museum where there's a huge art heist. And a dead body or two. I love the concept, but the plot isn't gelling."

"It will. You're not much of a drinker, but you've got the gift of blarney. Whether you're Irish or not."

Of course, Annie had no idea if she was Irish, French, or Tasmanian, though her dad often said she must be Scottish because of her black hair, hazel—not blue—eyes, and "outdoorsy" complexion, whatever that meant. Her mom and dad had adopted Annie when she was six weeks old; she'd never learned her heritage, not even later, when she'd had the chance.

"The truth is," Annie had explained, "my characters were best friends in college and are reunited when one gets a job at the museum where the other one volunteers. They're not us, though. Neither one of us knows squat about art history. And my characters are smarter, richer, and much more beautiful."

"No!" Murphy had screeched. "They can't possibly be smarter or more beautiful! But I do think the story sounds terrific. If you feel stuck, maybe you need a break. Even better, a vacation!" Then she'd grown uncharacteristically pensive. "Let's get serious. What's on your bucket list?"

"Stop! We're only fifty. It's too soon for one of those."

"No it isn't, Annie. Think about it. What would you want

to do if you weren't such an infernally sober stick-in-the-mud? If you shake things up a little, you might reignite your creative genius."

Annie had a good laugh at that. Still, she wondered if her friend was right. Murphy, after all, knew her like no one ever had. Not like her parents. Not like her first husband—her first love—Brian. And certainly not like the next one, Mark, the man she'd wasted too much of herself trying to please. "Okay," she said. "If I had a list—which is not to say that I'll make one—the first thing I would do would be to move here. Live on the Vineyard. At least for a while."

"Where you met Brian."

"A thousand years ago. But even then, I knew this place was more than romantic: it's magical." Annie had chosen to set two of her mysteries there. While doing the research, she'd fallen in love with the island again, not only for the breathtaking landscape, but also for its diversity of people, its immense support for art and culture, and its rich, unforgotten history—all of which combined to form an inspiring community.

"Do it," Murphy said in a serious whisper. "Make the move. It's time to open up your life." Annie knew that was Murphy's way of saying it was time to move on, time to shed the baggage of too many losses and disappointments. In hindsight, Annie wondered if her friend had had a premonition.

A month after that wonderful weekend, Murphy was diagnosed with a rare, swift-moving cancer. Carving out time between her family, work, and chemo treatments, she helped Annie find the cottage on Chappy, then, with her bald head cocooned in a gaily striped turban, she went with her the day that Annie moved. She said she needed to see Annie settled, to know that she was safe. That had been on Labor Day. Four weeks later, Murphy died. And Annie's heart had been irrevocably broken.

In some ways, Murphy's death had been Annie's greatest loss; no one was left now to help her navigate the day-to-day waters of life. But thanks to her advice, Annie was following her dream. She was here. On the Vineyard. Surrounded by unending beauty and the gentle rhythm of the place she now called home. And she knew that if she dared to leave, her old pal would come back to haunt her in her spunky, rap-on-the-knuckles kind of way.

Gazing out the window now, from the terrace up to the night sky, Annie saw the Milky Way, its wide, white ribbon shimmering like a twinkling sash. Just then, a comet streaked across, as if delivering a message of faith, hope, and love. With the curve of a soft smile, Annie felt her tears glisten like the stars. "I'm trying, my friend," she whispered to the heavens, up to Murphy, who surely was there.

Visit our website at
KensingtonBooks.com
to sign up for our newsletters, read
more from your favorite authors, see
books by series, view reading group
guides, and more!

Become a Part of Our
Between the Chapters Book Club
Community and Join the Conversation

Betweenthechapters.net

Submit your book review for a chance to win exclusive
Between the Chapters swag you can't get anywhere else!
https://www.kensingtonbooks.com/pages/review/